John Grant spen[...] before, in 1980, becoming a full-time writer and freelance editor. Since then he has written over twenty books under his own name and ghosted more; his articles, short stories and reviews have appeared in various magazines, anthologies and reference works. He has recently served as Technical Editor on the new edition of the Clute/Nicholls *Encyclopedia of Science Fiction*.

THE WORLD is John Grant's second adult fantasy novel and follows ALBION ('Great story-telling' *The Times*; 'A stunning debut novel' *Cult*; 'A grim, bloody and powerful book ... recommended' *Games Master International*; 'A truly amazing fantasy – some books feed the imagination, this one takes it to a banquet' *Samhain*).

Also by John Grant

Albion

The World

John Grant

HEADLINE
FEATURE

For Fay
with much love
(but she knows that already)
and considerable humility

Copyright © 1992 John Grant

The right of John Grant to be identified as the Author of
the Work has been asserted by him in accordance with the
Copyright, Designs and Patents Act 1988.

First published in 1992
by HEADLINE BOOK PUBLISHING PLC
First published in paperback in 1993
by HEADLINE BOOK PUBLISHING PLC
A HEADLINE FEATURE paperback

10 9 8 7 6 5 4 3 2 1

All rights reserved. No part of this publication may be
reproduced, stored in a retrieval system, or transmitted
in any form or by any means without the prior written
permission of the publisher, nor be otherwise circulated
in any form of binding or cover other than that in which
it is published and without a similar condition being
imposed on the subsequent purchaser.
All characters in this publication are fictitious
and any resemblance to real persons, living or dead,
is purely coincidental.

ISBN 0 7472 4041 8

Printed and bound in Great Britain by
HarperCollins Manufacturing, Glasgow

HEADLINE BOOK PUBLISHING PLC
Headline House, 79 Great Titchfield Street, London W1P 7FN

ACKNOWLEDGEMENTS

In general: Bill Bailey, Chris Barat, Catherine Barnett, Jane Barnett, Muriel Barnett, Struan and Zoe Barnett (both for lunatic reasons), Alberto Becattini, Judith Clute, Carolyn Couch, Malcolm Couch, Lydia Darbyshire, Joe Dever, Jane Judd, Roz Kaveney, Sharon Kent, Justin Knowles, David Langford, Hazel Langford, Barry Mather, Val Maund, Kim Munro, Caroline Oakley, Fionna O'Sullivan, Polly Powell, Fay Sampson, Paula Sigman-Lowery, Dave Smith, Liz Sourbut, Margaret Stewart, Joe Tercivia, Nancy Webber, Susan Willoughby and everyone listed below

For advice on sections of Part One: David Barrett, Chris Bell, Steve Cox, Susanna Drazin, Fox, Mary Gentle, Graham Higgins, Diana Wynne Jones, Christina Lake, Simon Lake, Zander Nyrond, Fay Sampson, Ron Tiner

For advice on sections of Part Two: Catherine Barnett, Jane Barnett, David Barrett, Mary Gentle, Colin Greenland, Diana Wynne Jones, Paul Kincaid, Christina Lake, Fay Sampson, Maureen Speller, Alex Stewart

For advice on the entirety: John Clute, Caroline Oakley

Backing musicians: Adam de la Halle, All About Eve, Apu, Virginia Astley, Pat Benatar, the *Brendan Voyage* musicians, Máire Brennan, Pat Brown (Silver), William Byrd, Peter Cadle, Mary-Chapin Carpenter, Clannad, Leonard Cohen, Enya, Mary Fagan, Flairck, Clive Gregson & Christine Collister, Heart, Incantation, Gael Kathryns (Baudino), Johann Kuhnau, Catherine-Ann McPhee, Gustav Mahler, Meatloaf, Carl Orff, Philip Pickett, Chris Rea, John B. Spencer, Bruce Springsteen, Savourna Stevenson, Igor Stravinsky, June Tabor, Thomas Tallis, John Taverner, Trees, Jennifer Warnes, Robin Williamson

Contents

Acknowledgements   v

PART ONE: THE SIX POINTS OF DEPARTURE
    Elsewhere & Elsewhen: one   3
1 Broken Strings   6
2 Cloak of Sky   51
3 The Painter's Eyes   89
4 Seven Realms   115
5 The Anonymous City   204
6 The Mistdom   246

PART TWO: A RENT IN THE FABRIC
    Elsewhere & Elsewhen: two   271
1 How I Slept with the Queen of China   273
2 Down to a Sinless Sea   282
3 A Rent in the Fabric   302

PART THREE: THE SEVEN ReLMS
    Elsewhere & Elsewhen: three   373
1 I NeVeR SAD IT WUOLD Be eASY   375
2 THe MUNKeY HOUOSe   403
3 BeYOND THe JADe GATe   424
4 DRABSVILL   448
5 JAM TOMOROW   479
6 MeN AT WORK OVeRHeAD   493
7 eMPIRe   523
    Elsewhere & Elsewhen: four   533

Bibliography   535

PART ONE
The Six Points of Departure

It is true, that which I have revealed to you: there is no God, no universe, no human race, no heaven, no hell. It is all Dream, a grotesque and foolish dream. Nothing exists but You. And you are but a Thought, a homeless Thought, wandering forlorn among the empty eternities!

Mark Twain, 'The Mysterious Stranger'

Elsewhere & Elsewhen

one

There is a way of looking far into the distant past and seeing everything that happened there. The same method can be used to observe distant events while they are actually happening – and also, of course, events that took place both long ago and far away. It is even possible to spy upon what is occurring in the alternative universes – those parts of the polycosmos which, unreified in our own time-line, exist for us only as the sites of dreams.

People who believe in breaking down everything into its constituents when there is no need to do so – analysts or vandals, depending upon your viewpoint – employ different words to describe all these different uses to which this single technique can be put: clairvoyance, precognition, far vision, timeslip, and many other terms. In fact, all these seemingly different phenomena are simply manifestations of one, and so people who fully understand the workings of the unconscious mind prefer to use a single word to describe what's going on.

Scrying.

Scrying requires no equipment, because the necessary 'equipment' is already present in your mind, if only you can reach it and learn how to manipulate it. But most of us require a *focus* in order to help us simultaneously relax and concentrate our minds in just such a manner that we can see those long-ago or faraway events. Some of the most able menticians use nothing more outlandish than the surface of some water in a bowl. They stare at it and stare at it, directing their thoughts as if they were asking it questions – although, of course, it is really to their own minds that they are addressing these questions. In due course the answers begin to make themselves heard: it is, to the mentician, as if he or she were watching moving pictures on the water's surface, and hearing tiny voices. In short, then, the surface of the water is serving as the focus towards which the mentician is directing his or her own inner knowledge.

For the moment you need to utilize an apparatus that is a little more complicated than a simple bowl of water. There are various possible designs, but here is the one which we have determined to be the most accessible to the beginner. You can construct it within minutes using easily obtainable household objects.

YOU WILL NEED:
- plenty of stiff paper (or thin card)
- a ruler
- a pencil
- a protractor *or* a pair of compasses (and do be careful of those sharp points!)
- a long needle (a darning needle is ideal)
- a cork
- an egg-sized lump of modelling clay (or similar material)
- some adhesive (sticky tape will do, at a pinch)

Using the ruler and the pencil draw a straight line rather more than 5cm (2in) long, then measure off a 5cm (2in) length of the line, marking both ends of this length with a point. Using either the protractor or a pair of compasses, construct an equilateral triangle using this length as the base.

Now use the right-hand side of the triangle as the base for another equilateral triangle, constructing the figure the same way as before; then use the left-hand side of the second triangle as the base for a third, and that of the third for a fourth. You should end up with the four triangles forming two-thirds of a hexagon. (The hexagon is a very important geometric figure in all matters to do with the psyche. Although you will not be using the remaining two equilateral triangles that would complete the hexagon, spend a few moments contemplating them. Even in their absence they will be contributing to the efficacy of your final apparatus.) Finally, use the inner free side of the fourth triangle as the base for a shallow trapezoidal flap.

Use the scissors to cut out the whole shape and, with the edge of one of the scissor-blades, crease firmly along the four lines that you have not cut. Fold along the creased lines to form a four-faced pyramid. With the adhesive, glue the flap to the relevant edge of the first triangle you drew. Leave the pyramid alone for a while to give the adhesive time to dry.

While waiting, roll out the lump of modelling clay on a firm surface, such as a clean table-top, as if you were rolling out pastry. Plant the cork securely in the modelling clay. Taking care not to prick your fingers, drive one end of the needle into the cork so that it stands as near vertical as you can manage it. Now balance your pyramid like a little hat on the point of the needle. If you have been very careful at every stage, you should now be able to spin the pyramid gently on the needle's point.

But don't do that just yet. Get your eyes down to the level of the sides of the pyramid, about 30cm (12in) away, and turn the pyramid so that one of its triangular faces is directly towards you. Concentrate very hard indeed on that plain little triangle of paper and ask yourself what is happening somewhere else in the World. At the moment you know nothing of this other place: you do not know where it is, or anything else about it, even its name – assuming, of course, that it has a name.

Very soon you will find that nothing at all seems to exist for you except the paper surface of the triangle, and a little while after *that* you will begin to see some tiny movements, and then to hear small sounds . . .

Chapter One
Broken Strings

1

The Anonymous City lies two hundred or more kilometres to the west of Arnas at a place where a minor river, the Marat, oozes reluctantly into the Sea of Hollows.

Few know of its existence, and fewer still choose to make the hazardous journey through the evil-smelling swamps, the Broken Marshes, that encircle it like the rotting tissue around an untended wound. The rare travellers who reach the gates of the Anonymous City usually do so by accident, and it is almost unknown for them to leave it. In truth, there is little for the visitor to see. Perhaps a thousand men, women and children inhabit its small and wealthy mercantile area, grown even wealthier now that trade with Albion, across the sea to the north, has opened up again; a further five thousand or more unfortunates live lives more savage than a cat's in the decaying mazes of the city's slum hinterland, where thin-faced children will insouciantly kill for the price of a beaker of unfouled water.

Crops can be grown with difficulty in the steaming swamps, but those that do are stunted and rank. Skinny domesticated animals stand huddled together by day around the battered city walls, gazing morosely out towards the Mistdom, perhaps realizing that freedom could be even worse. And for the people who dwell in the slums, where life is short and harsh, each day represents weary hours of corrosive hunger that will never be relieved for long. There are a few soup kitchens, but there are thousands of the poor: the opulence of One-Legged Tom's Kitchen is only a dream for them. The bodies of the dead do not lie long in the streets.

Yet the Anonymous City is rich.

Many centuries ago a ragged band of pious human beings – worshippers of the Sun, the God of Healing and Mercy – fled from the rest of the World and its wars to find a sanctuary where they could lead their lives in tranquillity. They sailed their crude vessels down the thick, creeping waters of the Marat until they came to its estuary, where they moored in a natural cove. From here a single wooden ship, the *Ellon*, set sail for Albion to find out if that land of travellers' tales was indeed a haven of plenty and peace. The remainder waited . . . and waited . . . and waited. The explorers never returned, and over the years it became plain that they never would. Another ship followed them northwestward, but all it found was the open sea.

As they waited, it became clear to the refugees that they had already found their sanctuary. Aside from themselves, no one ever came to this barren isthmus. Using boulders hauled up from the shore and wood from some of their vessels and from the skeletal trees that dotted the marshes, they built themselves a settlement. They survived the attacks of the vicious ffarg, the hostile, semi-intelligent beings who dwelled in the dank swamp called the Mistdom; they watched with pride as their rough stone walls withstood the onslaught of the storms and the hurricanes; even when, one year in those early times, plague came among their number, enough of them survived that their town was able to regenerate itself.

They gave the settlement no name, because without a name it had no real existence in the minds of the warring humans and other sentient creatures, elsewhere in the World, whose attentions they wished to avoid. Armed guards patrolled the walls, ready at any time to repel the ffarg, but this was the inhabitants' only physical reminder of combat. And daily the people of the Anonymous City performed their religious rites, thanking the benevolence of the ever-merciful Sun for having given them what little they had.

Centuries passed.

And then everything changed. Wealth came to the city – or, at least, to a part of it.

No one knows who first discovered that one of the unpromising-looking weeds of the swamplands, if dried and rolled tight and compacted with chalk dust and a little fresh water, could be eaten to produce euphoria. Collecting the herb was a dangerous business, because the ffarg were ever-vigilant and slaughtered barbarously any male humans they encountered; the females fared even worse, for it was the ungrounded vanity of the ffarg that they could cross-breed with human females to produce offspring that were stronger and more intelligent than either parent.

Yet to those who had once tasted bradz, as the narcotic came to be called, any risk was worth it. All of the body and all of the mind were filled with a joy that seemed to stretch to the furthest corner of the World. Even pain became an ecstasy to be welcomed. Hunger was a welcome old friend, to be greeted with embraces and small cries of delight. But most important was that for short periods the bradz-eater could fly – easily and gracefully, like a large-winged bird, floating among the high air currents before gliding gently back towards the ground. Flight was something that no one who had ever experienced it could possibly forget – or renounce.

Which was the trouble. The rapture had to be repeated. And repeated again and again, as the bradz-eater forgot about food and water and shrank in upon himself until his life ended somewhere high above swamps or rooftops, and the empty rag of his body fluttered to the ground.

The traditionally pious ways of the Anonymous City were dead within the year. Powerful men and women organized themselves into esoteric cartels – the guilds – excluding all except their own families and their closest friends, resisting the blandishments of bradz and turning their attentions instead towards the possibilities of covert trade with other areas. Soon bradz was outlawed in every land of the World, even in those whose knowledge of civilization was only at third hand.

The poor saw the wealthy families of the cartels, and they cursed them daily through their parched lips, but enough bradz was allowed to find its way into the slums to keep their furies subdued – at least for now.

And, it seemed to everyone, for an everlasting now.

2

The song used to run thus:

In one of the most dangerous slums of the Anonymous City there is a narrow, crooked alley joining two thoroughfares barely wider than itself. Years ago some joker called it Glory Row, and the name has stuck. The wooden houses, their paint long since gone, teeter inwards above the cracked cobblestones, as if trying to seize each other for support to stop themselves from falling in a heap of dusty fragments into the alleyway beneath. Only a brave man ventures here during the grey daylight hours; only a fool or a hero or one of the Vermin does so at night.

Windowframes hang at crazy angles and rotting doors slump on their hinges. There is no light here, for the people have no oil for lamps – and nothing with which to spark a flame. The windows are eyes into blackness. One would almost think the homes were empty were it not for the weak wail of a restive child or the uneasy shufflings of people trying to find paradise together on a pallet of damp straw.

But there is one house where the lamps are lit.

Half-way along the alley is the Kitchen of One-Legged Tom, where the lowest dregs from the Anonymous City's slums come at nights to eat and drink – thin, wiry men, creeping like cats through the shadows, their ragged capes drawn tight around their scarred bodies. Before they push open the heavy door of One-Legged Tom's Kitchen they cast their eyes backwards and forwards, their shoulders instinctively tensed for the dart of a blade. Then, all in a single movement, they are inside and the door is once more firmly closed behind them.

In an area where food is in such short supply that few children live long enough to say their first word, One-Legged Tom's Kitchen is an anomaly. Here there is food a-plenty for those who can afford to pay for it: crackling steaks, grease-dripping roast haunches of meat, steaming stews, pies, pasties, sausages . . .

There are two reasons why the Kitchen survives. The first concerns its regular clientele, the Vermin, who come here nightly to eat their fill. The Vermin are vicious and they are sly. Should anyone dare to attack Tom or raid his Kitchen, their name would soon reach the Vermin, who know only too well how to ensure that death is a protracted and far from enjoyable experience.

The second is more pleasing to the mind and the eye alike. Who knows when One-Legged Tom had a wife or what sort of a woman she was, but she left behind her a daughter, Kursten. Now Kursten is a woman herself, a woman whose face seems to shine with its own gentle light. Her hair is fine-spun gold, falling in thin drapes to her waist. Her lips are red as a ruby's red, and her eyes are the pale yellow of a winter's early sunrise. She helps her father by carrying wooden bowls full of food to where the Vermin wait eagerly on rough benches. She seems never to smile, and yet she kindles in them some sort of recognition of the kind of life they could be living if they were not in the here and now. The oaths and the ribald jokes die away when she is near. None of them would ever dare to lay a lustful hand upon her, and few of them would truly wish to, for she is their gateway to a different and infinitely distant world.

During the day Kursten sits in her attic bedroom, gazing out into the interminable distance, over the rooftops of the Anonymous City and over the Broken Marshes and the Mistdom beyond its walls. She plucks the strings of the small clarsach between her knees and sings to the notes its shining wooden frame produces. The songs she sings are songs to her lover, the lover she has yet to meet. They carry her away over the Mistdom that surrounds the city and the plains beyond it and the hills and the seas beyond them to some distant land unknown to any mapmaker, where he walks with her among green trees, the butterflies swirling around their faces or resting on their shoulders, the breeze taking her hair and turning it into a living thing.

As she is singing, she smiles.

3

Gnetz and Egroeg were among a couple of dozen Vermin enjoying their meal thoroughly and loudly that evening in One-Legged Tom's Kitchen when the door flew open. At first Gnetz thought it was just the wind again – it was a blustering night, and usually only the wind could open the door without first knocking and being granted admittance – and neither of them looked up from dipping their coarse hunks of bread into the deliciously oily stew.

But then the door slammed shut again, and the daggers in their fists were transformed suddenly from eating implements into weapons. Both stared at the person standing in the doorway, their bodies taut in readiness to fight.

The man who had come into the Kitchen was nearing middle age but seemed to have been gifted with youth – he looked about twenty, certainly no more than twenty-five, until one noticed the wrinkles at the edges of his eyes – and he was well, although not luxuriously, dressed. His cape was of a dark material much more finely woven than any fabric the eaters in the room had seen before, and his boots appeared to be made of real leather, although there was so much mud on them that it was hard to tell. At his belt there was the decorated pommel of a slender sword, but otherwise he seemed to be unarmed except for the customary dagger that everybody wore; also tucked into his belt, alongside his money-pouch, was an ancient cane flute, the wood worn white around its finger-holes. So the man was a singer. On his head was a brimmed green hat decorated with a single feather which, somewhere along the road, had been broken, so that its upper half dangled sadly.

He buffed his hands vigorously together and smiled openly at the closed faces.

'Windy night tonight,' he said.

'We know that,' grunted One-Legged Tom, his hand resting on the long black handle of a pan filled with boiling fat.

'Ah, landlord. Can you find it within yourself to feed a man that's hungry and cold? I have with me the money to pay you for your kindness.'

It was plain that the newcomer was beginning to suspect that perhaps he had strayed into forbidden territory, because a slight but distinct tone of anxiety had entered his voice.

'Go,' said One-Legged Tom, not impolitely, and a couple of his regular customers growled their agreement. 'I cannot be held responsible for your life if you choose to stay here any longer.'

The young-old man was turning to obey when Kursten silently entered the Kitchen's main room from the scullery behind. At first no one realized that she was there, as all their eyes were on the traveller.

'Father,' she said very softly, but it was enough that around the room bodies relaxed a little.

The intruder, his hand on the corroded brass doorlatch, turned to look, and paused. Slowly he drew himself to his full height, although there was still a certain nervousness in his movement. He smiled, a little weak fluttering gesture directed to her alone.

No one in that room except maybe her father had seen Kursten smile before, but she did so now – only slightly, and only for the briefest of moments. But there remained a warmth in her grave yellow eyes after the smile had gone from her lips.

'Father,' she repeated, a little louder this time, 'it's a foul night out there. Can't we let this traveller dine with us before he has to face the elements again?'

'Keep your meddling nose out of this, girl!' snapped One-Legged Tom at once.

'Ay,' agreed Egroeg. It was one of his rare words, and as soon as it had left his mouth he realized that he had been the only person to second the landlord's statement. Embarrassed, he crouched down over his bowl of stew and started to eat voraciously again, affecting lusty appreciation, doing his best to ignore the accusatory stares of his fellow Vermin.

The traveller took off his tired-looking hat and shuffled from foot to foot, staring unhappily at the broken feather.

One-Legged Tom suddenly relented.

'Ah, well,' he said. 'I reckon there's enough to go around for all. You eat up quick, mind, and then be off with you into the night, whoever you are.'

He cracked a grimy towel in the air and turned back to his flames and his pots and his pans, still glowering at his daughter. It was uncommon for her not to bend to his will.

She kissed him lightly on the side of the forehead, squeezed his shoulder affectionately, and moved past him and across the room to take the stranger's cape. She reached out to accept his flute as well when he drew it from his belt, but he waved her hand away, preferring to hold it close by him.

'Make room, you two,' Kursten said over her shoulder, flicking her pale hair back. 'Yes, you two – Egroeg and Gnetz. Come on, move over. There's plenty of space at your table for another.'

The traveller pulled up a stool and sat between them. The normal hubbub of conversation slowly returned to the Kitchen as the eaters at the other tables forgot the matter and picked up where they had left off.

The two Vermin looked at the stranger with distaste, Gnetz with his gap-toothed mouth open ready to swallow the congealing lump of stew skewered on the tip of his dagger. After a few moments Egroeg suddenly lost interest, and returned to mopping at the gravy in his bowl with a fistful of bread. But the little man Gnetz, by far the more intelligent of the pair, did not drop the matter so easily. His eyes narrowed as they took in the fine cloth of the stranger's clothing and the little silver medallion that hung on the stranger's chest: the head of a woman in whose eyes, even though the metal had been smoothed by time, there was the light of a warrior. Gnetz remembered that the man had told One-Legged Tom that he had enough money to pay for his meal, and the confident way in which he'd said it would seem to suggest that he had not just enough but more than enough.

Egroeg, his huge shoulders rounded under the dirty canvas of his jacket, started on a second bowl of stew.

'Is the food good here?' said the traveller. He smiled in a despairing way at Gnetz's forbidding, motionless stare. 'Mmm,' he added nervously, 'it certainly smells it.'

'What your name?'

Another gobbet of stew vanished into Egroeg's maw.

'Rehan,' said the traveller, startled. Gnetz's voice had been like a knife scratched across corrugated glass, but it had held a note of command. 'Barra 'ap Rteniadoli Me'gli'minter Rehan, to give me the full name that I hardly ever use.'

Gnetz raised his eyebrows on hearing the man's extended name. He knew what it meant, and wondered if its owner did. 'The little boy who wonders long enough to step through the gates which other people open for him.' Whoever had named the pipsqueak had seen the same dangerous inquisitiveness that Gnetz had suspected, yet had qualified the description with an expression of Rehan's passivity. Yet if the name had been given long ago . . . people can change. It would be as well not to relax too much in front of this singer.

All Gnetz said was: 'Where you come from?'

'From Albion originally, but this past year I have been dwelling in Rantang.'

Rehan motioned with his head towards the east, and Gnetz nodded slowly, putting down his dagger momentarily and picking up some bread. He knew the place. It was a fishing town – really no more than a village – about half-way to Dargen.

'Where you going?'

'Arnas.'

'Bit lost, then, you are,' said Gnetz. Of course, he'd never heard of Arnas before, but as a matter of principle he was putting doubts into the stranger's mind: those doubts might prove useful later.

'Just a little,' said Rehan with another of his uneasy smiles. He glanced towards Egroeg but saw nothing more than the balding top of his head, the scalp moving in tune to the giant man's jaws. Conversations didn't interest Egroeg much.

'Quite a lot,' Gnetz corrected. 'Got a horse?'

'I *had* a horse,' said Rehan eagerly, 'but it broke its leg in the swamp just a few kilometres from the walls of your fine city. I was hoping to be able to buy another tomorrow.'

Kursten arrived with Rehan's meal and Gnetz temporarily suspended his interrogation. He couldn't help noticing that the stranger's bowl was more generously filled than most, and that it came accompanied by a beaker of warm perry. Perry – even ale – was a rare luxury in the slums of the Anonymous City.

So the little angel has taken a shine to this halfwit, thought Gnetz dourly. *Never before known her to give any man so much as a second glance. Wondered if she were made of glass rather than flesh and blood, I did. Be a pity in the morning. Perhaps One-Legged Tom will recognize him later when he . . . no, be wisest to throw him in the river. Still, a pity's a pity, and that's all there is to be said about it. A man carrying enough gold to buy a horse must simply accept the fact that there's going to be a knife planted in his gullet.*

Rehan smelled the soft spring scent of her, even through the cooking odours, as she leaned forward over him to turn his flagon just a little, so that the handle was more convenient to his hand. He felt the soft touch of her gossamer-fine hair caress his cheek. Her breath stirred his own hair.

'I thank you,' he said with courteous formality.

'I thank you, too,' she whispered, so that even Gnetz's eager ears couldn't pick up the words, 'for simply being here.'

Ah, thought Rehan, *Anya and Reen, if you could only see me now. But one of you's secure on your throne in Albion with Ngur by your side and the other's wandering the World I know not where. And here am I being all but propositioned by a cook's daughter, and with half a mind to accept her . . .*

She left them, and he set about his food, moving his dagger in quick, economical sallies. His handling of the implement was graceful to the point of daintiness, yet it was in no way prissy.

Hmm, Gnetz thought, observing all of this with unobtrusive eyes, *so the poltroon knows how to use a dagger. Much good it'll do him, of course, but it would be as well for us to remember not to underestimate him.*

'Perhaps my good friend Egroeg and I could guide you back to your route,' he said out loud.

4

There was an argument going on in the scullery. The two of them kept their voices as low as possible so that the words wouldn't escape to reach the ears of the Vermin.

'Dammit, you stupid wench!' spat One-Legged Tom. 'You've condemned that poor misbegotten moron to his death!'

'Father, you . . .'

'Don't "Father" me this or "Father" me that! He's obviously got money with him – too much money. There's not a single man out there wouldn't gladly slit his throat for a solitary coin of what that fool's likely to have in his pouch. And you – oh, you're not content with that! Oh, no, not you! You have to go and sit him down beside Gnetz. Even those other wild bastards are terrified of what Gnetz can do when the mood's in him.'

'Father, you're always saying things like that, but I've known Gnetz since I was a child.' She smoothed her hands down over her long green dress. It was patched and faded, and soon she would have to abandon it and stitch herself another.

'May the gods in their heavens preserve us from the

maunderings of babes, fools and women!' said One-Legged Tom bitterly, and she could hear that he was losing control of himself. She put a thin finger to his lips to make him lower his voice. 'I wouldn't trust Gnetz not to slice off that poor boy's balls and send them to you on the morrow in a paper bag,' Tom continued more quietly. 'He's insane, I tell you: a mad dog. The others are bad enough, but he positively enjoys it all. It's like screwing, to him.'

She looked at him, horrified, because she realized suddenly that the unaccustomed bluntness of his words was a measure of the truth of what he was telling her. In the moment of finding that at last there was someone who'd come to her father's Kitchen who was neither furtive nor crooked, neither maliciously grinning nor cacklingly brutal – who was, by the whispered names of all the forbidden gods, nothing more nor less than a *normal human being* – she had forgotten everything else except her own joy at discovering a man who could, just could, bear some resemblance to the lover to whom she had been singing all these years. She'd sensed, too, that there had been a spark of response in him – not the usual unvoiced but readily invocable lust that she'd encountered so many times before: something quite different. The sound of a serendipitous nonce-chord on her harp, perhaps – a chord that, no matter how long or how determinedly her fingers sought it, they could never recapture.

And her reward to this stranger? To lead him to his death?

Father and daughter stood there, frozen, for a moment, his arms half up as if to draw her to his chest, she with low shoulders and with grief written in the soft lines of her face. There were tears at the corners of her pale eyes.

Then, with a sudden decisiveness, she stood up straight again.

'There's only one solution,' she said. 'He must stay here with us the night.'

'Here?'

'Yes, Father. He'll be safe with us.'

'There's nowhere in the city he'll be safe with that bag of money he's carrying. Not even here.'

One-Legged Tom shook his head wearily, and this time she did come into his arms. Her head made little convulsive jerking movements on his shoulder as she carefully wept into the cloth of his hot-smelling jerkin.

'Would he be safe with *me*?' she said unsteadily at last.

'Daughter . . .'

'He could sleep the night in my room. The Vermin would never dare disturb him there.'

'You'd throw away your virtue for him?'

'My reputation, yes – I'd gladly lose that for his sake. But surely that need not mean I lose my virtue.'

One-Legged Tom looked over her shoulder at the reflection of the pair of them in the blackness of the scullery window. He – and her own aura – had perhaps shielded her too well from the realities of the Anonymous City.

'He's a man,' the father said. 'He will want to lie with you.'

'Then I shall ask him not to.'

'D'you think it would be as easy as that?'

'Yes. It'll be as easy as that. I think so.'

The old man gently let go of her.

'Ach, then, let you have your way.' Reluctantly. Affectionately. Then, wiping away important matters as if with one of his dish-towels: 'Here, I must be getting back to tending the Vermin's appetites. Dry your eyes and come and help me when you feel able.'

He limped away from her, his crutch clacking on the stone floor, but he stopped just before leaving the scullery. He turned to give her a sad smile.

'Lass,' he said, 'you're a good wench and a courageous one – like your mother was, and if you'd ever known her you'd know what a compliment that is. If the morning comes and your maidenhead has fled with the night, I'll love you none the less for that.'

He pulled the curtain closed behind him.

5

Gnetz had just been explaining to Rehan about the venomous flora and malevolent fauna of the Broken Marshes – he barely needed to embroider the details of these but had done so anyway out of professional pride – and had paused to freshen his throat with a draught from the traveller's beaker of perry when both of them heard the crash of shattering glass and a swiftly muffled scream. Gnetz was about to laugh his high, scraping laugh when Rehan held up his hand to halt him.

'What was that?' the young-old man said.

None of the other diners in the Kitchen was paying any attention to the noise. Even One-Legged Tom, his face knotted, was too lost in his own thoughts to hear anything except the echoes of his argument with his daughter.

Egroeg, who had been looking bored ever since he'd finished eating, long before, broke his silence at last.

'Swiving,' he said, bubbles of gravy on his lips. 'Happens alla time. Some bitch asking for it. Fun.' He began to pick his teeth appreciatively with the point of his dagger. 'Join in, if you want. More the merrier.'

He grinned in the flickering lamplight.

Rehan toyed with his own dagger. Looking into the sewer of that subhuman leer, he found himself wanting to . . .

'It wasn't from outside,' he said. 'It came from beyond that doorway.' He pointed towards the scullery. 'What's there?'

'Just the scullery,' said Gnetz, laboriously uninterested.

'And where's that girl gone? The one who was here.'

'Dunno,' said Gnetz flatly, Egroeg having once more lost interest in the conversation. 'Pretty little thing, though, in't she? Make a good rolling for some man, someday, eh?'

'Landlord!' shouted Rehan across the room, his voice cutting through all the other sounds. 'Where's your daughter got herself to?'

One-Legged Tom came awake suddenly. Had there been a scream? He dropped the pan he had been tending and limped on his crutch as fast as he was able to the curtain shielding the scullery door.

He threw it open, and the Kitchen was filled with howling wind.

'Kursten!' the old man yelled despairingly.

A smooth leathery tail was just slithering out of the wreckage of the scullery window. 'Kursten! Kursten! Daughter! No no nonononono . . .'

Among his choking cries there was one word that kept on and on recurring.

'Ffarg.'

6

Within instants the Vermin were on their feet and tumbling out through the door into Glory Row. A lamp was knocked over onto the floor, and Rehan promptly stamped out the flames before they could spread. One-Legged Tom was left weeping where he lay, ignored.

'Which way have they taken her?' asked Rehan sharply. He ran his sword backwards and forwards in its sheath, testing the smoothness of its running.

'Who cares?' Gnetz replied off-handedly, speaking for them all. 'Get out of my way, you' – shoving at one of the other Vermin, who was blocking the doorway.

'Aren't we going to rescue her?' said Rehan, astonished by the Vermin's attitude.

Egroeg laughed. It was the sound of an imploding building.

'Us?' said Gnetz incredulously, turning to stare at Rehan.

'But I thought you . . . I mean, aren't we going to try to . . . ?'

'Don't be naïve, bucko. Ffarg are bloody dangerous, as you'd know if you'd been for more than five minutes in the Anonymous City. If there're any of them around, the best place for all of us to be is somewhere else. (May the forbidden gods shit on me, Freetin, but if you don't let me pass you'll have a dagger in your back.)'

Contempt arrived piecemeal on Rehan's face, but he said nothing else. Quietly, moving with exaggerated calmness, he knelt down and made the sobbing One-Legged Tom more comfortable, resting the man's head on a couple of cloaks left behind by the customers in their haste to escape from the restricting walls of the Kitchen. Then he took his own cape from the hook where Kursten had hung it such a short while ago, gathered a pair of discarded daggers from the tables and made his exit through the gaping space of the scullery window.

Behind him, Gnetz looked at Egroeg's puzzled eyes and laughed. 'He'll be back in good time,' said the little man derisively. 'The ffarg will be far from here by now.'

Once Rehan was outside he could hear off to his right the urgent footsteps of fleeing Vermin. He turned left.

The wind was directly in his face. This would make the going difficult, but was otherwise good news. The ffarg would be unlikely to pick up his scent, but with luck he would be brought some of the sounds of their progress during any short respite between the stronger gusts.

A dagger in his hand, his cape blown flat and snapping out behind him, his lips pulled back from his teeth and his eyes watering already from the thrust of the gale, he made his way as quickly as he could up the night-black centre of Glory Row.

He was terrified – more terrified than he could ever remember being except for the time, back in Albion, when he had entered the Ellonian encampment pitched on the field in front of Giorran, or the time, long before that, when first he'd bedded a woman – and yet he kept himself moving onwards. The reason for both terror and determination was the same one: what Gnetz had told him about the ffarg, added to the scant information he had been given before setting out for the Anonymous City – for he was not quite the straying wayfarer that he'd depicted himself to be, even though his ideas as to why he was here were distinctly fuzzy. The ffarg were as tall as or taller than a man, but far bulkier and twice as strongly muscled. Their thistle-like feet were vicious and effective weapons, as were the long, lashing tails of the warrior class, tipped by a bony excrescence that resembled – and could be used every bit as effectively as – a morningstar. Even the smooth tails of the ffarg's thralls – the smaller but rather similar trran – could be fatally dangerous because of the sheer bone-shattering force with which they could be wielded. And the ffarg ahead of Rehan would, in addition, be armed.

So far as he could understand, there were only two areas in which he had the advantage. First, ffarg were not very intelligent. Second, in the ffarg's snouted, tusked face there was only a single eye. The consequent lack of stereoscopic vision meant that they had much greater difficulty in accurately judging distances than humans did. *At least I won't have to contend with archery*. Because of their single eye the ffarg were one of the World's few intelligent or semi-intelligent species never to have developed the bow and arrow.

There were, Gnetz had been telling him, very few female ffarg. In fact, since they bore large litters, there was a sufficiency of them to keep the species' population at a fairly steady level, but it was the eternal fear of these creatures that their kind were in imminent danger of extinction. Therefore the belief – a conviction of almost religious intensity – had grown up among them that, through some quirk of evolution, ffarg males were capable of interbreeding with the females of the human and humanoid species of the World, the results of such bestial matings being perfectly formed ffarg with the sharp wits of the mother . . .

For all he knew, Kursten was just another tavern harlot, and her smiles to him the practised blandishments of one well versed in the skills of her trade. But he didn't think so, and at the moment the matter was irrelevant: no human being deserved to become futile breeding stock for the ffarg.

He heard a scream from up ahead.

Good girl, he thought. She couldn't know there was anyone following her, but as long as she could keep yelling from time to time his task of pursuit was going to be much easier. The ffarg were obviously not too much concerned about keeping Kursten quiet. Female screams were hardly rare occurrences in this part of the town – or anywhere in the Anonymous City, come to that. No one else but himself would bother coming to investigate.

He put as much more energy as he could summon into pressing forwards, dodging at the last moment as a broken window-shutter came dancing on the wind down the alley towards him. Had one of the moons not crept momentarily from behind the racing clouds he might have been felled in the darkness.

Luck, luck, luck, he thought urgently. *I can do with plenty of that from here on.*

He had finally reached the far end of Glory Row. The street that ran from left to right in front of him was somewhat wider and less dimly lit. He paused, once again uncertain which way to go. Directly across the thoroughfare from him was the black mouth of another narrow alley. Had he been a party of absconding ffarg he'd have chosen to go that way, but he could only make guesses about how the swamp creatures' minds might work.

The issue was soon settled by another scream. This time the sound was very faint, the wind no longer being in his favour, but he was certain that it had come from somewhere off to his right.

He scurried across to the far side of the street and started to run along in the lee of the houses. He made much swifter progress now. Not only was the light a little better but the buildings of the street shielded him from the worst of the wind's blast rather than funnelling it towards him. He smiled a grim smile as he felt his body smoothly obeying all the commands that had been drilled into it during his past year of self-imposed training in Rantang. Indeed, he was finding that there was a certain element of pleasurable excitement in the chase. This was, after all, what the servants of his master had been teaching him to do. Although his internal master had seemingly expected, when sending him here to the Anonymous City, that his acquired skills might have to be used only against the thugs of the bradz-runners, a skirmish with a band of ffarg would be looked upon as a suitable warming-up exercise.

Assuming, that is, that he survived it.

There was one thing puzzling him as he ran. From the sketchy information he had been given before setting out for the Anonymous City, and from what Gnetz had told him in One-Legged Tom's Kitchen, the ffarg rarely ventured out of the cloying mists of the Broken Marshes, and had certainly since the earliest days never been known to make an incursion within the city walls.

There were few people on the street tonight. The streets were in any event dangerous and hence little used during the hours of darkness, but tonight the boisterous wind had made many of even the most foolhardy citizens think twice before leaving the security of their homes. Those pedestrians that there were ducked swiftly out of the way when they saw the agile caped man running towards them, his twin daggers at the ready.

He came to a crossroads. Again there was a timely scream, this time from his left.

And then he saw something up ahead – a fluttering movement. Kursten's green dress? His mind, resolutely illogical, refused to believe that it could have been anything else.

Rehan began to move yet more swiftly, looking quickly from side to side as he ran. Because of their powerful tails, the worst direction from which to attack a ffarg was from the rear. Somehow he must get around them so that he could grapple with them head-on.

Or from above?

A much better idea. There was only one of him, so the more unexpected his direction of attack the better chance he would have.

They were approaching a slightly less seedy part of the Anonymous City, and the streets had grown wider. Here and there were small parks and gardens, in which grew shoddy imitations of the trees he had known in other parts of the World, their branches tossing and twisting in the gale like the arms of petulant children.

The moon Struan re-emerged from the clouds. Rehan saw to his astonishment that he had come dangerously close to catching up with the ffarg: their swiftly lumbering figures were no more than about twenty metres ahead of him. There were only four of the creatures, he saw with relief – two huge warriors and two of the less imposing trran. All four seemed bigger than he'd expected from the mental pictures he'd been shown.

Kursten was draped over the shoulder of one of the warriors, and, raising her head, spotted him immediately. He gestured her to silence and kept on running, slowing down a little to open up the gap.

He thanked the gods whose names he'd learned since coming to the World that they were once again running directly into the wind. Its screaming and the clatter of the ffarg's claws along the cobblestones drowned out any sounds that he might make. *If only one of them doesn't think to turn around . . .*

He waited until the next time they were crossing one of the open gardens and then, without breaking his stride, flipped the dagger in his right hand neatly backwards so that he was holding it by its thread-sharp blade. His forearm came up, and then he lazily threw, giving the dagger's tip a final flick just before he let it go, so that the weapon spun end over end as it flew through the air.

He ducked into the shelter of a tree.

The blade struck true, straight into the back of the squat neck of one of the trran.

The beast fell, dropping its weapons and clutching uselessly at the spot where the dagger's blade had irrupted into its spinal cord.

The others carried on regardless. Rehan, hiding behind a coarse bole, could hardly believe it. Either they hadn't noticed what had befallen their comrade or they simply didn't care. Again Rehan thanked the World's strange gods. *It's the single eye that's their problem*, he thought. *No real idea of ballistics. There's nobody close by them, ergo there can't be a weapon close by them, either.*

Dodging the still-flailing tail of the dying trran, he returned to the pursuit.

The sky had emptied of clouds, and the World's smaller second moon, Zoa, was climbing towards the first. In their joint silvery light he was better able to see where he was treading and what he was doing. The trouble was that the ffarg would be enjoying the same advantage . . .

But once more he had a dagger in his right hand, held firmly by the blade. Again he waited until they were in one of the little parks, and again the knife struck home, dropping the second trran in its tracks.

This time the two ffarg warriors certainly did notice that there was something going on.

They stopped with an abruptness that shocked him. One moment they were moving at a rapid run and the next they were stock-still. He dived for cover. The two great beasts stood there suspiciously as the trran squealed its last at their feet. They were sniffing the air around them, seeking the slightest sign of their attacker. Kursten screamed again, presumably hoping to distract their attention from the search.

Rehan pulled himself up the trunk of the tree in front of him. Bare twigs drew blood from his face but the coldness of the air was so intense that he hardly felt the pain. He settled himself warily between two branches, trying to make as little noise as possible, and then edged himself gently forwards astride the thicker of them, cursing the punishment his groin was taking from the roughly flaked bark.

But it seemed that again he was in luck – or, he congratulated himself, that his earlier ideas had been correct. Despite the evidence given to him by their reactions – or lack of reactions – to the death of the first trran, he had been dubious about the strategic speculations that had been turning inside his head ever since he had conceived the notion of assault from above. *The ffarg have only a single eye, and therefore cannot judge distance well. Therefore they have never developed the bow and arrow – or even, for that matter, the sling, the thrown dagger, or any other ballistic weapon. Therefore they have never had very much interest in flying creatures as a food source, because unless you have ballistic weapons there's no way you can bring down a bird in flight. And therefore, however much they might have seen flying creatures in their skirmishes with humans, the last place the ffarg would instinctively think of looking for an enemy would be directly above their heads. Add to that,* thought Rehan smugly, *the fact that the ffarg are intensely stupid creatures and you have a clear-cut case of QED. Rehan, the minstrel at whom some of Albion's peasant warriors scoffed, has shown his genius once again. Let's hear three lusty cheers for . . .*

The ffarg that was carrying Kursten stood well clear of the trees and watched all around it as its companion searched cautiously further afield. Kursten saw Rehan on his perch and once again he saw hope spreading back into her face. The questing ffarg, its tail swishing powerfully, was coming close to the tree in whose barren branches he was hiding. He leaned forwards, so that he was lying flat on the bough, gripping the rough bark with his thighs and calves to keep himself in position while leaving his hands free. He drew his own Rantang dagger from its sheath at his belt, feeling the metal scrollwork of its hilt digging into his palm.

The ffarg passed directly beneath him.

The stench of its sweat was nauseating, choking, but he forced himself to ignore it.

Moving swiftly, yet with his accustomed fastidiousness, he reached downwards and flipped the ffarg's leather helmet forwards over its eye and nose. Then, with all the power of his right arm, he drove the dagger directly down into the creature's cranium.

The ffarg collapsed instantly with a crash onto the scrubby grass. There was no other sound of its dying.

The remaining ffarg, Rehan could see, was unable to believe the evidence of its slow senses. One moment its accomplice had been alive; the next it had simply dropped down dead for no apparent reason. Rehan's strike had been so rapid that, in the poorish light from the moons, the creature had been unable to discern by what agency – mortal or occult – its comrade had met its end. And it had no urgent desire to solve the enigma.

The ffarg spun once in a full circle where it stood, and then turned again and fled with all the speed its stumpy legs could attain.

Rehan dropped lightly from his branch down onto the grass. He was aware that he was running low on weaponry: his sword was a light-swift weapon in his hand when used against human enemies, but he had little faith in the efficacy of its speed alone when used against the brute toughness of a ffarg's leathery skin. He spared a grunting moment or two to lug his dagger out of the dead ffarg's skull and return it to its sheath. As an afterthought he pulled the beast's great double-edged axe from its lifeless hand and hefted the heavy weapon over his shoulder.

The single remaining ffarg was running more fleetly now, and it was all that Rehan could do, especially burdened by the heavy axe, to keep up with it. His training-induced stamina was, he knew, beginning at last to ebb, and his chest was burning as if his pulsing heart had lit a fire in order to scorch its way free from the cage of his ribs.

There were more lamplit windows around them now, but this was offset by the fact that the light of Zoa was suddenly cut off. Rehan realized that they were coming close under the shadow of the city's walls. *The bastard must be making for the place where they managed to get through and into the city. I have to get closer. If that bloody ffarg just vanishes into the shadows and never comes out again then Kursten is as good as lost forever.* He thought of discarding the axe he'd so recently acquired, but it would probably be his only effective weapon should it come to straightforward hand-to-hand combat with the ffarg. From somewhere – perhaps from one of the various gods to whom he had learned to pay lip-service in the World – he found that he had just a little more strength.

And he was almost up on the ffarg now, just out of range of its lashing tail; Kursten was shouting encouragement at him. He remembered how abruptly the creatures had been able to stop, back there in the park when he'd dropped the second trran, and knew how vulnerable he was so close behind. But he was reluctant to let himself drop further back. He felt for the hilt of his dagger, but left the weapon in his belt; the neck of a ffarg was far tougher than that of a trran. The beast itself was slowing down. Clearly it was looking for something. There were many more lights now, and Rehan realized they were coming near to one of the Anonymous City's minor gateways. Surely there must be other human beings here who would be prepared to help him tackle the creature. But he could see no signs of anyone else.

Except, up there ahead of him, a couple of sentries standing by the gate.

In fact, the gate was hardly more than a massive wooden door, set perhaps a metre back into the wall. Although it had obviously been constructed with difficulty from the low-grade wood available to the inhabitants of the city and from scavenged pieces of metal, it looked stout enough to withstand even the full impact of a charging ffarg. Soon the beast must surely be at bay. With the help of the sentries Rehan would certainly triumph . . . so long as they could kill the ffarg without harming Kursten. That last was a priority as far as Rehan was concerned, but of course the sentries might see things otherwise.

Yet the sentries were making no move to raise their weapons towards the fleeing creature and its human burden. Instead, they were moving from their posts to strip back the bolts and bars of the door they were supposed to be guarding.

Rehan took in the situation instantly.

Here was treachery.

The ffarg raiding party could only have got into the Anonymous City with human collusion. Who better to collude with them than the gate-sentries themselves? The guards high on the walls need hear nothing and see nothing. The band of heavily armed ffarg could quietly sneak through the shadows, in by the welcoming gate, and off along the darkest parts of the city's streets. But there had to be more to it than that. For a start, the guards must have been bribed with money, and the ffarg, he had been told, had no conception of money. And Rehan refused to believe that the creatures would have gone to the effort and risk of crossing half of the Anonymous City on the off-chance that they might fortuitously stumble across a solitary woman. No, they'd have simply broken into the first house they'd come to, slaughtered the males, seized the girl-children and the women, and been gone before anyone could make a move to stop them.

They had wanted one woman in particular – Kursten. *And they knew where to find her!*

Rehan was close enough now to deal with one of the sentries. His dagger took the man in the eye. The sentry fell, screaming, in a gush of blood. The other was clearly in two minds. To face the onslaught of an enraged ffarg by helping Rehan and thereby maybe saving his own skin should the citizens hand out retributions later, or to let Rehan and the girl die, and then hope to escape from the Anonymous City in all the confusion. But where would he go to? Into the *Mistdom*?

Rehan could see on the man's face his sudden decision that the ffarg was closer to him and therefore the more immediately menacing of the two threats. The sentry began to tussle with the bolts even more eagerly than before.

And now he had the gate open. Hardly pausing, the ffarg rushed through, cruelly jouncing Kursten against the wall as it negotiated the strait opening. Thankfully the girl seemed to have fainted.

Rehan almost gave up all hope; but then, shouldering the gibbering sentry aside, he threw himself at the wooden door, slamming it shut with all the might at his command.

He'd hardly dared hope that the stratagem would work

– but it had. About a metre of the ffarg's tail still protruded, jammed between the edge of the door and the hard stone of the city wall. The mace-like protrusion at its end was jerked spasmically from side to side as the frantic creature tried to pull itself free. Still Rehan kept hold of the axe, in case it should prove necessary, but more and more he was doubting that: to sever the bony bulge would drive the beast into a terminal fury and thus almost certainly seal the girl's fate.

He half-turned, drawing his sword awkwardly with his left hand, ignoring the tug of the end of his flute at his cuff, and almost dreamily slashed out to take off the sentry's arm at the wrist in order to preclude a treacherous attack from that quarter. Then, as the man howled, he returned his attention to the ffarg's angry tail. He released his pressure against the gate a little, so that another few centimetres of tail disappeared into the darkness beyond. *Let it think that it's achieving these small gains through its own efforts.*

Rehan propped his sword carefully against the gate's hinges so that it'd be ready for when he needed it, and continued to play his teasing game with the swamp-creature's tail. He found the whole exercise oddly and dispassionately fascinating, like a perfectly executed dance in which you're certain that at any moment there is going to be some clumsiness but equally certain that there won't.

He could hear shouts and clatterings from above him as the guards scrambled down the precipitous stone steps from their posts on top of the walls. The sentry whom he had maimed was now standing quite motionless and quite silent, stupidly watching the blood spurt from the stump of his wrist. Most of the windows in the houses opposite the gate were now fully lit, and Rehan could see that in many of them the well-to-do citizens of the Anonymous City were avidly watching all that was going on. This was one of the richer parts of the city, as he'd guessed, and probably the only excitement these people ever got was a gratuitous execution. *What a pity for them*, thought Rehan with sarcastic sympathy, *that there will be so little for them to see tonight – and that with luck this clown of a traitor will have the sense to let me help him cheat the executioner. Sadistic bastards. All wrapped up warm in their furs and fineries – what fun it must be to watch a good, slow, gruesome death and hear the screams of the poor sod who's the star of the circus. 'Tra-la, tra-la, but wasn't that enjoyable, and now it's time to go home to a nice hot supper and tuck the kiddies into their beds. My dear, would you like me to pass your cloak?'*

In a way, Rehan concluded, he preferred the overt evil of the Vermin to the covert evil of these bradz-enriched burghers.

He let the tail slip the last few centimetres and watched with childish delight as, with a solid clunk, the bony morningstar caught the edge of the wooden gate firmly and held it immovably jammed.

There was a splintering of wood and a bellow of fury as the ffarg realized the trap its own body had created. Rehan's brow tensed as again he suddenly worried about what the creature might in its wrath start doing to Kursten. He shrugged the anxiety away – there was nothing he could do immediately to help her – threw the axe to one side, picked up his thin, light sword and waited for the ffarg to realize that any further struggles were in vain. The door shuddered a few times as the beast attacked it with its battle-axe, but the thick wood and the metal hinges held.

And then the racket subsided.

Rehan positioned himself so that the tip of his sword lay gently on the base of the gate's spy-hole. His hand held the pommel behind him as if he were clutching the shaft of a javelin, so that the blade ran horizontally over his shoulder and close under his chin and he could sight along the sword's length. In this slightly strained pose he waited for the ffarg to come to whatever passed for its senses. With his free hand he gestured to the arriving guards that they should stay well away.

There was silence on both sides of the gate, now.

And then slowly, stupidly, the great pallid single eye of the ffarg came into view at the spy-hole.

Rehan winked at it impudently.

'Keep down! Get clear!' he shouted through the wood, in case Kursten had recovered consciousness.

The eye continued to regard him moronically.

Rehan pulled his head to one side and plunged his sword up to its hilt through the spy-hole.

There was a single inhuman scream, and then the sound of a great weight slumping to the ground.

And I hope in the name of the few things in the World that are good that Kursten is not somewhere under all that, thought Rehan, severing the bony morningstar and wrenching at the lip of the gate to try to pull it open.

7

In the tunnel-like archway behind the gate she looked, under the uncertain light from the guards' torches, like nothing more than a pile of discarded rags. Fortunately, in its rage on finding that it had been trapped by its tail, the ffarg had thrown her aside, and she had nothing worse to show for her misadventures than a few bruises. She was less worried about these than about the fact that, at some stage during the chase, her bladder had responded to her terror, so that her dress was wet to Rehan's touch as he carried her out into the open.

'Home. Take me home,' she said. 'I must see what's happened to my father.'

'Kursten, there's just one more thing I have to do,' he said. 'Then I'll take you home.'

He passed his soft burden to one of the guards.

Rehan's sword had gone right through the ffarg's head and out the other side. He half-closed the gate and, with some difficulty, withdrew the weapon. He stepped back smartly as the suddenly released remaining weight of the creature collapsed, crashing the gate open so that it slammed back against the wall. Rehan *tch*ed as he looked at the blade, which was smeared with grey and red and green. Then he turned round.

'I wish a final word with that sentry,' he said.

'He's destined for the scaffold.' The voice was mournful. 'Unless you desire to have the killing of him.'

'He's dead already,' said Rehan. 'If he tells me what I wish to know I shall do him the great service of speeding his end. If not . . .'

He shrugged and let the words hang.

Two of the guards had the sentry firmly secured, his arms twisted behind his back. His face was ashen from loss of blood, and his eyes rolled in dread as he saw Rehan approaching. *So sad*, thought Rehan. *He's hardly more than a boy*. He held the tip of his sword directly to the boy's adam's apple, applying just enough pressure to prick the skin.

'You must have heard about what they do to traitors in this city,' he hissed after a few moments' pause. 'Perhaps you've even attended one or two executions yourself. They're not pretty sights, you know. I don't understand how you people can stomach watching them, myself, but then I'm a stranger to these parts, so I guess that it's just a question of different people, different customs. Come to think of it, my apologies: I suppose it was particularly insensitive of me to use the word "stomach" there – appropriate, though, if you happen to be the executioner or one of the spectators. That's where they normally start, you see.'

The sentry made a strangled noise.

'Oh,' said Rehan, with obviously feigned interest, 'so you've watched it all happen yourself, have you? They say that the bit with the stomach doesn't actually hurt as much as you'd expect it to, though for the life of me it's a mystery how they can know, since nobody's ever likely to be in much of a position to, as it were, report back on the details of the experience afterwards. Anyway' – he drew a breath and partly relaxed, so that his sword-tip took a tiny nick out of the sentry's throat – 'where was I? Oh, yes, now I remember: the stomach. Yes – whether it hurts or not doesn't much matter, I guess, because it must be infinitely *depressing*, don't you think, to be sitting up there on the scaffold with your guts all steaming in your arms and listening as all the fine pretty ladies laugh and jeer as they watch. The louder you scream – why, the louder they laugh at you! Of course, what they're really looking forward to is the saucy bit, when they get to see your balls, but that's not for a while yet, because the executioner likes to keep the best for last. So, right now, he's heating up the irons so that he can . . .'

Rehan spotted what was about to happen and withdrew his sword just in time as the sentry's head lolled forward and he vomited convulsively.

'Oh, I'm so sorry,' said Rehan cheerfully. 'I'm being tactless again. I just keep forgetting that it's *you* all this is going to happen to. How discourteous of me! How *stupid* of me! I feel a little ill just thinking about it being done to *anybody*, but I'm sure my antipathy to the whole notion would be every bit as strong as yours if someone told me it was going to be *me* up on the scaffold. Wouldn't you, Kursten?' he added over his shoulder.

'Yes,' came a tremulous reply. He half-turned and saw that she was looking distinctly unwell.

'There's an alternative, you know,' he said quizzically to the captive, putting his head to one side like an inquisitive bird. 'You could vanish from this existence with hardly a wink of pain or humiliation – if I were to allow you to. I don't know what your gods will do to you on the other side – probably something much worse than ever a mortal executioner could dream up. Still, take each moment as it comes has always been my motto, and leave the afterlife to take care of itself. If you'd like to reduce your suffering in *this* life, on the other hand – another tactless expression for which I apologize – all you have to do is tell me something.'

The youth's lips moved soundlessly. Rehan could work out from their shape that the silent word was 'What?'

'Someone paid you and your erstwhile chum to let those ffarg into the city. They probably didn't pay you nearly half enough, but then it's the established rôle of fools to be swindled and then to be hanged for it afterwards. Who was this person?'

For an instant's stillness the sentry said nothing. It was as if a terror even greater than that he had for the executioner were working behind the mask of his face. And then he said a single name so quietly and reluctantly that even Rehan, close in front of him, his face wrinkling from the smell of vomit, had to strain to hear it.

'Thank you,' said Rehan politely. His face became serious, his eyes strangely compassionate. 'And now it's time for me to keep my side of the bargain.'

He looked the captive in the eye.

'I'm really sorry about this,' he said earnestly, his voice shedding all traces of its former mocking note. 'You're very young, and you doubtless deserved a better life than any you've ever had. May your gods be merciful to you.'

And then Rehan skilfully cut the sentry's throat.

8

Two of the guards escorted them as far as they dared, through all the comparatively brightly lit districts and then those parts of the city where the lights were dim until eventually they reached the sea of almost-blackness that represented the fringe of the slums. To go beyond here, the soldiers explained apologetically to Rehan – and to a mercifully uninjured Kursten leaning wearily against him – was more than their lives were worth. In the meantime, would Rehan be so pleased as to accept from them this torch in order to guide the way?

He brushed away their words with a gesture and gave each of them a small coin from his pouch to thank them for their services.

'Kursten,' he said, then stopped.

'Yes?'

He thought about all the vileness and corruption and cruelty of the Anonymous City, and then he acknowledged that it wasn't the city itself that was evil: the evil sprang from the people who lived in it. Some of them had become evil through force of circumstance, but many had consciously chosen to enjoy the wealth they derived from their exploitation of the misery of others. Kursten – it was as if she simply weren't a viable component of this human cesspit.

'Ah, shit,' he said. 'Forget it.'

'No, tell me, Rehan. Tell me.'

And so he explained all the things he felt about the Anonymous City, and about her, and about the whole of the wide World where it seemed that people's worth was judged by the riches they enjoyed or by the cruelty with which they slaughtered their fellow sentient creatures, and how the two often meant the same. At the end of it, to his educated horror, he found himself telling her that he wanted to take her away from all this and that he realized that it must sound to her like a cliché but . . .

He ran out of words after a while.

'Rehan, I don't care if it's a cliché,' she said very quietly, putting her arms around his waist, ignoring the sentry's blood clotted on the front of his clothing and the weapons and flute at his belt. 'You saved my life tonight. Yes, I would like to be taken away from the Anonymous City. And I would like you to be the one who does the taking away.'

'Hey,' he said softly, 'that's what you say now. All right – if I can I'll take you with me when I go. But you're not to feel attached to me by any strings – all right? I only look good to you right now because you've got no one but the Vermin to compare me with. There are plenty of good men out there' – he waved his hand vaguely to indicate the World beyond the walls of the Anonymous City – 'and you may find that one of them proves to be more to your liking than I could ever be. I'd never wish to think for a moment that you were staying by my side because you felt *obliged* to. That would be almost as bad for you as being among the ffarg.'

'I can kiss you without committing myself to you too much?' she asked.

'You can do really quite a lot more to me than just

kissing without committing yourself,' he muttered, 'but I think a kiss is the traditional gesture.' He leaned down to her.

As they picked their way through the dark, seedy alleys of the slums towards Glory Row he had her walk ahead of him, so that he could keep a careful guard both to their front and to their rear. He had given her his dagger, so that at least she would have some form of weapon should he be jumped by some hurtling figure from the shadows, but all seemed deserted and dead. As they walked she told him about her plan to keep him safe for the night, but steered clear of the sensitive subject of what might happen once her bedroom door was closed. *Although*, she thought, *if you wish to share my bed with me I don't know that I will turn you away.*

'Your father and yourself offer me kind hospitality,' said Rehan mock-formally, 'but I'm afraid I have a little more hunting to do tonight, what's left of it, before I can permit myself to think of sleep. Don't worry, though: surely you must have seen that I'm capable of taking care of myself. Perhaps I may tell you the result of the night's work over breakfast tomorrow morning?'

She giggled. This was a man who had killed four ffarg and two traitors tonight without suffering a single scratch himself, save for what had been done to his face by a tree's lifeless twigs, and she was worrying about his safety! Yes, he was right: he'd live until morning, never fear. She was prepared to swear that he'd live forever.

'What – who – are you hunting?' she asked as they crossed into Glory Row.

'Whoever it was that sold you to the ffarg,' he replied lightly. 'I'm afraid the man must die.'

'Must he? I haven't been hurt badly. I'm alive and there aren't any bones broken, so do you really have to . . . ?'

'Leave him alive so that he'd be able to sell somebody else tomorrow? Some other young lass who's managed to keep a hold on her human-ness in this sewer? No – it would be a crime to allow him to do this ever again. Never.' His face was set. He had trained himself – and trained himself well – at the behest of his master to become a killing machine, but that didn't mean that he relished his task, any more than one might relish the prospect of culling a herd of animals.

They were nearing One-Legged Tom's Kitchen. It was easily distinguishable because, even though the lamps had burned low and some of them had run out of oil, it was still the only house in Glory Row to show light at the windows.

Kursten peeped nervously through one of the steamy windows and relief flowed through her. Wordlessly she passed Rehan's dagger back to him: she had no further use for it now. One-Legged Tom seemed somehow to have dragged himself up onto a stool. He was sitting at one of the tables with a tankard in front of him.

She let go of Rehan's hand and ran to the door.

'Wait, Kursten, wait! You don't . . .'

But she ignored him and burst through the door into the Kitchen.

'Father!' she cried, running to the old man and cradling his white-haired head to her bosom. 'I'm safe! I'm home!'

He looked up at her, and his foggy grey eyes were filled with tears.

'No, dear love,' he said brokenly. 'No, you're not safe.'

9

Rehan was only a moment behind her, but he stood in the doorway for a couple of seconds, cautiously sniffing the air, before coming on into the Kitchen. Her eyes had been only for the slumped, defeated figure of her father; his took in the room as a whole. He saw that lounging easily along one of the benches towards the rear of the room was a slight, weaselly figure, inevitably picking at his teeth with the point of a dagger. The little man chuckled, with that shrill, rebarbative laugh of his.

'Gnetz!' said Rehan, disgustedly.

'None other,' agreed the Vermin with a studiedly casual smile.

At once Rehan was all business and bustle. His face lined with scratches and his clothing covered in mud and blood, he nevertheless was able to gather about him the aura of a completely spick-and-span military officer.

He drew his light sword from its scabbard and directed it towards One-Legged Tom. 'You,' he said. 'You, old man. Take your daughter upstairs to her room and get her to lie down. She needs rest. See if you can persuade her to get some sleep.' He kicked the front door shut behind him.

Kursten looked at Rehan vexedly, but the expression on his face was sufficient to convince her that she should do as he said. With their arms around each other's shoulders, so that she could support the old man while permitting him the illusion that it was he who was supporting her, she and her father made their tortuous, stumbling way to the foot of the stairs. Rehan and Gnetz could soon hear them clumping around uncertainly overhead.

Still with his sword in front of him, Rehan moved sideways around to the scullery curtain and abruptly threw it open. The little room beyond was empty except for the wind whistling in through the shattered window. He pulled the curtain closed again and eased himself down onto the stool where One-Legged Tom had been sitting; the smooth wooden surface was still warm. He drew out his dagger and sheathed his sword, then leaned forward, his elbows on the rude tabletop in front of him, and cupped his face in his left palm.

For a long moment he stared at Gnetz before speaking. Then: 'You've spared me some work tonight, you know,' he said conversationally. 'I thought I was going to have to go to all the effort of hunting you down before I killed you, but instead you've served yourself up to me all politely, here on a platter. Perhaps you didn't expect that Kursten and I would ever return?' *But I bet you did. I'd wager my own tawdry life on it. I don't know why, but I'm convinced, little man, that you're even cleverer and more devious than you seem to be.*

'Course I knew you'd be here,' said Gnetz, equally

politely, swinging his body down off his bench and taking a stool for himself. 'News travels quick in the Anonymous City. To me most of all. Visiting singer kills four ffarg, two treacherous sentries, saves beautiful woman. Tale like that spreads faster'n if you stood on top of a roof and shouted.' He tittered. 'And they all want to be the first to tell good ol' Gnetz. Think they get a pat on the head, I think nicely of them in the tomorrows. Servile bastards, but no complaints from me, understand.'

'But *why*?' Rehan was genuinely baffled – had been ever since the young sentry had whispered the name. 'Everyone seemed to think – even Kursten herself – that she was the one person who was safe among you Vermin. And all the elaboration your scheme involved! Surely the ffarg can't have been offering you so much money that it was worth bribing the sentries, setting up this whole charade, telling the ffarg warriors how to find this . . . dump?'

'Market forces,' said Gnetz, and Rehan could see that for once the wizened Vermin was being frank.

There was a pause.

'Oil for the lamps in a bottle on shelf over near the stove,' said Gnetz suddenly, pointing. 'Be in total darkness we wait much longer. That it. Up there on the left.'

Moving carefully under the Vermin's watchful eye, his dagger held at the ready, Rehan fetched the bottle of oil and, as instructed, filled one of the lamps that had gone out. Sharing his gaze between Gnetz and the task, he trimmed the wick and then set light to it using the flame from one of the other lamps. He repeated the process several times, so that soon the Kitchen was brighter. Throughout the operation the little man made not the slightest threatening move. *But don't*, Rehan told himself, *give too much weight to that*.

' "Market forces",' Rehan repeated slowly. 'I still don't understand.'

'You very cunning fighter, bucko, and powerful adversary,' admitted Gnetz, but then he smiled maliciously, and Rehan realized that the compliments were over almost before they'd begun. 'Trouble is, though, that you are very naïve about the way people are in the Anonymous City. For 'sample, never once asked me what me and the rest of the Vermin do to keep ourselves alive. We just harmful parasites on society so far as you concerned. Never think about the fact that maybe we really *are* society: we the trading classes.'

'I have to confess that you don't exactly fit my picture of a successful merchant.' A practised supercilious smile on Rehan's lips.

Gnetz just shrugged in a matter-of-fact way.

'Different places, maybe merchants look different. You thinking of the fat cats' trade with rest of World in bradz and furs and other junk. Here in the Anonymous City traders among the people deal in food and clothing, look much like me, most of them much worse. Once a many-year ago, people call us "Vermin" to show that we scum, but we like the name, take pride in it, adopt it as our own.' He looked around him, quite content, it would seem, with the situation. 'Draw sword if you like, Rehan, but I going to get us some booze. Talking makes throat dry, 'specially when company boring. Won't try to attack you. Know you don't believe me which is why I say draw sword – but don't worry: not in my commercial interests attack you yet.'

Already a grey dawn was poking uncertain fingers in through the grimy windows.

Gnetz found a small barrel of perry just behind the scullery curtain. He hoisted it up onto one of the tables and filled two rough beakers from it. One of these he put down in front of Rehan. At a twitch of the sword-blade he nodded his understanding and exchanged the two mugs. Once he had settled himself back on his stool and Rehan had returned the sword to its scabbard, the Vermin carried on where he had left off.

'Don't seem much trade in the Anonymous City, does there? But there is.' He took a deep gulp, savoured the taste of the fizzy liquid in his mouth, and swallowed loudly. He put down the beaker and looked earnestly into the cupped palms of his hands.

He was still for fully a minute, and then he startled Rehan by bursting into explosive speech.

'You see the Anonymous City and you see that one part of it is very rich, the other part of it very poor, and you think to yourself: "Ah, that all right then. The rich people are rich because of all the money they get from bradz. They keep it to themselves and all the poor just carry on getting poorer." So simple, so neat, so orderly. So *wrong*!'

He was becoming vehement, and with it rapidly more articulate; as Rehan had suspected, the limping words that Gnetz normally used were part of a consciously assumed persona, a sham adopted so that he wouldn't stand out too much among his customary associates.

'But you don't take it any further than that,' the Vermin was saying. 'You don't, may you be tormented by eternal fire, ever stop to *think* about it all. Those rich people over there' – he waved a hand – 'has it ever occurred to you to wonder exactly what it is they spend their money *on*? They can import fine garments and jewellery, pretty trinkets for the ladies and big gold medals or diamond-encrusted daggers for the gentlemen. Exotic animals to keep as pets, slaves to tend to their most trivial needs, harlots of every sex to cater to the most bizarre of their sensual whims. They've got everything they could ever want except . . .'

He paused with an upraised finger and waited for Rehan to supply the word.

'Food.'

Rehan felt sick.

'Exactly. At last our boy's beginning to learn a thing or two about precisely how much one human being is prepared to make use of another – many others, maybe – just to give himself an extra soupçon of pleasure. The richies could bring in salted meats on their ships, or cured meats or all sorts of other meats from outside, but what they really want is *fresh* meat. And if you can't raise enough crops to keep cattle . . .'

'Human beings will do,' said Rehan deadly. The families in the cartels imported enough food to feed the city, just – as they could well afford to do – but the cargoes brought in on the merchant vessels hadn't tasted quite as splendid as the 'richies' would wish, so long ago they had turned the rest of the Anonymous City into a huge meat farm.

'That's right,' said Gnetz, following the singer's thought processes. 'So when I say I'm a trader I mean exactly what the word says. I'm a trader in edible flesh. If you like, we Vermin are simple, honest slaughterers, with the streets of the city as our abattoir. Don't think ill of us for it.' He held up a palm as if to ward off a blow. 'Some of us enjoy the job, others don't, but if we didn't do it then someone else would. It might seem abhorrent to you, bucko, but then you come from the World outside: you don't live here. The set-up has been this way inside the Anonymous City for centuries, and all of us have learned to accept that that's the way things work. I've heard about the rest of the World from the travellers who've been here before you, and I know that things could be done differently, but I'm one of the few who're getting along very well, thank you, with the system the way it is, and so it's not in my interests to let too many other people know that there's any alternative.

'And' – again the raised hand – 'don't start to criticize us butchers, us Vermin, until you've spent a few months out there in one of the houses on Glory Row, with nothing to eat except greening crusts and thin soup, or maybe if you're lucky a bone to chew at: no one ever cares much about the way their domesticated animals are kept, and the richies are no exception. Spend a while on Glory Row and, if you survive it, *then* you can come and tell me that I've made the wrong choice for my life.'

He took another gulp of perry.

'Plus, of course, we butchers have our little perquisites. Very occasionally, strangers come through . . . like yourself, for example' – a courteous little acknowledgement with the fingers – 'and they inevitably bring gold and coins with them, or fine clothes like the richies wear.' He grinned, and half-sang: 'Foodies for the richies, goodies for their faithful servants.' A mock bow. 'No one in the rest of the World ever knows where the strangers go, because of course the Anonymous City isn't on any of the maps.'

But it is! thought Rehan with a sort of sadistic glee, *and that's something you don't know. My master has found it after all these years, and she knows that it's where the bradz is coming from. Whether or not I return, she'll discover a way to send in other people, even better trained than me, so that there won't any longer be any 'richies' or their 'faithful servants'. And once this scrofulous society has been toppled – well, my smug little friend, I wouldn't like to be occupying your shoes when the 'cattle' have swords and daggers put in their hands.*

'And finally,' Gnetz continued, 'there are other advantages to my profession. We Vermin . . . ah . . . eat rather better than the rest of the populace.' He picked at his teeth again, pretending absentness, and Rehan knew that the purpose was to shock him.

'I've guessed the rest of it,' the singer said calmly, his initial nausea long dissipated. 'Whether or not you tell your customers, you keep back a few of the . . . carcasses . . . and supply them to One-Legged Tom, so that he can run his Kitchen and feed you all with the products of his rudimentary culinary skills. It's traditional in any society, I suppose, for the butcher to keep back all the best cuts for himself. You must have been laughing behind your face when I was eating here last night.'

'True,' confessed Gnetz, looking a little crestfallen.

'But that *still* leaves me in the dark,' said Rehan, shaking his head. He could sense that he had won some sort of hazily defined advantage, but he was uncertain how best he could press it home. Also, he was still trying to adjust to the knowledge that Kursten, too, had been raised on human meat. *But what else could she do? She's never known anything different . . .* 'I don't understand where arranging the abduction of Kursten comes in.'

'Told you,' said Gnetz, now abruptly sullen. 'I'm a trader in flesh, and of course I want my business to be as successful as possible. As far as I'm concerned, that girl up there' – he gestured over his shoulder with his thumb – 'she's pretty, oh yes, but really she's just another piece of flesh like all the rest of them. And she's got herself in my way. One-Legged Tom makes a good living out of the money we pay him when we eat in his Kitchen, but what if the Kitchen belonged to me, and I paid the old bastard half what he's getting now? Nice little income for myself, and I wouldn't have to do anything extra to earn it.'

He grimaced, as at a remembered frustration.

'But there's only one obstacle. The girl. None of the other Vermin would dream of laying a finger on her, so she'd be free to tell the news of the change to anyone and everyone she wanted to. I can cope with any of them singly – no problem – but if all of them together were out for my blood . . .' He made an expressive little spitting noise in his throat. 'So, it strikes me, I could have her removed from the scene, permanently, without seeming to have had anything to do with it – and perhaps I could even make a little profit on the side. Communicating with the ffarg isn't easy, but I managed to organize it in due course. That's another story. I told them that there was the best human breeding stock in the whole of the World sitting in this house – fit for their king or whatever it is they call their mighty numskull leader, worth a tower of diamonds, all of her family prone to giving birth in triplets, all the usual sort of crap you'd expect.'

He looked sour.

'Couldn't get any money out of them, though. Stupid bastards have never even heard of the stuff and didn't understand it when I tried to explain it to them. So I had to make a bit of a pecuniary loss on the deal; well, not so much a loss as an investment. Trouble is, thanks to you, my investment hasn't borne the anticipated fruit. Still, it shouldn't take me too long to earn it back again – especially since I'll also have the contents of your money-pouch, my friend.'

'And what makes you think that?'

Gnetz's eyes strayed towards the door, under which the daylight was showing a sickly pink.

'Oh, I just sort of know,' he said breezily.

There was a bulky, muscular forearm around Rehan's neck, half-throttling him.

He tried to raise his dagger, but a huge hand chopped down on his wrist, shattering its complex of carpal bones. Before Rehan could reach the pommel of his sword with his other hand, the great fist reached around and grabbed his unharmed wrist and twisted until the World seemed to be filled with nothing but tearing agony and the sound of splintering bones.

He pushed backwards, but the huge man behind him was immovable – it was like pushing against a solid stone wall.

Gnetz smiled at him.

'My associate Egroeg can move very quietly when he wants to, you know, however lumbering he might appear to be. If you want to be safe from attack you should always check out the minor details – things like whether or not a scullery window is firmly closed. A pity there was no way you could have closed it tonight, wasn't it?'

Now steel came into the thin voice.

'Tie him, Egroeg, and make sure you do it well. Even with his wrists smashed, our friend's not nearly such a pushover as we first thought.'

The big man moved swiftly, showing no mercy at all as he bound Rehan's crumpled wrists behind his back. In moments the ankles, too, had been tightly tied together, so that Rehan looked like nothing more than a wriggling rolled-up carpet on the dirty floor, the stains of dried blood on his clothing adding to the illusion.

Through a sea of bright red pain and humiliation he heard Gnetz say, quite solicitously, 'I hope that my associate hasn't hurt you too badly. But, you see, my dignity couldn't stand to take such a loss on my abortive dealings with the ffarg, so when you and the wench came back here last night it was as if the gods, in their infinite wisdom, had elected to give me the two of you as a small compensatory gift.'

Rehan felt the Vermin's thin, acquisitive fingers

burrowing inside his cape until at last they located his money-pouch.

'There,' said Gnetz happily, tossing the pouch up and down on his palm and listening to the cheerful sound of the coins clanking, 'now I've got the first part of the payment that I reckon the ffarg should have made to me. As for the rest? Why, I think Kursten will have the time to earn that for me before she becomes so pox-ridden that even the most desperate of men wouldn't want to mount her, and after that she'll make a perfect bride for some minor ffarg clan, don't you think?'

Rehan bellowed his hatred, his contempt, his pain, his loathing, his disgust, his . . .

'Calm down,' said Gnetz peremptorily, and Egroeg's meaty hand clamped over Rehan's mouth, stifling the noise.

'You see, while you were away slaughtering ffarg, I took a little time to do some thinking. The Vermin wouldn't lay a finger on Kursten – right now – because in their dumb, stupid way they see her as something pure, undefiled. But to them, of course, she's not really a person – she's just an image. Perhaps they don't know it themselves, but the taboo on fingers doesn't apply to the rest of their bodies. So all that needs to happen by way of apprenticeship for her new profession is that she, ah, becomes, as it were, defiled. She'll still be a non-person, still an image – except that now she'll be a tangible, malleable, fuckable image. I know you'd be only too pleased to volunteer your own services, but I feel that this is a chore that it is my own responsibility, as chief of operations, to perform. Hmmm?'

Rehan bit down hard on Egroeg's vast, sausage-like fingers. There was no reaction at all.

Gnetz paused at the bottom of the stairs, as if having an afterthought, and came back towards them.

'Oh, I wouldn't like to leave you with the impression that I'm just a common criminal and debaucher,' he said. 'Here's something in exchange for your gold – something that's worth far more than gold could ever be.'

He tossed a small leather bag over Rehan's head to Egroeg, who caught it at the second attempt.

'Don't kill him, good friend,' said the little man. 'I've come to like him too much to allow you to do that. Just give him a single pellet to start with, and let him go free – with the rest of the bag – as soon as he starts to float.'

Gnetz disappeared up the stairs, taking them one at a time with steady deliberation. Rehan felt his jaw being forced open; then there was an acrid taste on his tongue. Fat fingers pinched his nostrils: a well judged tap on his throat forced him to swallow.

And soon peace came to him as the bradz took its hold. He smiled dreamily as there was a loud crash overhead and, moments later, as One-Legged Tom's unconscious body came tumbling down the stairs. When the distant sound of screaming began he thought it was rather amusing, and giggled, but the noise went on too long and in the end he was forced to shut his mind to it.

10

Now the song runs thus:

During the day, when she isn't working, Kursten sits in her dowdy attic bedroom, the crumpled sheets uncomfortable beneath her. She gazes out into the interminable distance over the rooftops of the Anonymous City and over the Broken Marshes and the Mistdom beyond its walls. She strokes the strings, those of them that are left, of the small clarsach between her knees, and sings to the cracked notes that its battered wooden frame produces. The songs she sings are for her lover, the lover she met once, long ago, but lost. They carry her away over the Mistdom and the plains beyond it and the hills and the seas that are beyond them to some distant land unknown to any mapmaker.

But her lover is no longer there. Instead, he is floating high above the clouds, screaming his discoveries of ecstasy, his wing-tips dangling brokenly like the feather he once wore so proudly in his hat.

As she sings, she weeps, the tears running down over the bruises on her face, stinging her painfully when they reach her broken lips.

Chapter Two
Cloak of Sky

1

The night wind that was tormenting the Anonymous City was cold here in Albion as well, jabbing its bony fingers in through the gaps in Ngur's clothing, teasing folds of flesh that hadn't been there a few years ago, and that he was ashamed to admit he'd now come to accept as a permanent part of him. Back in the days when he'd been the Despot's Army-Master, riding proudly at the head of his well drilled army or practising his swordsmanship with officers who were careful never to be too skilled, he'd taken the trimness of his body to be a facet of his existence, unconscious of the ease and smoothness with which his muscles worked under their hard coating of flesh: he had *been* his body. Now, though he was not old, and though his stockiness was not corpulence, he felt as if he merely *inhabited* his body.

He moved the fingers of his right hand to form a fist, and felt the extra layer of flesh stretch across the outside of his knuckles.

Far above Ngur's head the swift-moving clouds were catching the icy light of Struan, the larger moon, so that they seemed like white horses as they frisked agitatedly across the sky. The moon was high, close to the zenith where the Sun had once hung perpetually, so that all around the horizon there seemed to be a great, black, menacing lake of cloud; it felt heavy to him, as if it were about to collapse inwards from all sides and engulf him. It seemed to him that he could see himself from the clouds' viewpoint, as a very small, very remote, very vulnerable figure, a tiny patch of darkness against the fickly lit stone of the ramparts.

Starveling was what they called the place now thanks to that jingle Barra 'ap Rteniadoli Me'gli'minter Rehan had made up during the wars, but, however hard Ngur tried to train himself to think of it as that, he still heard the name 'Giorran' in his mind whenever he looked upon the place. It had been here that he'd been inducted into the Ellonian Army, here that he had discovered the pleasures and the vicissitudes of the military regime, here that he had slowly and then more and more rapidly risen upwards through the ranks of the conscripted and the second sons until his abilities had come to the notice of Nadar, who had preceded him as Army-Master. Nadar had seen that Ngur was both useful and dangerously ambitious; had Nadar not died while glorying over the final degradation of the first great peasant leader, he would surely have soon seen to it that a blade in the darkness found Ngur's spine.

Ngur pulled his cape closer around his neck. The wind seemed to be mocking him. Twenty metres away, at a corner of the battlements, a sentry was watching him while pretending not to. The man was clearly concerned about his lord, who should have been safe in the warmth of one of Giorr . . . of Starveling's great chambers, sipping the heavy sweet wine imported from the World or biting into soft fruits, feeling the touch on his arm of Anya, She Who Leads, the queen in all but name of Albion.

The sentry turned his head rapidly away as Ngur glanced towards him.

The wind, swirling up under his cape, had found a gap where Ngur had failed to tuck his shirt properly into his embroidered breeches, and scraped his skin with its fingernails.

How things had changed. Ngur could remember when the peasants of Albion had been little more than domesticated animals, given their lives at and for the pleasure of the House of Ellon, content in their endless drudgery because the magic that the Ellonia had enlisted had not permitted the peasants to enjoy the faculty of memory. Then, somehow, a crude seaman called Terman had strayed through the encircling curtains of mist, bringing with him the plague of recollection. He had infected the serfs around him with his deadly disease, giving them names so that for the first time in their lives they had had the vanity to look upon themselves as something more than the beasts of the fields. Yet all could have been well – separated too far from Terman the peasants soon forgot their names and their conceits – had not the intruder sired a bastard, Lian. Once grown, Lian – He Who Leads – had led the first, doomed, uprising of the peasants; the House of Ellon had defeated him easily, but the Ellonian Despot, the fool, had failed to realize that great events can give small warnings.

Lian's daughter, Anya, had grown to become She Who Leads, and this time when the peasants had rebelled they had not been so easily abased. She had been helped by others who had chosen not to help her father – a disreputable dreamer, a singer, the Wind that had once upon a time toyed with the governance of Albion, and a spritish creature whose existence Ngur had never fully understood. But perhaps the most important of all Anya's aides had been a peasant woman, no different to look at than thousands of others, who had somehow developed a steeliness of spirit more adamantine than any resolve the Ellonia could breed or discipline into their soldiery. Had it not been for this woman, perhaps Anya would have died as ignominiously and as uselessly as her father had before her.

Ngur shivered, looking down at the brief stretch of trampled ground that the lights of Starveling dimly illuminated. Reen, the peasant woman, was gone from Albion now; she had seen Anya ascend to the throne and take as her consort the once-hated Ellonian Army-Master and briefly Despot, Ngur; had seen the rejoicings of the people as the hazy barrier that had cut off Albion had faded from the skies and the gift of memory had come to minds little prepared to accept it; had seen the deliria of delight diminish, as always they must do. And the small woman had quietly stolen sufficient gold and jewels from the treasury that had once been the Despot's, and embarked to find her fate in the unknown lands of the World.

It had been weeks before Anya had realized that her mentor had gone. Her mind had been on affairs of state and on more basic political matters. There had been rioting in the northeast, where the crops had proved incapable of resisting the unaccustomed onslaught of *seasons* – seasons that *changed* – and Anya had had to organize the despatch of a party of militia to quell the turmoil. The city of Ernestrad, at whose edge the newly named citadel of Starveling loomed, had become a rats' nest of criminals and murderers, as all sought to enjoy more than their share of the riches they assumed that Anya would now be free to bestow upon them; Ngur himself had led the struggle to calm the city, and the images of what he had seen during that time were still far too bright in his mind. The higher they'd raised their gibbets, it had seemed, the more protracted and numerous their executions, the worse the problem had become, until Anya had been forced to make Ernestrad what it still was today, a city of ever-temporary tranquillity, a wild beast caged by bars of fear.

There had been so many things for Anya to do, so many expedient cruelties, it was small wonder that she hadn't initially noticed the departure of Reen, even though the woman had been closer than a mother to her.

His watering eyes were telling Ngur that it was time for him to go inside, to do what the sentry was obviously willing him to do, to taste the luxuries that were his by right as the consort of She Who Leads.

He smiled at the soldier, but the soldier wasn't looking in his direction.

Ngur wondered where Reen was now – he wondered where they *all* were now. From time to time they heard rumours of the dreamer, Joli. His talent for reifying his visions had vanished, of course, now that Albion's magic had been freed from its self-imposed confinement, but the filthy old reprobate still never went hungry. He had taken to the roads again, boasting of his new-found prowess as a lover – justified claims, if even half of the tales and ballads about him were true. The singer, Rehan, had gone to sing his songs in the World; Alyss had returned to whichever corner of incomprehensible nothingness it was that she had come from.

Ngur descended the over-broad stone steps to Starveling's great courtyard. There were several people around, braving the fierce cold as they went about their duties, but still he felt lonely, unprotected despite the fur collar that he'd wrapped around his chin.

Not for the first time, he wondered what it was like to be one of his own servants. He had the power of life and death over the men and women who tended to his needs, and, although he chose not to exercise it, nevertheless the presence of that power must play an important part in their everyday lives. Each breath they took, each mouthful they ate, was with his permission; they must always have to accommodate in their minds the possibility that that permission could be withheld. In darker days, when the land had been ruled by the Ellonia – when Albion had been all of the World – summary, unpredictable death had been a very real presence among the serving classes of Giorran. Those harshest of times were past, and Ngur didn't regret their going, yet he was still aware of the apprehension on the faces of his attendants whenever he suffered indigestion or one of the streaming colds to which everyone was susceptible during Albion's unaccustomed winters.

A guard came briskly to attention as Ngur approached the ponderous granite doorway that led into the officers' quarters. Anya, ever mindful of the military experience of both herself and her consort, had arranged for the royal apartments to be set on the upper two floors of this wing; it was good for the officers to see that the two of them were still capable, despite the chasm that their rank had opened up, of mingling with the rest; besides, in the remote event of an attempt being made on her or Ngur's life, the would-be assassins would need to fight their way through several storeys of hardened soldiers.

A puff of wind came in with the consort, setting the torches along the corridor walls dancing. The door creaked shut behind him as he rubbed his hands together, restoring warmth to them.

Yet is my own life so very different from that of my servants? he mused. His existence was beholden to Anya, who had led the victors in Albion's short-lived and rather scrappy revolution. He did not delude himself that she loved him, any more than he had love for her; yet it was in her interests to retain him by her side – indeed, to be physically faithful to him most of the time – in order to maintain the semblance of union between the factions of Albion who still remembered the time when they had been at each other's throats. Should the situation change, however, Ngur had few illusions but that she would discard him as no longer suited to her purposes, like a once-trusted horse whose days of usefulness were done; whether she would decree that he be slaughtered or put out to grass would be a matter of whim.

Whatever the people believed, Anya's consort was nothing more than her indentured servant – worse: he was her slave.

And Anya herself?

She was, in a way, a slave as well; the slave of a dead woman.

2

A wench was rather worriedly turning down the ornate rugs on his bed when he entered his chamber. She looked up at him and smiled formally, standing to one side. He waved her from the room and watched her back as she retreated. She was a comely child, certainly not as old as twenty, and in an earlier age he might have requested that she stay with him to give him comfort for the night, so that he could use her youth and her warmth as shields against the loneliness that permeated him. Now . . . now it would warm him if once – only once – he were to see a genuine smile on the face of one of his attendants.

The opulent bedding beckoned temptingly. He unbelted his sword and dropped it on a chair. His clammy cape followed it. The room was oppressive, stifling, and the burning grease of the torches was making his eyes smart. He glanced speculatively at the closed window, but then remembered the honed gusts beyond. Restlessly he threw himself into a bulgingly upholstered demithrone, but he could settle himself there for only a moment before he sprang back to his feet and began to pace around the bed, backwards and forwards, as if it were a quicksand that he dared not approach any closer. He was impatient with something, but the trouble was that he didn't know what.

He'd been wrong to think merely that he was just as much a slave of circumstance as those who served him: in truth he was worse off than they were. The wench who'd been here a few moments ago was now free to be with her lover – or to be alone, if that was what she chose. He had – could have – no permanent lover, and nor could he ever seek out the embrace of voluntary solitude. Instead he was trapped in the pretence of affection for Anya; there was no one to hold his hand and mumble meaningless reassurances in the worst hours of the night. Anya would see nothing but weakness in any admission he might make of his own perceived inadequacies, whereas he had come to regard his acceptance of his own fallibility as a strength. Once, and only once, had he seen her confidence desert her. That had been when the five of them – Anya, Ngur, Reen, Joli and the singer, Barra 'ap Rteniadoli Me'gli'minter Rehan – had been watching as Alyss stripped Albion naked of its modest cloak of sky. Anya had looked up at Reen and in her eyes she had acknowledged the truth that the peasant woman, not herself, was She Who Leads.

But the moment hadn't lasted long.

And yet Anya's very arrogance was built on the most enormous confession of deficiency. Even now she would be . . .

Vexedly he clapped his hands together, abruptly ceasing his pacing. He looked at the door. He nodded, once, twice, reaching a decision.

As his hand rested on the door he paused. He crossed to the chair where he had cast his cape and his sword, and swiftly buckled the weapon to his waist: it would be as well to take precautions.

3

He heard the chanting long before he reached the chapel.

When Giorran had been rebuilt as Starveling after the devastation wrought by the Wind, Anya had insisted that this extra annexe be tacked on to the back of the officers' quarters for her own use. The years had weathered the buildings equally, yet the chapel still looked somehow like an unwanted guest at a party. Although there were no formal prohibitions or restrictions, few people visited it aside from Anya and her closest confidantes; Ngur himself had been here only a handful of times.

The finely crafted glass of the chapel's windows had been coloured rusty red. Now the flickering light of the torches within made them look like patches of fresh blood.

The wind hadn't let up. Even in the shelter of Starveling's high walls, Ngur wished he'd decided not to leave his cape behind him.

There was no guard at the chapel's door. There was no need of one.

Ngur felt the chilled, twisted metal of the latch-handle and once more he paused indecisively. He felt like an intruder into Anya's most intimate privacy, as if he were about to secretly touch her as she slept. The inchoate sensation of shame submerged any fears he might have had of her wrath.

He shrugged, and turned the handle.

The wind pushed him in through the entrance, and it was with difficulty that he backed against the door, forcing it closed behind him.

The chamber was brightly lit, most of the torches being

concentrated around the altar and the huge, crudely coloured painting that hung on the wall behind it. Anya was kneeling directly in front of the altar, her golden head bowed as she chanted; about a dozen other women, dressed in solemn grey, were standing around her, their high voices joining hers in the tuneless, iterative song.

Ngur felt even more strongly that he was engaged in some act of molestation, yet he made his legs carry him until he was standing in the narrow aisle that ran down the chapel's centre. On either side of him were rows of plain benches; all except those near the front were dusty. This was a place of worship intended for the people, yet it was effectively barred to the people.

He looked straight ahead of him down the aisle at the curve of Anya's back and, above, the great picture that was the building's sole decoration. One or two of the women had noticed his arrival, and a couple of heads were turned briefly in his direction; but otherwise it was as if he didn't exist.

Except for the eyes of the picture. They were staring directly at him; despite or perhaps because of the artist's cackhanded attempts to portray compassion in that oversized face, the eyes seemed to be regarding Ngur, the interloper, with cold malice. They were green, but the green was too bright – inhumanly bright. The pupils were too small and too dark.

The woman in the picture was dressed in mud-brown garments of roughly woven wool. The hair falling on either side of her face was of an indeterminate colour. She was seated at a loom, yet her gaze was not directed towards her plying fingers; perhaps the artist had been attempting to create the illusion that she had glanced up from her work to welcome someone who had just entered the clay-walled room in which she sat. Three balls of wool – one red, one yellow, one blue – were contributing to the tapestry she was weaving, a seascape seen from high on a cliff-top. Here the artist, in contrast with her ineptitude elsewhere, had managed to capture a slice of reality perfectly, so that in the uncertain light one could almost hear the clash of the breakers as they shattered themselves on the rocks at the cliff's base.

Syor – the woman in the picture – had shattered her own body on those rocks. Anya had been not quite a woman when that had happened; she had painted this picture of her mother from a memory blurred by her transition from childhood to adulthood. Reen, who had been Syor's lover after the death of He Who Leads, hadn't known whether to laugh or curse when first she'd seen the portrait, and in the end had done neither, opting instead never again to clap eyes on it.

Had Syor really been so cruel as Anya's memory had portrayed her? Or had Anya projected her own easy callousness onto the image of her mother? Ngur had never met Syor, so he had no way of knowing whether or not Reen's accounts of her essential kindness had been correct. Reen had mentioned, too, Syor's unpredictable moods; perhaps heartlessness had been included among her transient humours.

He stood there motionless for several minutes longer, until his presence could no longer be ignored and the chanting began to move uneasily towards its close. At last only Anya herself was still giving voice, as if unconscious of the fact that the other women had become silent; yet Ngur knew only too well that his wife was perfectly aware that there was an intruder in the chapel, and who the intruder was. Her continued song was a deliberate signal to him that his arrival was of no significance to her in comparison with the greatness of the presence of her mother's spirit.

Ngur sighed. All these pretences, all this constant play-acting in everything that Anya and he did. It seemed strange that Anya should wish so pettily to demonstrate her supremacy over him.

He waited until she was done.

At last she pulled herself easily to her feet and turned towards him, gesturing her attendants to leave them. Robes rustled and chamois shoes shuffled on the mosaic floor as the women wordlessly let themselves out into the whine of the night wind.

Anya, her head framed by light, stood watching him. Her eyes seemed to be as accusatory as those of the woman in the picture above her.

She said nothing. He must demonstrate his subservience by being the one to break the silence.

The trouble was that, now he had conquered the timorous beast inside him and gathered the courage to interrupt her here, he had no idea what he wanted to say to her.

She saw his confusion and smiled, but not in sympathy. A tiny move of her fingers was a command to him to speak, to justify himself.

'Anya . . .' he began. Still the words wouldn't come.

It had been enough.

'You choose to distract my attentions from my devotions, husband,' she said coldly, making it clear that he was guilty of being an irritation to not just the living: he was being discourteous to the dead. 'Your mission must be of considerable importance.'

'Yes,' he said after a few seconds. 'Of very considerable importance.'

And it was, he knew. So why did he feel like a small child who had interrupted the serious discussions of his elders in order to announce some matter which already he'd realized was negligible? His concern, rooted though it was in his own, personal disquiet, now embraced all the future of Albion. He was a surgeon who, on encountering what seemed to be merely a trivial little tumour, had recognized that in that growth lay the seeds of complete destruction.

'Your land – our land – of Albion is in danger,' he said lamely.

Her eyes narrowed. Ever since Alyss had dispersed the mists, Anya had been terrified that one of the nations of the World might send forces to subjugate her country. Sometimes Ngur wondered if she would have preferred it if somehow the barrier could have been preserved.

'Our spies in the World have heard rumours of war?' she snapped. Some of her dismissive hauteur had disappeared; she was granting him her dubious attention.

'No,' he said. 'The peril is far graver than that. We

could hope to fight off armies. No – don't look outward to the World for signs of impending disaster. The danger is to be found within our own shores. It's here, right here in this chapel.'

One thin eyebrow rose in supercilious disbelief.

'You have come here to kill me?' Her hand glided to the pommel of her sword; a martial queen, even in worship she declined to be weaponless. 'I admire the ambition you've found in your heart, husband, but I have to warn you that your optimism is misplaced. Unlike yourself, I haven't let our years of peace sap my skills.'

By way of answer Ngur drew his sword and threw it clatteringly down on the mosaic in front of him. Instants later his dagger followed. The brittle echoes faded swiftly.

Now, at last, she was beginning to take him seriously. Silently he breathed his relief. It would be a difficult climb to reach the plateau where Anya would accept him as an equal, and the handholds were few and precarious, yet at least she was permitting him to clamber onto the lowest slopes.

'Explain yourself,' she said, her hand still on her sword.

He groped for words. He wished that someone else – someone far more competent with words than himself – were here to speak for him. Rehan, perhaps: the singer would have been able to couch the meaning in a nest of fluent words, charming Anya with calculated mannerisms. Or no, not Rehan; not with Anya. Despite her pretences, Ngur knew that she had never forgiven the fey man for turning his love towards Reen. Alyss, then – or maybe even Joli, who would have farted and cursed until a smiling Anya listened. But Ngur was all too aware that she had grown accustomed to paying little heed to whatever he himself had to say to her; he was a conquered foe, and in ceding his power to her he had relinquished her respect for him.

'I would kill you gladly if I thought it would save Albion from the cancer that is eating it,' he said abruptly. 'There would be a song in my heart.'

His words shocked him: this was not at all what he'd

been planning to say. Even Anya was looking startled.

'You say you would save Albion,' she spat, 'yet surely killing me would be to destroy the nation I've created?'

'I believe you believe that,' said Ngur before his caution could stop him. 'I believe you truly consider it the truth: that you *are* Albion, and that Albion is you. In spite of all your rote protestations that you have sacrificed your desires to the good of the people over whom you reign, you've come to equate your country's well-being with your own, as if anyone who might disagree with you were seeking to attack Albion itself. Can't you see that this is a symptom of the malaise from which the whole country is suffering?'

' "Malaise"? What "malaise"?' She looked around her as if it might be a tangible thing.

'Can't you *feel* it? Strip away the layers of cloud from in front of your eyes and for once take a proper look at your domain. Can you honestly pretend that Albion is any happier a land than it was when it was ruled by the House of Ellon? You've given the peasants their freedom from the burden of mindless serfdom that the Ellonia imposed upon them for all those centuries, yet you've given them no way of expressing that freedom. You promised them a vision of glory where they could fulfil all their desires for happiness, and what have you given them instead?'

'All that I *can* give them.'

'Precisely. And that's not enough. They were looking forward to a paradise that no one could have created, and they've got to be content with reality. And of *course* some of them begin to resent this, to blame you for the shortfall between their expectations and the lives they find themselves living. It's irrational, naturally; it's naïve; but you can hardly expect them to think in any other way. They don't realize that any happiness they can ever achieve in their lives will be something that they'll have had to earn – through enduring the hard work and the pain of change that'll be needed before they can get there. They don't realize that, because *you* haven't told them. Instead, you've set yourself up as an absolute monarch, not so much a queen as a pitiless, unforgiving goddess. If they complain to you or if they show even the slightest inclination to disagree with whatever it is you might have decided to decree, in your *own* naïveté, you respond by killing them for their rebelliousness – to terrorize the others into stifling their desire for freedom.'

'It was I who gave them their freedom in the first place.' Her lips were taut, barely permitting the words to squeeze between them.

'*What* freedom? You've given them a word – nothing more! In so many ways they were better off under the Ellonia, when at least they couldn't recognize their misery for what it was! You've given them a glimpse of the open countryside and then slammed the prison door shut on them again! They know there's something wrong and, because you've identified yourself so closely with all of Albion, you're the only thing that they can blame. And you're too wilfully blind, too lost in your own glory, your self-accorded deity, to recognize this and try to do anything about it.'

He stopped, aghast at his own temerity. His tongue had stumbled over some of the syllables, but the words had come out in roughly the right order. Surely she would have him killed now for his audacity.

But do I actually care whether I live or die? he thought. *I said a little while ago that I'd gladly kill Anya if I thought it would save Albion from destruction. Surely the same is true for myself. It would give me little grief to depart this half-life.*

Anya said nothing for a while, as if she were daring him to carry on speaking. Amid the flood of his own words he hadn't noticed that she'd drawn her sword; he wondered if she herself had realized it. The weapon was twitching in her grasp, as if the blade were eager to be put to use, yet her eyes were fixed firmly on his face.

And then finally her gaze fell.

'What would you wish me to do?' she said, her voice softer than before.

'Explain to them. Tell them that all you are is a person who's trying to do her best for them.' He spread his hands, almost as if he were begging for something from her. 'Tell them something that they'd know for themselves if only they had the experience to realize it: that just because there's hardship at the moment doesn't mean that better times don't lie ahead – assuming that everyone's working together towards the same goal. At the moment your energies – and everybody else's energies – are being dissipated on squabbles and rebellions and oppressions. Soon those energies will have wasted away altogether, and the only future left for Albion will be to sink back into chaos.'

She tapped the tip of her sword on the floor reflectively. Ngur winced as he thought of what the stone must be doing to the fine-ground point. He could see that her lips were moving, as if she were having an argument with herself. There was hope then. She hadn't merely called for guards and ordered that he be taken away to his death.

Cautiously he took a few steps forward until he was standing closer to her.

She paid no attention to him, but half-turned away, raising her head.

Then a gleeless realization flooded into him. He'd been wrong to assume that Anya was debating the unpalatable truth with herself. Instead she was discussing it with her mother. Every now and then her lips would stop moving and she'd tilt her head as if she were listening to some other voice.

Automatically Ngur glanced up at the portrait, stupidly expecting to see signs of animation on Syor's relentlessly hostile face. He silently cursed himself for imbecility – the face was nothing more than a dead thing of paint – but then he stilled. It seemed to him as if the lips on that face had curved themselves into a malicious smile of triumph, directed not at Anya but at himself. The illusion persisted for only a moment, disappearing so swiftly that he could hardly believe that he'd seen it, and yet . . .

Now Anya was making sounds. At first all he could

hear were the plosives, but then he was able to make out a long, urgent, susurrating whisper, punctuated by pauses as she listened to her mother speaking. Finally she turned to him.

'Thank you for your honesty, husband,' she said. Her earlier sarcasm seemed to have vanished entirely. She brushed his stubbly cheek with her lips. 'Leave me here with my thoughts a while. I will join you in your bedchamber – later.'

Ngur was confused, his mind a mixture of suspicion and elation. He'd expected a hard and possibly unsuccessful argument before persuading Anya to bend even a little, and yet here she was apparently capitulating to his view almost immediately. Had the unexpected fluency that had captured his tongue succeeded in swaying her so easily?

'Leave me,' she insisted softly. 'I won't be long.'

Uncertainly he reached out to touch her forehead with the back of his fingers; it was a gesture of affection that had sprung up between them back in the early days when there had seemed to be some chance of deriving more than practical benefits from their union. She smiled now, her eyes warm on his. She reached up and took his hand, lowered it to her lips, and lightly kissed his knuckles.

He looked back at her as he opened the door.

She was kneeling towards the altar again, her shoulders moving slightly as she soundlessly requested Syor's guidance.

From where he stood he couldn't observe the caustic smile on her lips, and nor could he see through her eyes as she watched a responsive expression of mockery appear on the features of her mother, poised on the wall above her.

Ngur, Anya heard Syor saying, *is so unsubtle and so easy to delude. His years of powerlessness have softened him, so that now he listens too much to gossip. He's like a drunkard weeping copious tears at the thought of a fly being killed. You must pamper him for a little longer, Anya, until he believes that he shares your throne – that your decisions are his as well. Then he'll forget this compassionate, jelly-hearted nonsense of*

*his. The peasants of Albion are like children – your children
– and they require for the moment the same sort of strictness
that a mother would exercise. It's for their own good that you
need to be so harsh with them. In due course, Anya, they'll
grow up into adulthood and then, maybe, you can treat them
the way that Ngur wants you to. But, until then . . .*

Anya crept into his bed an hour later and delighted him
with her submissiveness until dawn trickled greyly into
the room.

4

Someone had imported a trained wolf from the World
and had been trying to persuade it to perform tricks to ill
rendered tunes on a flageolet in one of the minor marketplaces of Ernestrad. But the wolf had become swiftly
terrified of the jostling crowds around it and had forgotten
all that its unknown master had taught it. The beast had
turned and freed itself by biting once right through the
tethering arm of its captor, then fled through the press,
savaging any limb that happened to be in its course,
dragging the bloody forearm, now mercifully sans flageolet, behind it on the end of its leash. The screams had
attracted the attention of a platoon of soldiers who'd been
sitting outside a tavern debating whether or not they'd
consumed too much cider to go whoring, as had been
their intention. With pikes and swords they'd soon
despatched the frightened creature, but not before one of
them had had his guts torn out and another had accidentally slashed a blade across his own hamstrings. After the
surviving soldiers had calmed their jangling nerves with a
further infusion of cider the tavern-keeper had been
unwise and unpatriotic enough to demand from them
some payment for those of his wares they had consumed;
for his persistence he had been rewarded with a metal-
studded fist in his eye, which had burst, to the great
amusement of the soldiers.

Now he had come to Anya's twice-weekly audience in
Starveling to seek some recompense for his injury.

She held her audiences in the same great hall as the Despot had used for his formal consultations with his courtiers, a coincidence that Ngur always found disconcerting. The room had been completely refurbished since then, of course, smoke stains and Ellonian erotic murals covered by white paint and woven hangings executed by peasant artists in a style that could best be described as 'vigorous'. Even so, on the rare occasions that Ngur attended his wife's public appearances here he found himself subject to alarming double-shifts of perception; unless he concentrated hard on what was going on, the trim figure of his wife, seated upright on her plain wooden throne, was apt to haze into the corpulent bloat of the Despot, wallowing across and beyond hectares of ostentatious gilt.

The tavern-keeper could not have been very prepossessing even before the assault, mused Ngur, whose sympathies in the matter lay largely with the wolf. The man was on his feet, surrounded by a restless crowd of squatting citizens totally uninterested in his case, enduring him until such time as they could present their own grievances. Either he was an amateur mummer or he had been watching too many itinerant theatrical presentations. His hands were never still as he declaimed; Ngur was fascinatedly identifying each of the various attitudes they adopted, playing a guessing-game with himself to try to identify the emotions they were intended to convey. The ferocity of the wolf's attack on a defenceless child sparked off a remarkably evocative imitation of a windmill followed by what was apparently intended to be a seduction scene that Ngur had difficulty fitting into the overall narrative. The soldiers' violence instigated a prolonged period of histrionics which Anya had to raise a hand to still. The tavern-keeper, visibly affronted, concluded his peroration by holding a dramatic pose, his right-hand index finger pointing accusingly at the purple scab where his eye had once been.

'Why do you not take this issue before the magistrates?' said Anya in her clear voice. Ngur, glancing sideways, was impressed by the way that she was able to banish all traces of impatience from her face; instead she had arranged its lines and creases into an expression of almost maternal condolence.

'Because the magistrates . . .' the man stammered, wondering what to do with his right hand, now that it had served its purpose. 'Because your magistrates, while they will protect your citizenry against the depredations of the soldiers who once served under the Ellonia, will but rarely find against those who fought in your army.'

Only Ngur was close enough to hear the little hiss of annoyance that escaped from Anya's lips. It was accepted that in theory the people could bring *any* complaint before her on these occasions, but there were some topics that were tacitly regarded as taboo. The integrity of her cobbled-together judiciary system was one of them.

'You suggest that my magistrates, in whom I place my utmost trust, are corrupt?' she said, a trenchant eyebrow raised. 'Or are you trying to intimate that they are in fear of my officers?'

'I . . . I . . .'

Ngur knew what the tavern-keeper's difficulty was, and wondered if he could make a tactful translation on the man's behalf. The peasant militia had little respect for the judiciary because the judiciary were ultimately responsible to Anya herself, who found it hard to credit that any of those who had followed her during the rebellion could be guilty of any crime. An appeal by a peasant warrior over the heads of the magistrates, to Anya herself, was almost certain to be successful; although there would be no physical manifestations of her displeasure with those who had clearly perpetrated a miscarriage of justice, the luckless magistrates responsible would find that they might be better occupied for the future pursuing careers in agriculture – swineherding, for example.

'It seems to us clear in this instance,' Anya was saying, 'that some of our soldiers, over-exuberant in the aftermath of their success in saving the citizens of Ernestrad from further depredations by the dangerous beast, their inhibitions perhaps lessened by their intoxication, certainly did behave uncivilly to the extent of committing a crime against your person. But we are not magistrates, and it is for our magistrates to deal with such matters. I can only suggest that you pursue your grievance in the customary manner. Should it be that you remain dissatisfied after our law has taken its course, then return here and present your cause before us again.'

She dismissed the tavern-keeper with a wave of her hand. He sat down, scowling, and a fulsomely pregnant wench rose with difficulty to her feet, her mouth already open to speak.

'Wait,' Ngur said.

For a moment neither Anya nor the pregnant woman realized that he'd spoken. Then they both turned incredulously towards him.

'Yes, my dear?' said Anya softly, reaching out to brush his wrist caressingly. The fire in her eyes was quenched before he had had the chance to notice its flicker.

'Our friend the tavern-keeper . . .' Ngur began.

The man looked up from his cursing, his remaining eye filled with alarm: was the consort about to propose that he, not the warriors, had been the guilty party?

' "Our friend the tavern-keeper",' Anya prompted.

'We wouldn't wish him to leave here feeling that his injuries have been belittled,' said Ngur.

'We – both of us – recognize the true seriousness of the crime to which he was subjected, do we not?' said Anya, a trace of waspishness creeping into her voice.

'Yet the man clearly believes that he will gain scant satisfaction from your magistrates,' Ngur continued, gaining confidence. The gathered citizens were looking up at him amazedly. 'And I believe that he has good grounds for that belief.'

'You denigrate the honour of our justices?' Her head was cocked endearingly towards him, and her question was politely spoken, but now Ngur could see the fury behind her smile.

'Your magistrates,' said Ngur, sighing, unconsciously

accenting the *your*, 'will indubitably find the soldiers guilty, but the sentence they deliver will be paltry and the reparation they award this poor unfortunate will be likewise. They fear for their well-being should they interpret the law too harshly in dealing with those whom you regard as your own.'

There was a mumble of agreement from the watchers. The sound stopped when one of the guards reached instinctively for her sword.

'Surely not!' Anya protested. 'Surely we would dismiss in ignominy any magistrate who abused justice through fear of our displeasure?'

Ngur just looked at her. There were pinknesses at the points of her cheekbones. After several seconds she turned to gaze at the tavern-keeper who, bewildered by the unexpected turn of events, was doing his best to be invisible.

'My consort,' Anya said tightly, 'has expressed a point of view. Is it one with which you agree?'

Unable, in the heat of the moment, to decide which was the right answer, the citizen chose at random.

'Yes,' he blurted.

He tried immediately to correct himself, but stage-fright knotted his tongue.

Anya drummed her fingernails on the arm of her chair.

'Is this a view shared by all?' asked Ngur hastily of the crowd.

Their assent was obvious. The guards looked to Anya for instruction, but she was lost in thought, her eyes blank.

'We thank our fellow-citizen for having brought this matter to our attention,' said Ngur courteously, wishing that he could pass the burden of judgement over to Anya so that she could reclaim some of her self-esteem. 'Be assured, all of you, that this terrible crime will be thoroughly investigated by a senior officer selected by ourselves, and that the culprit or culprits will be prosecuted with the full zeal of the law. In the meantime, we shall arrange for some small token of recompense – five horses from our own stables – to be given to you, our friend' – a nod towards the stunned tavern-keeper – 'as an earnest of our sorrow that you should have been so abused by warriors under our command.'

There was a long silence and then a sudden, astonished outcry. Anya gazed out sightlessly over the roiling heads. Ngur looked at her nervously, wondering what might be going on behind that frozen visage. He felt little satisfaction in having righted an incipient wrong: he realized that in many ways his judgement was indistinguishable from giving the man a bribe to get him to go away. For a few moments he was apprehensive about the forms Anya's wrath might take, but then he angrily banished such thoughts. She had accepted – hadn't she? – that the rot that had been devouring Albion was a product of the way that all things devolved upon herself. This mistrust of the common people for the judiciary she had appointed was yet another symptom of the same disease – as surely she would come to recognize once the brief anger had left her . . .

Uncertainly, he apologized to the pregnant woman for having interrupted her complaint, and bade her continue where she had left off.

5

Joli, crouching in the back row of the great hall where no one would notice him except as an extra grubby face, nodded his approval in Ngur's general direction. He'd known the Ellonian whippersnapper for only a brief period, and had judged him to be a jumped-up time-server whose sole priority was the protection of his own skin. This was customarily Joli's sole priority, too, and he'd respected the symptoms of dawning wisdom. None the less, he was pleased to see momentary evidence that Ngur was made of sterner stuff – much sterner stuff, indeed, if he were prepared to risk the raw edge of Anya's temper. Joli had known the woman since she'd been barely departing adolescence, and the memories of some of her more spectacular tantrums still made him shiver. And, later, the executions she'd ordered when she'd believed her army was being infiltrated by Ellonian spies . . .

Maybe, Joli thought, he'd been wrong. He hadn't stayed around very long after the conquest of Ernestrad and the installation of Anya on the throne. He'd seen her take Ngur as her consort, and had vaguely approved. The peasants had won the war, and so had earned the right to rule; yet the surviving Ellonia had considerably more experience and expertise in the arts of governance and administration, and it would have been criminal to have wasted that knowledge. So, as he'd slipped unostentatiously away from Ernestrad, Joli had been as content as ever he was about the prospects for the future.

Part of him had wanted to stay on in the city. As one of Anya's most senior and powerful allies, he would have been assured of ample opportunity to revel in the fruits of triumph: wenches, good food, wenches, fine wines, wenches, soft beds, wenches . . . But, after a few debilitating weeks, he'd found himself restless, yearning for his old life among the byways and the open fields. Reen had acidly diagnosed the reason for his wanderlust as overwenching, but that hadn't been it at all. In those days he'd felt like a brand-new person – which he quite literally was. Not only had the most important part of his previous personality been taken from him, for his dreams had become of no more significance than anybody else's nighttime fancies, but also he'd experienced death and rebirth. Quite how Alyss had engineered the latter he still wasn't certain but, having clear memories of the afterlife, he was everlastingly grateful to her for having done so. He'd spent a short time in a place of perdition where existence was dominated by the growls and roars of mindless monsters, a she-demon called Leonora had delighted in devising ever more refined torments to which she could subject him, and the wenches had been unwilling and the hangovers severe. On returning to reality he'd been so relieved that he'd have gratefully spent the rest of his years on a rack if doing so would have extended his life by an hour.

So the new – the genuinely new – Joli had taken to the roads as a professional peripatetic wencher. Business had been brisk – he had been the first to break into a hitherto unsuspected and hence untapped market – and the next few years had been happy ones. He looked back with a mixture of pity and contempt on his old sybaritic self, and thanked his good fortune that he'd discovered the satisfactions of virtuous toil. Yet now, after all this time, curiosity – and, maybe, something else, but mainly curiosity – had lured him back to Ernestrad to see how things had been getting along without him.

If Ngur's unexpected firmness were anything to judge by, then at least here in the capital things had been getting along rather well – better, certainly, than they had in the provinces.

He picked his nose ruminatively, prised the sticky gum out from under his fingernail, rolled it into a little ball, and flicked it at the back of the neck of the still spouting mother-to-be.

Bullseye.

She started at the impact, and mercifully lost the flow of what she'd been saying for long enough that Anya's consort was able to interpose a swift judgement of the woman's case: yes, she should return the offending apricots to the vendor.

On the throne, glad to be rid of the woman's whining, Ngur grinned inwardly. He'd spotted Joli at the back there some moments before, and his eyes had followed the arc of the invisibly small missile's trajectory. The distraction had performed its intended purpose perfectly. He gestured to the next complainant to rise.

While the hall was filled with the beginning of what promised to be a tortuous account of a land dispute, Ngur beckoned one of the guards to him and pointed out the wrinkled, dirty little face at the rear of the crowd. The soldiers at the door saw the exchange, and moved to bar Joli's immediate attempt to escape. The guard to whom

Ngur had spoken unobtrusively skirted the walls until she reached the back of the room, where she took charge of the struggling man. After a brief but intense altercation, a rather subdued Joli agreed to accompany her to an antechamber, his throat pulsing nervously as she fingered the hilt of her dagger.

Ngur smiled, and tried to concentrate his mind on the hotly argued case of the neighbour's fence. He looked once again at Anya, but still she seemed to be lost in another world. Her lips were moving slightly, and Ngur guessed – correctly – that she was communing with the internal voice that she believed to be her mother's. He wished that he could eavesdrop, just once, on their frequent conversations, but Syor apparently chose to speak only to Anya.

Perhaps an hour went by before a jolt seemed to pass through the queen's body and her eyes suddenly came to life again. Ngur shook off his drowsiness and smiled warmly at her; he was relieved when she smiled back. He winked and made a slight movement of his head. As requested, Anya promptly declared that the audience was over for the day.

Her demeanour remained amicable as the citizens untidily left the hall, some still muttering, others looking smug. The guards waited until the last of the people had vanished and then, at a nod from Anya, themselves departed.

'You bastard!' she said to Ngur as soon as she was sure they were alone.

He was shocked. Since recovering consciousness she'd acted her part so well that he'd believed that she had indeed realized the justice of what he'd done.

'I . . .' he said.

'Silence, before I have your tongue plucked from your throat, you little shit!'

'Anya . . .' He reached out a conciliatory arm.

'Fuck off.'

'We agreed that . . .'

'Get out of my sight! Thank that bloody Sun you

worship that I still need you . . . for a while.'

He shrugged helplessly. As she knew, he didn't worship the Sun; nevertheless, he thanked it for giving him the prescience to have had Joli detained. The little man would act as a useful buffer until time had had the chance to moderate Anya's temper.

'There's a friend of yours here,' he said cautiously.

'Go!' Her fist missed his mouth by a hair's-breadth as he stepped backwards. 'I don't want to see any fucking friends, and especially I don't want to see *you*!'

In fact, it was Anya who went, her hands worrying at the hem of her jacket and her feet beating out a staccato on the tiles. Ngur watched her go, and shrugged yet again. This wasn't at all like the yielding, compliant Anya who'd been his bedmate these past few weeks. He began to wonder if her softening had been all a pretence – but no: he knew her too well not to have penetrated any attempted dissimulation.

A minute or two later he found Joli sitting glumly on a stone bench in the antechamber, the guard standing threateningly over him, her dagger drawn.

'Go on,' said the little man morosely as Ngur appeared. 'Cut it off. You'll be destroying my professional livelihood, of course, but don't let that worry you.'

'What are you talking about?' said Ngur. 'It's good to see you after all these years.'

'This bitch said she was going to . . .'

'It was difficult to persuade the prisoner to remain in custody, my lord,' said the guard rapidly.

Ngur laughed. 'This isn't a prisoner, soldier,' he said. 'This is an old friend of ours. I wanted to be sure that he wouldn't run away before Anya and I had the opportunity of giving him the welcome he deserves.'

The guard looked frightened.

'An honest mistake,' said Ngur.

She returned her dagger to its scabbard, her movements more relaxed, the beginnings of a smile at the corner of her mouth. 'I beg your forgiveness,' she said formally to Joli, who smirked.

'Dismissed, soldier,' said Ngur.

The two men – one upright and elegantly dressed, the other bent and ragged – walked arm in arm along a sequence of corridors until they reached Ngur's study. The room was filled with a friendly litter of parchments and half-read books. Ngur swept a pile of these off an easy-chair onto the floor and gestured to Joli that he should sit himself down. The consort himself ignored the upright chair behind the cluttered desk and went to stand by the window, through which he could see a vista of Ernestrad's rooftops. There had been a cloying mist over them this morning, but now it had cleared and the Sun was shining brightly, feigning spring.

'Anya is . . . indisposed for the moment,' he said.

'I could do with a piss myself,' said Joli. 'I don't suppose there's a . . . ?'

When he returned to the room a little later Ngur was still staring out across the city. Joli immediately noticed the wistfulness in that gaze, and said nothing as he quietly sat down. In his absence a large flagon of wine and a pair of copper goblets had been set on a corner of the desk, and he helped himself eagerly.

'What brings you back here?' asked Ngur at last.

'Curiosity,' explained Joli. He described in some detail his journeyings to all corners of the land, and by the time he'd finished Ngur was sitting on the floor, his back resting against the wall beneath the window, affairs of state forgotten, his face a little boy's. The two of them, eyes locked dancingly, raised their goblets and silently toasted each other in the dusk.

It couldn't last. Ngur felt the weight of graver matters flopping down over him like a blanket cutting out the light. His limbs seemed stiff with age as he pulled himself up and went to sit behind his desk. None of the documents scattered across it seemed to be of any significance – most of them were standard forms filled out by World merchants requesting permission to land their goods in Qazar, the rudimentary fishing port to Ernestrad's east that had been hastily enlarged to cope with merchant traffic once the shores of Albion had been opened. Ngur knew he was supposed to have signed them all – some of them quite a long time ago – but he hadn't bothered and wasn't going to: the traders would land their wares whether or not they were legally entitled to – in one of Albion's countless natural harbours if they were too mean to pay the necessary bribes at Qazar. For the hundredth time he made a mental note to ensure that something was done about the nation's coastal security – there were rumours that soul-destroying drugs were beginning to trickle into Albion – and for the hundredth time he promptly forgot all about it.

Joli was looking at him with shrewd eyes. 'Anya is . . . displeased with you.'

It wasn't a question.

'Yes,' said Ngur with a sigh, watching his fingers play with the shaft of his rarely used pen. 'Yes . . . but she'll soon be over it.'

'Not unless she's changed a deal since last I knew her,' said Joli.

There was an uncomfortable silence between them.

Ngur was the one to break it.

'How much do you know of how things have been, here in Ernestrad?' he said abruptly.

'A little. As much as anyone out in the sticks has heard. People have largely stopped caring about events here in the capital, you know, unless the executioners should happen to come their way. A more pertinent subject might be how much *you* know of how things have been in the country.'

'I gather there has been . . . discontent.'

' "Discontent"? Too bloody right there's been "discontent"! The people had to *learn* to love Anya when she was leading them against the Ellonia. Now most of that love has been forgotten again. Many of them are wishing that Reen had taken the throne in Anya's place, and there's a pretty powerful rumour going the rounds that Reen's stuck in some dungeon somewhere, or even that she's dead.'

Ngur gave a wintry smile. 'Be assured, friend, that there's no truth in that. She bought a passage on a trawler and went off to explore the World.'

He stopped, the smile vanishing like a snuffed flame. *I have no proof of that*, he thought sickly. *I never saw her embark. Anya could have lied to me when she professed to be so startled to discover that Reen had left us. Maybe the rumour is . . .*

'And maybe it's wrong,' said Joli, finishing off his thought for him. 'I think it's just a good story to be told when people are getting newted of an evening and they want to find an extra reason for disliking She Who Leads. As if they needed extra reasons,' he added darkly.

'It's that bad?' said Ngur softly.

'Worse,' said Joli. 'There are a lot worse tales than that being bandied about. Even if people only half-believe them, they pass them on to others more credulous than themselves. And the gibbets have been busy all over the land. You can dismiss a rumour as just so much gossip, but you can't deny the evidence of a corpse swinging in the breeze, when you hope the marks on it were put there by the birds after the poor sod had died, not by Anya's executioners before. And those aren't just cadavers, you know, not just hunks of meat: for too many people they're reminders of their daughters or sons or sisters or brothers or mothers or fathers or . . .'

'Enough,' said Ngur wearily.

'The people are living on hope,' said Joli, 'but that hope's fast ebbing. I doubt it'll be long before it's gone altogether, and then . . . *pfft!*' He made an expressive shape in the air with his hands.

'They hope that Anya will meliorate her reign?' said Ngur.

'No.' Joli clapped his thigh annoyedly. 'They've given up any expectation of that – long ago. What they're hoping is that Reen isn't dead after all, that she'll come back to claim the throne they believe is hers by right. Or they hope that you'll depose Anya yourself, because, while they may not have any great love for you, they trust you in a way that they don't trust your wife: you'd be that strangest of things, a popular usurper. Or, if they get really stuck for bright sides to look on, they just hope that someone – anyone – will have the luck and the bravery and the guile to murder her.'

'Is that why you came here?' said Ngur quietly. 'You fought against us – against the Ellonia – to end tyranny. Have you come here to complete your old task?'

'Me?' Joli began to laugh bitterly. 'No, never me. I'm no killer – never have been, never could be. That's probably why I have such san-guin-ar-y nightmares, to compensate for my waking milquetoastery. But there are plenty of other people around who'd have less compunction than me.'

'Then why *are* you here?'

'I told you: curiosity. One night, a couple of weeks ago, I found that I had to call it a day after the seventh – pretty little thing the eighth was, too – and that reminded me that I can't expect to spend too many more years in this life, so I decided to come to Ernestrad and see for myself how things were going.' Joli shuddered. It hadn't been the seventh; it had, embarrassingly, been only the fourth, and the intended fifth had mocked him cruelly and publicly. He determined that he wouldn't tell Ngur about the afterlife, where such failures had seemed to be *de rigueur*.

Ngur wasn't paying much attention. He'd disguised his astonishment at one thing that Joli had said – that Anya's subjects would be glad to see him usurp his wife's throne. He'd rarely given much thought to how the citizens regarded him; he'd always assumed he was of little importance in their eyes, a moon to Anya's Sun. The people of Ernestrad, of course, being closer to him, would regard him as either much more or much less than that, precisely because of their propinquity. But he'd guessed that, to the peasantry of the far-flung rural regions, he was nothing more than a figurehead, a political convenience.

And maybe – his mind took a jump forward – his supposition had been correct.

'Tell me,' he said, breaking into whatever it was that

Joli was prattling about, 'tell me more about this hope of the people's that I might become ruler of Albion in Anya's stead.'

Joli launched into an ocean of words. Ngur let its waves crash about him, listening only to as much as he needed to. If the little man's account was to be credited, the people of a tormented land were crying out for the beneficent reign of a new monarch, and the person they desired above all to be that monarch (assuming that Reen was unavailable) was none other than Ngur himself. Joli waxed enthusiastic over the glories of such a reign, and he was beginning to startle even himself by his passionate articulacy when Ngur suddenly slapped the table, so that parchments flapped and pens leapt.

'Enough!' snapped the consort. Then, more softly: 'Enough. You say that you're not a killer, but it seems that you have indeed come to Ernestrad with the intent of an assassin. You're an artist of speech, Joli, and your words paint alluring landscapes. But you've been painting canvases of a scene that no longer exists: Anya has listened to the advice of myself and' – he waved an embarrassed hand – 'her mother, and has realized the error of her ways. She has forsworn tyranny. Already, as you must have seen for yourself during this afternoon's audience, she has passed some of the responsibilities of governance to me . . .'

'That's not what I saw at all,' said Joli, his eyes hot. 'I saw, instead, a puppet daring to move a step without the tug of a string.'

'You underestimate your queen,' said Ngur sadly, wishing that he were wholly confident that this was true.

'Do I?' said Joli. 'I doubt it. I may not admire her, but there are a deal of things about her that impress me, mightily. When she was hardly yet a woman, I learnt not to underestimate some of her qualities: her ruthlessness, for example; her ability to manipulate people, even though she's unable to make them love her; her single-mindedness; her faith in herself. I could go on listing her attributes for a long time, friend, but there'd be little point in it.' Joli helped himself to the last of the wine; gulped; belched. 'You can't see the situation with Anya as it really is, because you're an integral part of it yourself. If you looked deep enough into your soul you'd find guilt: even though no one pretended that your contract of loving marriage with Anya was anything more than a charade, you're still ashamed of the fact that you can't find husbandly affection for her in your heart, and so you overcompensate, hoping that if you act the part of a lover earnestly enough and long enough the time will arrive when the counterfeit becomes a reality. Anya knows this, and uses your guilt and your response to it. And she knows, too, of your other dissimulation: the way that, for all your protestations of modesty and humility, you unconsciously desire to believe that you are your wife's equal in all things. Again Anya can see more clearly through the sham than you can, and she knows how to turn it to her advantage.'

'You talk of her as if she were a cold, calculating . . .'

'She *is*!' Joli found that his goblet was empty and tossed it into a corner, where it joined the rest of the room's untidiness. 'You've told her what you'd like her to become and she's looked behind your words to discover what the illogical part of you believes she could actually be. It's been easy for her to adopt a disguise to trick you, because you've done most of the trickery yourself. You've persuaded yourself, despite all good sense, that Anya has become the person of your ideals. Look at the way you are now. You've told me yourself how her mask slipped off this afternoon, so that the truth about her real feelings was as blatant as a fist in the mouth, and yet still you're trying to convince yourself that it was just an accidental tantrum, that she's not like that *really*.' Joli's voice was becoming ever more bitter. 'You're like a fawning dog that wants to believe that its master's kick was a kindness and comes back, tail wagging and tongue lolling out, for more.'

'I don't believe you,' said Ngur, his eyes stinging; he wiped swiftly at them with the back of his sleeve, telling himself that the tears were of tiredness. 'And it's as well that you've spoken these . . . aberrations to me rather than in front of anyone else. We are not like our predecessors, seeing treason in every curl of a lip, but what you have been talking is surely incitement to rebel, and no state will tolerate that. No' – a suddenly aggressive glare at Joli, who was half-rising from his chair – 'be silent and hear me out. You're mistaken, too, in your belief that I have ambitions to usurp Anya and grasp power for myself. I sipped at the flask of power when the Wind slew the old Despot and I took his throne, but I did not acquire the taste for it, and have no wish to. If you seek someone to depose her then you must seek elsewhere, and you must bear it in mind that, for all the length of our acquaintanceship, as her husband and as her dutiful consort I will do everything within my abilities to thwart your aims. Have I made myself clear?'

Joli was miserable; Ngur thought it was because the little man had failed in his persuasions. He didn't see the look of pity in Joli's eyes.

'Transparently so, my lord.'

'Then let us forget such things, eh? Let us remember instead the tales you were telling me of your many acts of generosity.'

But Joli wasn't to be so easily sidetracked.

'If you believe that I was speaking treason, sire,' he said, 'you should hear what the wenches whose antics you laughed over are saying. If you would wish to prosecute all those you deem to be traitors – because their loyalty is to our land, not to its self-appointed symbol – then you'd better set your factors to building a thousand gallows, and you'd better train up a whole generation of executioners. If that is what you wish. But I beg you not to accuse *me*. I had no intention that either you or Anya should know that I was here, still less of speaking with you as I have. All that I've done is to report to you, as honestly as I know how – and however much honesty may run against my natural preferences – what your subjects are saying, and the reasons for their saying it.'

'Please,' said Ngur unhappily, 'please don't continue, Joli. Already I've heard far more than I should have without calling for the soldiers to carry you away. Please don't force my hand. Please.'

Now there was no mistaking Joli's look of pity. The two men held each other's gaze for a long while in the grey evening light and then, as if by mutual agreement, they both shifted their attention elsewhere, Ngur picking a stray hair from the smooth linen of his breeches and Joli finding something of sudden interest in the darkening sky outside the window.

'Anya will be wishing to see you,' said Ngur eventually.

'I'm not sure that I'm wishing to see *her*,' said Joli caustically, getting to his feet, 'but I suppose I'd better, and get it over with. Lead me into her august presence, my lord. That is, if you can still remember how to lead.'

'You . . .' Ngur began, raising his arm, his lips white, the aftertaste of the wine suddenly sickly in his mouth.

But then he forced down the swell of his anger.

The man was bent and frail, after all, and slight. It would have been the act of a bully to crush him.

'Come, Joli,' he said. 'Let me lead you to Anya's chambers.'

6

Although the basic structure was unchanged since the time before fire had swept through Giorran, there was much that was new in Starveling, and so the two men dawdled on their way to Anya's quarters, stopping frequently to gaze from windows that had been hacked through the stone or to admire ornaments and curios brought in from the World. The soldier who had been sent to eavesdrop at Ngur's door therefore had plenty of time to report to his queen on all that he had heard.

She listened without expression, then, after issuing a brief command, waved him from the room.

By the time Joli and Ngur were admitted to her chambers a tray of shrimps and oysters had been laid out on a side-table alongside goblets and a jug of strong white wine. Anya, too, was in white: a simple, sheer nightgown of silk. She had brushed her curly yellow hair back over her ears, securing it with a loose clasp. She had dabbed a few drops of a lemony scent beneath her jaws and at her temples. Her only ornaments were the silver betrothal ring on her finger and, on a chain around her neck, a tiny plain copper case within which hid a miniature portrait of her mother. For once Anya bore no weapon.

'Joli!' she cried, rushing forward, arms wide, to embrace the little man. 'You're a sight for sore eyes.' She kissed him on both cheeks, then hugged him again. 'I knew you'd come back to Starveling for a bath one day.'

The little man laughed, breathing the freshness of her gown.

Ngur smiled as he watched them. It was hard to reconcile this sibling mock-flirtation with the harsh words that Joli had been speaking only a short while before. Now the fellow was whispering something in Anya's ear that was making her blush like a maiden. It was as if the various dissonant events of the afternoon had been nothing but a bad dream.

He poured himself some wine, reminding himself to go easy: his mind already felt insulated thanks to the flagon he'd shared in his study. He broke a shrimp and tugged with his teeth at its succulent contents.

Finally Anya unpeeled Joli and joined her consort by the table. She was laughing silently, a picture of unmarked happiness. She filled the two remaining goblets and passed one of them to Joli.

'You'll dine with me, of course?' she said.

'As long as you don't cook it yourself,' said Joli, 'and as long as you can think up an errand to occupy your husband the while.' He fluttered his eyebrows.

'The wine would serve as adequate chaperone,' said Ngur comfortably.

'Nonsense!' cried Joli. 'Didn't I remember to tell you about the fertility festival I invented as a promotional stunt? I was a little apprehensive beforehand, I can tell you, so I drank a hogshead of usquebaugh to steady my nerves and *still* I was able to . . .'

They were laughing, some time later, as they entered a side-room where a table had been set out for them. The lights were bright, the food was ample and good and the servants who attended them were jovial, but still for some reason the laughter soon drained away and the conversation became strained. Joli tried to gloss over the tension with a further string of ribald stories, but Anya had stopped smiling at his jokes and so in the end he gave up. Ngur, looking back and forward between their two faces, felt strangely left out of things, as if there were some conversation going on between them that he could not hear.

Finally Anya yawned decorously, patting her lips with her fingers.

'It's been a long day, and a tiring one, Joli,' she said. 'The burdens of state are heavier than you might imagine. Forgive us if we say goodnight to you. I've arranged for a room to be prepared for you in the officers' quarters downstairs.' She grinned suddenly. 'You must tell me in the morning how well your wiles succeed with the women under our command. Come, husband.'

She reached her arm across the table to Ngur.

Before Joli was led from her chambers, however, Anya called the two men to her side. She kissed both of them on the lips, and then asked to borrow Ngur's dagger. Moving neatly, she clipped from each of the men a small lock of hair and then, from her own head, two of her curls. Twining one of these with Joli's lank knot she passed it to Ngur; the other, tied with Ngur's hair, she gave to Joli. As they looked at her inquiringly she explained: 'They are tokens of the fact that I love you both, each in your own very different way. And I would like the same bond to exist, through my love, between you.'

Joli had no quip to make as he tucked away the knot of hair in his pouch. Ngur beamed at the pair of them as he kissed and then pocketed the one that Anya had given to him. He would keep it near him always, he vowed to himself.

That night, in her richly furnished bed, she was like a wild animal with him. She pinned him on his back, holding his outstretched hands tight against the mattress, and rode him frenziedly until his ecstasy became pain and he had to call out above her hoarse shouts, begging her to stop. But even then she wouldn't let him be, covering him with kisses and moaning at the back of her throat as she rubbed herself against him until she had coaxed him back to hardness. His final climax felt like the lingering touch of a red-hot wire, and his scream was only partly one of release.

Sleep was a welcomed analgesic.

7

A young cadet was being sick in the corridor when Ngur arrived.

'It's that bad?' he said, pausing by the retching man.

'Worse.'

Ngur sucked in his cheeks. Anya hadn't been beside him when one of her servants had woken him with the news. He'd thrown a robe over his nakedness and hurried down here as swiftly as he could. Even over the stink of vomit he could smell the stench of death.

'I must look for myself,' he said, gently patting the cadet on the shoulder.

Joli's remains were spreadeagled across the bed. Where his genitals should have been there was only a dark-red, ripped emptiness. Ngur looked down to the uncarpeted floor and saw the torn scraps of flesh. He remembered a guard's jesting threat. He remembered an ecstasy that had been transformed into pain. On the stone beside the pitiful bundle he saw a tangle of hair, gold mixed with steel; he stooped and picked it up, running his thumb over its roughness. He remembered the strong white hand that had given it to Joli. He remembered words of love.

He stood with his head thrown back, the taut flesh of

his throat rippling as a scream of agony and misery came bubbling up, only to falter and fail before it reached his lips.

Shoulders slumped, he fancied that, in the distance, he could hear voices chanting.

Chapter Three
The Painter's Eyes

1

It was in the late weeks of the season the World calls spring – the one among these new things named seasons that we find hardest to understand – that the Painter first came among us. Like the dreamers and the singers who used to wander in the old days – the days we can hardly remember – across the hills and along the trodden paths between the villages, he seemed then and still seems to bear with him nothing but the implements of his trade: brushes broad and narrow, and cloths for spreading; two scooped buckets of wood, their holes chocked with clay, for mixing; and, in a sack slung over his shoulder, a paltry supply of the coarse and gritty pigments he has gathered from the gods know where. Aside from that he has only the fronded clothes on his back, a stick broken from a tree somewhere along his endless road, and a pig that runs in its heavy, laborious, eagerly reluctant way from his walking legs to the terrain in front of him, and back again. The pig, which has a name, but not one that the Painter would share with any but a lover (and he has no lovers), is not only his companion of the road but also his guard animal, his friend, and perhaps also his critic, for as he works it sits on its haunches and watches him, its head tilted and its mouth half open, its small eyes alert on the movements of his arms.

Was there a first village he visited, in that spring? When we initially became conscious of his presence among us we became aware also that he had been on his wanderings for some short while, and that already his paintings decked more than one scarp. Yet we cannot clearly recall the very first of those creations, although those of us who dwell in Embrace-of-the-Forest are very insistent that it was they whom the Painter and his pig first graced with their presence. Let us, for the sake of argument (or, more accurately, for the sake of *no* argument), agree with them that yes, it was in Embrace-of-the-Forest that the Painter first appeared.

Already, by then, the folk of Embrace-of-the-Forest were become suspicious of newcomers, and the Painter was at first not privileged by any greater a welcome than if he'd been one of the many Worldsmen who'd come before him. Some of the people from the World who come to explore our ways are honest enough, and many have settled among us and even taken mates; but often enough they are tricksters or thieves who have fled to the shores of Albion to escape retribution or simply to open up new territories for their maleficent endeavours: we are even now unaccustomed to the idea of possession, and still less to that of covetousness, so we are easy prey. Be that as it may, there were no trumpets sounded or flowers strewn in the narrow streets of Embrace-of-the-Forest the day that the tall, undernourished figure of the Painter teetered on its stick-legs to the door of Halgiad's cottage; Halgiad, an urchin had told him, might take in a lodger because she was all alone with the children these days.

And it was one of her children who answered – that small girl of hers who keeps herself tidier than the others do. The child saw first the pig, and a grin came to her face. Then she noticed the stranger's trousers, two columns of what had once been soft black velvet with lacings along the seams, now creased and muddied and rent from their travels. Then the girl's gaze travelled upwards to the Painter's face, and she screamed and ran wailing for her mother's skirts . . .

That is what happened in Embrace-of-the-Forest. Maybe it had already happened in much the same way in others of the villages before, and maybe it hadn't. We do not know, and it hardly matters.

But a few days later, after Halgiad's daughter had

learned the playfulness of the Painter's smile and the softness of his chapped hand around hers as he told her one of his stories of great people and their doings in faraway places, he found his way – stumbling along, hands outreached ahead of him, rarely cursing when he tripped and fell (although that too was rarely, for his pig usually shouldered him gently aside from any dangerous obstacle) – to a place at the fringes of the village where a long-forgotten caprice of the Wind (of course it was long-forgotten, for now that we can remember it the Wind no longer plagues us) had ripped two slabs of the ground asunder to create a wall of naked rock half as high again as a tall man. Once he discovered this place – so Halgiad's daughter was later to tell her mother – he stood stone-still, as if he himself were of the rock, and then a smile grew on his face that seemed to warm the fields all around them. He told the child to mark the place well, so that she could bring him back to it by a more direct route than the circuitous one they had taken, and then they returned to Halgiad's house, where the Painter was paying in the soft yellow metal to dwell, and they collected a little clean, fresh water in his buckets and he arranged his sack of pigments on his back and, with the child's questions like birdsong in his ears, they went back, the three of them – man, girl and pig – to the rent in the land.

Halgiad's daughter sat with an arm around the pig for much of the rest of the day, returning home only the once to fetch bread and lard for a meal she and the pig shared. She watched as, for a long time, the Painter left his colours unmixed, instead just running his fingertips and the palms of his hands over the texturing of the crystal-winking rock, allowing its hard sharpnesses to become soft pliant warmths against his flesh. He sang a song to himself as he did so, a song we have often enough heard since the days that the Ellonia ruled and Barra 'ap Rteniadoli Me'gli'-minter Rehan the singer himself composed it as a memory:

Seven women rode down through the town of Starveling
  that night,

*Horses' hooves spitting galaxies in the pale moons' empty
  light.
And their eyes sought out the corners where the shadows
  grew
As deep and as dark as wine . . .*

Even the child was well acquainted with the song, and sometimes her own discordant voice quietly joined his; and then he would smile that *deep* smile again, and shift his singing so that the notes of his own voice twined themselves around her cracked ones and made the whole seem flawless. The pig, then, seemed to be laughing at the two of them, its head moving easily on its fat neck as it shifted its attention back and forth.

The Sun was looking wistfully towards the horizon when at last the Painter turned and told Halgiad's daughter that she could watch him as he mixed his colours.

He picked up his sack from the ground where he'd tossed it and spilled out onto the grass a cluster of small leather bags, tied at their necks with lengths of torn linen. The pig stayed where it was as she drew closer; this was the first time that she'd been permitted to see the contents of his secret sack, and her thumb absent-mindedly crept towards her mouth as she watched him pick up each of the little bags and heft its weight in his palm, muttering as he did so, until he'd identified each of them. Then he put two of them to one side and packed the rest of them away.

His dirty fingernails made short work of the first of the linen knots, and the girl gasped as the leather drooped aside to reveal a neatly crested pile of an ochreous yellow purer than any she could ever recall seeing (although in truth it was no yellower than the sands of our shores). The second bag opened, and this time the dust was of sparkling green, the brightest colour the sky might show in one of the dawns that Alyss has brought to us.

The child reached out to touch, but behind her the pig grunted a warning and she stilled her hand. The Painter, too, raised a palm in her direction, bidding her stay clear of his mysteries.

He told her to run and fetch some mud from the bank of a nearby stream. When she returned with it, laughing excitedly as it dribbled along the insides of her arms and over the front of her grey woollen dress, he gravely accepted it from her and kneaded it between his fingers, testing its consistency. Then, in one of the buckets, he mixed it with some of the clean water they'd brought until it had the viscosity of a thick lentil broth. Once he was satisfied, he began to pour in some of the ochre, stirring it with fingers that seemed to move quicker than sight, then adding a little more . . .

The girl's mouth pursed as she saw the pure colour clouding dirtily; it was as if he were deliberately destroying its light. But then, as she watched, the colour seemed to grow back into the mixture, still with that same elusive purity but now with a greater strength, as if the pigment and the mud were singing together in harmony (rather as she and the Painter had been singing earlier) and thereby producing a sound of a greater than imaginable richness. Framed by the bucket's irregular rim she saw a pool of a substance that seemed not altogether to be a part of the world she knew; she was gazing through a window into outwithness.

She was at once thrilled and frightened. She drew the hard, skimpy, matted wool of her dress around her shoulders.

'Have I caught the sunlight?' he asked her at last.

'Yes,' she said. Yes, now that he'd used the word 'sunlight' she realized that that was what he'd created, and why the hue repelled her at the same time as it attracted her. It was everyday yet alien. It was comforting yet it bore the unhidden threat of flames' voracity. And yet it wasn't the same colour as the sunlight at all: it still possessed the yellowness of the solar disc, but it was also more of a brownish colour, like the fine hairs on the backs of Halgiad's arms.

'Then I may begin to bring the goddess into this place,' he said gently.

An hour or two later and it was sunset.

The Painter didn't notice the cold springtime shadows,

but kept on working, splashing the single colour exuberantly yet carefully against the rock's surface. Finally Halgiad's daughter, shivering but too nervous to interrupt him herself, elbowed the pig sharply; it agreed with her, and snorted imperiously.

The Painter stopped work immediately. He held his dripping hands out to his sides, one squeezing a sodden cloth, and turned to grin in her direction.

'So soon, the end of the day,' he said.

Then he was all business and hustle. At his behest, she ran with the bucket he'd used, and a couple of brushes and the cloth, and rinsed them out in the now-dark stream. The ochreous mess seemed to mix reluctantly with the water, clinging to the materials and to her fingers as if she were trying to drown it, but eventually, in trickles, it floated away from her downstream, stretching into drab curves on the water's surface, collecting around a protruding stone for a while before abandoning itself once more to the current.

She ran back to where the Painter stood, waiting.

He'd packed away the two leather bags, one now a little lighter than before, and he had his sack up on his shoulder again. The pig was by his thighs. Both of them seemed to smile at her noisy approach.

As they set off for home she hung back a little at first, giving the rockface a last look in the grey-red light of early evening. The bright yellow-brown was still catching the late rays of the Sun so that it could call out like a clarion across the empty fields, yet it wasn't using any words that she could comprehend. All that the Painter seemed to have created was a tumbling, amorphous form that held no meaning that she could perceive. And yet it was clear from the shape of his body as he picked his way along the path that they'd created with their feet earlier in the day that he was satisfied with the work that he'd done.

Even the pig seemed satisfied.

They were foreigners, she concluded, just as she turned to run after them. Her mother had been wrong to think that they were, as the Painter had claimed, people of

Albion like everyone else in Embrace-of-the-Forest. The reason that the message of the painting was impenetrable to her was that it was being spoken in a foreign language.

Satisfied with her own explanation, on the way home she took his hand and joined him in singing yet again of the seven women.

2

That night at supper, as Halgiad and her four children sat around the table with the Painter, eating soup with fistfuls of the good gritty bread that Qat the baker baked, the girl prompted him to tell another of his stories of glorious deeds. After an apologetic smile at her mother, he began to tell them about the day when Albion's misty curtains had been dissolved. He himself, he told them, had been there, sitting on a hillside with Anya and Reen and Rehan and Joli while, in front of them, Alyss had flown across the canvas of the sky as one of his own paintbrushes might do tomorrow.

The girl doubted much of this, of course: she was old enough to accept the convention that every tale-teller will, without in any way marring the truth, claim to have been present at the more dramatic of the scenes described. Yet she knew, too, that what he was telling them must be very close – almost *exactly* close – to what had really happened, so she said nothing. Her younger sister, more credulous, listened agape; her older sister and her brother displayed the part-patronizing smiles that said that they knew they were listening to something that was more embellishment than truth, yet admired the telling. Curiously, however, her mother was accepting it all matter-of-factly, as if their guest were merely recounting some anecdote of a minor adventure in the streets of Ernestrad – excitingly distant from them, yet a part of tangible things.

Then the Painter's voice grew gloomier. He told them of how he had married an imaginary – surely imaginary – woman of gold, uniting himself with her not only in body but also as a support for the peasants of Albion to lean on whenever they grew weary or fearful of the incursions of the World. The girl and her siblings were too young to remember, but they'd heard their mother talk about those years and knew that they'd been times of great harshness. The children could only vaguely comprehend what it must have been like to face the inhumane might of the torrent of awareness – of *self*-awareness – that had rushed foaming across the previously barren plains of minds, but they knew that the ecstasy it had brought had been mingled also with a bitter pain whose shocks, often enough, had turned people into drooling fools or sharp-clawed creatures of night. Their mother sometimes told them that it had been like having been locked up in an utterly dark room for all of your life and then, abruptly, being thrust out into the most brilliant of all summer days. Even the Ellonia hadn't been immune to the glare. All of a sudden the world was the World: instead of being measured from side to side in days of riding it was now infinite, stretching out in all directions as far as the human ken could compass.

And the World was full of strangers. Some had come to Albion out of interest or to trade, and they had been possible to accept, with however much difficulty. But others had had motives that the people of Albion had been unable to understand: they hadn't been human beings at all, in the way that the Albionians had understood human beings to be. They had been like the worst of the Ellonia of the old days – no, worse, because at least the Ellonians' cruelties had been predictable.

The golden lady and himself, the Painter was now telling them, had apprehended and anticipated much of this, yet even they hadn't been able to appreciate the true magnitude of the effect – not even while it was happening. Encased in Starveling, they hadn't understood much of what was going on among the people of the rest of Albion. They had seen the World as a physical threat; they had prepared to ward off armies. They hadn't observed it furtively creeping in behind them, hiding behind the curtains of their naïveté.

They had done foolish things. Cruel things.

And the Painter had found that his golden lady had a golden heart, not a fleshly one. Finally she had destroyed an old friend of theirs in a way too bestial for him to speak of (the girl saw Halgiad's lips whiten and tighten), and driven the Painter from Starveling to make his own way as best he could, and he'd been glad of the banishment.

He smiled as he talked of what his golden lady had done to him, even though the room was now silent. And when he'd done – when the set of his cheeks told them tonight's stories were over and that there was an end of it – he smiled again, this time with the deep smile she'd seen out by the rock, and turned his lovely, hideously eyeless face towards her.

She saw the beauty in his clawed, burnt scars, and loved him even though her soup was cold.

3

The next day Halgiad's daughter and the pig were not alone with the Painter out by the rock. Maybe a dozen children had joined them – for Halgiad's son was an eager talker – and even a couple of the adults had come along, too . . . just to keep an eye on the children, they said. There was quite a festive atmosphere to the gathering, with girls and boys yipping as they played various running and hiding games, pausing every now and then in their merriment to come and spend a few minutes gaping at the stranger as he worked.

The Painter paid little attention to the hubbub surrounding him beyond nodding his thanks to whichever child next volunteered to fetch fresh mud or water from the stream. His pig, too, was unconcerned, sitting with its eyes on the daubed rockface, often enough with the arm of Halgiad's daughter around it. In the way of small children she had insisted on giving the beast a name and then had dubbed it simply Piggy; but it didn't seem to object, turning its head in response every time she tried out the sound.

All day long the painting grew.

About mid-afternoon the Painter was done with the yellow pigment. At his request, Halgiad's daughter, accompanied by the pig, which seemed eager to stretch its legs, led him to the stream, where he carefully rinsed out his cloth, his mixing bucket and, his fingers teasing through their bristles, his brushes. Once he sensed that the last vestiges of yellow had been banished from his implements he carefully laved his hands, continuing to rub them over and over each other long after Halgiad's daughter's eyes told her that the skin was clean. At last he stroked his flattened palms on the grass to dry them.

Halgiad's daughter was puzzled when they returned to the scar. Perhaps one third of its surface was now coloured, and yet still the decoration had no perceptible purpose. She supposed that an embellished rock was better than an unembellished one, but otherwise she could see little point in his labours. She concluded that this must be, like so many other things, an adult mystery; when she grew older she would be able to understand it.

For a short while the Painter didn't go near his sack of pigments. Instead, thoughtfully, as if his forefinger were a chalk, he began to make invisible lines on the stone. First he drew the roll of a slow hill and then, after a few moments' contemplation, directly beneath it he traced its reflection in still water. For a long time he was lost in meditation, cupping his torn chin in his hand, and then, perhaps half a metre to the right, he repeated the simple pattern.

Halgiad's daughter was becoming ever more bemused. She hugged the pig's warmth as if somehow the beast could transmit an explanation to her through their touching skins. Perhaps it did, because she suddenly realized that of course, to a blind man, lines sketched with a finger were every bit as visible as if drawn with a charcoal. Yet that still didn't explain why he should want to make lentil-shapes . . .

The Painter nodded to her (how did he always seem to know where she was?) and she got to her feet and hurried to him. Her movement attracted the attention of some of the other children, and a little group of them clustered around her as the Painter explained to her what he wanted her to do next.

'All the great artists in Ernestrad have assistants to help them prepare their paints,' he said, smiling, 'and I don't see why I should be any different, just because I choose to work out here in Embrace-of-the-Forest. You saw me mixing the yellow ochre yesterday and again this morning. This time I need some white and – how late is it?'

She told him.

'I thought so. My stomach's been telling me that it's long past midday. Well, just white for today.'

As he listened to her movements, she fetched out the leather bags and prised open the fastening of each of them just enough to be able to peek inside. The fourth bag contained a powder of a brilliant white, like the cold stuff called snow that had briefly decked the hills around Embrace-of-the-Forest a few months ago.

'Now,' he said, 'we don't want to blend in the burn's mud, like we did with the yellow, because that would make the white just look dirty. But we do want to add something from the World to the mixture, because without it the colour would be only a colour – not real. What would you suggest?'

He was smiling again, his face pointed questioningly towards her, as if he were watching for her reactions.

She looked at the pig, but it was watching a couple of the boys wrestling and paid her no attention.

'There's my own spit,' she said at last, hesitantly. 'That's white. It wouldn't muddy the paint.'

He laughed.

'You're a clever child,' he said. 'That's a better and easier reply than I was expecting. I was going to propose that we squeeze the sap from some dandelions, but that'd take us both a lot of effort.'

'And it smells yuk,' said Halgiad's daughter, wrinkling her face.

'Quite right. It'd take us forever to wash the stink away before supper tonight.'

He knelt down beside her and took a little of the powder

into his hand. Once he was satisfied that he had precisely the right quantity he dropped it into the empty mixing bucket.

'Next,' he said, 'I want you to pretend that you've just come across something *really* disgusting! OK?'

Halgiad's daughter thought of her elder brother – no, her elder brother's smelliest poo ever – and screwed up her face.

'Now spit!' commanded the Painter.

She spat once, and then again, and then the third time she managed just a few drops and realized that there wouldn't be a fourth time. Her spittle formed bubbly splashes on and around the powder in the bucket.

'Good,' he said. 'Now there'll be a little of *you* in the picture for as long as it survives.'

Moving easily, he splashed in some water and stirred it up with the powder and her spittle until, as before, the stuff had the consistency of runny mud.

She felt herself dismissed. The children who'd been watching all this dispersed. Halgiad's daughter herself went to sit with the pig, again.

By the time the sun was touching the hills in the distance the Painter had filled with white the two invisible lentil-shapes he'd traced out earlier. Above and to either side of the circles there was the cloud-like tumble of yellow-brown. A natural ridge of the rock ran partway down the centre of the unpainted space, so that Halgiad's daughter began to wonder if the Painter were trying to make the face of the stone look like a human face, in the same way that the Worldly coins that sometimes came to Embrace-of-the-Forest as trinkets had flat shapes on them that looked like people's faces if you caught the light on them aright. It seemed a very strange thing to want to do – to build a face – when if you wanted to look at one all you had to do was to go out into the street and wait for somebody to come by. Besides, people's faces – *real* people's faces – were capable of moving, of shaping themselves into grins or glowers, which was something that dead stone couldn't do. Maybe, when the picture was complete, the rock would indeed be able to move, so that the Painter's creation would be able to laugh and cry like everybody else.

Halgiad's daughter wasn't sure she wanted a gigantic living face planted permanently on the outskirts of *her* village, but adults were wilful creatures and she knew that there wouldn't be any point in registering her protest.

4

The next few days showed her that her guess was at least right in part. The Painter's work had been slow from the start, and it grew even slower as the days passed, for more and more of the adult villagers found excuses to be passing by the rock, and of course they all wanted to stop for a while and ask him what he was doing and how the work was progressing and if he wanted them to take their children away so that he wouldn't be interrupted so often; he got rid of the grown-ups as quickly as he courteously could, but paid no attention to the children's games. Halgiad came sometimes and sat with her daughter and the pig, talking to them a little but never to the Painter except to ask him briefly if he wanted some of the food she'd brought, which inevitably he didn't; despite this minor behavioural blemish, her daughter was proud of her for her good sense.

One day a party of grown-ups came from the next village, Streamdance, to twit the madman they'd heard about, but Halgiad's daughter confronted them a few tens of metres from the rockface and, terrifying in her tiny fury, dismissed them.

By now the picture was definitely recognizable as a human face. The yellow-brown which had at first seemed so meaningless was a cascade of hair, bushing out on either side and puffing up above. The lentil-shapes were where the eyes would be, although the Painter had left them still blankly white; they were rather creepy-seeming, so Halgiad's daughter tried not to look at them very often. Combinations of several pigments from the

Painter's leather bags had been used to daub in the flesh colours of a firm chin, a smooth forehead and cheeks moulded over a well delineated jaw-structure; the lines of the eyebrows were almost black.

'Tomorrow I'll finish,' said the Painter to Halgiad's daughter one evening as the three of them trooped tiredly home together.

'Just the eyes to finish,' she said, skipping over a grassy bump.

'That's right,' the Painter said. 'Just the eyes.'

Halgiad's daughter didn't speak for a minute or two. She knew what she wanted to ask him, but wondered if she ought to. Grown-ups could be so enigmatically secretive about the most extraordinary things – like why people's fathers wouldn't be coming back again, and what the meaning was of the word that Halgiad only ever used when talking about one of the Streamdance women – and the child didn't want the Painter to get angry with her and accuse her of prying into things that were none of her concern. Still, the Painter wasn't really like other adults. He wasn't quite a child, either. In the end she decided that he was good enough to be a sort of honorary child, like Piggy was.

'Whose face is it you're painting?' she said at last. 'Is it the golden lady you sometimes tell us about?'

'No,' he said quietly, not biting her head off as she'd thought he might.

'No,' he repeated, 'she's not the golden lady at all.'

'Then did you just make her up?'

'No, not that either.'

He paused where he was, and Halgiad's daughter could see that he was thinking very hard about how he could explain something to her.

'You could say,' he mumbled after a little while, 'that in a way she's the golden lady's mother. That wouldn't be quite right, but it'd be near enough.'

It was getting cold and Halgiad's daughter was hungry, but now her curiosity was fully aroused.

'Why wouldn't that be quite right?' she persisted.

'Because I never saw her mother. Her mother's dead. She died long before I ever met the golden lady. Or, at least, she's not really dead.'

Halgiad's daughter stared at him annoyedly. His answers were doing nothing but raise further questions. She wasn't in the mood for riddling games.

'She's either dead or not dead,' she said flatly. 'I know. Qat the baker's father died last winter, and once he was dead he stayed dead.'

'Sit down for a moment,' he said, dropping onto the grass.

She joined him, despite the air's coldness. The pig looked up at them briefly, then returned to snuffling among the grasses.

'You're right in a way,' said the Painter, patting her on the knee. 'Long ago, before Alyss cleared the sky, when I was still one of the Ellonia rather than being just an Albionian like everybody else, I used to half-believe that when people's bodies died there was some fragment of them – a soul – that kept on living, somehow. But I wasn't very happy with that idea then, and I don't accept it at all these days. Maybe I'll be proven wrong, but as far as I'm concerned we all have just the time we spend here in the World and, when it's over, that's it. Done. Finished. Only . . .'

'Only what?' she pressed, her forehead wrinkled.

'Well, it's only that some people *seem* to keep on living after they're dead, as if everyone else's memories of them were so strong that somehow those memories could knit themselves together to make a living soul. Try shutting your eyes and find out if you can still see . . . who was it? . . . Qat the baker's father.'

She did so, and discovered that she was looking at the toothless, almost imbecilic face of an ill tempered old billy-goat. It wasn't the face of Qat the baker's father, quite, but it was the way she'd always seen him in her mind's eye.

'So,' said the Painter, sensing something of this, 'in a way you could say that Qat the baker's father is still alive, even though you just said that in reality he's very, very dead. Now think of thousands and thousands of people, all having the same moving picture of Qat the baker's father in their minds.'

She did her best. It was difficult to conceive why anyone might want to think about the old man, but . . .

'Can you see how all those pictures could sort of come together and join up with each other, so that they became almost as real as a real person? Everyone's ideas about Qat the baker's father mixed up to make one great big idea. A strong idea. An idea that comes to have a life, so that it no longer does exactly what people expect it to do, as if it had a will of its own. Like the characters in stories. You must have heard the tales about Alyss and Reen and Barra 'ap Rteniadoli Me'gli'minter Rehan and all the other heroes who burst the chains the Ellonia had tied around Albion. Pick your favourite of them.'

'Um.' A little hard thought. 'Barra 'ap Rteniadoli Me'gli'minter Rehan. The singer. I like him the best.'

'Right. Let's take Rehan. A very good choice, if I might say so, because I liked him a lot, too, for the short time I knew him. It's sad that I don't know any longer if he's dead or living; let's hope he's alive. But everybody knows about Rehan, because they sing his songs – like we sometimes do – and they know about the music that he and Alyss used to create. Well, if you take all the pictures people have in their heads of Rehan and put them together you get somebody who's quite different from the real Rehan. If you could see the imagined Rehan and the living one standing side by side, you'd notice at once that they weren't at all alike. And as soon as they started talking . . .' He waved his hand, as if brushing away an insect.

'Yes,' she said. 'I can picture that.' It was like Qat the baker's father and the billy-goat's face. They didn't look much like each other but in a way they were both the same thing.

'Would you be prepared to say that the imagined Rehan

wasn't just as alive as the other one?'

'Yes. No. It's as if it – he – were living but . . . somewhere else.'

'That's the way I think of it, too,' said the Painter, gazing at her earnestly. ' "Somewhere else." The only trouble is that I haven't the first notion where that "somewhere else" might be.'

'Neither have I,' she said, squeezing his hand reassuringly to let him know that he wasn't alone in his ignorance.

'Never mind,' said the Painter, looking a little baffled. 'Wherever it is, it's as if there were someone – something – living there that has the name Barra 'ap Rteniadoli Me'gli'minter Rehan and does lots of the things that Rehan himself might do – like play on the flute and the bodhran, or make a fool of itself with women – but isn't altogether the same person as Rehan, because it's made up of lots of other people's ideas.'

'And the golden lady's mother's like that?'

'Sort of. Syor – that's her name – died years ago, but the golden lady herself alone believes so strongly that Syor is still alive that the *other* Syor, the golden lady's imagined Syor, really does exist. You couldn't find her however hard you looked, but she's still there, "somewhere else", wherever "somewhere else" is. If you'd ever known her you'd be able to close your eyes and see her, just like you did with Qat the baker's father. Well, you can't do that, of course, and neither can I, because neither of us ever met the real Syor when she was still alive, but if you get close to the golden lady you can begin to be able to see the imagined Syor-being through her eyes. That's how I first saw Syor. Or you can get the same sort of effect by looking at a picture, like the one I'm making, if you look at it hard enough and think about it long enough, until you can see right through the pigments to the realness underneath them.'

'That's why you wanted other things in with the paints? Like spit and mud and wee?'

'That's right. They're *real* things – not abstract, like hues are. They're needed if the picture's going to be able to capture the wholeness of the Syor the golden lady believes in.'

Halgiad's daughter chewed all this over for quite a long while as the two of them sat comfortably together, watching the sky cleanse itself of colour. Zoa was above the horizon and glaring at the wakening light of a bright star that was chasing the long-gone Sun into oblivion.

'Why do you *want* to keep the golden lady's mother alive with your pictures?' she said. 'The golden lady's cruel. You've told us what she's done to you, and Mummy gets a funny crimped-up look on her face every time she mentions her name. They say it was the golden lady who sent the soldiers to garotte some of the men in Streamdance last summer. Surely you should want the golden lady to be dead, and her mother to stay even deader?'

'Oh, yes,' said the Painter, plucking a blade of grass and then throwing it so that it glided away into the gloom, 'my golden lady's cruel, all right, even crueller than people know, but not because she's really evil. She's stubborn and she's ignorant and she's rather stupid, in a way, and most of all she's frightened, and frightened of being frightened. But she's not truly bad. She thinks she's doing all the right things, and that her cruelties are necessary if everyone in Albion's going to have a chance of being happy. And I don't think that, deep down, I really would wish her death. When I was an Ellonian I killed people myself, and I ordered people to be killed – sometimes most painfully.'

Halgiad's daughter looked at him in horror. He was telling another of his make-believes. The Painter was a gentle person, a kind man.

He felt her scepticism.

'I've changed since then. I had too much of killing when I was younger. And maybe Alyss changed me a little, too. Nowadays I find it very hard to wish anyone's death – *anyone's*, even the golden lady's.'

'But her mother's already dead! Couldn't you just leave her be?'

The Painter laughed, a little dourly. 'When the golden

lady was young there was only one person who could curb her,' he said, 'and that was Reen. Or so Reen tells me. Part of the reason why her mother died was to do with that – she saw the cruelty that was latent in her child and recognized that she herself was powerless to tame it. But the imagined Syor – ah, that's another person. The golden lady does what the *other* Syor tells her to do. Except, as you'd expect, at the moment that's exactly the same as what the golden lady herself wants to do, because hers is the only idea that's gone to making up the other Syor.'

'Oh.'

The child was beginning to understand.

'You want to change the other Syor by adding in my ideas and Mummy's ideas and . . . and everybody else's ideas?'

'I've said you were a clever child.'

'Well,' said Halgiad's daughter, 'if I were you I'd keep my brother away from your picture.'

'No,' the Painter said, grinning. 'We want his ideas, too. He's got something good to contribute to the new other Syor we're all creating – everyone has.'

'Hmmmf.'

They sat for a time longer, saying nothing, thinking a lot, until the night's chill began to finger them a little too firmly, as if it wished to insinuate itself right into them. Then they got up and went home to supper.

5

'I'm going to finish the picture tomorrow,' the Painter announced after they'd all finished eating, 'and then I'm afraid I must be on my way.'

Halgiad's head whipped round. Shock and distress were written all over her face. The children looked equally appalled at the prospect of the Painter's departure. And Piggy's.

'You can't do that!' said Halgiad. 'I mean, d'you have to?'

'Yes,' he said, spreading his hands. Mixed in with his

evident unhappiness there was also a trace of pleasure, as if it gratified him that they should be so concerned.

'Even if my picture were still only part-done,' he said to Halgiad, 'I'd have to leave your home tomorrow.'

'The gold isn't important,' she said angrily. 'I've only been taking the stuff to keep you happy. I've got little use for it.'

'That's kind of you, to say that.' A grave nod of the head. 'But my . . . duties lie elsewhere, now that my picture is almost done.'

'The children! Especially this one! You can't just . . . dump them like this! Me too. We've all got accustomed to having you kicking around the place. And your pig. *Even* your pig.'

'I will be sad to leave,' admitted the Painter, 'because I've grown fond of all of you. But I meant what I said about my duties. They override any preferences of my own.'

Halgiad's daughter understood what he meant. He was like a fisherman, spreading his net as widely as possible in order to catch as many people's ideas as he could. Just as a fisherman couldn't turn for home until he'd caught enough to make sure that his family would be fed and housed, so the Painter couldn't stop here – or anywhere else – until he'd built up a strong enough other Syor to safeguard the future well-being of Albion. But understanding his priorities and the necessity for them didn't make them any easier to accept. She felt as if someone were taking tongs to her insides, pulling away the softnesses of her. Her chest felt tight, like it did when she'd been running too fast for too long. Her eyes stung.

'Must . . . ?' she began.

The Painter turned his blindness in her direction, and she stifled the words, looking down immediately to where her hands shuffled together in her lap. She knew, too, why her mother was so upset. There'd been nothing spoken or even hinted, but all of the children had observed that Halgiad had enjoyed having another man to speak to and to share opaque, grown-up jokes with. They knew, too, that she yearned to have someone else in her life to replace their father. Her dream hadn't yet been fleshed out, but it had become substantial enough that it was painful for her to watch it being demolished so firmly.

'Well,' Halgiad was saying, 'if that's the way it is, then that's the way it is. We'll be sorry to see you go, of course, but a woman's got to earn her way in the world, and, if you can't afford to pay for your keep, you can't afford to pay for your keep. If circumstances were otherwise I'd say you could pay for your lodging a little while longer by doing some work around the house, but in your condition . . .'

She let the words hang. Her daughter marvelled for the millionth time at the way her mother could alter her whole perception of affairs so swiftly and so apparently effortlessly. A moment ago her mother had seen the Painter's departure as a disaster inflicted upon her; now it was a natural consequence of her own desire to vacate the spare room for some other traveller whose rent-money might be paid in some more easily exchangeable commodity.

'Please,' the child said, not really aware that she'd decided to start speaking. 'Please, Mummy, please let him stay just an extra night or two.'

Halgiad grunted vexedly and started wiping a soup-stain from the table.

'And please,' the girl added to the Painter, 'please say that you and Piggy can be with us for a little while longer.'

The Painter looked troubled, and said nothing.

'Well,' muttered Halgiad grumpily, still wiping, 'if he's got anything to pay for his board . . .'

'I haven't,' said the Painter drily.

'Not gold,' the woman snapped. 'I don't need your gold.'

'I've nothing else that you might want.'

'Your jacket,' said Halgiad, making it plain that the matter really wasn't of any interest to her.

The Painter began to laugh.

'If you really needed my jacket, poor forlorn thing that

it is, to keep away the cold at night or to protect you from the wind, then you could have it, and with my good will. But I'm not going to give it up just so that you can have a few extra dusters that you don't really want.'

'I didn't mean the jacket itself,' she said impatiently. 'It's not even worth dusters. But there's a button on the cuff that's taken my fancy. Let me have it in exchange for a wooden one I'll give you, and we'll count that as an extra couple of nights' lodging.'

The Painter looked dubious, but after a little further coaxing from Halgiad's daughter he eventually conceded, and went to fetch the garment from the boxroom where he'd been sleeping. Soon the blackened, hemispherical metal button was lying on the table, shorn threads sprouting from its rear, while Halgiad, having waved aside the Painter's offers of help, was sewing on its replacement. And, while she was about it and just because she didn't like to see a job left half-uncompleted, she was sewing a partner to it onto the other cuff.

Halgiad's daughter picked up the Painter's button and looked at it. It was covered with raised, rope-like ridges which were wound together to form a picture. Rubbing the metal with her sleeve and turning it towards one of the sputtering candles so that she could see it better, she made out the simplified, stylized likeness of a wild wolfish dog impaled through its midriff by a sword or a spear. It was a disturbing image.

She put the button back down on the table-top again and looked at the Painter's gentle face, remembering what he'd said earlier about having been an Ellonian and having killed people.

Halgiad's daughter shuddered.

It was a long time before she could sleep that night. In the darkness of the top room, which she shared with her two sisters, she lay awake long after the others were snorting in their sleep, half-expecting to hear Halgiad and the Painter both go to the same room for the night. But, when they finally did go to bed, it was separately.

She was a little sad about that.

6

Next day, she and Piggy were the only ones to accompany the Painter to the rockface. He was tired and unhappy, as if he'd lain awake worrying all night, and so she didn't disturb him more often than was necessary. He seemed almost bitter as he unceremoniously dumped his sack down on the trampled grass in front of the picture of the golden lady's other mother, and his voice was curt as he instructed the child to fetch him two flat stones and a handful of leaves from the trees at the forest's edge.

She scurried to obey, then watched him as he ground the leaves until they were a green smear. She knew the green would be brown by the end of the day, but she said nothing.

Then he asked her to find a dry branch and bring it to him. This took her some while, because most of the dead wood of the forest floor had rotted into moistness. When at last she returned to him she found that he had mixed up the green pigment with the crushed leaves and was already at work on the last stages of his portrait.

On the white lentils of the eyes he had scratched circles with the sharp edge of one of the stones, and now he was brushing on a bold block of solid colour. He wasn't taking any of the painstaking care he'd used earlier, yet his strokes were following the circles' circumferences exactly. Looking at him as he worked, Halgiad's daughter got the impression that it wasn't really him at all who was applying the paint; it was more as if somebody else were operating through the medium of his body. Could it be that the presence of the golden lady's other mother was here with them, not just watching but making her will felt? Halgiad's daughter didn't know where that notion had come from, and it filled her with unease. Quietly she put the dry branch down near the Painter's buckets and retreated to seek solace from the pig.

It wasn't long before the luridly green irises were complete, and the Painter took a couple of paces backwards and let his shoulders slump. He had seemed exhausted earlier; now it was as if all the energy had been squeezed right out of him.

He felt around fumblingly until his fingers found the branch Halgiad's daughter had brought. Ignoring her completely, he squatted down with the bough between his knees and pulled from his trouser pocket a pair of flints. After he'd frayed the fibres at the broken ends of the branch a little, he began striking the two stones together, leaning forward intently as if he were trying to see more clearly whether or not his efforts were being successful. At last a hesitant spiral of smoke rose.

Halgiad's daughter knew better than to interrupt him to ask what he was doing. If he wanted to have a torch to brighten what was already a very bright day, then it was none of her concern. She whispered as much in Piggy's ear, and as far as she could tell Piggy agreed with her.

As soon as the wood was well ablaze the Painter began to beat it against the ground in order to douse the flames. This was even odder than making a torch in the first place, but still Halgiad's daughter said nothing.

When the flames were dead, although there were bright embers glowing among the blackness, the Painter got back to his feet and turned for the last time towards the picture, the branch hanging easily in his hand.

Then his grip tightened, and with a forced, pained cry he sprang forward and plunged the charred end of the wood directly at the centre of one of the green circles. The embers hissed and sang as they encountered the still-wet paint. He screwed the wood around, thrusting it against the unyielding surface with such force that Halgiad's daughter was sure the branch was going to break or that the Painter himself would collapse from his exertions.

Then, so suddenly that she jumped, he took a couple of paces to the right and attacked the other green circle in the same way as the first. His breath was coming in ragged gasps now; all at once she realized that he was sobbing, but had no eyes to shed his tears.

A few moments later he was standing half a dozen

metres away from the rockface. The expression he turned towards it was of such impossibly intense hatred that Halgiad's daughter cowered away from him in terror.

He snarled a curse that meant nothing to her. Turning, he raised the wood high behind his shoulder and flung it from him as hard as he could, so that it went whooping away end-over-end above the grass until it fell to perform a few crazed dance-steps along the ground before lying still.

Halgiad's daughter looked at him silently.

For a full minute he said nothing.

Then: 'The painting's finished,' he mumbled, collapsing to the grass.

The black pupils at the centres of the other Syor's green eyes were like holes ripped out by a clawed instrument.

7

One morning, perhaps two days later, when Halgiad and her family awoke they found that the Painter was gone. There was nothing left in the house at all to show that he had ever been there. The pig's foul-smelling straw in the yard outside had been removed, and the bed in the boxroom had been stripped and its blankets neatly folded and put on top of the cupboard. Dreading the worst, Halgiad's daughter ran through the village and out to the outcrop where she had spent so much of the past fortnight or so, but the picture of the golden lady's other mother was exactly as they'd left it. The face was gazing out across the fields with a placidity born of its infinite vision. Halgiad's daughter, as she looked at it in her relief, felt that it was the face of someone whom she knew and loved – not someone as close to her heart as the Painter had been and as her mother and her sisters and (if she dredged her conscience) her brother still were, but nevertheless someone integral to her own existence.

She went back again about a week later, after a night when a thunderstorm had drenched the World, and in the sparklingly clean morning light she found that the rain had washed away all the colours from the rock, but that the picture was still there.

Chapter Four
Seven Realms

1

His parents had impressed it upon Alven that he should never, *ever* stare directly at the Sun and so, during the long hours when he was alone in the hills with nothing but the bleats of the sheep to keep him company, he made a frequent practice of doing so.

Today the dome of the sky was an artificially bright blue, as if someone had painted it with thick, glossy colour. Near to the zenith was a flock of heavy-looking white clouds. Closer to the horizon was a gibbous Struan, a bowl of mother-of-pearl shaved to a translucent thinness, paradoxically visible despite the brilliance of the day. Alven imagined to himself that it was the gleaming blade of an exotic conqueror, hung by the gods in the skies of the World to token their respect for him and to warn the territories that he was still to conquer. Or perhaps the sign was meant for his, Alven's, eyes alone? The singers told of stranger happenings than that a shepherd might rise above the incessant growls of his stomach to lord it over the lands as far as the horizons and beyond.

He hugged the thought to himself. It smelt better to him than the reluctant odour of the crushed grasses around where he sat.

He stared at the Sun's disc and saw in its engulfing brightness the glory of the magnificence that would one day be his. Its brazen yellowness sounded in his ears like a fanfare.

A sheep wailed in parody, and he glanced away from his dreams. For a moment he could see nothing at all through the broth of colours that filled his eyes; then he made out that the call of distress had been part of an ovine argument that was already over, lost from the animals' memories. Alven wished he could find it within himself to feel fondness for his flock.

He laid himself back on the grass and gazed up at the sky, trying but failing to recapture his glorious train of thought. There was a coin of many colours on the surface of the gravid clouds above him – the afterimage of the Sun, of course. It seemed to be moving slowly from left to right as his eyes wandered idly, and he grinned to himself at the thought that it might be a god or a goddess traversing the ceil of the heavens, shrouded in an incandescence of power, plying whatever inscrutable business the gods and goddesses plied. Could this be yet another emblem of the future greatness of Alven the Beneficent, known for his fearless courage and ferocity in battle yet blessed by his grateful people – and even by his myriad vanquished foes – for his goodness and mercy and generosity and . . .

Modestly he shifted his eyes, expecting the corona of the deity to follow the changed direction of his gaze.

It didn't. The afterimage had somehow coalesced into reality, adopting an existence of its own independent of his sight. It continued to move in its own direction.

Alven scowled. He'd grown so accustomed over the years to his feigned encounters with the gods that it annoyed him to think that, just for once, his vision might be real. Frightened him, too. The squabbling gods had vast powers – they could carve the earth and incinerate the skies – and their motives were impenetrable to the human understanding; their villainies, which were perhaps virtues in some ethical spectrum incomprehensible to mere mortals, were countless and unpredictable. It was safe to shudder at the histories of their callousnesses when wrapped in the cocoon of the goatskin temple his parents occasionally took him to – where an old woman of parchment with a long white beard and polished-pebble eyes would berate you for your transgressions and a handful of coinage – but it was a different matter altogether to contemplate seeing physical evidence of the gods' activities. Or – and Alven shivered – even meeting one.

It required an effort of will to concentrate on the disc of light again, but he did so. Surely, this far away, the deity would leave him unmolested? He was only a shepherd, after all; a lowly person, a humble one, beneath the contempt of one so mighty. Surely he could just *watch* . . .

The glow was moving very sluggishly against the backdrop of dirty unskeined wool, and yet there was purpose in its motion. Instinctively Alven looked ahead of it, to see where it was going. There seemed to be nothing there except a further empty tract of soiled whiteness, and then he saw that one of the specks of the clouds' grime was darker than the rest, and that it too was moving of its own volition – yet purposelessly and sporadically, like one of the fine particles of smoke above a campfire. The aura of the god seemed to be chasing after this mote, as if somehow the tiny darkness must be absorbed into the brightness, thereby incongruously to contribute to its splendour.

There was someone standing beside him, he suddenly realized. He hadn't heard the person approaching, so obviously it must be some kind of avatar, some projection into corporeal form of the god who was sporting overhead. Alven, terrified, looked up at an infinitely long expanse of much-patched grey cloth to a belted waist, a crumpled jerkin and a pair of dark eyes that were staring back down at him. In the periphery of his vision he could see a weatherbeaten face framed by silver hair that had been wrought by the smith into a luxuriant tangle. The adopted image of transcendence smiled sourly at him, causing herds of grime-filled wrinkles to appear at the corners of its mouth, only to disappear as the false smile faded.

'Have mercy,' said Alven, without thinking.

'I'm not going to harm you,' said the avatar, looking startled.

'Spare my soul,' he gabbled. 'My transgressions have all been accidental, all of them. You must know that.'

'Consider it spared,' said the almighty, impatiently.

'Some of the sheep are pretty sinful . . .'

'I'm not after your sheep.' Now the herds of lines had flitted to the space between and above the image's eyebrows, lengthening its nose. 'I'm looking for someone I was told might be found around here.'

'It's not me, not me. I'm . . . someone quite different. You must mean . . .'

'What are you blithering about, boy?' said the taut, omnipotent lips. 'Sit up, why can't you, and speak to me like a normal human being – don't just lie there writhing like something the dog's thrown up.'

'As you command,' said Alven unwillingly, forcing his hands and arms to push him up. His mind was confused. Somehow he'd never conceived that the emissaries of the gods would speak this way. And he resented being compared to something the dog had thrown up.

'I don't "command" anything,' said the avatar, now beginning to look weary of him. This was unsurprising, since the patience of the gods was notoriously short. Now that Alven could look at it more normally he could see that the deity had adopted the form of a perilously ancient woman – older than his mother even – yet by no means a frail one. She, if it was sensible to think of her as a she, was clearly stained from long travel, and there were elements of both fatigue and age in the angles of her stance, yet there was a certain undefinable essence of resolution in the way she was looking at him. The sword and dagger at her belt were obviously not mere decorations. The expression on her face was neither friendly nor hostile; he decided swiftly that he had no wish ever to see her angry.

'That's a bit better,' she was saying. 'Now, do you think we could start this conversation all over again?'

He bowed his head.

'I was told I'd be able to find a shepherd called Alven around here,' she said.

'I'm not . . .' He quailed. 'That is, I'm Alven.'

'Good. I thought as much. Presumably you've been expecting me.'

'No.'

'You mean she didn't tell you? Oh.'

The avatar thought deeply for a few moments, and Alven began to wonder if possibly she was just another human being like himself.

'Who should have told me something?' he said at last.

'Alyss, of course.'

'I don't know anyone called Alyss.' Apart from his mother, the only women he ever met were those who came to the market in Naraleen on the days of Struan's fullness.

'You ought to surprise me,' said the woman, hunkering down onto her ankles so that her dark eyes were on a level with his own, 'but you don't. That girl's so damn' flighty and inconsiderate. It's as much as a woman can do to refrain from clipping her around the ear, get some sense into her head.'

'Who're you talking about? Who's this person who's forgotten to tell me something?'

'Oh – she won't have forgotten. She's as near omniscient as makes no difference; she can probably remember all of your thoughts and mine, so she shouldn't have any difficulty remembering her own. No, she'll just have found something more entertaining she could be doing instead of visiting you to warn you I was going to be here today. That's what I said: inconsiderate. It never crossed her mind that I might be hungry when I got here, so that it'd be a good idea if you were told to bring extra food with you . . .'

'You can have . . .'

A talon-fingered hand flipped away his words before they'd been properly spoken.

'Damn her and damn her and damn her,' the woman was muttering intensely, digging into the earth between her thighs with her dagger. 'Never had any parents to keep her in line when she was young, and she's spoilt herself rotten all her life. And,' she added, turning to stare directly into Alven's eyes, 'she's had a lot of life to spoil herself rotten in.'

Alven was perplexed. 'You're not making yourself very

clear,' he said nervously, half-raising an arm in preparation for a blow.

A leather-hard hand caressed his cheek roughly.

'No, I'm not,' said the woman's voice. Reassured, he opened his eyes again. She was smiling at him, her head a little on one side. There was still anger in the lines of her face, but he could see that it wasn't directed at him.

'You're a human being,' he said abruptly.

The woman laughed.

'Yes,' she said. 'I'll admit to that.'

'I thought you were an incarnation of a god,' said Alven, feeling increasingly stupid as he spoke. He looked away from her, cheeks warm.

'How kind,' she said. Her hand touched his to take the edge off the sarcasm. 'No, I'm not that – except insofar as we're all of us incarnations of the gods.'

'I saw a light, you see,' he began, pointing vaguely upwards in the general direction of the clouds, 'and I thought . . .' Embarrassed, he ran out of words.

'Ah.'

He glanced at her. She wasn't looking at him any longer. Instead she was staring intently towards the sky, her eyes slits.

'You weren't as far wrong as you think,' she said casually. 'In fact – yes, there she is.'

'Then you *are* a . . .' he started, but she wasn't listening to him.

'Bloody Alyss,' Reen was murmuring. 'Always has to make a bloody *entrance*, doesn't she?'

2

Alyss adjusted the temperature of the air blowing in her face until it was refreshingly cool rather than numbingly chilly and, without breaking her flight, dragged her fingers through a tendril of cloud to pull away a wisp of nothingness that became a linnet in her palm. The bird's bewilderment at its sudden rush into existence vanished instantly; it flew away from her, spiralling off downwards on confident wings. For a few moments she watched it go, her lips pulled back in a smile from her sharp teeth, and then she tumbled her body in an aerial somersault that was beneath her dignity but nevertheless essential to the moment.

At a time like this she could quite literally have seen forever had she wanted to, but instead she preferred to limit herself to the World, bathing in its freshness to her, for she had permitted herself the experiences of many lifetimes since last she had been in this chamber of existence's mansion. She had been . . . elsewhere – to many elsewheres – so that her glimpses of the World had been restricted to the visions she had conjured from the minds of those who in their dreams – her own dreams? – had willy-nilly followed her from the World into one of the countless othernesses.

She spared another glance downward and saw that Reen and the boy, Alven, had encountered each other, as instructed. A part of her mind felt touches of the boy's perplexity and the woman's resentment, and she giggled maliciously. It wasn't her fault that the path of Alven's silent-mind had never crossed hers among the othernesses, so that she could have spoken to it the way that she had spoken to Reen's. Besides, the boy was just a landmark, really – the physical aspect of a location in space and time where she wanted Reen to be.

A kestrel squawked vexedly at her. As startled as it was, she froze it with an imperious glare. It plummeted.

It was because of unexpected occurrences like that, that she was here. She wasn't accustomed to the unexpected, yet recently it had been interfering with her existence – not just once, but many times.

Ahead of her, growing larger as she caught up with it, there was a thin black figure lurching through the sky with all the erratic uncertainty of a daddy-longlegs. At every moment it seemed just about to give up its struggle with the air and fall towards the ground, but then to catch itself and somehow manage to make just sufficient effort to keep itself aloft until the next moment. She knew that within the next few minutes, were she not to intervene as planned, it would lose the battle against gravity for good. Not that that would happen.

She hoped.

Now Alyss was frowning. There was an impediment along that particular future road as well, and it was a road about whose destination she cared.

She flew a little faster, her lips moving silently to the words of a song more forgotten than learnt.

3

'Well met,' said a voice out of the fog that surrounded the surviving kernel of Rehan's consciousness.

'Well met,' he muttered in response. He was a beggar dragging his weariness through the night-time streets of Ernestrad towards the ditch where he sometimes slept. The grip of the freezing mist around him hurt less than the twisting knife that was mincing the inside of his empty belly; his mouth was a shapeless mass of raw pain. He shuffled onwards, not looking up to see who had addressed him. It could as likely be a killer as a kindheart, and he had no wish for the knife within him to be matched by a real knife of iron from without. He imagined himself into invisibility.

'Rehan,' said the voice. He recognized it, but had neither the ability nor the desire to identify it.

'Barra 'ap Rteniadoli Me'gli'minter Rehan,' it expanded. 'Listen to me.'

The syllables laboriously unscrambled themselves and he dimly perceived that they were forming his name. So what. That the disembodied voice knew him by name meant nothing. Killers. Kindhearts. Lots of people knew his name. He wished whoever it was would go away and leave him alone with his agony. He wished the person would touch him on the shoulder and lead him off to a warm room where the fire crackled and there was steaming food on the table. He almost wished just that the stranger could be one of the city's untold street assassins because death, too, would be a way of alleviating his misery. His only relief was that the night cold had long since driven all sensation from his naked feet. Maybe his feet had left him completely, rejected the hardships to which he'd subjected them, eloped from him to join themselves onto a pair of legs that would treat them more considerately. It was possible, all perfectly possible. It was too dark and foggy for him to be able to see the packed clay of the street beneath him in order to check whether or not his feet were still there. He wouldn't blame them if they'd decamped, of course; he wasn't the sort of man who held a grudge like that.

It had been a long time since he'd seen a light through the mist, but there seemed to be one now.

'Barra 'ap Rteniadoli Me'gli'minter Rehan. Kindly do me the courtesy of paying attention when I speak.'

The voice was waspish. A woman's voice, he realized. The muffling mist was unable to ameliorate its sharpness.

Yet again he recognized it. Yet again he knew nothing more than that he recognized it. He tried to pull his sacking garments more tightly about himself, but they were suddenly as insubstantial as gossamer. Grey like the mist, their strands floated away to become lost in it. The flesh of his body exposed by their departure would be the same grey, he knew; even through all the other pains he could feel it unravelling into its constituent threads and pulling away from him.

And then, in turn, his soul would be exposed in nudity. His modesty forbade him to permit even a stranger to gaze upon this greatest nakedness, even though the fog would partly garb him. He, who had thought he had long ago bartered away all his shame, now found that there was such a potency of it left inside him.

He might have smiled had he had any smiles left.

Instead he allowed his rediscovered modesty to fuel his will, to spur his gaze as the mist partly cleared and the light in front of him brightened.

He could see fractions of a face in that light. There was a small mouth with narrow yet pronounced lips, parted slightly. Eyebrows were etched in precise curves. Cheekbones pressed flesh outward. A tatter of cropped hair above a snowfield of forehead. A nose.

The first dripless nose he had seen in a billion centuries of cold nightmare.

'Alyss!' he said. The mist drank the name.

'Who else?'

He fell to what he imagined were his knees.

'Give me warmth,' he begged.

'Stop being so foolish. There's warmth all around you, if only you'd let yourself see it.'

The fog fled. He was in a crucible of sunlight. Its golden caresses should have warmed him, but his body was still ice.

'Help me,' he said, his voice little more than a sigh.

'What's the magic word?'

'Damn you!' he shouted. A torrent of his self foamed into him. Immediately he realized that he'd been totally wrong about his situation. He was no beggar, and he was not in the streets of Ernestrad, and the world was awash with heat. Strong and proud in his strength, clad only in a gladiatorial loincloth, a massive mace a feather in his grip, he looked arrogantly around him at the wondering throngs encircling the arena where he stood, a woman cowering in front of him. Other men's blood was as hot as fire against his skin.

'Alyss!' he bellowed.

The mob echoed him in a protracted lowing.

'Alyss!'

Five thousand thousand drunken throats raping her with their noise.

'Kneel before me, woman! Acknowledge me!' he yelled, feeling that his voice was great enough to crack the walls of the heavens.

'I think I preferred you as a beggar,' said a cool, thoughtful voice in his ear.

Again the illusion was shattered, to be replaced by a third.

He was flying just beneath the clouds, his last reserves

of strength nearly drained from him. Many kilometres below, hazed by the distance, he could see the tiny haphazard features of the ground. He forced his spirit to keep him aloft for just one further second.

'Rehan,' said the voice. 'I'm grateful that at last you've decided to join me.'

He looked to one side and there, sitting with her knees crossed as if the emptiness beneath her were a comfortable old armchair, was Alyss. She was scratching her chin as she watched him, and her mouth formed a sudden smile as she saw that he had seen her.

Is this the real reality, at last? he thought resignedly in her direction.

Oh yes, came her voice, speaking to him now from just inside his skin. *Welcome back to the World.*

I could say the same to you, I guess.

The thought used up the last drops of him.

Some seconds passed before he noticed that the patterns on the ground were getting larger.

4

Reen looked into Rehan's eyes and saw a blackness in them that stretched away forever. Yet it wasn't the blackness of empty space; rather it was as if an artist had mixed every conceivable colour onto the palette to create the jet of a raven's wing. Rehan's eyes were telling her that they had seen too many things, flared to too many colours, narrowed too often to the lungeing lances of brightness that wove themselves together to form the succeeding events of the World. She looked for the song that had always been in his gaze and couldn't find it.

That his eyes were open at all was a miracle. A couple of hours ago she'd thought he was dead. A kestrel the size of a horse had come looping down out of the sky carrying in its talons what looked more like a sack of branches than a human body and had settled its burden down none too gently in front of Reen and Alven. Then it had shrugged its wings and *changed*; the effect had been less one of metamorphosis than as if the two of them had been, up until then, looking at the bird from the wrong angle and so had been misperceiving its true form. Alyss was standing before them – had already been standing before them – with a normal-sized kestrel perched disconcertingly on her thin shoulder. After looking at them with a couple of incredulous jerks of its head, the bird had launched itself away to become lost in the azure of the sky.

'Rehan,' Alyss had explained, gesturing towards the motionless bundle.

Moments later the singer had begun to twitch. The ghastly pallor of his parchment face had been relieved by a blue-pink brush of life, and there had been a tiny, tentative motion in the small veins across his upper eyelids. His lips had sucked into his gap-toothed mouth and made a small, painful hiss, and his fingers had begun to stretch and flex, as if trying to grab the air. Reen, throwing a quick look up from where she'd found herself kneeling beside him, had seen the intensity of Alyss's concentration on the singer's crumpled body, and had realized that the small woman was forcing the life back into him. Reen had picked up one of his straining hands and rubbed it between her own, had tried to give him some of her own life.

And soon enough he'd been sitting up and talking to them in a curious, jerky, nervous way that he hadn't had before – back at the dawn of history when he'd been Reen's sometimes lover and, more important, always friend. By then Alven had managed to light the fire that she'd curtly ordered him to build, and Rehan was weakly struggling towards it, desperate for its heat despite the warmth of the day.

And now Reen herself was glad of the fire's warmth. Alyss had sent the boy home as soon as dusk had begun to fall, and the three of them had gathered close to watch the flames and to toast their palms and feet. In the night around them the sheep made occasional shuffling noises or low cries of protest, and Reen's horse, tethered nearby, whinnied once, but otherwise there was stillness except for Rehan's urgent, convulsive words. He was expelling speech from his mouth as if, in so doing, he could simultaneously expel from his body the memories that he was describing.

Poor, fragmented memories they were, too. His recollection was as staccato as his voice. Amid the incoherence only a single theme kept recurring: that of the master who had trained him in some undescribed way and then sent him into the pits of the Anonymous City. When he was talking he never once looked up at their faces; he watched only the movements of the flames and the climbing, dying sparks.

Unnoticed by Reen, Alyss was louring like a child whose parents have just realized that it's past bedtime. She didn't need to listen to much of what Rehan was saying, because she'd already read it from the surface of his mind. The trouble was that she found herself unable to delve beneath that surface. It was as frustrating as her encounters with the obstacles in the future-roads. At first all she had wanted to do was to clarify the nature of the enigmatic figure that Rehan described as his master, but then the puzzle of the barrier's very existence had become far more important to her than any specific enigma it might shield. Although she told herself that there was a simple explanation for what was thwarting her – that the bradz had solidified his thinking processes so that much of his mind had become like fire-hardened clay – she knew that this was only a tiny portion of the whole truth. Clay she could have bored into or shattered open: she could have penetrated to his greatest depths without much effort, even if only to find out that there was nothing there. No, it wasn't at all as if someone had put a rocky shell around what might be left of his inner mind. It was instead as if that area of his existence had been marked off as taboo, forbidden to her with absolute finality, so that as far as she was concerned the territory did not exist.

But who could have done the forbidding? Only rarely in her timelong voyagings through the othernesses had Alyss encountered any being with power on the same scale as her own. Even the countless gods who existed throughout the polycosmos were each confined exclusively to their own otherness; their power was sometimes greater than Alyss's, but it was easily enough escaped.

This was different.

The artefact that Rehan's mind had become wasn't trying to fight her off or counter her will in any way; had that been the case she could comfortably have settled down to match her strength against it, secure in the knowledge that she must surely, in the end, prevail. Instead – like the obstacles that barred her way to the future – this barrier simply *was*.

It shouldn't have been there.

It had been put there.

It had been put there by a being who should never have existed, not in this nor in any of the othernesses.

It shouldn't have been put there.

She stared through the heavy cast of the night clouds and saw the distant stars shining coldly and clearly: if she hadn't known them for what they were she might have asked them for their advice; their help, even. And beyond the stars all she saw was endless, mindless vacuum. She tried to probe the infinite expanse in search of some responsive flicker from whatever it was that had entered Rehan's mind and settled itself there; but, as she'd known, there was nothing.

Rehan was still talking. Reen was still listening. Alyss gazed at them for a few moments. She experienced a wash of an emotion that in a mortal mind would have been called fondness. She had done right to bring them together as lovers in Albion, back in the time when the Ellonia had still kept that land under their iron heel. She had needed the two of them whole if they were to fulfil her wishes, and both of them had been broken strings, twanging discordantly on the clarsach of their existences. Rehan, more sensitive than most men because he was a singer, yet still so untutored in his knowledge of affection. And Reen, the adult to his child, the rock of strength whenever those around her were frail, the stalwart stoic who showed no tears as her lovers died – she too had been incomplete, unable to recognize the worth of the childishness that dwelled inside her, and the different kind of strength that it could give her in the times after Syor killed herself, when Anya was becoming . . . Anya.

Again, reflexively, Alyss sent her mind towards Rehan. She visualized it as a money-spider, reeling itself down from nowhere to catch hold of the upper curl of his ear, then cautiously lowering itself still further until it could creep into the dark tunnel that led to his brain.

Nothing. The money-spider, rebuffed, paused for a foiled moment and then slowly faded from her consciousness.

Struan, now sinking towards the western horizon, reddened as it bore the impact of Alyss's frustrated thought. That night, for as long as it took to vanish from view, the dead moon smouldered.

Finally Rehan's monologue lurched to a halt. Alyss, smiling with all the sweetness at her command, plucked a burning log from the fire to light her way into the darkness – it was unnecessary, of course, but she felt it proper to observe the customs of the country so long as doing so didn't inconvenience her – and, with a few muttered pleasantries, went off to find a place where she could be on her own.

Reen watched her go. Rehan kept on staring at the waning firelight for a short while longer and then slowly turned his head so that his overloaded eyes were on Reen's face. His lips worked, as if he were trying to say something more in that thick, tongue-tangled voice. Reen was suddenly acutely aware of the fact that so many of his teeth had been lost or broken during the past months. For a moment the lack seemed more pitiful to her than the fragile thinness of his body and the bent boughs of his shoulders. Perhaps he'd have seemed a wholer man to her if he'd been carrying his flute or his bodhran, but of course both of them had been lost somewhere along the way. Somehow, incongruously, he'd retained his hat; it had a long feather in its band, but the feather was bedraggled and broken in many places, so that it dangled like a chain. His body would have seemed more recognizably *him* to her had the essence of him still been in his eyes, but of course there was only the blackness.

She left him for a few moments while she went to check her horse and to pee. When she returned, a couple of coarse blankets in her arms, he was still sitting immobile, eyes fixedly staring at the place where her face had been as if he were watching for some change in her expression.

'Here,' she said roughly, tossing a blanket down on the ground behind him. 'You're well enough to be able to make yourself comfortable, are you not? It's late.'

Like a marionette he turned and grappled with the bedding. She left him and walked a few metres away from the fire, not trusting herself to bid him goodnight. She supposed that she ought to take him in her arms and nurse him through the remaining hours of darkness with soft words and mumbled endearments, but she'd never felt less maternal in her life.

Zoa, the lesser moon, watched her dispassionately as she lay wrapped in her blanket, her eyes firmly closed, her mind obdurately wakeful.

When finally sleep did come to Reen it was leaden, and lumpish, and short.

5

The dawn brought Alven, face broad with curiosity. He'd decided that Reen was the most approachable of the three strangers – and hadn't he met her the first of them? – so she woke to find herself staring at his breechcloth. She raised her heavy eyes to look at him, then immediately shushed him as his mouth began to move.

'Quiet with you,' she croaked, and then, as his face crumpled: 'We old bags need a little while in the mornings before we're at our best.'

She was aware of his eyes on her as she groped her way out of the blanket's tenacious folds, pushed clumsy feet into wool-lined suede boots, scratched her armpits and sucked in cold morning air through the spaces between her teeth. 'If I catch you watching me at any time during the next ten minutes or so,' she said after a while, 'I'll put your eyes on my necklace as a souvenir. Make us a fire and get some water boiling.'

Some time later she and the boy were sitting side by side, each sipping in turn from her battered tin mug. Rehan still lay asleep, sprawled like a dead chick beneath a nest, his chest unmoving although he was sounding thin snores. Alyss hadn't yet made an appearance; Reen allowed Alven to continue believing that 'the scrawny bint', as he called her, was still unconscious somewhere out of sight.

'Why did you come here?' he said. 'How did you know my name, and where I'd be? I wanted to ask you yesterday, but you were busy with the others.'

'Talking too much, the way adults always do,' said Reen, nodding her head gravely.

He matched her nod automatically, then shook his head rapidly, then half-nodded, then grinned weakly.

'As for where I've come from,' said Reen, 'that's a question with many answers. Originally I was from Albion – you've heard of Albion?'

He looked at her glumly: no.

She explained about the island nation and what had happened there. 'So a while ago I decided to see if this World of yours was really all you Worldlings cracked it up to be. I came through these parts – I can't have passed more than twenty or thirty kilometres from this very spot – but I didn't stop. Things around here aren't all that much different from Albion, and I was in quest of the exotic.' She smiled painfully at him. 'I'd got a lot of things I wanted to wash out of my mind, you see. So I didn't tarry long around here, but headed for the east, where people'd told me I might find, you know, marvels.'

Again the smile that twisted his heart.

'Did you find them?' he said.

'Oh, yes. Oh . . . yes.' She looked at the faded colours of Rehan's blanket; the singer was still motionless. She wasn't going to tell the boy the half of it, and especially not the parts she wasn't so proud of. And nor would she tell him about Qinefer, the black woman she'd met, with the eyes that seemed to see the World differently from the rest of humanity; she'd loved Qinefer, she thought, more closely than perhaps she'd ever loved anyone else, even the bundle of rags in front of her now. But then Alyss had seized her arm one night as she'd been walking down a dream-street and told her that it was important that she give up everything of her new life – even Qinefer – and come west again . . .

'I worked as a herder of alliberis for a while,' she admitted, smiling with practised grumpiness. 'So you could say we're fellow professionals.'

'A herder of . . . what?'

'Alliberis. If you've never met an alliberi you don't know how lucky you are to be missing one of life's great enrichments. The same sort of size and shape as donkeys, only never tell a donkey that if you want to keep its friendship . . .'

Alven's eyes grew wide as she told of distant hardships.

'And so,' she said at last, 'every time things get really so bad I want to die, I say to myself, "Well, at least you're not an alliberi herder any longer, so things could be worse," and that cheers me up.' Abruptly she was smiling at him again. 'You ought to try it yourself. Whenever you get bored watching this lot' – she waved an arm to embrace his flock around them – 'just remind yourself that they could all be alliberis.'

'I will,' he said. 'I will.'

'Will what?' said Alyss's voice behind them.

Reen told her, grinning.

Alyss turned to look sternly at Alven. 'I should inform you, young man,' she said, 'that I'm not particularly enamoured of the word "bint". You're lucky that I have a forgiving disposition.'

'I'll fetch some wood for the fire,' Alven muttered, going.

Reen, too, got to her feet. 'The boy didn't mean any harm,' she said.

'That's what they all say,' snapped Alyss. 'Still, let's forget about it for the while.'

Reen looked down at Rehan.

'He looks like he's dead,' she said. 'Is he all right?'

Alyss concentrated on his still form for a split second. 'Yes,' she said. 'He's just catching up on a year's missing sleep. If undisturbed, he'll awaken in a little over eight hours and seventeen minutes from now, and feel like a new man; he'll be very hungry, though, so it might be as well for us to have some food ready. Something simple. Lightly toasted bannocks smothered in warm acacia honey and lashings of fresh butter might be just the thing.'

Reen put her hands on her hips. 'Where in all the World do you . . . ?'

Alyss smiled at her, raising one hand. 'Find some grass and catch me a bee, and get the boy to milk one of his sheep,' she said. 'I'll do the rest. Before that, though, I want to do something with Rehan while he's still asleep.'

Reen looked at her with a raised eyebrow. Was Alyss proposing to perform some kind of operation on him, or something?

'You could say that,' said Alyss lightly, 'but the surgery I want to try to do doesn't need knives. Our whimsical friend may have the answer to a puzzle locked away in his mind, and I want to try to find out if he has or not. The trouble is, I can't get into his mind while he's awake – there's something stopping me doing that. But I think that if I have a shot at it while he's asleep I might be able to inveigle my way past his defences – well, past *its* defences, whatever *it* is.'

Reen was looking baffled. Alyss, deliberately misunderstanding the reason, added: 'Oh, I really can be surprisingly persuasive when I choose to be, you know.'

'He won't suffer?' Reen said harshly. 'There's no risk that you'll be doing him any damage, is there?'

Alyss looked at her sharply. 'I won't kill him intentionally unless there's no other choice,' she said flatly.

'Thanks,' said Reen, staring at her with level eyes. 'Thanks. I thought that was the case.'

Alyss saw Reen's body shift its posture as the woman

accepted Rehan's death. It was more than likely that the singer would live, even that Alyss's ministrations might restore the old Barra 'ap Rteniadoli Me'gli'minter Rehan rather than the jerky puppet who'd been with them last night. But he might die. And the bradz had robbed him of so much of himself that, this time, even she might not be able to engineer his return to the World from whatever otherness he was in.

'What're you going to do, exactly?' Reen said, her voice betraying no emotion beyond casual interest.

'I'm not sure,' said Alyss, turning away with rapid grace and folding herself up until she was sitting cross-legged on the crushed grass by Rehan's grey-skinned face. She touched the fingertips of one hand to his forehead, as if in a brief, informal benediction.

Alven reappeared, arms full of brush and branches. Reen beckoned him to come and stand beside her; she helped him chuck the fuel onto the fire, then laid an arm around his shoulders as the thinner twigs began to crackle.

Alyss waited patiently for the sound to die down a little, then looked up at them, her face betraying an unaccustomed uncertainty. 'I really won't be very long,' she said quietly. 'Not so far as you'll notice, anyway.'

Her fingers moving more swiftly and precisely than mortal fingers could, she pulled back the blanket from Rehan's immobile torso and then stripped away the upper part of his ripped shirt, so that she could run her eager little palms across his narrow chest. Abruptly she froze, as if she'd found the exact spot she'd been searching for; her mouth formed a little 'o', and her eyes closed in seeming relaxation.

'Nice fire,' remarked Reen. 'Want me to tell you a bit more about alliberis while we're waiting?'

6

Alyss felt herself stepping through an invisible doorway.

There was a road made of crystals that stretched out from beneath her to flow away in gentle meanders among breast-curved hills. Above her the sky was completely black, and yet all the countryside around her was brightly lit, as if the midday Sun were high above her. Birds sang and butterflies danced. She looked down at herself and saw that she was clad in her favourite costume: a tunic of silver velvet above breeches of the same material, torn off just below the knees. Her feet were bare and she wriggled her toes a couple of times to admire the way that they creased and flexed. She put up a hand to feel her face and head, and found that everything was much as normal except that her lips were perhaps a trifle fuller than she'd have ideally liked. She started to change them but found that she suddenly lost interest in doing so.

That stopped her mind in its tracks. She tried again but much more determinedly to alter the cast of her lips, but once more her determination seemed to evaporate before she'd got properly started. Then she attempted to change the colours of some of the multifaceted crystals underfoot, but again there was that strange loss of concentration.

She put her head to one side, thinking this through. Once before, in a quite different otherness, she'd found herself in an environment where the sky had been shinily ink-black, as it was here, and in that place, too, she'd found herself deprived of the aptitude to exercise her very considerable powers of tailoring reality to her will. She hadn't enjoyed the experience one whit. The whole venture had had about it a nauseating nuance of mortality, and she'd resolved never to let that happen again. Now it looked as though it had.

She took a pace and was reminded of her predicament by the sharp crystals digging painfully into the soles of her feet. She winced and swore an oath that had been old before humanity's amphibian ancestors had struggled up from the swamps. The surrounding hills didn't even look like flinching from her wrath, and that convinced her more than anything that here, truly, she had been stripped naked of her ability to mould reality.

Steeling herself against the pain, she took another

tentative stride, and then another.

Distance, she discovered, disobeyed all the natural laws here. She'd taken no more than half a dozen steps when she found herself rounding the curve of a hill and saw on the horizon ahead of her a grotesque castle projecting upwards in jagged confusion like a carious tooth, gleaming yellow-grey against the blackness of the sky beyond. She looked at it in dismay. It seemed so remote from her, yet it was obvious that the road she was on led there. Oddly, it never occurred to her to attempt to leave the road, to see if the glassy-looking grasses of the verges would be kinder to her feet than the gems.

She shrugged. In this place she'd come to, it didn't matter if the castle were a day's walk away or just a few paces; it would still seem like an eternity of agony. Her feet were already covered in blood from the cuts they'd suffered; her blood was red, she noted, like the blood of the mortals in the World. She wondered if, assuming she spent sufficient subjective time here, she might discover what it was like to menstruate. Satisfying her long-standing but minor curiosity about that particular sensation would be small consolation on its own, she mused; she hoped there would be others to set alongside it.

She took the next step and almost screamed as the blade-sharp corners dug into the already raw meat of her sole. Her vision slipped out of focus for a long moment, and the small trees dotting the slopes to either side seemed to bend in towards her, as if she were looking at them through a distorting lens. She shook her head impatiently until it was clear.

Pain, she told herself despairingly, *need not necessarily be disagreeable. It was programmed into mortals as a part of their defences, so that they would be warned when they were doing something that was inflicting tissue damage on their bodies, and would know to stop it. It's only indoctrination that makes them regard pain with such horror. In reality it's not really either pleasant or unpleasant . . .*

Yee – ow!

Tears starting from her eyes, she confessed to herself

miserably that there was a considerable gulf between philosophical theory and practical fact. When she'd put her foot down it had hurt like fuck all through her body – there was no getting away from it. Pain *was* unpleasant, distinctly so. If she ever got out of here and had the chance to catch the creators unawares, she'd apprise them of the fact most forcefully.

What was most demoralizing of all was that she knew that the mortals of the World had learnt of ways of dealing with pain much more effectively than she was doing now. She recalled discussing the matter with Anya's mother once. Syor had told her that there were only two things that made pain so harrowing: one was the memory of the experience of the pain, and the other was the lack of knowledge that the experience would extend for only a finite time. Of course, Alyss told herself self-justifyingly as fresh waves of agony from her foot surged through her, she had no guarantee that there *would* be any end to the pain she was experiencing now, here, in this hinterland of Rehan's mind. Perhaps she had accidentally crossed into a different otherness, one hitherto unknown to her, where not only distance but the passage of time disobeyed natural laws. Maybe she'd somehow, without noticing it, already penetrated the odd barrier she'd earlier sensed and was now imprisoned in a pocket universe no bigger than the singer's skull.

Well, the anguish wouldn't end if she just stayed where she was. A sudden horrific image of her wounds scabbing themselves inseparably to the surfaces where she stood spurred (no, in the circumstances, think of a different word), *urged* (yes, that was better), urged her on to take the next step.

At the end of which she found herself, slightly to her surprise, standing not more than twenty metres from a vast but dilapidated wooden gate. In places there were cracks between the boards as broad as her thigh, and the whole edifice slouched on its hinges as if the merest touch of drifting thistledown might be enough to bring it crashing to the ground.

On either side of the gate, like a pair of firedogs, stood two tarnished metal sculptures. The one on the left was of a tall young man, no more than nineteen or twenty years old. He was strongly yet gracefully built, and his face was handsomely carved, as if he enjoyed wisdom far beyond his years. On his left arm he bore a bodhran; in his right hand there was the short, double-headed stick with which he had obviously until a moment ago been beating the instrument's taut pigskin. Alyss suspected that if she glanced away he would pick up the rhythm exactly where he'd left off. The statue on the right was quite different. This time the minstrel was a young woman, and she was frozen in the middle of performing a fantastic, gravity-defying pirouette, one leg straight as a stave, the foot pointed so that its toes seemed barely in contact with the ground, the other leg thrown crazily off at an angle so that its knee seemed almost on a level with the statue's shoulders; the foot of that leg was cloven. The woman had a flute to her lips, and her face was a caricature of spiteless impudence. Her skirts were leaves falling in the wind of her dance.

Alyss smiled. The statues were self-portraits. The castle gate couldn't have been more clearly labelled to indicate that it was also the gate to Rehan's mind.

Around each of the minstrels' necks was hung a hand-lettered pasteboard sign. Again Alyss smiled as she noticed that the one on the flautist had been carefully placed in as indecorous a conjunction as possible with the woman's naked breasts. *Definitely the handiwork of Barra 'ap Rteniadoli Me'gli'minter Rehan*, she thought.

The writing on the sign on the left was in simple, uncluttered letters:

WeLCOM

On the other notice the writing was cramped, not just because there was more of it but because Rehan had chosen to embellish it with all sorts of ungainly curlicues, much as a bored child would elaborate its written name on the cover of a notebook:

TO THe SeVeN ReLMS

The eyes of the dancing figure seemed to reflect Alyss's own amusement at the childishness of the spelling. And Alyss was more than just amused: that Rehan should choose to be so playful was surely an indication that a great deal of his mentality still survived. Then her face became sterner. She couldn't assume, as she had been doing, that this gate had been decorated for her benefit by Rehan himself. The evil that had become him – if indeed it was evil – might have deliberately imitated the singer's thought patterns in order to lull her suspicions. Even if that wasn't the case, there were still good reasons for her to be wary of what lay beyond the castle gate: Rehan had always had a habit of dressing up bad news in the guise of a jest.

She took a step forward onto soft grass. For a moment the agony was even worse than it had been on the road, as if the grass's acid juices were attacking the torn flesh. But then, almost at once, there was a cessation of pain – a feeling as if the pain had never really existed, as if her memory must have been at fault. It felt as if her legs and then, very soon after, her whole body had been roughly bathed in warm, scented water, then buffed dry with a vast towel. With the complete physical restitution there came as well a mental languor, a torpidity that she instantly and suspiciously flushed out of her mind. She looked down at her gleamingly clean tunic and trousers and noticed without surprise that, like the sculpture of the flautist, she now possessed a cloven right foot.

Now that she was on the grass, the traversal of distance seemed to have reverted to orthodoxy. She had no sensation of strangeness as she strolled loosely yet warily towards the ramshackle gate. She suddenly wished that she had Reen by her side for support, and was irritated by the unexpected yen. To require the presence of a mortal was surely demeaning . . . and yet, of course, *here* she herself was as much a mortal as anyone else . . .

139

When she was close to it she found that the gate was nothing more than a perfectly executed trompe l'oeil, each knot and worm-hole painstakingly painted onto a huge sheet of paper that was stretched tightly on a crudely nailed wooden frame. She blew on the surface of the paper and watched the ripples receding outwards, away from her. Then she reached out to tear a hole through which she might enter, but stopped her fingers just before they started to rip downwards. Why destroy such an immaculate artifice?

Tutting at herself for her almost-vandalism, she pushed cautiously against the frame.

The gate swung open easily. She glanced backwards and forwards, unbelievingly, from her fingers on the side of the stretcher to the rusted hinges at the far edge. She could see the way that the metal surfaces were grating against each other and hear their whines and squeals as they shed flakes like brown snow, but at the same time her touch and her eyes were telling her that the gate was gliding easily.

Too easily. She felt at her belt and discovered she had no sword, not even a dirk.

Distractedly she wondered if perhaps there was a gateman who would suddenly appear, rearranging his breeches, to demand of her testily what her business was. Or perhaps to ask her three riddles. But there was no gatekeeper — indeed, no indication at all, apart from the castle and its walls themselves, that any human foot had ever trod in the courtyard other than her own. On either side of a grilled door there were rings screwed into the stained, greasy-looking grey walls, three on the left and four on the right, making seven in all. Seven rings for seven horses. Seven horses for seven riders, and suddenly Alyss knew that she was standing in front of the original Starvling of which Rehan had sung. And within Starveling there were, it seemed, seven realms – or 'ReLMS', as the notice outside the paper gate would have had her believe. She found herself singing his doggerel:

Seven women rode down through the town of Starveling that night,
Horses' hooves spitting galaxies in the pale moons' empty light.
And their eyes sought out the corners where the shadows grew
As deep and as dark as wine . . .

And at the time she'd never been sufficiently inquisitive to wonder why it was that a singer who'd spent all of his life sealed off behind the encircling mists of Albion, the Sun perpetually opaquing the sky, had known about the moons and the galaxies. Clearly he'd watched them in the night sky while standing on the ramparts of Starveling, looking out over the infinite empire that stretched all the way from one side of his skull to the other. *And*, she thought, *there was more to it than that. There was the other stanza, the one he hardly ever sang. 'The walls screamed out their agonies of age – too young for resignation, but much too old for rage. But the women, with their grey hair flying, still rode on, isolated in their own time.'* Which last must have been precisely what they were when Rehan watched them arrive here, and tether their horses, and let themselves into his castle. Only what he didn't say in the song was that he, too, was alienated in that other-time from the rest of his fellow-mortals. *Poor Rehan. He must have felt very lonely.*

She looked around her. If ever the courtyard had been paved or flattened down, there was no indication of it any longer. Instead, the ground was covered in flowers of every conceivable shade of blue and gold and green and blood-red; rarely there was a spot of soft purple, as if those few flowers were shy intruders among the throng. And then Alyss noticed that none of them were really flowers at all, just as the rotting old gate hadn't been a gate; there was no touch of them against the smooth skin of her calves as she stepped among them. They were completely insubstantial, mere projections of different-tinted lights into the vacant air. Yet the illusion was, again like the false gate, near-perfect, so that she had to bend down and run her hands through their nonexistent petals and stalks before she could finally convince herself that there was nothing there.

She looked up at the metal grille of Starveling's door and wondered if it, too, would prove to be as immaterial as the un-plants. Somehow she doubted it.

But she was wrong, as she discovered a few moments later when she pressed her face against one of what she'd assumed to be bars in order to get a better look at the interior, where trailing ropes of spiderwebs drooped menacingly from tall, gloomy walls that seemed to rear up to a chink of light infinitely far above her. The bar yielded against her cheek, and a quick check with her fingertips confirmed that the castle door, like the gate, was merely painted on thin paper. This time, however, there was a stout lock which looked to be new, and it refused to give when she shoved against it. Shrugging despondently, looking nervously to right and left in a sudden illogical fear that someone might be watching her, she raked with her nails until she'd created a rent large enough for her to step through.

The interior wasn't at all like the painted scene. The room in which she found herself was roughly cubical, its ceiling no more than about three metres above her head. A hideous fireplace done in green and silver tiling was to her left; within it was what seemed at first to be a snarlingly welcoming log fire but proved, on closer inspection, to be an electrical imitation, with a tinted bulb and fan under a thin plastic moulding to give the illusion of flickering. Alyss frowned at this, and equally at the plastic-veneered reception desk – it couldn't have any other function – on the other side of the room, facing the false fire. On the desk was an anglepoise electric lamp, switched on to illuminate the pages of a large open book; beside the book, in a quillholder, was a cheap ballpoint pen. That there wasn't a feignedly smiling over-madeup receptionist behind the desk seemed to Alyss something of an omission.

The flesh on her spine crawling – *yet another of these unfamiliar sensations that mortals must endure throughout their lives!* – she made her way edgily towards the desk. As she'd expected, the book was a registration book for guests. The whole place was like the foyer of a cheap hotel trying to pretend it was a more luxurious one. Alyss looked gloomily at the columns ruled in the book by someone with an uncertain grasp of their ruler; at the top of the page, poorly centred, someone had scrawled in an uneducated fist:

> WELCOM TO THE STARVELING ARMS
> Colour TV in Every Room
> Bedwarmers Negociable
> *Licensed*
> Tradicional Hot and Cold Roasts Served Daly

Picking up the ballpoint pen to write her name in the book, Alyss discovered that it didn't work. *Doesn't matter*, she thought idly. *I never know what to put in the 'Nationality' column anyway.*

She recognized so much of Rehan in the lobby. The whole set-up was a parody, and a somewhat juvenile one at that, littered with puerile jokes. The trouble was that it was a parody of a scene that a mortal like Rehan, tied forever to his existence in the World, should never have encountered. Electric fires were common to the cultures Alyss had infiltrated on countless other worlds – many of them parochially called something much like 'the World' – some of them within this particular otherness but the vast majority of them outside it. Anglepoise lamps, being so logical in design, were another standard. Ballpoint pens were comparatively rare, but certainly not uncommon enough for her to hope to be able to pinpoint the set-up as being from any particular culture. The fitted carpet beneath her feet was machine-made, of course, but again that was hardly a diagnostic help; neither was the portrait on the wall behind the desk, showing a woman with a blue-green face.

Set in the wall opposite the torn entrance she'd made for herself was a tall red door, closed but somehow inviting her. She looked at it distrustfully. In the cocoon of her customary powers she wouldn't have thought twice about opening it to find out what was on the other side, but she was becoming exaggeratedly aware of her current vulnerability. And the Rehan who had camouflaged so many secrets from her – from everyone else, of course, but most remarkably from her – might also have concealed from her unsuspected evils of character. The Rehan who was capable of, if not actual migrations between the other-nesses, then at least glimpses into them, might also be driven by motives quite different from those she'd always attributed to him.

You're being a coward, Alyss, she thought suddenly. *You've probably always been a coward, but it's never shown itself so obviously before.* She was vexed to find that she was asking herself what Reen would be doing in this situation. *Opening the door, but cautiously*, her mind responded before she could stop it from doing so.

Once again she wished she had a weapon of some sort. She picked up the ballpoint pen, looked at it, and put it down again.

There was nothing else for it.

Sighing, trying to draw together all the strength her small body could hold, she walked across to the red door and tried the handle.

The door didn't open, but there was an immediate reaction to her touch on the handle. On either side of the doorframe there popped into existence half-sized burlesques of the metal sculptures she'd seen outside Starveling's main gate. The two figures were the same as before, but their faces were turned up towards her and the expressions had been subtly modified, so that the man's stern austerity bore a taint of bovine bigotry and the woman's youthful mischief had become slyness. Where the others had been of metal, these statues were of what seemed to her sight and tentative touch to be yielding flesh, but cold – not so much dead as never-was-alive. The wording on the signs hung around their necks had been altered, too.

BeWARe

said the one on the left, and

OF THe SeVeN HeLLS

said the one on the right, beneath the flautist's knowing sneer. Without quite knowing why, Alyss immediately reached out and turned the latter sign around, only to find that the same message was repeated on the reverse, but in mirror-writing, as if it had penetrated right through the pasteboard.

So 'WeLCOM' has become 'BeWARe', she thought, *and 'ReLMS' was a much more welcoming thought than 'HeLLS'. Well, at least the alien-Rehan is being honest with me, or seemingly so.*

This time the door sprang open as soon as she put her hand against it. Behind her the pseudo-cosy lobby vanished.

She was standing in the middle of what seemed to be an infinitely large field of some grey cereal. Above her the sky was a livid red with, at its exact centre, a glowing ball of near-violet flame that seemed more like a hole punched through the sky than a sun. Alyss looked at it briefly, forgetting that she was burdened with mortal eyes; for the next several seconds she was completely blind, and only over a much longer period did her vision return in full. Despite the lurid display of the heavens, the air wasn't particularly hot; there was no breeze against her skin, but otherwise she might have been enjoying the afternoon of an indian summer on the World.

There was no breeze against her skin, but she could *hear* the sound of a breeze. And the stalks of grain all around her were in motion, as if a gentle wind were playing among them.

She squatted down and looked at them more carefully, just as she'd done with the non-flowers in Starveling's courtyard. These were substantial enough, though, but they were unlike any heads of grain that she'd come across before in all of the othernesses. Each of them took the form of a desiccated manikin, features distorted almost beyond the semblance of humanity, yet instantly recognizable as such. The faces and chests were collapsed in upon themselves, like those of a long-mummified corpse. They were light, too, as if the internal organs had centuries ago turned to powder. She brushed several of them with her hand, and saw their grey ash come away on her fingertips.

She plucked one and, standing, watched as it turned into a delicate latticework on her palm. When she clapped her hands together, lightly, the lines flattened into two dimensions, but, to her surprise, persisted. She shook the outline figure away, in sudden terror that it might have branded itself permanently into her skin, but the indestructible network floated away from her like a falling feather, circling down to land among its still-whole fellows a metre or more away.

Alyss looked down at her feet and saw around them a litter of similar lines, squashed into abstract shapes. She felt an abrupt and illogical twinge of guilt, as if these were living souls that she had pulverized out of existence.

And maybe they were. Kneeling down so that her face was once more level with the forest of mummies, she discovered the source of the hushed breeze-like soughing that she'd been hearing. Each of the untold billions of them was keening almost imperceptibly, its leather lips open just a fraction to let an iota of flimsy sound emerge. The tiny noise was continuous, with never a pause for breath, and it sounded to her infinitely miserable.

Slowly, aghast, she pulled herself erect and looked around her across the slowly moving heads of the not-grasses to the place where the plain met the sky. There was no horizon there, only a slow fading of the surfaces into each other, as distance made even the clashing contrast between the plain's grey and the sky's crimson no longer distinct. This was no bounded prairie on a curved world, she realized, but a truly infinite tract, absolutely level. It was an impossibility in any of the othernesses. It was a construct, brought into existence by the mind of the singer whom she'd thought she'd fully understood. It was a portrait that he'd created of his own perception of the reality of existence.

Of mortal existence.

Call the cobs souls, because that was near enough what they symbolized. They were indistinguishable from each other, uniformly grey. And their existence was an eternity of low, impotent, inexpressible misery. Was. Had been. And forever would continue to be. The only significant variations in the monotony of the grief were the casual ailments brought on them by fate or the capricious torments inflicted upon them by tyrants who had some glimmering of the dreary futility of it all and tried to escape from it by transforming featureless misery into some positive, more individual agony.

She was surrounded by the massed consciousnesses of all the othernesses, the sum of all creation.

And she, Alyss, was the bright immortal, clothed in gaudy colours as she sprang carelessly into and out of this existence or the other.

The luminously blind immortal.

Hell – for surely the first of the seven hells that Rehan's mind was presenting to her was Hell itself – was not some distant otherness, not some to-be-shunned afterlife, nor even the twisted artifice of mortals' malevolent nightmares. It was the slow, inexorable, unavoidable, eternal march of mortality.

No wonder mortals of all the othernesses personified Death as a culler, and looked upon Death's image with such ambivalent emotions. Their fear of Death was not that the reaper's blade would inevitably end their lives but merely childish apprehension of the unknown state of existence that they believed would follow life – even the blankness of nonexistence was terrifying in its own way. But the cruellest deception of all that the creators had wrought upon their creations was the dream that life, that consciousness, might ever come to an end. Instead, it was eternal. Each of the cobs in that infinite field was an immortal as much as Alyss herself was – in a way, she'd always known that – but, unlike her, they had no conception that they had been *condemned* to their immortality.

Just as they had been condemned by their creators to inflict upon themselves their perpetual misery. Truly the creators had built in their own image.

She was weeping, she found. At first she didn't know why the skin around her catlike eyes was wet, or why her vision had blurred and cloyed, but then she remembered having seen mortals – no, other *im*mortals – conquered by tears, and she guessed that this was what was happening to her in this spiritual otherness that Rehan or Rehan's usurper had fabricated for her. Brushing away the worst of the wetness with the back of her wrist, she looked around her and saw yet again the neverending sprawl of the field of grain and heard that long, soft, almost inaudible sigh of eternal grief, and she felt the totality of all those individual tininesses crushing her with their collective magnitude.

She covered her eyes with her hands and let herself drown in her tears.

After a long time had passed she became aware that, without her noticing it, a little while ago the ambience surrounding her had changed. The dreadful drearisome soughing of misery had gone, too, and the temperature had become so close to that of her body that she couldn't sense it as temperature at all.

She took her hands down and saw that once again she was standing in front of a door. This time it had been painted in searingly bright chrome yellow, a shout of colour; hanging crookedly on it was yet another of the signs of which the secret Rehan's mind seemed to be so fond:

WeLCOM TO THe
MUNKeY HOUOSe

Before she had properly had time to read the message, it and the door were receding from her, faster and faster, until all there was in the emptiness surrounding her was a distant point of light, which brightened momentarily before yielding to its final invisibility.

She could feel the way her head moved on her neck as she turned it to look around, but somehow the direction of her gaze didn't seem to have changed in response. She ran her hands fitfully over the front of her body to reassure herself that they and it were still there; she felt the plain of her stomach and the protrusions of her pelvic girdle, yet somehow the confirmation failed to hearten her. She breathed in deeply, but had no sense of any air coming into her nostrils; there wasn't any air in the second ReLM. The effect wasn't smothering or choking, as she might have expected it to have been had she been suddenly hurled into a vacuum; instead, her body seemed simply to have no need of the energy that air would have brought. For a moment the familiarity of not needing to breathe encouraged her, but then the other way of looking at the situation struck her: might it not be that, instead of her body not needing her to inhale, her body had no way of utilizing any energy she garnered from her surroundings? Her limbs were still capable of motion, as she'd discovered, and that motion surely required the expenditure of energy, yet the movements didn't seem to be having any effect relative to anything else other than her own body. It was as if she were a completely self-contained system, as if beyond the confines of her flesh there wasn't just nothing but *nothing*.

Certainly that seemed to be the message that the non-evidence of her vision was conveying to her. To say that she was surrounded by darkness or blackness or emptiness would have been to fail to describe the situation. She found that she could see more with her eyes shut, the random accidental, reasonless flickerings of the sense-cells in her retinas causing seeming flecks of light that were prevented from vanishing into the non-being by the penning curtains of her eyelids.

No, it was more than that.

Eyes still tight shut, she found that she was indeed able dimly to see fixed shapes around her. But those shapes didn't demarcate solid objects, or even any pattern of insubstantial light and shade. Instead she could see, quite definitely, that over *there* was a stolid, upright wall of anxiety; that the even floor beneath her feet was made up of neatly squared tiles of fear; that the low ceiling above her, thousands of metres thick and sinking ponderously down towards her, was composed of depression. Instinctively she raised her hands in a weak attempt to push against its descent, but she could see nothing of her hands or fingers; only the implacably approaching flat surface beyond them.

There were other moving shapes that she could see, as well. Somehow they seemed to her, as they flitted and danced around and over her, to be like excitable terriers or kittens. She half-expected to feel the touch of a rough warm soggy tongue on her legs or her hands, but of course there was no sensation in her flesh at all. Then one of them swept across her and she felt an immediate surge of hunger – hunger so all-embracing that it transcended all possible physical needs. She wanted to devour . . . she knew not what: everything and anything, edible or poisonous, palatable or vile. And then the shape was away from her, and the omnivorous yearning with it, leaving her weak and soulless in the aftermath of its going. Another shape seemed to nuzzle her inquisitively, and eroticism flared through every cell of her with the intensity of an electric shock, so that the pores of her skin seemed to enter into simultaneous climax and her groin was an agony of orgasm. As soon as the shape had gone on its haphazard way there was another in its place, and her mind was lost in a savage yearning, more voracious than perhaps even the hunger or the lust: the tiny atom of her consciousness that remained had no conception of what the yearning was *for*, any more than a starving baby might know that what it required to assuage its overarching need was food. She wanted everything that there was that she could have, and everything else as well, whatever it might be. She wanted to flounder in a sea of sensualities, to inflate her spirit with hastily gorged experiences, to become greater than all the cosmos.

And then the need was gone, and her consciousness filled her once again. But now it wasn't composed of self-knowledge but was instead a wailing, gibbering, terrorized, broken creature, its screams knives and its moans thorns. It had no sense of time, no knowledge of the past nor any expectation of the future, doomed to dwell in an eternal present. A detached part of her could watch it – detached but not dispassionate. It was a witness to the destruction of her *self*, and was wrenchingly aware of its inability to halt that destruction. It was racked with guilt, sorrow, pity, empathy, despair, hollowness . . .

How long she remained in this situation not even the remotely rational part of her could tell. The motile emotions touched her as they would, exhausting her body until it was drenched with fluids and sensations that felt like fluids; she could no longer distinguish hunger from lust, pride from humility, or complacency from need.

And then it was over.

She found herself on her hands and knees, looking directly at a filthy carpet littered with scraps of food and crumpled papers, tattooed with cigarette burns. The stink in her nostrils was from her own faeces, larded clammily down her thighs. The air around her was blue-grey with smoke, but it didn't muffle the clangorous discords that pulsed through her head or the pungent flashes of varicoloured light that seemed to ebb and flow around her. Convulsively she threw up in great steaming masses the emotions that had been cramming her body, and then watched as the pool of vomit on the sluttish carpet fizzled and evaporated away.

The shit on her legs, too, abruptly dried and fell in great flakes that became dissipating puffs of powder before they reached the floor.

She forced herself to look up, and saw the base of a door. Craning her neck yet further, she saw a foreshortened rectangle – yet another of Rehan's rebarbative little notices. Using the front of the door as a support, she managed to drag herself up onto uncertain, heavy legs.

Then she turned and leaned against the door, her palms flat on its puce-painted hardboard, and looked at the room in which Rehan had dumped her.

It's a pub! she thought incredulously. *A pub or a disco. I don't believe it!*

The room was jammed full of hundreds of people, all talking very loudly so that they could hear themselves above the thunderously distorted electrical sounds that shook the walls. No one was listening to the music or to any of the shouted words their fellows were uttering. She could just discern, through the throng, a small, raised stage where two almost naked limbo dancers performed raggedly under the merciless glare of steel-blue spotlights.

The technology wasn't of the World. Like the electric fire and the anglepoise lamp she'd seen in Starveling's lobby, it was the product of a quite differently oriented and scientifically more advanced culture. Over the aeons she'd encountered numerous such cultures scattered through the othernesses; they were all very similar. She tried to make out something of the blaring music, to give herself some sort of clue that might help her identify the particular culture from which Rehan's – or the false Rehan's – mind might have derived these images, but the sound was too loud for her to be able to hear it. And individual words were indistinguishable in the babble of voices, so that there was no chance of her guessing the language that was in use.

No one was paying her any attention at all. She felt lonelier than she had been even in the midst of the field of souls.

She turned away, intending wearily to read the latest sign. First, though, her eye was caught by another piece of printing, further up the door, formed out of individual plastic letters screwed into place:

LADIES

If she could trust the evidence of her eyes, this was a clue – unless it was something bogus placed there to deceive her, or unless her mind was translating the image into its own inner language. She shrugged. It was impossible for her to think it through properly, even on the periphery of the turmoil. She stored the memory of the pattern of lines away inside her head, and turned her attention instead to the card beneath:

OPeN THe JADe GATe
NO LUCTUReY SPAReD

Rather sullenly, Alyss kicked the front of the door, then yelped at the pain in her toes. Rather than swing open, the door at first merely quivered; then the wood began to split apart in the centre of the central panel. Rapidly the leading edges of the rent ran upwards and downwards; the gap opened more slowly to each side. Within moments there was in front of her a tall oval aperture wide enough for her to step through. Beyond she could see nothing but the sort of blankness that had surrounded her in the MUNKeY HOUOSe.

Alyss shuddered at the prospect of returning to that quicksand of unfettered emotions. However, with a last glance over her shoulder, she daintily put one questing foot forward through the gap then, all in a lurch, allowed the rest of her body to follow it.

The spicy, smoky scent of narcotics instantly invaded her nostrils, making her half-choke for a few seconds before a soothing sensation began to spread through her mind. She blinked a couple of times, then looked leisurely at her surroundings through half-closed, sleepily alert eyes. She rubbed her palms lazily along the fronts of her thighs, smoothing down on them the brushed silk of her dress.

She was standing in a great bell tent, perhaps fifty metres across, its thick, gnarled central pole standing perhaps seventy metres tall and supporting hectares of billowing squares of coloured cloth; the apex of the tent dissolved mistily far above her. Her toes, their nails painted blood red, wrinkled appreciatively against the soft luxuriant rug beneath her; glancing down, she saw that the rug was embroidered to depict a scene of sylvan ribaldry, the pubic hair of the participants picked out in elaborately stitched thread of gold. All around her were divans, each separated from the next by no more than a metre or two, and on each of the divans stretched a young woman dressed, like herself, in skimpy, semi-transparent silks. The women were of many colours and sizes, but all shared the same generous bulbous curvatures; Alyss took another hasty glance down at herself and was relieved to discover that Rehan had not tampered with her own trimness.

The air was filled not only with the smell of the drugs but also with the soft rustling of silks and a perpetual, slow sensual sighing noise, born of many throats. All of the women were in lethargic motion, sliding their thighs together or massaging their sides or bulging breasts, and Alyss suddenly noticed that there were gossamer-thin lines joining each of their limbs to some invisible point high overhead, up near the tent's apex. Then, to her horror, she realized that similar threads led upwards from her own wrists, elbows, shoulders, head, ears, back, buttocks, hips, knees and feet. At the moment of this discovery she felt an insistent tug on one of the strings, the one joined to her right knee. As her leg raised itself obediently there were counterbalancing pulls on other strings so that her body remained upright. She willed her head to tilt backwards and narrowed her eyes to peer towards the tent's hazy peak, but still she could make out nothing of the puppeteer.

Having little option, she allowed her manipulated body to lead her along one of the aisles between the cushioned divans, then left past a steaming, perfumed, sunken marble bath where two of the marionettes languorously rubbed each other's glistening bodies with phallic loofahs, then along to the right until she was standing in front of an untenanted divan – obviously intended for her to occupy.

Acting in concert, the strings hauled her body clear of

the floor, swung it around and laid it flat, face upwards, on the pneumatic surface. Then their tension relaxed; simultaneously she felt a degree of voluntary control return to her muscles. To her dismay she found that, its normal spikiness rubbed smooth by the narcotics she'd inhaled, all her mind wanted her to do was start fondling her body lethargically the way that the other women were doing.

I'd thought that you were old enough to have grown out of this sort of fantasy, Rehan, her mind muttered sleepy-grumpily as she touched her knees with her fingers and then ran her hands higher, up over the thin yet firm rounds of her thighs until they were playing with the resilient mat her groin hair formed under the silk of her dress. She arched her back, luxuriating in the taut feel of her stomach and sides.

None of the rest of the women were paying her any attention. Sometimes, out of the corner of a not very interested eye, she would notice one of the others slowly, controlledly making her way to or from the places where rising columns of pale steam betrayed the presence of a bath, but otherwise there was no change in the scene. Alyss idly wondered if perhaps attendants came round periodically to give the women food and drink, but she could see no crumbs or empty goblets. Aside from the baths, whose purposes seemed purely cosmetic and/or titillatory, there were no visible lavatory facilities of any sort. *Rule one in adolescent mortals' fantasies, male or female*, she thought. *Dream ladies never crap.*

The trouble was that, even while she was thinking these things, almost the whole of her mind was eagerly anticipating the moment when she, too, would be given the opportunity willingly to submit. She felt a lovely heavy smokiness seeping all through her, a sort of active passivity; all over her body, although especially around her hips and loins, there seemed to be a gentle, firm, warm outward pressure. She sought the pleasure of pleasuring. She recalled the orgasms that had battered her in the MUNKeY HOUOSe, and recognized some of the same eroticism, although without any of the violence. The cool, dissociated part of her mind noted the sensations, and catalogued them for future analysis; although Alyss had engaged in sexual activity with mortals of varying morphology before, out of a spirit of scientific enquiry, she'd never derived any especial physical delight from the contortions. On occasion she'd achieved some aesthetic pleasure through coupling among species whose mating was dancelike, but the deeper satisfactions of lovemaking would have required her to draw upon emotions that were alien to her. So this inchoate yearning that her body was experiencing was entirely novel, and therefore worthy of her attention; it was that fact alone that maintained her mind at any level of conscious perception.

'Hi, there, pretty lady,' said a voice beside her, startling her.

'I . . . oh, hello,' she said, blushing as she sat up on the divan, putting her arms about her knees. She noticed absently that the puppeteer's strings slid through each other easily to avoid tangling.

A somewhat embarrassed-looking two-dimensional blue rabbit, not quite as tall as Alyss herself, was standing there, moving nervously from one enormous hind leg to the other. It had a protruding rack of front teeth and bad breath.

'I wonder,' said the rabbit, 'now you've had time to acclim . . . acclim . . . get used to da joint, if you'd like to see da movie show? You're a new goil here, an' da sky-massa always likes da new goils to iron out da wrinkles by seein' da video.'

He looked down at the large digital watch painted on his chest. 'Dere's gonna be a showin' in tree minutes and tirteen, no, twelve, no, eleven . . .'

'I understand,' said Alyss, staying him with a finger. Her arm moved slowly in the gesture, as if she were having to press the limb through water. 'Yes, I'll watch your video.'

More confusion of the cultural tropes . . . . the detached part of her was thinking, but it hadn't the energy to pursue the thought any further.

'Well, cutesy, all ya gotta do is look up into da air. Dat's where da gadget . . . da . . . what's it da massa call it? . . . da . . . sumpin' ta do wit' social diseases . . . anyhow, babes, da gadget appears up dere, an' all you gotta do is watch da pretty pictchas move.'

Alyss started to tilt her head complaisantly, but the strings pre-empted her, pulling her around so that she was flat on her back again. New lateral strings tugged her eyelids open and held them that way, so that she had no option but to stare directly upwards at the rolling cloth of the tent's roof. She constructed a mental chronometer inside her mind's eye – she was delighted to find that she was still sufficiently sentient to be able to do this – synchronized it with her recollection of the watch on the blue rabbit's breast, and watched it as the seconds pocked downwards towards the zero. When only five of them remained a screen materialized above her. It was filled at first with nothing but multicoloured static, and she heard the blue rabbit swearing gaudily, but then almost immediately it cleared to show a picture.

The scene was an arena. In the centre of the blood-soaked sand and sawdust stood a pitifully gaunt-looking man, the ribs on his chest standing out as clearly as if the meat had been plucked from them. He seemed to be exhausted, his shoulders drooping. He was naked. In one hand he had a small club; the other was empty, its fingers bloodily shattered.

'Dat's da sukka,' explained the rabbit self-satisfiedly.

Alyss looked at the man coolly. His face was distorted into a caricature that was barely recognizable. It was as if the artist had deliberately chosen to stress every weakness beyond the extreme to which it could reasonably be stressed, while also eliminating all of the characteristics that might have countered those deficiencies. It was no longer really the face of Rehan, let alone that of Barra 'ap Rteniadoli Me'gli'minter Rehan.

And the same could have been said of the face of the big, strapping individual who now ambled casually into the picture. The same artist had been at work on his features, but this time the exaggerations had been done in exactly the opposite way. The results, however, had not been as the artist had perhaps intended, for determination had become obstinacy, strength of will ruthlessness, courage insanity. Yet Alyss found that she looked at the newcomer approvingly, admiring his rippling, oiled muscles and the brute ease with which his limbs moved. And she could hardly help noticing the disparity in the sizes of the two men's genitalia; despite the slightly hysterical mockery of the small island of her mind that remained aloof from the proceedings, her mouth opened in awe when she saw that the muscular caricature's scrotum, housing testicles the size of goose-eggs, dangled almost to his knees, his arm-thick penis yet further.

'Da massa don't normally have much call for da phillos . . . da sensitive collock . . . collock . . . aw, shit, ya know, da bit when you're pullin' da dames by showin' 'em you ain't tick,' whispered the blue rabbit.

The two pseudo-Rehans were circling each other, the smaller one nervously and reluctantly, the other with the air of a cat deciding which barbarity to inflict on a vole. In his mighty fist was clutched a mace the size of a half-grown tree. The crowd were bellowing at him to hurry up and get on with the bloodletting; Alyss found that she, too, was yelling for him to hurry, to splatter the runt's brains across the arena's floor.

A brisk movement of the great mace smashed the small man's arm, so that he dropped his own weapon. Blood sprayed. Crumpled yellow bone-ends showed.

'Bet dat hoit,' said the rabbit merrily.

The mob roared approval.

The shrunken Rehan screamed. At the same time, paradoxically, his minuscule penis began to stir and swell. The same was happening, more explicably, to that of the brawny gladiator. The watchers were going berserk. Alyss, to her horror, found herself unable to tear her gaze away from the two growing erections – found herself, spittle flying from the corners of her mouth, shrieking spiteful ridicule at the smaller man's puny offering and lewd approbation of the great bole jabbing outward beneath the huge man's knotted belly. Already it was bigger than his mace, which he threw away from him, and still it expanded.

Again the men were circling each other, their erections jutting in front of them. The gladiator with the shattered arm was hobbling, clearly disabled by his injuries and in agony yet, realizing that there was no escape, prepared to put up one last futile battle to preserve whatever shreds of dignity remained to him. The cool part of Alyss admired his courage while the rest of her clamoured bestially for his annihilation.

Then the men, both now fully aroused, closed to commence a bizarre contest of cross-staves, a twig against a mainboom. It was clear that the twig had no chance of prevailing, that the combat should have ended before it had even begun, yet the mainboom played with the anticipations of its public – Alyss included – by extending the combat as long as possible. She found that her screamed entreaties for the smaller man's death had become completely incoherent, that she was up on her hands and knees on the divan, her head raked back until her neck was almost breaking so that she did not have to tear her gaze away from the ferocity depicted on the screen, her buttocks searching the air behind her.

'Most o' da goils like this next bit,' reassured the rabbit. 'You wait an' see. Wan' some popcorn?'

A final colossal swing of the grossly engorged penis crushed the smaller man's head, so that the skull splintered and the pink brains flew in gobbets all over the screen, some of them sticking there and, as they slid slowly downwards, partly obscuring the view. Alyss reached a trembling hand upwards as if to wipe them away.

And then she was not only on the divan but also inside the skull of the prancing victor as he paraded his gargantuan weapon to the awe of the mob.

Strong and proud in his strength, she looked arrogantly

around her at the wondering throngs encircling the arena. The dead man's blood was as hot as fire against her skin.

'Alyss!' s/he bellowed.

The mob echoed her in a protracted lowing. 'Alyss!' Five thousand thousand drunken throats raping her with their noise.

'Kneel before me, woman! Acknowledge me!' s/he yelled, feeling that his voice was great enough to crack the walls of the heavens.

The erection, rising in front of her, hid almost everything else. Beyond its empurpled skin and its blue, bulging veins she could catch just glimpses, sometimes of the hysterical masses, sometimes of a man's shoulders and, behind them, billowing canvas. She was both herself and the titanic Rehan.

'Now comes da actual fuck,' explained the rabbit's voice, 'if you'll poidon my French.'

What there was left of Alyss's own personality could see that she was alone on the divan, but its corrective whisper was lost in the bawled delirium of her lust. On her back again, she stretched her legs as wide apart as they would go and advanced between her spread, supplicatory legs. She shoved the rounded head of his penis towards her openness and grabbed at it with both her hands and rammed/hauled it into herself until there was nothing left except the sensation of being torn into a million rags and gripped as by a relaxing vice and . . .

'I think I preferred you as a beggar,' her lips said coldly.

The harem, the lust, the spicy aroma, the ecstatic pain and, mercifully, the blue rabbit all evaporated. In their place was a tall, thick hedge covered in bluebells, forget-menots, honeysuckle, toadstools and michaelmas daisies; here and there a protruding stalk was further adorned with a neat bow tied in red-and-white spotted calico. As Alyss stood staring at it in blank exhaustion a chorus of skylarks and bluebirds above her head launched into a piping rendition of 'Tiptoe Through the Tulips'.

In the hedge was, as she would have anticipated, a door. It was low and squalid looking, its lardy surface-panelling contrasting with the almost suffocating wholesomeness of its surroundings. This time she could see not one but two little pasteboard signs, both curling at their yellowed edges. The upper one read:

I NeVeR SAD IT WUOLD Be eASY DID I?

The lower and smaller sign simply said:

DRABSVILL

Wearily accepting the inevitable, she took a few steps forward and wrenched at the door-handle. Her hand slipped on the greasy metal, and the door remained motionless. Just as she was about to step back, fire returning to her eyes, and expostulate at the object, unseen hands seized her and rapidly bundled her up until she was a small rubbery package, which was firmly shoved by the same unseen hands through the door's letterbox, to land with a plop on a coir doormat on the far side.

Alyss shouted a protest at the indignity of this treatment, but all that came out was a petulant squeak. Then she felt her body expanding jerkily as if it were being inflated by a hand-pump until, seconds later, she was standing at her normal height.

The other dimensions of her body were very different, though, as she immediately realized. She was squat, heavy and hirsute, her limbs like mouldering sausages beneath her costume, which was a set of soiled blue dungarees. Into her mind popped a full memory as to who she was and why she was here. She looked down at the pot of black gloss paint and the brush she carried in one hand and then up at the top of the aluminium ladder she bore on her other shoulder. A grimy handkerchief, knotted at its four corners, served as her headgear. The bluebirds and larks were still singing as they had been on the far side of the hedge, only now the tune was 'The Windmills of Your Mind'.

It took her a moment or two to realize something that was strange about the world in which she'd been so unceremoniously dumped. Aside from the cloth of her dungarees, everything else around her – the trees, the sky, the flowers, the grass, the distant hillside and the pebbles of the winding path under her – seemed to have been drained of all its colours. This was a place depicted in blacks, whites and an infinite number of qualities of grey. The effect was to make everything seem somehow fragile, like a thin curl of ash; she felt that if she were to tap one of the thick treetrunks hard enough it would collapse into a cloud of memories.

As before, when she had been still outside Starveling, she knew that she was intended to walk along the path, and so without further ado, hefting her two burdens, she set off in the rolling, sturdy gait that seemed appropriate to her new body with its cloven foot. The cluster of songbirds followed her, and soon she discovered that she'd pursed her lips and was whistling 'The Teddy Bears' Picnic' along with them. The lacklustre scenery went past her, showing little variation, as she joggled along, scarcely noticing the weight of the paint and the brush and the stepladder. She could hardly wait to get to the end of the path so that she'd be able to set up the stepladder and climb up it and . . .

She rounded a corner. In front of her, at the foot of a shallow hill, was spread a small field. At exactly the same moment as she saw this, her ears were filled with huffety-puffing noise, as if the sound were somehow inextricably linked with the light from the scene, both having been blocked off from her in exactly the same way by the intervening banks. The racket was coming from a smoking steamroller squatting weightily in the centre of the field; beside the gasping machine stood a human figure. As Alyss watched, the person bent down to fiddle with something on the ground, then stepped back, looked at his or her handiwork with evident frustration, scrambled up into the steamroller's cab, and sent the vehicle forward with a great clashing of pistons to flatten whatever it was she'd been fiddling with.

Alyss kept on walking down the hill, and the figure kept on repeating this same process.

As Alyss came nearer she saw that the person was a young woman dressed in dungarees similar to her own, but in a printed check. She was of adult size, but her proportions were those of a child, as was the language of her gestures: she reminded Alyss of a cross toddler whose work is never done. The woman's hair was bundled up on top of her head, where it was tied with a bow just like the ones that had been on the hedge. Her cheeks were puffed out in a parody of vexedness.

'It'th not my fault, you know,' she said before Alyss could open her mouth in greeting. 'Nothing ever ith, ath a matter of fact, and certainly it ithn't thith time. Ooooh, thethe nurtherymen, don't they jutht make you want to thcweam and thcweam?'

Alyss carefully put down her burdens and leaned her elbows on the fence. 'Whatever are you talking about?' she said, bewildered. Her voice came out in a harsh, unsubtle grating that she didn't much care for. 'Who are you?'

'My name'th Thomathina,' said the girl-child, popping her thumb briefly into her mouth, 'and I'm the word-farmer for thith . . . ooh, thith whole wide world. It'th my job to grow the wordth that everyone can uthe, and it'th a very, very rethponthible job, too, I can tell you.'

Alyss suppressed a giggle.

'And thethe wotten nurtherymen who thupply me,' said the child, 'keep thending me the wrong thortth of theedth. Come here and look at thith.'

Obediently Alyss clambered up and over the wooden fence, dropped her oddly heavy form down, and walked across the packed earth to where Thomasina was standing, elbows fractiously akimbo.

'Look at thethe thackth, will you,' said the girl-child.

Alyss looked. They appeared to her like nothing more than two full sacks. She said as much.

Thomasina gave her a frustrated glare, then dipped a hand into one of them, bringing out a seed about the size of a cherry-stone.

'Here'th a typical one,' she said, holding it out. 'Abtholute rubbith, ath you can thee. The nurtherymen mutht think I'm thimple, or thomething, if they think I'll fall for thith thort of tripe.'

Engraved in tiny letters into the meat of the seed was the word 'malodorous'.

'That's a "malodorous" seed?' Alyss guessed. 'I mean, when you plant it, it grows until it becomes the word "malodorous"?'

'Yeth. Exactly. Now you thee why I'm tho very, very angry. Who wantth to grow a "malodorouth" when a "thmellth bad" ith every bit ath good?'

Alyss looked at her bemusedly, worrying in case she was just about to find herself caught in the middle of a one-sided argument. Thomasina looked ready to explode into some kind of tantrum. The thumb had been jammed aggressively back into the rosebud-lipped mouth, so that the girl-child's cheeks bulged.

'Er,' said Alyss, wishing she could keep herself quiet, 'doesn't it, um, sort of depend on what you're using the words *for*?'

The thumb emerged with an enraged floop.

'You're jutht ath bad ath the nurtherymen!' hissed Thomasina hotly. She plunged her still moist hand into one of the sacks and pulled out a squirming fistful of what seemed to Alyss's untrained eye to be polysyllables. 'Jutht you take a pwoper look at *thith*, then!'

She scattered the seeds on the ground and almost immediately they had burrowed away into the earth, leaving only little dusty piles to show where they'd been. Several seconds passed, interrupted only by the sounds of Thomasina's wrathful breathing, and then shoots began to emerge from the soil. They were a light, bright, buoyant, joyous green; and as Alyss watched they grew and sprouted to form petals in a glorious array of different colours. Each of the petals formed a letter, and so each of the plants' many-floreted heads spelled out a word. The contrast with the drabness of the grey world around them made the colours seem even more vibrant. Alyss saw them as if they were songs.

'Thee what I mean?' asked Thomasina belligerently.

'They're beautiful,' breathed Alyss. 'Serene' she read in blues and greens. 'Rebarbative' was a cluster of spiky oranges and too-bright yellows, all jostling together in a somehow robustly pleasing way, despite the word's hostility. A fair, shy plant was 'velleity', made of subtle curves of pale purple and paler green. She saw the cold steel-blue of 'ratiocinate', spider-thin petals knitted precisely together; 'rumbustious' was a shout of reds; 'incandescent' an eruption of more hot colours than she could have found names for; 'tranquillity' a cool but not chilly harmonious blend of soft violet and hazed blue. And there were other flowers, perhaps fifty others, all of them perfectly formed to match the words that their petals spelt out.

'Abtholute codthwollop,' said Thomasina, ignoring Alyss, who had stooped down to let her face bathe in the colours from the plants. 'They've been thending me all their blathted trath, ath uthual.' She crossed one foot over the other and flounced her ridiculous bob of incongruously grey hair. 'You jutht wait until you get a look at what *I* do with all thothe weedth!'

And she was off and into the steamroller's cockpit and, before Alyss could do anything to stop her, had driven the ponderous vehicle a couple of metres forward to pulverize the offending flowers into the soil. She put the steamroller into heavy reverse and pulled it back to reveal the flattened ground. As Alyss watched, the flowers died, their colours fading. Dismally black on the grey earth showed 'still', 'cross-making', 'wish', 'suppose', 'noisy', 'burning', 'quiet' . . . Then these words, too, dissolved away into the overall drabness.

'Ithn't *that* a jolly lot better?' said Thomasina, beside her once again.

Silently – wordlessly – Alyss turned away from her and sadly went back to the side of the field. A minute or so later she had resumed her trudging progress along the path. Just before passing out of sight she paused to look back at Thomasina, who was still sowing seeds, jumping up and down in a grotesque tantrum every time they flourished as a crop of vivid hues, and then obliterating them with a pass of the steamroller.

How tragic, thought Alyss, *that colour and gaiety should be destroyed by a child's ignorant whim. And I know that, even though I don't want to, I'm going to have to perpetrate the same sort of murder.*

It was a long time until the natural stolidity of her borrowed body was able to oust her depression, and she must have walked several kilometres before she began once more to look around her at the scenery through which she was passing. The shapes of the trees were sometimes interesting, when their greys contrasted enough with the greys of the sky behind them, but most of the time there was just the same soulless procession of sombreness. Once she came across a place where a spring emerged from the ground at a tumble of rocks on a steep bank near to the path; but the water didn't bubble or shine, just lifelessly oozed forth to congeal in squalid, flat-looking pools. The songbirds overhead seemed to have been at 'Horse With No Name' for a very long time, but of course it was hard to be sure.

And then, as she'd known it must, the rain came.

The shower didn't last for very long, and nor was it very heavy, but it was enough to drench her from head to foot. In the normal way she wouldn't have minded too much, would have accepted that the chilly inconvenience was adequately balanced by the refreshing tang of the stinging droplets, but the rain felt grey against her skin, as if it were lifeless, somehow attempting through sheer lack of vivacity to match itself to the dreariness of the world into which it was falling. She found herself aching for even the pain of a vicious hailstorm or the soul-piercing iciness of a full-scale hurricane – anything but this half-hearted, soggy drizzle.

As soon as the rain ceased, a pallid, colourless sun emerged from clouds barely dimmer than itself, and then, again as Alyss had anticipated, the sky burst into precocious life as a great arch of colours stretched across it, seemingly from one horizon to the other. She found herself grinning at the effrontery of the rainbow, and paused to watch as the clouds picked up something of its generous and varied brightnesses. The grasses and the leaves on the trees reflected the greens to her; there were glisterings of yellow among the pebbles; blues and violets suffused the sky.

Then Alyss's face became drawn and sour.

The knowledge was inside her that it was her allotted task to put an end to all this.

Yet again hefting her loads, she turned away from the sky and plodded onwards along the path. She had free will enough only to resent what she was about to do; not sufficient to refuse to do it.

It wasn't long before she was standing at the rainbow's end beside a sullen-looking lead cauldron that could have done with a good wash. Dropping the stepladder and dumping the pot of paint and the brush on the grey grass beside it, she scratched at the metal with her fingernails. Sure enough, the tarnish scraped away to reveal a warm glint beneath. The sight spurred the rancour inside her.

She found herself, nevertheless, propping her stepladder against the rainbow, looping the handle of the paint-pot over her arm, climbing up the first few steps, sloshing the brush around in the deep gloss, and getting stuck into her chore.

The first brushful of paint went on with an angry dash, and the entire rainbow, all across the sky as far as she could see, seemed to dim and recoil from the blow, as if she had touched it with some poison.

For a moment she felt a thrill of megalomaniac power, and then it drained from her as shockingly swiftly as it had arrived.

'No!' she shouted, throwing the brush away from her. 'No!' The paint-pot followed, scattering blackness on the grey of the grass. 'No!' She jumped to the ground, grabbed the ladder in both hands, hurled it down. 'No! I will not do this!'

'OH YETH YOU WILL!' boomed the sky.

A deep shadow washed across her.

Alyss looked behind her and upwards. Towering over her, bulking out to cover almost all of the sky, was a gigantic Thomasina, her far-distant face blown out with pique. Her feet in their knitted bootees were tapping agitatedly, each tap shaking the ground. The holes between the woollen strands were each nearly as large as Alyss herself.

'I TELL YOU YOU WILL PAINT THE WAINBOW THE WAY I WANT IT, YETH YOU WILL THO, BECAUTHE ITTH NATHTY COLOURTH ARE ALL PUKY AND THEY'RE NOT RIGHT FOR THITH WORLD, AND IF YOU DON'T LET ME HAVE IT MY WAY I'M GOING TO THTOMP YOU, I AM, I AM, I AM!'

'You're not a god!' Alyss shrieked, cowering away from the gargantuan woman-toddler. 'You don't . . .'

'OH YETH I AM. I KNEW ATH THOON ATH I THAW YOUR WOTTEN DUNGAREETH THAT YOU WERE A HERETIC THENT HERE BY THE FORTHETH OF EVIL TO PERVERT MY WILL! WELL, YOU CAN'T THWART ME, AND YOU'LL BE THORRY YOU EVER THOUGHT OF TRYING TO! I'M THE THENTRE OF THE UNIVERTHE AND I WANT TO THTAY THAT WAY ALWAYTH, AND I'M NOT GOING TO LET YOU THTOP ME! IF *I* CAN'T ENJOY THE COLOURTH, THEN ANYONE ELTHE WHO TRIETH TO ITH A THIN-NER, A THTINKER, A WOTTEN THWINE AND A BEATHT!'

'But . . .'

Alyss wasn't allowed the time to think up a word to follow her strangled 'but'. One of Thomasina's huge booteed feet rose high in the lacklustre air and then stamped crushingly down, spreading out Alyss's body into a great flat splat on the insipid grey grass, so that the blue of her dungarees became one with the soil.

Just before her consciousness fled, Alyss made her blackness spell out 'merkin' on the ground, but even as she did so she knew that it was a very petty revenge, and anyway Thomasina didn't know what the word meant.

The long sucking process of dragging together the thin film that her being had become was exhausting, and her breath was coming in ragged coughs when finally she regained coherent awareness of her new environment. At first it seemed to be made up of a kaleidoscope of random colours that ebbed and flowed, near and distant, contorting as they went as though she were trying to look at the world downwards through a full tumbler of tinted water. At last things settled down – her vision and her breathing together – and she found herself standing in the middle of a snowy courtyard, facing a much smaller and even more run-down version of Starveling: the castle of an impecunious minor line of the aristocracy, perhaps. It was night, but there was enough light spilling out through the walls' embrasures for her to be able to make out the humped forms of carts and dead braziers cloaked in ashen snow. Drifting flakes caked themselves wetly against her coarse fur, and her dispirited tail hung rat-like between her hind legs. She shivered and snuffled, her breath a cushion that was whipped away from her each time she tried to put her head forward to rest on it.

Mixed in with the wind was the sound of her own whining.

For want of anything better to do, she made her way stiffly through the coldness to a dark shape that seemed to be the castle's door. Just as she reached it, a moon came out from behind the clouds. In its wan light she was able to perceive that this door, like all the others, bore a sign:

JAM TOMOROW

She sank her head back into her skimpily furred shoulders and stared mournfully around the courtyard, becoming conscious of her own thinness. The only part of her that felt large was her stomach, and it was achingly so. The whole of the rest of her body was weak, and she was only dimly aware of what she might do to bolster her meagre reserves of strength. She had shadowy memories of having just eaten some snow, but that had had no effect except to make her feel ill.

She could sense that there was some warmth – not much, but more than there was out here – on the other side of the door, and she began to mewl even more plaintively and persistently than before. For a long time there seemed to be no response, and she just slouched there while the wind and the snow and her own exhaustion conspired to turn her internal organs to ice; the remotely floating intellectual part of her was reminded of the way that silicates leach into the bones of dead creatures and replace them to form rocky fossils, and she had a sudden picture of herself being found like that, a million years hence, still begging admission at a long-vanished door.

But at last the door did open.

Half-falling, she staggered into the bath of warmth. All around her, investigating her like fleas, were countless odours of delicious corruption – rotting meat, stale cheese, urine-drenched walls, hanging poultry, ratshit, forgotten scraps, a bitch tantalizingly coming into heat, mouldering bones and the much-loved unwashed arsehole of the door-keeper. His rough hand between and behind her ears, affectionately tousling and bullying her head, warmed her more than the castle's heat.

'Are you glad to see your old Lian, then, Fanglord?' said the drink-slurred voice as Alyss wagged her tail furiously, twisting and turning to perform clumsy appreciative circles, whacking her shoulders against the man's wool-covered legs. 'Hey, hey, hey, hey, now old Lian wouldn't forget you out there in the coldy-wold, old fellow, would he, now?'

She eyed his unshaven face speculatively but decided that her strength wasn't quite up to leaping and licking it, the way humans generally seemed to enjoy. As the door boomed shut, cutting out the cold night gusts, she felt her icicle bones begin to thaw, and the mindless weariness that had filled her receded a little, so that her thinking processes, clumsily at first, started once more to function. She was inside, the creators be praised, and it was worth her while to perpetuate her demonstrations of joy long past the time when the emotion itself had been forgotten, so that Lian – the one human of whom she was genuinely fond – would remember to open the door to her all the other nights when she might be shut out. So she buried her head in his crotch and pushed playfully with her muzzle against his balls while he held her strait shoulders in his hands and muttered his endearments.

Finally he saw her tail beginning to flag, and released her. She set off towards the corridor that led through into the back kitchen, but he stopped her with a word.

'Not the kitchen tonight, my fine fellow,' he said, slapping his thigh. 'Tonight your lord and mine wants you to eat in the Great Hall, along with him and his guests. Nothing but the tastiest veals and hams, I shouldn't wonder, and pretty ladies' lacy kerchiefs for you to wipe your mouth on after. Now you be sure, Fanglord, my old comrade-in-arms, that you remember your table manners as was taught you by me and the late lady wife, d'you hear? I do be a having said to our lord, I do be, that 'ee'd be a credit to all o' us'n.'

Alyss looked at the scrubby fellow critically. She hadn't noticed before that his straw nicky-tams were the home for a prolific family of shrews, or that he was chewing a long grass, so that its head traced out intricate patterns in the air. His rustic dialect seemed to be getting more ersatz with every word he spoke. It would appear that Rehan's – or the pseudo-Rehan's – imagination was beginning to run out of inspiration. This oaf who'd taken the name of Albion's Lian – He Who Leads – was behaving the way that the projections sent by mortals into different othernesses sometimes did. He was becoming inconsistent – yes, now he was wearing a kilt complete with sheepskin sporran, and she was sure the mirror-shades hadn't been there before – and his bodily posture was shifting like his accent into caricature.

But Rehan never met Lian, she thought cumbersomely. *Surely it's not Rehan's fantasies alone that I'm trapped in.*

She pondered this, wondering what if anything it meant, as she half-lay down and began to lick and nip the inside of her rear thighs, bumping her nose a couple of times against the knot of her genitals before she realized what they were. She noticed dully that one of her hindpaws was cloven: had it *always* been that way?

'Oi'll be a buggered right down dead, oi'll be, if'n you doan' be a bein' of goin' inter the marster's ruddy Great 'All,' said the burlesque door-keeper, bent over almost double and scratching his armpits. From head to foot he was clad in a robe of green-leafed branches; as she watched, the leaves went from green to yellow to brown to silver and back to fresh spring green again. 'Be a gettin' along of 'ou, Fanglord, y'ald bumswipe, or I be pickled for 's lordship's pleasure, I be . . .'

The tent of branches was falling in on itself, and Lian's speech, though continuing on a steady course, was becoming an incoherent string of rounded monosyllables. She sat up on her haunches and watched, whining thinly, as the leaves reached the silver phase of their cycle once again, but this time, instead of reviving anew, blackened and liquefied. The assemblage of clichés that had been the door-keeper was now nothing more than a slowly shrinking puddle of steaming dark fluid on the paved floor.

She gave the liquid a couple of experimental laps, but it tasted bitter and so she turned and trotted off down the corridor that led to the Great Hall.

Had her host body never been there before, Alyss would have been guided by the noise. She shoved open one leaf of the hall's oak double door and found that there were perhaps a couple of dozen guests ranged along the two sides of the ancient elm trestle table which had served the Despot's family for generations. The men and women, dressed in plush and lace fineries, were laughing and jesting as they peeled fruits, or carved joints, or sipped or gulped from perilously thin crystal goblets, or speared delicacies on little pointed sticks.

When the door creaked, the Despot looked up, and the company hushed.

'Aha!' he boomed, clapping a fat palm down on the polished elm in front of him so that the silver cutlery danced. 'It's my hound, Fanglord! I asked the doorkeeper to send him through to join us.'

A footman leaned forward, a cloth poised to wipe the spittle from his master's lips, but he was dismissed with a violent gesture.

'Come in, faithful friend,' said the Despot, 'come in. Tonight you will see a feast the like of which you cannot have imagined even in the wildest of your doggy dreams! Eh! Eh! You hear that? Eh!'

The Despot had the shape, texture and colour of a giant doughball. He was sweating profusely, not from the heat – the only flames in the room were the candles arranged in an untidy single row down the table's length – nor even from the strain of gorging himself on the gargantuan meal, but merely from his own corporeal grossness.

'And in return, noble Fanglord, you shall . . .' Attempting to laugh, eat and speak at the same time, the Despot was seized by a choking fit. The footman, looking weary, clapped him three times on the bulging back with practised skill, and soon the Despot's face changed back from purple to its customary pallor. One of the young women tittered uncertainly. 'In return, I was saying before I was so in*suff*erably rudely interrupted, you, you scrounging little bag of bones, will contribute to the entertainment of the evening.'

The dog's eyes rolled as Alyss looked doubtfully among the faces turned towards her. Some of them appeared unhappy, even repelled, but most of the men and women were smiling broadly, as if privy to some jest that had yet to be explained to her. She began to feel very nervous indeed. On countless worlds she'd seen mobs look like this when condemned prisoners were being brought forth for execution. Mutilation, disembowelment and finally death were great jokes for sentient beings to play upon each other.

Then her eyes locked onto a half-eaten haunch of venison, its grey gravy congealing around it, and she found it very difficult to think of anything else.

'Come here, come here, my champion,' burbled the Despot, reaching out a pudgy hand under the table. There were some splodges of sauce on his fingers, and Alyss trotted forward eagerly, circumnavigating the legs of the diners, some of whom shrieked in forced gaiety, pulling their feet away as if the touch of the dog's rough fur might scratch them.

The sauce had been made with beef juices, flour and redcurrants, and it tasted very good.

'Now,' said the Despot, ignoring the dog still licking uselessly at his hand, 'let me show to you how even the proudest of men can be made into the most abject of servants. Or,' he added to the sound of strained giggles, 'the proudest of women for that matter. I say "servant", not "slave", because of course I, as employer, will pay for the services rendered to me. Now, pass me a platter.'

Alyss, looking up as the fat hand vanished, could just see that he was choosing small, tasty cuts from those of the serving-dishes within easy reach of where he sat. In moments he had assembled a miniature feast of different morsels: not enough to make a full meal for a hungry hound but certainly quite sufficient to assuage the worst of her hunger pangs. Saliva washed around her teeth.

'Fanglord,' said the Despot in cooing tones, 'here's a dish beyond your wildest dreams. It can be yours, all yours, if you will simply show my guests what a grateful beast you are to me for my many kindnesses by performing a simple trick to divert them. Sit up on your hind legs for me, and show us all how you can beg for your supper.'

It wasn't an unreasonable request, Alyss concluded, although she resented its pointlessness. Obediently she adjusted her strangely proportioned canine body so that her paws were up under her chin in a parody of supplication; for good measure she beat her tail against the floor a couple of times. The plate was hardly a tongue's-length from her face. She could taste the combinations of rich smells and . . .

The dish was withdrawn.

'Not yet,' said the Despot, grinning around the table

as he held the plate aloft so that she couldn't reach it. 'The best things in life are worth waiting for, are they not? Besides, I wish you truly to enjoy this delicious meal that I'm giving you, Fanglord.' He chuckled, and one or two of his guests joined in. 'So I'm going to make it even nicer for you.'

Pursing his lips as he made his selection, he put an oozingly succulent crescent of rich pork crackling on the plate along with the other viands, and nodded his head gravely.

'See, Fanglord,' he said, turning back to the hound and showing it the augmented dish. 'I've added a little extra goody for you, out of the kindness of my heart. But, of course, it's only reasonable that I should expect you to demonstrate a little further your appreciation of my generosity. You've begged already – my friends are weary of that trick – so this time I ask you to roll over on your back and play dead for me.'

Alyss mentally scratched her head in exasperation. Why couldn't the old bastard let her have the food first and perform all the indignities afterwards? Weren't thanks as good as pleases? Still . . .

Lying on her back with her paws curled up, imitating not so much a corpse as a baby in its cot, she closed her eyes and pretended to enjoy it when the Despot's balloonlike fingers tickled her breast clumsily. The odours of the meats swirling in her nose, exciting all sorts of memories and connotations in her mind, she wondered how long she was supposed to keep this up. Even though her eyes were closed, she knew that the plateful of delicacies was directly above her head, floating there, so close that she could have grabbed its edge just by opening her mouth, snatching at it with her long front teeth . . .

The aromas receded abruptly.

She opened her eyes.

The Despot was looking down at her, his face a mask of benevolence, his eyes gems of malice. 'No,' he was saying, half to her, half to the company, 'for a dog as fine as my Fanglord – a hound fit to lead the pack of a monarch

– only a monarch's supper is good enough. Let me prepare that for you, my faithful friend: be patient, be patient. These things always take a little time, you know.'

Alyss growled softly, scrambling to her feet again. She couldn't recall ever having felt hunger as intense as this, not even when she'd been preyed upon in the MUNKeY HOUOSe. Her starvation was a solid, rasping presence in her guts. If she could have wept, she would have.

'Quiet now,' said the Despot, a trace of nervousness creeping into his voice. Then, when he saw that she wasn't going to attack him, he chuckled confidently again. 'It's not that I'm withholding the food from you, you understand. It'll all be yours in due time, just as soon as I've finished putting on your plate all the very finest things that I can find. But, as I say, it'll be a little while before I'll have been able to do that. There's no avoiding it. That's just the way things are. *You* know that. It can't be helped.'

He shrugged histrionically. Alyss dimly remembered that he'd tormented her this way a million times before, and realized that on this occasion, as on all the others, there was absolutely nothing she could do except endure his sadism until eventually he tired of it and fed her. The worst of it was that she had no guarantee that he would indeed feed her: there was always the awareness that he might, out of malicious caprice – although oh-so-carefully rationalized such that it bore the guise of sweet reason – decide that after all she wasn't worthy of her supper that night, or any other night. And then, when her prolonged anticipation had raised her to a frenzy of desire, her starvation would remain for hours inside her like a raging carnivore attacking her intestines, so that her head throbbed and her whole body trembled. There was always that possibility . . .

'These things just take time,' the Despot repeated to the others. 'It can't be helped. Now' – turning back to the fawning dog – 'while I'm preparing this banquet for you, perhaps you could show your gratitude for my huge-hearted beneficence by licking my boots for me. I was out inspecting the cattle today, and I haven't had the time to wipe their sharn away from my feet, so if you could be so kind . . .'

He smiled. The guests were now watching blankly.

Alyss saw that at least he was keeping the first part of his promise. Half a smoked ham, the bone yellow-white with the promise of good sucking, had been added to the platter. And a couple of firm, bulging, fat-soaked sausages.

Head low, she slunk forwards and began to run her tongue along the creases of his leather boots, scooping out the tart-tasting dried cowshit and forcing herself to swallow it before the taste had a proper chance to take hold in her mouth. Her stomach seized upon the stuff, transmitting cramps all over her body as it tried to pretend that the small scraps were food. Once she had finished one boot, once it was all shiny and clean, she turned miserably to the other.

The Despot was laughing uproariously. Some of the other diners were joining in feebly with their host.

When she had finished she backed off, looking up at the plate he was holding out towards her. The food was piled high on it: juices and gravies awash around a mountain of tender, greasy, savoury flesh. Her tongue hung from her mouth, and every muscle in her body strained forwards as he lowered it slowly, nearer and nearer to her nose. She knew that she mustn't break her pose: although the Despot had issued no command, it was clear that her demonstration of self-control was yet another trick with which he wished to impress his visitors.

Closer and closer.

And, inevitably, snatched away again.

'Hmmm,' he said. 'This feast is *almost* good enough for you, but still it could stand a little final improvement, don't you think, Fanglord? Perhaps an extra soupçon of gravy, or a devilled kidney or two – I think I missed out the devilled kidneys last time, and they're ever so tasty.'

She growled again, but slumped meekly.

'Well,' bubbled the Despot oleaginously, 'while I'm

just taking a trifle of extra time adjusting the final perfection of your dinner, my friend, perhaps there's one last caper you could execute for our delight.'

She hung her head hopelessly in acquiescence.

'This is the most difficult trick of them all,' he said, depositing the plate briefly on the table and bending down to wag his forefinger at her, as if he were tutoring a wayward child. 'But because you're faithful to me, Fanglord – because you're so infinitely faithful and adoring – I'm sure you won't find it an imposition. You see, my friend, not everyone is as loyal to me as you are, my fine hound. No' – he sat up and looked around the pale faces of the diners, his voice beginning to liquefy with hilarity – 'hard as it may seem to you to comprehend, there are some who would secretly betray me, who would practise deception against me. No, Kursten' – a prohibiting palm raised as the liquid of his voice froze – 'there's no need to leave us so precipitately. Your bladder will retain its contents for as long as it needs to. Lifting your skirts to bare your pretty little arse has, in rather different context, for far too long been your method of solving problems. You just stay where you are, this time. I won't delay you long.'

'Hasn't this gone far . . . ?' began one of the men, his fist clenched as he half-rose. Suddenly Alyss recognized him. Now wasn't the moment to renew her friendship with him.

'No, Barra 'ap Rteniadoli Me'gli'minter Rehan, it hasn't gone far enough yet – and it won't until it's run its full course. *Sit down, you shit!*'

The echoes petered out. The footman and the diners were like statues, caught by the sculptor in frozen moments of horror.

'And now, Fanglord,' said the Despot amiably, 'it's time for your last trick, the one that'll earn you this banquet I've prepared for you so generously. You and I are friends, are we not? The staunchest of friends. And, as even your doggy brain will realize, that means that anyone who is a traitor towards me is likewise a traitor towards *you*. The logic is simple, no? So, just to protect us both from future perils, naturally the sensible thing for you to do is to destroy the traitor, so that she'll never again plot against us, will she?'

He began to laugh again, clutching his robe where it stretched over his fat sides.

'Go on, Fanglord. The final trick.'

Alyss sprang up onto the table, her hunger driving her. Ignoring the piled plate the Despot had been preparing for her, ignoring all the other dishes that littered the broad elm, she advanced down the length of the table, shrugging the candles aside, her lips drawn back from her teeth, her hackles bristling, a deep growl pushing its way up from the depths of her throat. The fragile-seeming blonde woman at the far end pushed her chair scrapingly back and got too slowly to her feet, her hands flying up in front of her breasts.

'No!' she screamed, the cords in her neck like harpstrings. 'No! Get this—'

Alyss was at her throat, her long ripping teeth at last finding sustenance as they tore into the white flesh. All she could see was a sea of redness as blood burst all over her head and body, spraying the table and the diners; the sweet, rich, aromatic, warm blood . . .

There was no time, no need for chewing. She swallowed the first wet gobbet whole. The woman was flat on the floor now, Alyss astride her head tearing at the wreckage of her throat. At last the guests had started to move. Some vomited where they sat; others were reaching for their weapons; a man screamed shrilly – even through the haze of her bloodlust Alyss recognized the voice as Rehan's. She put a dripping paw on the woman's forehead to steady the head and wrenched away the freckled nose, gulped, shifted her position so as better to be able to attack a rounded cheek. Inside it there would be the succulent tongue . . .

A little while later, and the room was almost empty.

Alyss looked up from the shambles that had once been the blonde woman's head. She licked her whiskery lips, tasting the blood's saltness. Only the Despot was left at the table – the Despot and, standing motionlessly formal behind him, his whey-faced footman.

Grinning greasily, the Despot clapped his hands languidly a couple of times.

'A pretty trick, my faithful hound,' he said. He half-turned towards the footman, keeping his eyes on Alyss. 'A fine jest to culminate our evening of merriment, eh?'

'Sire,' agreed the footman.

'And now, Fanglord,' continued the Despot, 'I should say that you've had enough supper for one night.'

He looked at the heaped plate in front of him, the one that he'd spent so tantalizingly long preparing for her.

'I don't think you'll be needing this now, will you? And' – he shrugged – 'it would be a shame to see it go to waste.'

At the command of a finger the footman tucked in a napkin around his master's bulging neck.

'*Bon appetit*,' said the Despot, raising his fork eagerly.

Once again the red of blood washed over Alyss's vision, so that she was drowning in its clammy warmth. The dog's body stayed where it was, as if made of stone, as her consciousness swam away, struggling to keep its head above the water as the current seized it.

Nothing but blinding redness for a very long time.

Then:

'Wake up, dearie. You've been having another of your bad dreams. Shouting and screaming like nobody's business, you've been. Wake up, wake up!'

Bony fingers tugging at her shoulder.

Alyss opened her eyes.

There was a chilly draught blowing across her face. High, high above her, almost at the limits of her visibility, a moist-seeming rocky ceiling patchily luminesced coldly white. Closer to her there was an equally pale face, hovering anxiously over her; through its features Alyss could just see some of the ceiling's darknesses.

'Ah, dearie, you're back with us at last,' said the translucent face, showing ghosts of broken teeth. 'No time to shake away your dreams, dearie; there's work to be done. When is there ever not? I think Barra 'ap Rteniadoli Me'gli'minter Rehan's master works us all too hard, and I'll say that to anyone who's prepared to listen, but there's nothing as anyone can do about it, so it's best for us just to accept it, isn't it, sweets?'

Wearily Alyss hauled herself erect. Her whole body seemed to be aching, as if someone had been kicking it while she slept. *At least*, she thought as she pulled her clothes into order, *it's one of my own bodies*. She examined herself cursorily, noting with approval her thin hips, her trim breasts, her dainty hands. All were as pale as the face she'd seen on waking – even her jerkin and breeches were the same silvery grey – but at least they were recognizably *hers*.

She was only slightly surprised to find that she floated a few centimetres above the cobwebby ground, rather than standing directly on it. All around her there was the sound of dripping; also a slow, deep, smooth continuous sound, as of a great body of water flowing in massive, inexorable tranquillity towards some distant ocean.

'Still half asleep, aren't we, dearie?' said the woman beside her. Alyss looked at her properly for the first time, and was startled. Add a half-dozen decades of cruel ageing, and the woman was surely Anya.

'Anya?' said Alyss shakily.

'Anya as always,' confirmed the hag. 'My, but we are the sleepy-head, aren't we? Now, come on with me, there's a door we've got to go through before we can start work. I don't know why the master wants us to go through a door this waking-period of all waking-periods, but those are the orders and we can't change orders, as I always say, don't I, sweets?'

' "The master",' Alyss repeated. The bright clashing images of that loathsome banquet table were still hideously fresh in her mind. 'We're not the vassals of the Despot, are we?'

Anya's face cracked into a gappy grin. 'Oh, no, dearie,' she cackled. 'Not the Despot at all, not at all. Whatever gave you *that* idea? What a naughty nightmare that must have been! Now, follow me, ducks, and let's forget all those silly dreamsy-weams, shall we?'

Mutely, Alyss followed her. She heard Anya snort 'The Despot!' once, and then, a moment later, 'We should be so lucky' as they floated up and over various piles of broken shale and heaped quartzes. Their route took them for a while along the bank of the great watercourse whose progress Alyss had been hearing ever since awakening. Refusing to obey Anya's impatient tug on her arm, she stopped briefly to look out across the black, shining surface of the river. Here and there the perfection of the mirror was disrupted by a bobbing white shape. When one of these passed close to where Alyss was standing she saw that it was the still, waxen body of a child, its eyes wide open, unseeing. One hand lay across the stomach; there was a brighter white glow on a finger, like a ring.

'Come *on*, ducks!' said Anya vexedly. 'We don't want to get into trouble, do we?'

Reluctantly Alyss allowed the hag to drag her away.

Then they were rising, floating smoothly up the side of a huge rock-fall that led towards one of the cavern walls. Alyss could feel the bulk of the roof coming closer and closer above her as they climbed. Soon she could see that there was a small door let into the side of the chamber, and it was towards this that their course was unerringly taking them.

'Stop!' she snapped at Anya. 'Wait just a moment. Even this master of yours – ours – can't object to us pausing to . . . to get our breath back, or something.'

'Get our breath back? That's a good one, dearie!' wheezed Anya, batting her ethereal hand against Alyss's equally ethereal shoulder. 'Do tell us another one, do!'

'No,' said Alyss firmly, trying unsuccessfully to sit down on a shelf of black rock. 'No, it's your turn to tell *me* a few things. I won't budge one single millimetre from here until you do.'

'Oooh!' said Anya. 'All hoity-toity today, are we, you little minx? Well, you'll be smiling on the other side of your face when . . .'

'I've little doubt that I already am,' said Alyss sweetly. 'So tell me where we are, what that river is, why there are corpses floating in it . . . everything.'

'And just why should I, little miss muck, I ask you?' said Anya, hands on her scraggy hips. 'Oh, well' – she relented – 'you always were the stubborn one, I s'pose. I'd better humour you, since you insist – otherwise we'll never get anywhere, and then the master will get so, so cross I hardly like to think of it. Though why you should need to be told things you already know . . .'

She let the words drift. Alyss just stared quietly at her until her eyes fell. Anya began picking at the wispy rags of her dress.

'The river is the way between the othernesses,' she explained wearily, 'and all mortals must travel along it when their time in one otherness is done. Further down-river the master will fish them in to the shore and decide which otherness each of them must dwell in next. Our task, of course, is to strip the people of their memories – the imprints they bear of their favourite times or their most terrifying, the relics of those they loved, other people or just treasured objects. You saw the ring the child back there had been given to betoken its coming-of-age as clear as I did.'

'It wasn't a ring,' said Alyss. 'It was just a shining light where a ring might have been.'

'The memory of a ring,' said Anya impatiently. 'What's wrong with you this waking-period? Couldn't you see the remembered exultation of the child when the matriarchy's acolytes bestowed it in the Festival of the Hundred Aloes on the Island of Cups on H'kllim"rtx?'

'No.'

'Were you blind to the mind-sight of the red sun-goddess Veer-Han at the zenith, her consort, blue Mard-ragon, poised at her core so that the pair of them together formed the eye of heaven? Couldn't you hear the blaring of the horns and the ecstatic screams of the sacrificial victims as the ring of adulthood was slipped onto the child's finger? Those memories were so very very bright and clear – you can't have failed to notice them, dearie!

Or has something gone awry with your senses?'

'Yes – no. No, there's nothing gone wrong with my senses. It's just that I'm not who you think I am, and I don't have the senses you think I have.'

Anya glared at her unbelievingly.

'Have your nightmares driven you mad?' she said, voice quiet with fear.

'No, no. I'll explain it all to you some time. These memories – why can't the people take them into their new othernesses?' Knowing the answer already, Alyss paid no attention as Anya launched into a new burst of explanation. *This is all wrong*, she thought. *I've seen people pass between the othernesses often enough to know that it's nothing like this. There's just the instant of non-knowledge before they're returned to the torment of existence; there is no time in between, no floating down a river, no period of relief from the pains of living before, cleansed of memory, the essence is brought screaming into the next otherness . . .*

The cobs in the field of souls had it right . . .

This is just a picture of the transition of souls, something dreamt up by a mortal mind in an attempt to depict something that mortal minds cannot bring themselves to comprehend. Knowledge of the truth would be too painful, too spirit-extinguishing for them, and so they refuse to accept it, pretending instead that pretty pictures like these are the reality. And, if their faith in the sham is strong enough, the sham becomes a reality of sorts, just as fresh messiahs come to peoples who pray hard enough for them . . .

'We've been talking long enough,' she said abruptly, cutting off Anya in mid-stream. The crone, open-mouthed, gawped at her. 'It's time for us to pass through this next door of yours, into the sixth ReLM.'

'Well, ducks, it's good to see that at last you've come to your senses,' said Anya crossly, gathering her floating skirts. 'I never did!' she muttered, deliberately just loudly enough for Alyss to be informed of her displeasure.

The door, when they came to it a few minutes later, seemed to have been designed for dwarfs. Even Alyss, small as she was, was going to have to crouch down to get through it. The wood was painted an unsubtle vermilion, the first pigmentation she'd seen since awakening here; she was reminded of the word-flowers that Thomasina had been destroying back in DRABSVILL. Now, however, the colour was strangely uncheering.

To each side of the door was a heap of metal helmets shaped to represent the heads of predatory birds and reptiles; along their sides were etched obscene friezes.

She was reaching for the door-handle when Anya stopped her.

'Read the notice, you fool!' the old woman said angrily. 'Don't you have the first idea of protocol?'

Alyss read:

THe PeNULTIMATe OF THe CONCeNTRIC HeLLS
BeWARe – MeN AT WORK OVeRHeAD
WeAR YOUR HARD HAT AT ALL TIMeS
THIS MeANS YOU!!

Anya passed her a helmet in the form of a unicorn's head. The long spike jutting up from the centre of the brow was needle-tipped, and its length was encrusted with knife-edged diamonds. There were pointed metal studs along the bars of its visor; across the front of the helmet was painted a double line of hooked teeth. As Alyss raised the hideous structure, looking at it in awe at its gaucheness, Anya was tucking her wispy hair into a stylized boar's head. 'The unicorn,' she was cackling. 'The symbol of the virgin. How very suitable, very fitting, ducks.'

Alyss merely shrugged at this, donning the helmet at last. Once it was on, her head instantly felt warm, although the rest of her body was still at the mercy of the cavern's chilly draught. She adjusted the thing on her shoulders so that she could see more easily through the grille of the visor, then gestured to Anya to precede her through the door.

The boar's head split in a malevolent leer, and shook from side to side.

'Oh, no, dearie,' Anya said. Her body was rapidly

solidifying, the floating shreds of gauze coming in together to knit and form hard, hairy flesh. She dropped down onto all fours as her legs and arms shortened and her torso barrelled outwards. 'No, dearie,' she repeated, her voice becoming a harsh grunt. 'From here on, only one of us can proceed, and it's not going to be me. I'm happy to stay here in the hinterland of the sixth HeLL: I've no wish to be incinerated by the brilliance of the master's direct gaze. Leave me here to my chills and my quiet task of plucking memories from the transients.'

With a shake of its broad hindquarters, the boar turned and trotted off carefully down over the jumbled rocks, ignoring the tiny avalanches its every step produced, balancing with obvious effort.

Alyss, the muscles at the corners of her mouth tightening in resignation, reached out for the handle again. This time she turned it, then flinched as the door opened and a blast of noise and colour came through the gap. She crouched down and edged herself warily through into a scene of heat, industry, din and unnaturally bright blue-white light. All around her were men dressed in oily white coats and fantastically wrought helmets like her own. They were walking swiftly and purposefully in all directions, paying her no attention at all except that some instinct seemed to make them always evade her, so that where she stood she was in a small oasis of emptiness. A voice was booming out over the scene, but its sound was so distorted and cloaked by static that it was impossible to pick out individual words. All around her there were huge metal structures, like the hulls of steel sailing vessels, yet unmarked by rivets; complicated stands of scaffolding ran up their sides, and on these human figures were moving like busy ants. Here and there she saw arches of blue and yellow sparks as people worked with powered cutting devices or oxyacetylene torches.

She looked around her helplessly.

A gloved hand clamped her shoulder, and she almost screamed.

'Boy!' said a gruff voice.

'I'm not a boy,' Alyss retaliated. 'I may not exactly be suffering from an excess of steatopygia, but . . .'

'Shut up! Don't you recall having humiliated me before?'

'No, I . . .'

She'd been about to say that it was unreasonable to expect her to remember any particular instance of her having humbled an individual during her travels through the othernesses. Abashed, she silenced herself.

'Well, now it's my turn to humiliate you!'

The big man who had grabbed her was wearing the masked helmet of a berserker. It was battered and beaten, as if it had served him in many battles; it had two animal horns curving upwards from the crown, one of them broken. A swarm of flies surrounded the entire headpiece, buzzing companionably.

'I . . .' she began again.

The huge frame seemed to relax. 'But I can't hold a grudge forever,' said the hoarse voice. 'Never let it be said that Thog the Mighty is the vengeful sort. I've got more blood on my soul than you'll find in an abattoir, but it's all of it been honestly shed in fair combat, and some of it's my own. I wouldn't want to add yours to it, young whippersnapper, just on account of a mischievous prank you played on me a hundred lifetimes ago. I'll accept it as an apology if you take this parcel up to the master's office.'

He proffered a small, oily package wrapped in brown paper. She'd assumed that it was his lunch.

'The master?' she said shyly. 'Are you sure you're not sending me to my death at the master's hands?'

He stood quite rigid for a moment, then began to guffaw.

'No one kinder than the master,' he said finally. 'No need at all for you to be frightened. Here, take it.'

He turned and was lost among all the other hundreds of scurrying white coats. Alyss looked stupidly at the scruffy brown package in her hand, and squeezed it experimentally. It even felt like a couple of sandwiches, with a hard spherical lump at one end that could have been an apple. Still, if it was her destiny to take this thing to the master . . .

Some of the other workers were willing to pause long enough in their rapid trajectories to give her directions, and she found her way reasonably easily across the great dockyard until she stood beneath a gleamingly polished metal ladder that stretched upwards towards a meshed catwalk. The last worker whom she'd asked had told her that the master's office was near the top of this ladder.

As her foot reached for the first rung of the ladder, it crossed her mind that the office itself might be the last of the seven HeLLS. If so, it seemed likely that in it she would indeed come face to face with the master, the creator and controller of all the ReLMS. Although this had surely been her whole purpose in entering Starveling in the first place, she was now perversely loath to take the culminating few steps of her quest. She had assumed for much of the time that the master must be Rehan, or at least some hitherto unknown aspect of the singer, and she was certain that Rehan in any guise would be, if not positively friendly towards her, then at least easily copable with. Now that she was so close to the final encounter, however, that small possibility she'd kept alive in her mind only as a sort of academic *caveat* seemed to be growing in importance until it outweighed her main thesis. After all, before she had come to Starveling she'd assumed that someone or something had usurped Rehan's mind, but thereafter she'd seen so many symptoms of his idiosyncratic personality – the irritating little notices, the adolescent fantasies, the self-indulgent quirks as when Anya had turned into a boar for no particular reason except that, as Alyss had interpreted it, Rehan's one-time love for the woman had soured so much that he wanted to debase her image in this petty fashion . . . so many symptoms, yet was it possible that she'd read those in such a way as to come to a false diagnosis, the diagnosis that she preferred as the truth rather than the truth itself?

Besides, if the ReLMS had been Rehan's creations alone, surely there'd have been more music? Looking back on them, she realized how music had been remarkable by its absence. There'd been only the discords of the pub, the travesties committed by the songbirds in DRABSVILL . . . and in the pornotopia, where surely the presence of music should have been compulsory, there'd been nothing.

Her encounters in the six HeLLS had seemed all to be telling her something about power. The power of the polycosmos's original creators to condemn all mortals to an eternity of misery. The power of animality, in the MUNKeY HOUOSe, to dominate her temporarily human mind. The stupid abuse of power focused on the image of the mightiest phallus. The power of Thomasina to paint all of the world in her own dreary shades of grey ignorance and self-belief. The power that the Despot had so delighted in exercising over the starving dog and then the frail human in his thrall. The power of the wraith Anya to steal memories, and even that of the bluff stranger to compel her, using the most genial of emotional blackmails, to run his errand for him . . .

His errand. She looked at the negligible-seeming package in her hand. In the various HeLLS she should surely have learnt by now that few things were as they at first appeared. Glancing agitatedly from side to side, she swiftly peeled away the paper wrappings.

She was holding a single, complex, composite memory. As she ran her fingers over it, she understood the nature of the senses to which Anya had been referring down by the riverbank. Alyss found herself able to read the memory in all its almost infinite nuances and glances, until at last she was able to fit them together to paint an entire sensual scene.

Someone's single most treasured keepsake had been a copy of the entirety of Albion – or, to be accurate, the country's own composite memory, distilled down so that it could be encapsulated within a single mortal consciousness. Someone had left the otherness that called itself the World bearing *that* along with them as the one thing they held most dearly. And if they had borne even a vestige of it into the next otherness into which chance had determined that they should be incarnated . . .

Alyss shuddered.

If a mark is stamped deeply enough, no one can ever, try as they might, completely erase it.

She had seen all the symbols of the six HeLLS and their hinterlands as symptoms of Rehan's mentality, and to be sure traces had been plentiful of his distinctive patterns of thought. But suppose those traces had been merely remnants, things ignored when some usurper – gentle or tyrannous – had remoulded the contents of the ReLMS. Moreover, whereas she had interpreted the various examples of power as demonstrations of the fantasized abilities of whoever's mind it was that she had been exploring, suppose it was all the other way around? Suppose the fantasies were not of exercising power but of *enduring the exercise of power*? Might the usurper be not tyrant but *victim*?

Yes, surely that must be it. She'd been too easily assuming, all along, that she'd been being subjected to the various torments of the HeLLS because the mind into whose fantasies she'd stepped was taking joy from her humiliation. But it all began to make more sense if the controlling mind was making her *share* its experiences of the HeLLS. This was a mind that had been anguished through being subject to other people's caprices of power. It was trying to ameliorate that lonely anguish by *sharing* it. It had been condemned to immortality, and now it had been given *knowledge* of that immortality. It was a mind ruled by the drives of the body or bodies that it inhabited – now including, presumably, Rehan's. It had been powerless before a tyrant's brute and stupid force, and it had groaned under the yoke of a tyrant's childlike and irrational whims. It had been tortured by promises of happiness capriciously broken. Its will had been so dominated by others around it that it no longer could rely on its own true memories . . .

Yet, as Alyss knew, there was no such thing as a true memory. The past was in a state of constant flux, but mortals were unaware of this. The mind whose HeLLS she had been sharing must transcend the realities to which mortals so touchingly clung. It was too human to be the mind of one of the creators – and, besides, no creator would ever permit itself to be cast into the role of a victim.

That was surely the key to it all: that the mind whose fantasies Alyss had been dragged through was, for all its transcendence of the mortal state, a victim.

A human being, surely – but a human being who had been given at least the minor trappings of deity, the abilities that Alyss herself had always taken for granted as a natural part of her own existence, but which must seem inordinately strange to someone who had come to them afresh. No wonder that the mind that had usurped Rehan's – had usurped Starveling – required to share the HeLLS with another of a similar kind: Alyss. Mortal miseries, symbolized in such a very mortal-like way, could never have been projected onto a large enough screen that a being like Alyss could experience them. And so Alyss had herself been shrunk down into a semblance of a mortal's existence.

The usurper mind must be a mortal that she had known, somewhere along the line: there were clear signs that the symbolism of the HeLLS had, here and there, been tailored for her. It had surely been deliberate that in the MUNKeY HOUOSe she had been more humiliated than a mortal, accustomed to the bullying of uncontrollable emotions, could ever have been. In the caricatured harem, and in the gladiatorial arena that was *also* the harem, she had been forced to behave in ways that were too precisely opposed to her normal self for coincidence to have been solely responsible. No, the mind had known her, either in some mortal reality or – and she felt a touch of despair – in the interstices between the othernesses: in the greater reality that was the polycosmos.

And yet her thoughts kept circling back to one undeniable fact: this mortal-who-had-become-at-least-partway-a-god was also a *victim*.

Alyss felt further despair. A victim who had carried

glimmerings of his or her experiences of the World into some next otherness? Someone who had seen the naked face of the polycosmos? Someone who had unwittingly discovered how to dwell in two realities at once? Someone who would thereby be capable of forging a link between two mutually contradictory othernesses? If so, the future could surely hold nothing but the destruction of both, for the inconsistencies between them must inevitably lead to annihilation. A cold-blooded tyrant – someone like the Despot but necessarily more intelligent – might be able to control the fusion of the two othernesses, but if Alyss's thesis were correct and the ReLMS were the introspective fantasies of a sufferer, of a victim . . .

She still had an errand to run.

Tucking the lumpy memory carefully into a breast pocket and moving with something of her accustomed agility for the first time since she had infiltrated Starveling, she shinned rapidly up the ladder.

It was a matt-grey metal door. Stencilled neatly on it was:

THe MASTeRS OFICe!
NOW YOU See Me—
NOW YOU DO

She pushed the door open, and found herself once more in darkness.

7

In the darkness that was the empire of someone else's thoughts . . .

It had all begun so very long ago, of course. Or, no, it hadn't been that long. It was becoming so difficult to tell how long things had lasted.

She shook her head, trying to get rid of the dustiness in her mind.

She had first met He Who Leads two years ago – no, longer, must have been three or more. Through all of her life until then she'd lived hazily from one moment to the next – literally. She'd been a prostitute somewhere down near Qazar Harbour, touting around for any hirsute sailor that might take her. And it was all very odd, because she had a vague half-memory that, the waking-period before, she'd been an Ellonian princess, picking and choosing among the many admirably qualified suitors who came here to the palace. But that might have been a false memory, of course: maybe she'd been a prostitute for all of her life. Yet she hadn't felt like a woman of broad experience . . . nor like a virgin, which was what the royal princesses were decreed to be.

Lian had discovered her on the docks. She'd been looking out over the river waters, watching the sunlight being scattered by the ripples and thinking about . . .

No, that wasn't the truth at all. Albion had no docks where prostitutes could hang around, leaning against the wall and taunting the passers-by with suggestions about their virility or lack of it. She'd been a princess. She'd been strolling in the forest one time when she'd . . .

She had no clear remembrance of that, either. All she could remember was the times she'd had with Lian, either just the two of them or riding beside him at the head of his army, the army that he'd raised among the people of Albion to challenge the ancient tyranny of the Ellonia.

The Sun was a white-hot disc at the zenith. She veiled her eyes to look at it, ignoring the crescendo of sound from within the palace. A dark speck moving across the dazzling light was a high-flying bird, its destination unknown to her. She settled down so that she was almost lying, only her head supported by the stones, her knees exposed to the air just as they had been that long-ago night – when she had been exercising one of the privileges of her regality by exploring the dockland area of Qazar Harbour, her merchant father having given her his smiling approval.

And a voice had said: 'Tell me that you are not evil.'

She had said: 'I touch nothing, so I cannot be evil.'

She was a princess. She was of the Ellonia.

'There is no evil in touching.'

'Of course there is. But a nice evil.'

She was a whore.

'Forget this.'

'There's nothing to be forgotten,' she said lightly. And there hadn't been – because until now she hadn't been able to remember anything.

'Who are you?'

'Syor,' she had said into the darkness.

'My name is Lian,' he had said. 'You and I will have great joy before we die.'

'What kind of a name is "Lian"?' she had said.

'The name I was given by my mother,' he said.

She picked idly at an old scab on her calf.

'It's because of my hair,' he had said.

Then he had come out into the light in front of her, so that she could see him properly. He was of no more than average height, but he was very stocky; standing there in the docks that had never existed except in the imaginings that she was now experiencing, a distance away from him, she could feel his weight. His blond hair rattled down over his shoulders. He was wearing a leather vest, short leather trousers and very little else except for a scabbard at his belt; the hilt of the sword was covered in gimcrack jewels.

He had smiled at her.

'Syor,' he had said, 'you and I, we'll conquer all of Albion.'

Only . . .

Only that hadn't been the way it had happened at all.

She recalled having been at a curtained ball, watching detachedly as the merry young women had, one by one, peeled off into the gardens with the merry young men. There had been hustle and bustle all around her, and the flickering hot lights from the candelabra had glinted into her eyes, so that she had had to half-close them, as if – but only as if – she had been squinting at the sintered reflection of the Sun on the choppy water of a river in spate . . .

He had approached her then. He was dressed in the most exquisite satin from slim shoulders to elegantly pointed shoes. His beard had been neatly trimmed; the hairs of it were finely spun bronze. The opulent stones on his black velvet scabbard and on the hilt of his sword had shone like stars, twinkling in the candlelight. His froth of fair hair had seemed to fill all of her vision as he had bowed, dropping onto one knee in front of her, removing a brown cap that held an impossibly long feather.

And his voice had said: 'Tell me that you are not evil.'

She had said: 'I touch nothing, so I cannot be evil.'

She was a whore, you see . . .

Her father had nudged her, hiccupping at the same time so that the mouthful of red wine he had just taken spurted out from his lips, spraying down over his own white robes, and her white robes, and the face of the man in front of her.

The stains looked like blood.

'I touch nothing,' she had repeated.

'Touch me.'

Ignoring the splattered wine – ignoring the angry glare of her father – he had reached out his hand towards her, the rings on his fingers glowing in soft, fiery colours, like dying embers. And she had reached out her own thin hand, her arm so white that it silenced the din of the musicians and merrymakers, and their fingers had interlaced . . .

And that wasn't it either.

They'd met some other way.

She was neither princess nor harlot: she knew this for a fact.

She had been . . .

And there *was an interesting conundrum. Who had she been? Her memories of the time before Lian were better than most, but . . .*

No, she hadn't been a princess. If she'd been a princess she'd be able to remember things more clearly now.

A scream came from behind her, penetrating through all the others to which she had long inured herself. She let her green eyes scan the landscape in front of her, seeing the soft, feminine curves of the hills and the scrubby patches of forest embracing them. Giorran, the palace-fortress of the Ellonia, had been built on a high point. Ditches had been dug around it, longer ago than even the Ellonia could remember, so that attacking armies would be fatally slowed. There had only ever been the one attacking army, of course: the one led by her mate and herself.

Lian.

Lian was dying.

She was alive.

The surviving guards of the Ellonia were being put to the sword by her lover's mercenaries; in due course, she knew, they themselves would be put to death as the House of Ellon exacted its vengeance for this impertinence.

Lian was dying.

The worst of it was that she didn't care.

The Sun seemed to have become a swollen orange bag. The sky was filled with an unhappy mixture of reds and blues and greens. Peace was smearing towards her from all the land of Albion . . .

8

Alyss, reeling, sent a tendril of thought into the darkness.

Syor?

Yes. The response was very muted, almost undetectable.

That was when Lian was killed, wasn't it?

Yes. Again Alyss had to strain to pick up the wisp of thought.

You never got over your grief for him, did you? You told yourself that you had, that you'd found new love in Reen and in Anya – and of course you had – but it wasn't ever quite enough to replace what you'd had with Lian . . . because you couldn't allow it to be, in the same way that, even when he was still alive, you made sure that your emotions towards him remained ambivalent as a means of protecting yourself. If you'd been able to permit yourself to feel proper grief when the Ellonia killed him, then perhaps it would have been different, but instead you let the grief stay inside you, growing like a shell around your love for Lian, isolating it, so that it couldn't develop and become a part of the love that you felt for the other two.

Yes. There was the catching of a tear in the faint assent.

Yet you loved all of Albion enough that, even though you chose to end your own existence in its otherness, you bore out of it a version of the country's own memory?

I did. Everything I loved seemed doomed to be destroyed, in one way or another. Lian – you know how Lian died. Anya – I could see the marks in her even when she was still a child, and I was both repelled and terrified by the adult she would become. Reen – she kept faith with me, and that was maybe worst of all. Albion – only Albion itself could I love wholeheartedly, without shame or fear, and yet Albion itself was condemned to perpetual suffering under either the Ellonia or, worse, the daughter I'd brought into the World. So it was Albion-the-way-it-should-have-been that I brought with me, and it had become such a part of me that the valkyries of the caverns were unable to expunge it completely from the essence of me.

Alyss sensed a shifting in the darkness, as if Syor's act of confession were making the woman more companionable towards her. *But you could have let it alone*, she thought. *Lots of mortals in the othernesses have odd memories, scattered images that they come across in the less used corners of their minds. Usually all that's happened is that their silent-mind has brought back something unjumbled from one of its dream forays among the othernesses, but sometimes, like you, they've carried a special memory through the barrier between corporeal existences. Whatever the case, most mortals just look on those images as curios – laugh at them, maybe, or exaggerate them, imbuing them with doleful meaning as dire portents of disasters to come. But you, you seem to have retained too many surviving images for that. Or maybe you deliberately worked to piece them together until finally you had a picture of the whole.*

I didn't, came the reply. *They'd have meant nothing to me if it hadn't been for the fact that people from* this *otherness are trying to pull me back through the barrier. It's as if the hem of my dress had caught in the door as I closed it behind me, and they're hauling on the protruding corner of cloth so hard that they're bringing back all the rest of me with it. It's not very pl . . . it can be – painful.*

Alyss considered briefly. She was beginning to understand the nature of Rehan's 'master', but . . .

So you find yourself in two othernesses at once, as it were? she projected. She wondered what it could possibly feel like. Although she was accustomed to making the transitions between the othernesses as mortals might pass through a door from one room to the next, it had never crossed her mind to attempt to be in more than one of them simultaneously. She was sure that she could do it, of course, if she wanted to. She determined to experiment with the notion as soon as she . . . *if* she emerged from Starvling's concentric ReLMS with her abilities intact.

Yes. The focus of me – my physical presence – is elsewhere, but more and more I find myself becoming a part of the World again. And I'm not sure that I want to be. In fact, I know I don't want to be. I'm being driven mad in two different minds – in two different universes – at the same time! I know it must sound like something of a joke to you . . .

Bloody hilarious, thought Alyss sarcastically. She shielded the reflection carefully from any possibility of detection by Syor's consciousness, instead asking her: *Who is it that's doing the pulling you mentioned? How are they doing it? Are they . . . like me, or are they mortals like yourself?*

Oh, came Syor's wistful thought, *they're mortals, all right. Anya is pulling me back through the sheer force of her will. She has determined that my essence is still to be alive within this otherness, and now that she has made up her mind that this is to be so it takes a great effort of self-stabilization on the part of the otherness itself to counter her will. You must know yourself how blind faith can alter reality: consider, then, the power of* focused, directed, deliberate *faith to achieve the same end. And the daughter I bore has become a woman of considerable determination, as I'm sure you must be aware. Even so, Anya on her own wouldn't be capable of disrupting reality this way – no, not on her own. She might cause an eddy on the surface of the ocean of verity, but it would be a very short-term affair, and soon the water would have washed away all traces of the petty swirling. No, she's being assisted, for reasons I can't perceive, by her consort – by Ngur. And Ngur's is the stronger pull.*

Alyss was shocked. *Ngur!*

Yes.

But . . . but that can't be. She'd always dimissed Ngur

as just another ordinary mortal. He had risen to prominence among the Ellonia when that clan had been ruling Albion, and so it had been a fitting resolution of the conflict there when he'd been married off to the triumphant rebel leader, but she'd assumed that by now there'd have been a discreet assassination – an 'accident' – and that Anya would have relieved herself of the encumbrance of his presence. Ngur had never had any magical or mystical potential whatsoever. Even if he'd enlisted the assistance of the most powerful magician in all the World – Alyss sniffed, having little respect for the abilities of mortal magicians – Ngur would have been unable to affect reality at this level, or indeed at *any* level. Trying to inculcate the rudiments of magic into Ngur's essence would be like sowing seeds on sterile ground.

She explained some of this briefly to Syor.

Ngur has a magic you don't understand, Syor replied, *the magic of understanding how people think, of how things want to turn out. He can't himself alter reality, but he can see the way that reality is flowing and the possible courses it might follow in the future, and he can subtly change the prevailing conditions such that the course reality actually* does *take is the one that accords most nearly with what he desires.*

Alyss was fuming. *You say that I can't understand this magic of Ngur's!* she expostulated. *Can't you see that exactly the opposite is true? That's the way that* all *magic works, by persuading reality to adopt a prescribed course, rather than compelling it to do so! Even an individual as powerful as myself can't force reality to do something that it doesn't want to do. Don't be alarmed – it's not you that I'm furious with. It's me. I'm such a blithering, lackwitted fool not to have paid any attention to Ngur's powers of insight. Anyone* can *manipulate reality that way, if they have the insight to realize it. How else do you think the diversity of othernesses are generated?*

She fell to steadfast cursing, drawing upon oaths that were fortunately meaningless to Syor.

Finally Syor intervened shyly. *There's more.*

More? By all the babes as yet unborn, you say there's more*?*

Can't you understand that your status in two othernesses could lead to the destruction of both of them? Isn't that enough for you?

Syor was silent.

I'm sorry, said Alyss after a time. *Tell me. Let's get it over with.*

I'm with someone else, now, in my new otherness, who I used to know when I was in the World. He has no knowledge of this. It's all very difficult. He was my enemy in the World, you see, and yet here he's the same person – not only does he bear the same name, but he has all the same characteristics, so that I'd know it was him even if I didn't know, if you see what I mean – only here it's as if an artist had tried to make the same painting twice: even though everything about him's the same, he's different as well. Here he's my friend. Here he may become my lover.

Who is he? spat Alyss.

Nadar.

There was a long pause before Alyss sighed: *Oh, shit.*

I thought you were going to say something a lot worse than that, thought Syor tremulously. *I thought . . .*

Oh, shut up for a moment, can't you. I want to do some thinking - private *thinking.*

There was too much going on for Alyss's liking, too many 'coincidences', as mortals described the acausal principles which largely governed the othernesses. In all the infinity of universes within the polycosmos, the chances of two mortals who'd known each other in one incarnation reappearing subsequently in the same otherness was minuscule. The likelihood that they should do so at the same chronological time was vanishingly small. The possibility of them *meeting* . . . even Alyss's mathematics quailed at the idea of a number so close to the infinitesimal – the Absolute Zero of statistics. So there had to be some guiding principle at work, which would imply that forces of at least similar magnitude to her own were interfering with the customary acausal running of the othernesses. Who/what could they possibly be? And, ignoring that fundamental question for the moment, if it were indeed the case that they were in operation, how many further as yet undiscovered 'coincidences' might she find screwing up the non-pattern of reality? *Three coincidental incarnations in an afterlife?*

And all this had been going on while she'd been idly farting about in an otherness so remote from this one – and, evidently, from Syor's – that matter took the form of musical phrases. She damned herself a thousand times over for having indulged herself for so long, basking relaxedly among . . .

Music.

Why Rehan? she thought suddenly towards Syor. *Why is it his mind that you've chosen to take over?*

There was no choosing in it. I found myself here. I believe it was because, in one of the ways that I saw Lian, he had a long feather in his hat. And, when I came across Rehan, he too had a feather. I think there was nothing more complicated to it than that. I think it must have been the feather that caught the hem of my dress as I was travelling into the next otherness. Or something. Maybe it was because his mind was free, too: with nothing but the bradz inside it, he wasn't really using it himself. There was room for a squatter.

Rehan, thought Alyss, *was a fine mortal, if that isn't a contradiction in terms. Did you have to destroy him?*

I don't think I have. He felt me arrive, you know, and he welcomed me. He knew who I was, and he realized how much my essence needed protection from the World outside. It was at his suggestion that we began to construct the seven ReLMS. Only then . . . only then, as we worked, he somehow came to be excluded from them, so that for a long time he's been locked out of Starveling, not knowing how to get in, while me, I've been alone inside Starveling, not knowing how to open up its portals to let him in. I could go outside to join him, I suppose, but then what would happen if neither of us could work out how to open the gates?

Well, thought Alyss, *that much I can help you with. Take me outside Starveling and I can do the rest for you. Take me outside Starveling anyway – what you've told me is terrifying. There are things I'm going to have to do to try to repair the damage you and Anya and Ngur have been doing – or at least to ameliorate its consequences – and I'm not going to be able to do them if I'm stuck in here for the rest of time.*

Oh, came Syor's thought, sounding like a young girl's laugh, *I can lead you outside if you wish. Take my hand and we can leave immediately.*

No – no, wait just a moment more. Tell me just one more thing before we go.

What?

The sixth HeLL. I don't understand it. In all the others I was humiliated in some sense or another, but in the sixth all that happened to me was that a big gorilla of a man asked me to come up here to be with you. I can understand why this place we're in now is the seventh HeLL, because it's the HeLL of your existence – and, come to that, I've been humiliated here, too, in a way. But the sixth? It seemed all right to me. A bit noisy and messy, but . . .

Ah, the sixth HeLL. Syor's thought was a drape of sorrow. *The sixth HeLL is the most tragic of all of them.*

Alyss was silent, waiting for an explanation. In the end she said: *Why?*

Because, Syor replied, *it's the HeLL that hasn't happened yet.*

9

The three of them stood outside Starveling's main gate. The crystals of the road were hurting the soles of Alyss's feet like perdition; guiltily she hoped that the same was true for Syor and Rehan as well, so that she wouldn't be the only one. She looked down. Hmmm. If she'd still had a cloven foot, that might have reduced the pain by a full fifty per cent.

The paper gate was still ajar, and Alyss led them through the courtyard of flowering light, luxuriating once more in the sensation of her healed feet. The trompe l'oeil doorway had been repaired, and the two mortal essences gasped as she showed them that the brilliantly executed paintwork was indeed nothing more than that. Rehan tried to tear it with his fingers, as she instructed him, but the doorway might as well have been constructed of metal bars for all the difference it made; Syor, too, was powerless to rip it.

So Alyss pulled away the paper, piling it up in big tattered scrolls behind her as she worked. It seemed to take much longer than she'd expected, and certainly the quantities of torn pieces were much greater than she'd have thought possible, but at last the job was done. Looking around, she saw a poppy's hot flower and, after speaking very respectfully to the pattern of light of which it was a part, she took a single petal and brought it to the heap of tatters and kissed it into flame.

The white smoke was rising steadily over the battlements of Starveling to lighten the sky as Rehan and Syor re-entered their ReLMS together. When they glanced back through the doorway that would now remain forever open they saw that Alyss had already left.

Chapter Five
The Anonymous City

1

Gnetz looked up as the door opened.

The place was still called One-Legged Tom's Kitchen, out of an ironic respect for its one-time owner, who had long ago vanished – some said on the arm of a beautiful young maiden to seek his fortunes with her in a faraway land: Albion, if the rumours were to be believed. Gnetz and his allies among the Vermin took care never to contradict such tales, although jokes about One-Legged Tom's toughness had enjoyed a temporary vogue among them. There was a new man to cook the food now. Sometimes the customers were served by One-Legged Tom's daughter, Kursten, whom most of them assumed now to be the proprietor; but more often she was upstairs, plying her primary trade on a well used bed. She had become a well-to-do woman, over the months since her father's departure, and would even have been a wealthy one had her customers' assumptions been correct. If there was an occasional wistfulness in her gaze, it was well disguised.

Tonight business was good. There had been an execution earlier in the day, and so a band of the more courageous youths from the richer suburbs had dared to venture into the slums so that in days to come they could shock their elders by recounting their exploits among the city's scum. Besides, the new cook had a more expert hand with the stews than One-Legged Tom could ever have aspired to, and the reputation of the food had crept out of the slums like the vapour drifting away from one of his pots. The young men were laughing and joking too loudly, smacking their lips with impossible relish, secure in the knowledge that, while they were far from invulnerable to a concerted attack, the Vermin would never dare to harm a group of this size: one wealthy scion lost could be written off as misadventure, but the disappearance of a score or more might attract attention.

The man standing in the doorway was dimly familiar to Gnetz. He was nearing middle age but held himself more like a young man, as if his mind had somehow forgotten to age along with the rest of him; yet the lines on his weatherbeaten face and the depths of his gaze as he scanned the room seemed more weary than time. Perhaps long ago his clothing had been of highest quality, his dark cape much more finely woven than any fabric Gnetz had seen before, but now it was torn in many places and the few patches that had been crudely applied were of sacking. His boots, Gnetz's expert eye observed, were made of real leather, but they were barely holding together; perhaps they had been stolen from a rich man's midden. At his belt there was the clumsy pommel of a sword, but otherwise he seemed to be unarmed except for the customary dagger that everybody wore; also tucked into his belt, alongside his money-pouch, was a flute new cut from a reed that still showed traces of green along its shining length. So the man was a singer. On his head was a battered green hat – and Gnetz caught his breath. There was something missing from the hat, and for the moment Gnetz couldn't think what it might be: surely it was anyway a nonsense to be trying to guess what was absent from a stranger's hat?

A feather.

A broken feather.

'Oh, shit,' breathed Gnetz at his gravy. He glanced up to see if Egroeg had registered the arrival, but the big man was concentrating his attention on the antics of the buffoons in the far corner.

Gnetz reached out furtively and tapped him on the arm.

'What?' said Egroeg, turning towards him reluctantly.

'Don't make a commotion about it,' said Gnetz peevishly.

The broad brow furrowed. 'Dunno what not to make commotion about,' grumbled Egroeg, but mercifully he kept his voice low.

Someone else had followed the singer – the bastard, shit-sucking singer who should have been dead by now – in through the doorway. It was a woman, and she was standing on the slightly raised entrance platform a metre or two apart from her companion and a little behind him. She had silvery grey hair and there was more about her that betrayed her age, yet time had chosen kindly when selecting lines to carve upon her face; her body, so far as Gnetz could judge, wasn't that of a girl or even of a young woman, yet it was perfectly poised, and there was a confidence in the way that she held her arms that indicated that she was in complete control of it. Her eyes were very dark and very alive as they took in the details of the Kitchen and its raucous clientele. She had a dagger casually in one hand, another protruding above the lip of her boot, a bow slung around her shoulders and a sword that looked much used at her belt. Those were the weapons he could see.

'D'you remember the singer?' he hissed to Egroeg. 'You know,' he added as the giant's face looked confused, 'the one who stopped the ffarg from . . .' He nodded towards the cracked ceiling, beyond which Kursten was presumably bringing shoddy joy to someone.

Revelation lit up Egroeg's face. 'You mean the weedy . . . ?' he began.

'Shut up!' said Gnetz urgently, grabbing him by the front of his waistcoat. Then, in a less agitated voice: 'Don't look, but he's behind you.'

To Gnetz's astonishment Egroeg didn't turn his head. 'Should've killed him,' he said. 'Thought so at the time. Should've. 'S he alone, or has he got cronies?'

'There's a woman with him.' Gnetz was using the big man's head as a shield around which he could glance occasionally at the two newcomers. No one else seemed to be paying them any notice except Focks, the cook, who was wiping his greasy hands on his apron and looking backwards and forwards between the strangers and Gnetz's table, as if asking silently for guidance.

'Ha!' said Egroeg. 'Just a fuckin' woman. This time we kill him, like we should've earlier. Wench can help out Kursten during the rush-hour.'

'Not this one,' said Gnetz. 'She's a bit long in the tooth for one thing, and . . . and I wouldn't like to take her on in a fair fight.'

'Who said anything 'bout a fair fight?' whispered Egroeg, beginning to giggle silently.

'She doesn't look the type who'd fight fair anyway,' responded Gnetz impatiently, his mind more on the movements of the singer and his companion. The two of them were advancing down the aisle between the crowded tables, looking this way and that, the woman aimlessly turning the dagger in her hand so that from time to time its blade caught the yellow light from the wall-torches; she maintained her apparently subservient position a metre or so to the singer's rear. Gnetz could see that all the while she was prepared to spin around should she hear some untoward noise behind her. Now some of the diners were beginning to be distracted by the pair's arrival, and were looking up at them in vague perplexity – not yet alarmed, but not wholly at ease either. One or two hands clasped a little more firmly around sharp eating-knives, just as a precaution.

Focks gave Gnetz one last despairing gape and then hurried forwards.

'We have little room tonight,' he blustered, gesturing around him. 'Loath though I am to turn away such fine-looking customers as yourselves . . .'

'We're not hungry,' said the woman, very precisely. Although her voice was quite quiet it was enough to silence most of the merry-makers near to her. Again there was that restless motionlessness as more of the Vermin put their palms to their weapons.

'Then . . .' stammered Focks.

'There was a woman here,' said the singer. 'It was . . . a time ago. When I was last here.' Vagueness darted across his eyes and was gone. 'Her name was Kursten. The daughter of an old man with a leg missing. She's who we've come to see. Kursten.'

Focks looked embarrassed. He was quite accustomed to Kursten's clients having to be asked to wait their turn, but this man didn't look like any of her normal purchasers. 'She's . . . she's busy,' he said, waving his hands in a gesture of confusion.

'I would be grateful,' said the singer, 'if you could see your way to unbusying her.' Now his dagger was drawn as well, and Focks looked at it with fascination, unable to drag his eyes away from the bright edge. 'If,' added the stranger with heavy courtesy, 'that wouldn't be too much trouble.'

'I . . . I can't disturb her,' Focks wailed. 'It's just not possible.' He darted another look at Gnetz, pleading to be let off the hook; he was a cook, his eyes were saying, not a protector.

Barra 'ap Rteniadoli Me'gli'minter Rehan's eyes followed the nervous cook's glance, and a smile came to his face as he recognized Gnetz. 'Please inform Kursten that she has guests who would wish to speak with her,' he said more animatedly to Focks, brushing the man aside with a neat motion of his shoulder. 'My friend and I will be able to find plenty to occupy our attention until she is ready to receive us.'

Mumbling, Focks turned away towards the stairway. He glanced up into the gloom above, then back at the stranger, spreading his hands in an effort to explain his predicament. But the stranger wasn't looking at him, and neither was the bag he'd brought with him; so, after a moment's further consideration, Focks made for his kitchen and its simmering pans. His scuttling walk and the slump of his shoulders were a clear enough message to Gnetz that, whoever's problem this might be, it was no longer the cook's.

'Well met!' cried Rehan, putting one hand on Egroeg's shoulder as if it were a piece of the furniture. The vast man, grimacing furiously at Gnetz, kept his face turned away from Rehan's sight.

Gnetz half-stood, forcing himself to adopt the comradely smile of someone greeting a casual acquaintance. He extended his right hand, ostentatiously empty; the woman's eyes were alternating between his face and the place under his cloak where his left hand was concealed. He knew that she was watching for the tiny involuntary contractions of his facial muscles that would precede any sudden movement.

Rehan ignored the proffered hand; he too was evidently more concerned about the hidden one. There was a pool of anxious quietness around them now, and it was slowly spreading out across the rest of the room as ruffians and dandies alike felt the tension emanating from the little group.

'Would you care to join us, old chum?' said Gnetz, his low voice seemingly unperturbed. 'I've finished eating, myself, and Egroeg here' – an acknowledging nod – 'has as good as; but we'll willingly raise a flagon or two of wine with yourself and your merrywoman. Budge up, Egroeg, budge up; make a little space for an old friend and a new one. Budge up, I say.'

'I'd starve before I ate with you,' said Rehan lightly. 'I'd starve before I ate what you were eating. I'd rather eat your shit than share your company.'

Egroeg growled. In the warren of the Anonymous City no one dared to speak to the boss like that.

Gnetz stilled him with a flick of his hand. 'You have lost your courtesy, singer,' he observed mildly.

'I have lost much else besides, this past year or more, thanks to you,' said Rehan. Both of them were speaking as casually as if the topic were the price of horseflesh. 'I might have lost everything had it not been for . . . some friends.'

Gnetz's eyes moved towards the woman. A less wary eye would have thought that she was relaxing. 'Not many friends,' he said.

'Three of us,' said Rehan. 'Enough.'

'I can see only the two.'

'But we are three.'

Some of the youths from the suburbs were

inconspicuously slipping out through the door, leaving reckonings unpaid. Blood was fine in its proper place, on the executioners' dais; pain was just as fine, when it wasn't theirs.

For the first time Gnetz looked disconcerted. His eyes flickered around the watching faces suspiciously, trying to see if there might be a sniper or a backstabber among them. He cursed the fact that there were so many rich layabouts in the place tonight; it would have been easy enough for an assassin to slip in, camouflaged by their overdemonstrative amity. He felt a little tickling sensation on his spine, just between his shoulderblades; it was lucky that, as always, he'd chosen to sit with his back to the wall.

'Your friend is well hidden,' he said.

Rehan nodded slightly. 'You could say that.'

'I'll take the big one,' said the woman impatiently. 'You can cope with this little ferret on your own, Rehan, can you not?'

'No,' said the singer. He held up a decisive hand. 'No – we came for Kursten, not for these turds. If we could hope to change a whole city, I'd take great pleasure in seeing them die, but we can't so it's not worth killing them. They'd only be replaced by some even viler species.'

'You've come a long way to insult me,' said Gnetz, clasping his hands easily over his stomach and rocking backwards and forwards on the balls of his feet. Reen's eyes narrowed, and she stopped turning the knife in her hand.

Egroeg's patience suddenly expired, and he erupted to his feet, twisting as he rose, throwing Rehan a couple of paces backwards.

'You bastards,' yelled the giant into a suddenly quiet room. He reached for his sword.

Reen's dagger, moving more quickly than seemed possible, pounced at him and sliced through the sleeve of his hessian jacket and across the tendons on the inside of his elbow. Egroeg let out a bellow of anger and agony and clutched his left hand to the sudden flush of blood. All around, chairs scraped backwards and toppled onto the floor; perhaps two-thirds of the diners, including all of the slummers, made a charge for the door. The remainder, the Vermin, moved swiftly and quietly into positions where they could use their now-drawn daggers and swords freely.

'That was a mite premature, Reen,' murmured the singer. 'Remind me to have a word with you one day about your impetuosity.'

'You won't *see* another day!' spat Gnetz.

Egroeg, moaning, sat down on his bench with a thump.

'Go,' said Reen curtly to the Vermin surrounding them. 'Get out of here. This isn't your quarrel. This is strictly between us and the little rat.'

Gnetz noticed that she discounted Egroeg. That might prove a dangerous mistake, if only the great bovine hulk could stop fussing like a child over his scratch and start pulling himself together.

Some of the Vermin looked at her, at the blood running down the blade of her dagger; and turned to go. Others were more courageous and stood their ground, but it was obvious that even they were apprehensive. It was rare in the Anonymous City for a woman to dare to strike a man, still rarer for one of the cunts to possess a weapon and know how to use it. They were frightened not just by her dagger but also by the alienness of it all.

'Get a move on, you cretins!' she snapped.

Some of them shuffled away and out into the night, looking at anything except Gnetz's accusatory stare.

'Nice to have a bit more air to breathe in here,' said Rehan pleasantly.

'Haven't you lot got wives and families to be getting on home to?' said Reen to the remaining Vermin. 'No, come to that, I don't suppose you have. Can't imagine any woman wanting to bed one of you lot and, even if there were such a pudding-brain, she couldn't make children on her own, could she? I bet there isn't one of you knows how to . . .'

A flick of an angry hand towards the pommel of a sword. Even faster, Reen's hand throwing her dagger; she stooped to tug its mate from her boot and was standing alert again by the time the fool felt a sudden pain in his shoulder and realized that her blade had stabbed right through the muscle, just under his armpit.

'Tut,' she said as he bellowed in agony. 'I'll trouble you to return my knife to me before you go, if I may.'

There were only four of the Vermin left now. Silently Gnetz swore all sorts of hideous revenge on those who had deserted him. Egroeg sobbed, his shoulders jerking. Rehan's eyes had not left Gnetz's face.

A clatter and a curse. The last of the Vermin, holding his shoulder and glaring resentfully at the woman, had thrown her dagger at her feet. He cursed her again as he disappeared through the door.

'So now it's three against two,' said Reen lazily. In a single movement she returned one dagger to her boot and picked the other up from the floor.

'I will kill you,' said Gnetz, stating fact. 'Not now, perhaps, but soon.'

'We only came to see Kursten,' said Rehan, almost apologetically. 'If your friend here hadn't made such a palaver out of our perfectly reasonable request, we might have been gone by now. With Kursten, of course. Where is she, by the way? I do very much hope she's well.'

Gnetz let a smile shape his mouth. 'She's the best fuck in the Anonymous City. Which is not a compliment I bestow lightly. Everyone else agrees with me.'

Rehan slapped him, hard, across the face. For a few seconds Gnetz could see nothing but a blackly, redly pulsing cloud. His jaw felt as if it had been broken; he dropped forwards, supporting his weight with one hand on the tabletop in front of him while the other went up to his face. There was blood in his mouth from where one of his few surviving molars had champed viciously down on the side of his tongue.

'I wish you hadn't done that,' he said, his words slurred.

It was as if he'd given a cue to Egroeg. Not even Reen had noticed that the giant's moans had trailed away during the past minute or so. Now Egroeg was roaring to his feet once more, in his left hand the knife he had been eating with earlier; as he waved it wildly to and fro, droplets of sticky brown gravy flew through the air.

Rehan stepped back.

The giant's red eyes were focused implacably on his throat. He brought up his own dagger to defend himself, taking yet another backwards pace. He didn't hear Reen shout a warning to him; he wasn't aware of the sudden movement hidden from him by Egroeg's huge, blood-streaked body. Suddenly the knife was swinging around towards him, as if Egroeg thought he was handling a cutlass rather than a dirk. He dropped his own hand a little, instinctively, and the two blades missed each other by a hair's-breadth; however, the edge of the great fist caught the back of Rehan's knuckles, jarring him all the way up his arm. His dagger shot from his hand, skittering away across the floor to be lost from view under one of the rough-hewn benches. He staggered, half-twisting his body as if to dive after it before he realized that it'd be futile to try. He fell onto his hands and knees, his head up, looking at the colossal silhouette of Egroeg as the man raised his meaty arm high, the dagger like a toy in his hand – a sharp toy, directed downwards. Awkwardly Rehan wormed away, reaching up onto a nearby tabletop, groping for any implement that someone might have left behind. His foot caught on the leg of a stool, slowing him down just enough that Egroeg's enraged kick missed him; the vast boot whistled by directly in front of his face. His hand had found something – a heavy wooden platter. Left-handed, he hurled it upwards at the giant, not in any hope of hurting him but simply in an attempt to distract him. The plate missed; Egroeg seemed not to notice it fly past him. The Vermin's lips were drawn back to reveal an irregular line of blackened, broken and missing teeth; Rehan knew his foe was smiling in anticipated triumph, ready to administer the final blow. His fumbling hand again found something on the table, this time a knife, but it was going to be too late because Egroeg had caught his balance once more after his failed kick and was readying himself to plunge his dirk downwards, his eyes wet with glee . . .

And then Egroeg's expression changed to one of wonderment. For a moment Rehan saw how the man must have looked when he was still an infant, before the bestialities of daily life in the rat-runs of the Anonymous City had had a chance to turn him into what he had become. The evil, malevolent joy cleared from the big man's face like a streak wiped from a windowpane with a single sweep of the cloth; and in its place there was suddenly a radiant innocence. His dirk dropped from his hand, narrowly missing Rehan's arm as it fell to the floor; the pain at his elbow forgotten, Egroeg raised both hands as if to cover his face in the presence of some vast and benevolent brilliance.

Then, slowly, like someone trying to dance underwater, he collapsed forwards across the backs of Rehan's legs. The huge form twitched once, twice; a cupful of blood flowed almost coyly from the Vermin's still gently smiling mouth; and finally there was stillness.

Rehan, his eyes fixed on the dagger jutting out from Egroeg's back, with difficulty extricated his feet from under the heavy corpse.

'He's gone,' Reen said. 'The little one – Gnetz.'

She was sitting on the far side of a table, her elbows on it, looking at him calmly as he picked himself up.

'It's a pity that I had to kill the lard-tub,' she said, 'but I didn't have time to aim a blow that'd only disable him. We might have been able to get out of him where Gnetz could have fled to – any favourite rat-holes the scum might have.'

Rehan's mind was slowly beginning to function again.

'There's still the cook,' he said, gesturing towards the kitchen at the rear.

'Not worth it,' said Reen flatly. 'He's either a craven or he's the wisest man in the whole of this stinking city, depending on your point of view. Myself, I subscribe to the latter opinion, but no matter. If he's still there – which I sincerely doubt he's stupid enough to be – he'd tell us whatever he thought we wanted to hear, which'd be bugger all use to us because of course we wouldn't know which bits of it, if any, were the truth. Leave him be.'

Ignoring her final remark, Rehan swiftly checked the kitchen. Sure enough, the window was open; there was no sign of Focks. The singer smiled as he saw that the heat under the pots had been carefully damped down; clearly Focks was a cook first and a fugitive afterwards.

'Damn,' he said, putting no power into the oath. 'Any good ideas? Reen?'

She shook her head.

'Syor?' he said.

His face changed. The shape of his mouth became quite different as another voice, with the same timbre as his own but otherwise utterly unlike it, spoke. The effect was as if a musician from a foreign land had suddenly, mid-phrase, taken over the playing of an instrument.

'The girl,' said the third of them, speaking the words aloud for Reen's benefit. 'Kursten. She may still be in the building somewhere. When you asked the cook about her he checked the stairs.'

'Ever felt thick?' said Reen.

'Yes,' Rehan replied briskly. He emerged from under a table, holding his knife as if it were an heirloom. 'Lots of times. But not usually that thick.'

'Hello, Barra 'ap Rteniadoli Me'gli'minter Rehan,' said a woman's voice from the stairway.

2

It had been Alyss who'd told the three of them, rather crossly, to go to the Anonymous City. Reen and Alven had been watching her during the few minutes she'd been exploring the ReLMS: both she and the recumbent Rehan had held absolutely motionless for that short time, so that only the ebbing and flowing of the fire's glow and its lazily rising grey-white feathers of smoke had destroyed the illusion that they were elements of a startlingly vivid painting. Then Alyss had moved, lurching forwards abruptly before catching herself; at the same moment Rehan, too, had stirred – only a flexing of the shoulders, but nevertheless a clear sign to Reen that the man's consciousness was returning to him.

His own consciousness.

But, as Reen had soon discovered, not *just* his own consciousness. While Alyss had tottered off, her arms thrown around Alven's shoulders for support – it was the first time that Reen had ever seen the girl seem in any way physically affected by her exertions – Rehan had begun to talk. At first his words had been incomprehensible, but at last he had responded to her entreaties to slow down a bit. It had been then that she'd recognized the prime cause of his jumbled speech: there had been two independent voices competing for control of his lips and tongue, both of them trying to greet her in their own different ways. At last Reen, feeling like a dominie attempting to control a class of rowdy infants, had slapped her hands together and somehow restored order. After a few moments' internal debate, the singer – the angle of his shoulders showing that for the moment he was robust with freshly rediscovered self-confidence, that he was Barra 'ap Rteniadoli Me'gli'minter Rehan, rather than just plain Rehan – had started to give her a sketchy account of Alyss's venturings inside him. He had talked in terms of half-perceived probings succeeded by sudden reawakenings of aspects of his former self. Once, grinning, he had compared the experience to a first lovemaking, in the darkness, after a long period of abstinence, when unseen hands suddenly touch forgotten places, sparking off sensual reactions that derive their intensity from the fact that, like a flash-flood, they are pursuing long-dusty courses. And then, in another moment, he had talked of being locked in an unlit room and watching as the windows were abruptly thrown open, one by one, with no pattern to their opening. Reen had followed his account as best she could; smiling affectionately at his eagerness, she'd reached a hand out over the warm embers to touch his arm, reminding him that she was still there.

After a long while Rehan had given up the reins of his speech to the other occupant of Starveling, and Syor had spoken to Reen for the first time in many years. There had been tears in the woman's clumsy voice as she'd told Reen what it had *really* been like, of the alien ReLMS that she'd discovered when first she'd found herself within Rehan's awareness, and of how she'd moulded them until they were more in accordance with her own perceptions; until Alyss had ventured in through the seemingly impregnable walls of Starveling to quest through the six outer HeLLS until at last she'd encountered Syor lurking in the gloom of the seventh. And Syor had told Reen of other things, too; scenes that were drawn not from the seven ReLMS but from somewhere utterly outwith Reen's experience, a place where giant animals of iron rent the skies with their roaring, where the people swarmed in crowds and the ground was stone, where a created time had usurped the body's own, where superhuman enchanters cast their tenuous simulacra to weave webs all around the world and so ensnare the minds of mortals, where . . .

Reen had held her hands up, laughing as she'd begged Syor to stop. Had she been able to assimilate the half of all these images, she knew, she'd have found them rich and wondersome; but her mind, paralysed by the onrushing torrent, had scrambled back to dry land. 'Tell me more slowly – tell me another day,' Reen had said, both of them knowing that she meant 'never'.

They hadn't seen Alven or Alyss all morning. Hand in hand, the three of them had strolled around aimlessly, talking to each other and sometimes to the sheep. Once, Reen had found herself being embraced, avid lips prying against her mouth, but she hadn't known whose lips they were and so, embarrassedly, she'd shoved Rehan's body away from her. She'd realized then that the time must inevitably come when they would make love, and the notion had frightened her and fascinated her in equal measure; she'd resolved to postpone the moment of discovery for as long as she could, until her mind had had the opportunity to accept that the hand now once again resting quiescent in hers belonged not to one but to two of the few people she had loved.

Later, with the Sun an hour or more past the zenith, she'd killed a rabbit – feeling almost guilty as she did so, for the creatures had been all over the hillside and were so unafraid of humans as to be almost tame – and they'd gathered around the refuelled fire to cook its tough flesh on the points of sharpened sticks. Even Alyss had joined in the meal, which had surprised Reen: she knew that Alyss had no nutritional need of the food, and had wondered if the girl were eating with them as an expression of companionship or if the very act of devouring satisfied some more spiritual hunger.

Then, wiping the juices from her lips, Alyss had begun to talk intensely to Syor, pointedly leaving Reen, Alven and Rehan out of the conversation. Able to understand very little of what was being said, Reen had wandered off, followed by the boy, who was keen to hear more of her exploits in far lands where creatures even wilder than the alliberi roamed.

The afternoon had passed rapidly.

Blinded by invented marvels, unaware of all that had been going on around him, the boy had left them at dusk, but not before extracting from them the promise that they would still be there when he returned the following morning.

That night Alyss and Syor between them had tried to explain to Reen and Rehan what was concerning them. Even though they'd used easy words and were obviously going to considerable lengths to try to simplify the situation, Reen had very soon found herself floundering in a pool of concepts that were entirely alien to her; however hard she'd tried to reach out and catch hold of their misty shapes, they'd remained stubbornly indefinite, seeming to wait for her fingers with mischievous pleasure before, just as she'd begun to believe that they were within her grip, slipping off from her in some way that she couldn't properly see.

When finally they'd given up, all that Reen had gathered was that an integral part of Syor was somewhere else. This part, it had been patiently explained, was not Syor's body: Syor's body had long since rotted away in an unmarked grave near some nameless village in Albion. At the same time, though, it was intimately connected with Syor's body – her different body, which she was occupying in the different place. At first Reen had baulked at the notion that a single person could tenant two separate bodies, but then she realized that it was no more arcane a concept than that of two people occupying a single body, as Rehan and Syor were currently doing; if she could accept one of these circumstances as a reality then it was illogical of her peremptorily to reject the other. But such acceptance hadn't made the idea of the 'somewhere else' any easier to grasp. In the end she'd conceived of it as being rather like the places she'd created for Alven and herself during the afternoon; and Alyss, looking at her with bright eyes, had nodded and said that that was as good an explanation as any.

The idea's extension, that Syor's presence both in the World and in the 'somewhere else' was dragging the two locations together in such a way that their fusion must lead to the destruction of both, had held no meaning at all for Reen that she could analyse in any way, much less imagine the physical consequences. It had been put inside a separate room in her mind's library; every now and then the librarian might pass the closed door and try to recall exactly what was behind it, but the librarian would always be busy about other, more demanding business, and so there'd never be time to stop, to open the door, to take the books down from their shelves and attempt to decipher their outlandish script.

She'd been able to understand, however, that Alyss intended to travel to the different place where the missing part of Syor was dwelling and there attempt to draw the two components back together again. Whether this reunion would be in the other place or here in the World, Reen couldn't quite make out; she'd tried to get Alyss to clarify, but the girl had been evasive, and Reen had concluded that she didn't know either. It had been pleasing to discover that Alyss was capable of the human failing of indecision.

'If I bring the other soul of Syor here,' Alyss had said enigmatically, 'I may bring others with her.'

She'd refused to expand on that remark, and Rehan's puzzled expression showed that he, too, hadn't known what Alyss was talking about. Reen had watched him closely as he'd silently asked Syor to explain; then the muscles in his face had abruptly clamped tight, as if his request for explanation had been curtly refused.

Reen hadn't thought too much further about it. In the midst of so many impenetrables, what difference did an extra one make?

But she'd been eager enough to find out how long Alyss planned to be away from them.

'I don't know,' the small woman had said acidly, her mouth crooked with frustration. 'It's difficult for me to calculate,' she'd added, 'because of the way time is constructed within the polycosmos.'

Reen had effectively switched off at that point, listening to Alyss's convoluted words as if they'd been pretty but forgettable tunes. There'd been something about how there was a greater time that functioned within the interstices between the shadow-universes, and of how the lesser times that operated inside the universes themselves depended from this greater time, so that disparate moments within the lesser times were synchronous in the greater time; Reen's thoughts had become a muddle of times. Alyss had speculated briefly as to whether there might be some kind of supreme time, from which greater time itself depended – or perhaps there might even be a whole hierarchy of times, comprehensible to and surveyable by only the creators. Reen had agreed that this was a mind-rockingly fascinating idea and had put another log on the fire.

The gist of it had been that Alyss expected to return to the World within about six weeks. 'And it'll be in Albion,' she'd added, nodding intently. 'That's where Anya is. That's where Ngur is. I can't yet see the whole of the solution, but I can see enough to know that they must be a part of it. Above all else, I have to try to stop them dragging Syor back into the World the way they're doing. I'll have barriers to repair, if I can, and I won't be able to plug the gaps if those two are splintering them at the edges again the whole time.'

Rehan had bullied her to be more precise about the when and the where, but she'd resisted him. 'It's not that I won't tell you,' she'd explained, as if to a child. 'It's that I can't. But I'll do my best to encounter your silent-minds, individually or together, on the nights when they're exploring the othernesses; I'll tell you that way. Trust me.'

'But where?' Reen had insisted. 'At least you could make a stab at telling us that. Albion's a big island, you know. You can't expect us to be everywhere in it at once.'

Alyss had thought for a moment. 'It's hard for me to be exact,' she'd repeated, then raised a palm to forestall their shouts of protest. 'There's a plateau above Giorran; I think some used to call it Giorran-stage. I suppose it's Starveling-stage these days.' She had paused again, as if the name 'Starveling' had come to mean something different to her than merely the fortress and the stage. 'I'll try to make it there that I return. If not, I'll try to give your silent-minds as much warning as I can. It's pleasing,' she'd added, some of her old vigour returning to oust her uncertainty, 'that the three of you are all so concerned for my welfare, and so eager that my absence from you should be as brief as possible. Understandable, of course; but pleasing nonetheless.'

Reen had laughed at the show of vanity.

Alyss hadn't joined in. Instead she'd looked with weasel sharpness at Rehan's smiling face and said: 'This girl of yours. Your floozie in the Anonymous City.'

His grin had vanished.

'Kursten,' he'd said sullenly.

'As it happens,' Alyss had said, grinning, 'it would fit in well with my plans should you choose to return to Albion by way of the Anonymous City. If you care to extend your sojourn there a trifle by rescuing your damsel in distress, Barra 'ap Rteniadoli Me'gli'minter Rehan, then I have no objections. It's up to you if you want to be a shining saviour. She's still alive.'

'Why do you want us to go to the Anonymous City?' Reen had said.

'The ffarg. They puzzle me. Before I had the pleasure of being welcomed to the ReLMS I was more concerned about the "master" whom Rehan kept mentioning to us. The ffarg represented nothing more than a minor riddle. But the very fact that I should find anything at all a riddle, however trivial, is actually a rather large mystery. I would like to speak with one of those creatures, if I might. Befriend one, and bring it to Albion with you.'

'I don't think they much want to be friends,' Rehan had muttered bitterly. 'If you knew as much as I did about them, you'd . . .'

'Oh but Barra 'ap Rteniadoli Me'gli'minter Rehan,' Alyss had said with courteous sarcasm, 'you don't seem to understand that I know considerably more about them than you do. That's why they're a conundrum to me.'

'You want us to try to bring you a monster,' Reen had said resignedly.

'Quite so.' Alyss's voice had been warm and ingenuous. 'But I'd like you to bring me a ffarg as well.'

3

Rehan hardly recognized her as she stood there in the opening that led to the stairs, her hand on the lintel. The scruffy little man who had descended behind her took one rapid glance around the ominously empty room, ducked under her arm and streaked for the door. Reen watched him go.

'Kursten,' Rehan said numbly.

'Who else?' she said. 'I'm glad to see you. Night after

night I've prayed to the gods that you'd come back here, one day, and help me.' She glanced at the dead Egroeg.

Rapidly, all the while watching her, Rehan explained what had happened. Her face was patterned with the red lines of burst blood vessels. Her skin seemed to have been rewoven using a rougher fabric and a broader stitch. Her lips were thicker, and they seemed reluctant to obey her commands when she smiled. Her eyes were bleak. Her hair was darker than he had remembered it, and it was cropped shorter, so that it seemed to have lost a lot of its softness. Her face as a whole seemed to have retreated in on itself, even though it had in fact gained a little flesh, so that there was a bulge of throat under the line of her jaw. Rehan was alarmed to discover that, had this been the woman who'd first welcomed him to One-Legged Tom's Kitchen, a lifetime ago, he wouldn't even have noticed her.

And yet she *was* Kursten. Now that he looked at her more carefully, he could see that she was unmistakably the same person whom he'd recovered from the clutches of the ffarg.

'It's taken me longer to get back here than I'd thought it would,' he said apologetically.

'You've changed, too,' she said. Her voice was harsher now than it had once been, yet its rough edges didn't grate on his ears; instead they seemed caressing, like the coarse fibres of a warm blanket.

'We've all changed,' said Reen impatiently, 'but we can talk about it later. For the moment it'd be best if we could concentrate on getting you out of this accursed burg, grab us a ffarg, and then slither off Albionwards as fast as our legs can carry us. You two can get in your smooching on board whatever vessel we manage to filch – you know how romantic the rocking of the sea can be, with Struan's light on the water-crests . . .'

'Shut up, Reen,' said the singer. 'Shove off and kill Gnetz or something for an hour or two, will you?'

'Gnetz!' said Kursten, her face blazing loathing. She spat at Egroeg's corpse, folded her arms across her chest and turned half away from them. 'As long as that swine still breathes, I'll never be safe.'

'I was beginning to come to that conclusion myself,' said Reen thoughtfully. Absentmindedly she'd begun carving on the tabletop in front of her with her dirk. The tip of her tongue peeped out from the corner of her mouth.

'Kursten . . .' Rehan began.

'Never safe,' the stranger repeated.

She shook her head as if her face were still framed by flowing curls, then raised her head, with a haughtiness he'd never seen before, to stare at him directly.

'He's done everything he could to debase me,' she said. 'Me! I've got few illusions about myself – I know I'm nothing much, just another woman lost in a city that the gods'd be glad to forget – but that doesn't mean I'm an animal, dammit. And yet he's treated me worse than if I were. Him and his friends . . . oh, Rehan!'

'Do you have a secondary name, Kursten?' said Reen.

'No,' the woman responded, startled out of her imminent tearfulness. 'Why d'you ask?'

'Nothing important. Carry on. You were just getting to the good bit.'

Rehan's face had become even paler than it had been ever since Alyss had recovered him from the skies. He was twisting the hem of his cloak brutally, as if to test the endurance of the cloth to destruction.

'Kursten,' he mumbled.

In a moment she was in his arms, sobbing against his shoulder. He cradled the back of her head in his hand, feeling the skin move against his palm. There were tears in his own eyes, now. At last, quietened, the shuddering gone from her shoulders, she turned her face up towards him, running a little row of shy, experimental kisses along the sides of his jaw. Finally she reached his mouth, set in a firm line of misery, and probed timorously at the creased corner of his lips. He turned slowly towards her, pulling her body tightly against his, so that he could feel the softness of her breasts against his chest and the hard crib of her pelvis against his hip, and put his mouth fully over hers. She squirmed even closer to him, throwing her arms around his neck and catching his hair in her fingers so that she could press his face down to her, as if she were eager to devour him, all of him, and to be devoured in her turn.

Reen carried on carving, softly whistling a nonce-tune.

Finally they broke their embrace, gasping, retreating slightly from each other, staring into each other's eyes, their fingers intertwined so that their arms formed a cradle between them.

'Shall we go and kill Gnetz, now that you've finished?' said Reen cheerfully.

At once the steel came back into Kursten's stance. She shook her hands free of Rehan's.

'Yes,' she said. 'Yes, we must. That's the only way I'll ever be free of him. I've dreamed of his death so many times.'

'Well, first we'll have to find him, won't we?' explained Reen tolerantly. 'I've never been in the Anonymous City before, and my friend's sole visit a while ago was, shall we say, a flying one. Besides, you know the little runt better than we do. We'll need you as a guide.'

'Right,' she said.

'So where do you think he's likely to have run to?'

Kursten sucked her lower lip in thought.

'If he's run anywhere,' said Rehan, looking suddenly worried. 'He might be on his way back here, with a gang of his Vermin to support him.' He glanced at the main door, then at the opening into the scullery; he drew his sword.

'No,' said Kursten. 'There's no fear of that. The tale of how you outfaced a whole band of them, even Gnetz himself – not to mention the minor matter of slaying Egroeg – it'll be all over the warren by now. However much they fear him, they won't willingly come against you. But they'll defend themselves, if need be. If I read Gnetz aright, what he'll have done is find somewhere that he can gather a few score of them around him, so that in order to attack him you'll have to attack them as well.

And that'll probably be out in one of the big houses in Sunland.'

Reen looked at her, eyebrows arched inquisitively.

'Sunland,' Kursten continued. 'That's up near the docks. The richies have their homes there, but Gnetz has one of the houses, too – not for living in all the time, just to show that he *can*, if you know what I mean. I could lead you there, if you liked.'

'Can we trust you?' said Reen sharply.

Kursten's mouth dropped open in astonishment.

'Well, of course you can . . .'

'What are you talking about, Reen?' shouted Rehan. 'Of course we can trust Kursten, dammit! I'd stake my . . .'

'That's just what you're going to do,' said Reen very quietly, cutting across his bluster. 'But that doesn't mean I've got to stake *my* life on her, too. So far she seems a reasonable enough wench, and she's obviously got a good armlock, but apart from that I don't know anything about her except for what you've told me in your somewhat starstruck way. So I repeat my question to you, Kursten: Can we trust you?'

'Yes,' the woman breathed angrily. 'I swear it on my heart that I will not betray you, that I will do everything that I can to help you slay that scum. Look at me!'

Reen did. She seemed unimpressed by what she saw, but nodded nevertheless. 'You'll do,' she said.

'Who is this bitch, anyway?' said Kursten, turning violently towards Rehan. 'Your mother, or something?'

Seemingly paying them no further attention, Reen was viciously scoring through her unfinished carving. Sharp spills of wood were already jutting up at acute angles from the tabletop. 'She's a very dear friend,' she heard Rehan explaining. She grinned inside herself, keeping her face stony. Reen was quite happy to be the age she was. Now that the girl was thoroughly unsettled, she might let slip a clue as to whether or not she was indeed to be relied upon, as she claimed. Reen resolved, whatever the outcome of the continuing quarrel, not to take Kursten into account in any of the plans she might have to make during the course of this night. As far as strategy was concerned, there'd be just the two of them – three, if you counted Syor, except Syor didn't have a body of her own. Rehan's strumpet would be just an extra piece of baggage that had to be protected – Reen would have to make sure that Rehan understood that, so that he could help to forestall the girl from doing anything too dimwitted. Like kill Gnetz out of hand. According to Rehan, the Vermin had treated successfully with the ffarg: any information that Reen could get out of him before . . . well, just *before* . . . would be well worth any effort she had to expend to get it. It'd be a bloody nuisance if the girl tried to do something dramatic like slit the little bastard's throat – the Revenge of a Woman Wronged, or some such drek. But in the meantime, of course, Kursten must lead them . . .

'I apologize,' Kursten was saying to her. Her voice was too candid for Reen's liking, but the concession seemed to satisfy Rehan.

'Apology accepted,' said Reen. 'Best if we got moving right away. If you've got a sword, fetch it; there're enough daggers lying around here to fit out an army, so grab a couple of them as well. Do you need a cloak, or anything? The night's quite warm – at least, it was earlier.'

'What were you carving?' said Rehan curiously as Kursten went to the door to test the air.

'Nothing,' said Reen. 'Doesn't matter. You're going to have some pretty tricksy explaining to do, once you get your doxy on your own. About the fact that you won't actually be on your own, if you see what I mean.'

'That can wait,' he said softly, looking towards the girl. 'Not forever, of course, but it can wait for now. Please tell me what you were engraving.'

After a last, deepest slash, Reen returned her dagger to her belt and rubbed her palms together in a businesslike way. 'I told you,' she said. 'It wasn't anything important. Anyway, though *she* was all right' – a belligerent nod in Kursten's direction – 'with just the single name to worry about, you had too many bloody initials, Barra 'ap

Rteniadoli Me'gli'minter Rehan, for me to fit them all in, even at the top.'

4

There was a brisk wind in Glory Row. Reen pulled the collar of her cape up around her cheeks as she and Rehan trotted along behind Kursten. The wind was making all the rickety wooden houses crowding in on them creak and rattle, as if they were rocking in their moorings like loose teeth. The sky was reasonably clear, just a few tendrilled clouds drifting across it indolently, barely dimming the light of Struan even when they shrouded the moon's semicircle. A dog fled from them, scuttling up a side-alley so strait that it was hard to believe it was used by human beings. *Correction*, thought Reen, holding the handle of her sword even more tightly. *That wasn't a dog. They breed their rats big here. Two types of vermin to keep an eye out for* . . . There was a distant crash of shattering glass; some screaming; a too-rapid cessation of the screaming. She shrugged. There were a lot of animal and human turds underfoot, so they had to pick their way carefully; there were other, less pleasant things to avoid, too. It'd have been nice if they could have had Anya with them, or Lian – poor, dead Lian.

Lucky dead Lian. This dump was worse than any she'd yet come across in the World, which was saying something. There'd been that street in Marg'phelin which had been illuminated on the night of the Garayan Emperor's birthday by criminals, soused in oil, strung up from the lamp-posts, and lit while they were still kicking and struggling. Still enough life left in them to be able to scream. Some of them hardly more than children. The sight and sound had made her sick in the stomach for weeks afterwards, but even so it hadn't all been so *squalidly* cruel as this city, somehow.

Yet Kursten didn't seem overly concerned. The girl was being sensibly cautious, of course, not stepping too near the pools of even blacker blackness that betrayed the entrances to the narrowest wynds; but that was prudence at work, rather than fear. Not fear like the fear that Reen was experiencing. Not fear – a sideways glance – not fear like the fear that Rehan was experiencing, either. Well, Reen supposed, if you lived in a place like this you must get inured to the horrors that the night might hold, used to the idea that the next shriek to split the darkness might be your own.

They were soon onto a broader thoroughfare, and Reen could see Kursten relaxing her vigilance a little. The pubs were still open, and their windows splashed warm light out across the road; people were standing outside them in groups, chatting amicably enough, or wandering from one to the next. The street could have been in any prosperous town, Reen reflected; it was difficult to remember that only a matter of metres away, not far behind the respectable façades of the houses and shuttered shops on either side, lay the territory of the Vermin. One or two of the people bade the trio good evening with a smile and a comment about the mildness of the evening.

Not long afterwards, they were once again among deserted streets. There was a tart smell of the sea in the air. Here there were no shops or other overtly commercial buildings; clearly this was a wealthy suburb, the grand houses fronted by extensive, well tended gardens. They passed one where the precisely arranged shrubs and the neatly trimmed lawns were juxtaposed oddly with a heap of toys – a tricycle, a broken bucket (sans spade), a bow, a ball – clearly dropped where they were by the children of the house when they'd been called in for bed. Reen smiled: even in the Anonymous City life went on. Lights shone placidly from generous windows.

Kursten slowed them with an outstretched arm, led them into the shade of a spreading tree, and pointed towards a solid-looking town-house directly ahead of them; the road split in front of it, so that the garden formed the upper part of a triangle. The house itself was not especially large, and its skewed position within the garden made it seem even smaller. There were no lights in the windows of the two walls that they could see, no smoke coming from either of the chimneys. The place looked deserted, and Rehan said as much to Kursten.

'You'd hardly expect the Vermin to advertise their presence,' she whispered. 'But that's the house that Gnetz owns, and that's the house they'll be in if I'm right and he's fled here to Sunland. Be careful: they're bound to have sentries posted.'

'Is there a back entrance?' Rehan asked the girl.

'I don't know,' she said hesitantly. 'Gnetz doesn't often invite guests. I've only been here a couple of times. But it must have one – all these houses do – unless he's had it blocked up.'

'Pity there's only the two of us,' said Reen. She was about to correct herself when she noticed the lack of reaction from Kursten. Good. So the girl had recognized her status as a noncombatant already. That might save a lot of problems later.

'Remember Giorran,' said Rehan. His brief fit of peevishness over, he was smiling at her. In fact, her memories of storming the Ellonian fortress single-handed were only hazy and muddled, but she took his point. Glumly. Wounds still hurt, even when you're victorious. And the wound of the knowledge that Alyss might have permitted the victory without any of the bloodshed still pained her. But Rehan would understand nothing of all this, of course: he'd been dead at the time, and had had to derive all his knowledge of what had happened from the highly coloured accounts people had given him afterwards.

'This is no Giorran,' she said. 'Wish it were. It's more dangerous attacking houses than it is fortresses. At least with fortresses you've got a pretty clear idea in advance where the defenders are likely to be.'

For a few minutes the three were silent, Kursten and Rehan both quite consciously leaving Reen in peace to think through their best course of action. She wished that she could produce some sort of instant result for them, to justify their confidence in her as the master-strategist. But all she could think of was that everything would have been so much easier if only human beings could have acted like logical, rational creatures: then none of them would ever have been in this situation in the first place. Gnetz wouldn't have allowed himself to be so corrupted by greed that inevitably he'd have found himself hunted like this; Rehan and Reen wouldn't have become his necessary foes – instead might even have been his friends, and could simply have asked him for his tips on how to treat with the ffarg.

Get your mind back on the job at hand, woman!
There's no way of telling how many of them might be in there, nor how well they're armed, or with what, or if they know how to use their weapons, or if they've got any guts or'll leap at the first opportunity to abandon Gnetz to his fate. Hmmm. Probably the last is true, at any rate. Rats like him construct their empires using fear, and fear's a lousy glue to fasten a man's soul to yours with.

She squinted up at a nearby lamp, guttering at the top of its pole, as an idea struck her.

'Give me your cape, Rehan,' she said suddenly. 'Yes – yours too, Kursten.' She stripped off her own and threw it down to the ground in front of her; the other two garments joined it moments later.

She stooped and spread the three cloaks out flat. 'Your flute'd be useful, too, Rehan.' Out of the corner of her eye she saw his body tense, so she added: 'Aw, come on, dammit – you can always make another one. Kursten: are you good at shrieking like a dervish?'

'What's a dervish?'

'Good point. Making a hell of a racket. Distraught damsel. Scared shitless and making sure everyone knows about it. Pretend someone's stuck a red-hot poker up your bum.'

'Oh.'

Standing, Reen explained tersely to the other two what she wanted them to do. Begging Rehan's pardon politely, she then briefly consulted Syor, who gave her approval.

'Right,' said Reen finally. She made a conscious effort to keep a brusque, matter-of-fact exterior; inside, all she felt was vaguely depressed. Assuming they were successful, the brunt of the killing that would have to be done was going to fall on her. In her mind she saw Qinefer's face watching her, and she read in the woman's strange unfocused eyes the same resignation that she herself felt: ending human lives was a distasteful business, but sometimes there was no alternative. Or so it seemed. Maybe there was a place somewhere that people didn't have to kill each other. No, that couldn't be. If word got around, the place'd soon be jammed full of people wanting to live there, killing each other in the rush . . .

'Go,' she said to Rehan.

The thin body of the singer was immediately in motion. Holding his flute ahead of him like a spear, he sprinted silently to one of the nearby lamp-posts and deftly plucked the burning basket from its top. Balancing the burden precariously on the end of his flute, he scampered back to them. As the basket dropped into the centre of one of the spread cloaks, he spun on his heels and raced off to fetch another. While he did so, Reen quickly pulled up the corners of the garment to form an elongated bag which she swung around her head a couple of times as the cloth began to smoke. Then she let fly with it, and the heavy basket with its smouldering tail of cloth crashed through the main window of one of the merchants' houses. Instantly there was commotion from within.

'Good shot,' panted Rehan, dropping a second flaming bundle beside her.

'Get screaming, Kursten!' snapped Reen, ignoring him.

The girl ran out into the centre of the street, beating at herself and yelling 'Fire! Fire!' at the top of her voice. Reen was impressed. A doughty scream. You could mug a lot of girls before you found one that . . .

'There!' said Rehan, arriving with a third blazing basket. He grabbed the primitive missile she passed him and darted off across to the other side of the street. Moments later there was a satisfying shattering of glass and then a cacophony of horrified shrieks.

Reen herself ran, half-bent over, the third torch muffled by a cloak against her midriff, directly towards Gnetz's stronghold. Without allowing herself to pause long enough to contemplate the risks, she sprinted boldly along the front pathway, straightening her body as she went. There was a broad, blank, uncurtained window just to the right of the main door, and she hurled her burden straight at it, putting into the effort all the disgust and loathing she felt for what she was doing.

Glass everywhere. Must be ten times worse inside. Already flames beginning to show from the first of the houses she'd bombarded. Kursten still screaming as if her death-god were after her – good girl. Now there was a score of other voices joining her chorus of 'Fire! Fire!' Neighbours pouring horrified out into the street. Back, Reen, back into the shadows of a bush that some clot of a gardener thought looked better pruned into a perfect sphere. *Watch the front of the house. Rehan should be round the back by now, letting the Vermin flee if that's the way they want to go. But I doubt it. Even the stupidest of them must realize they'd be safer coming out here at the front, where the neighbours are: there could be an army waiting for them at the rear.*

The noise in the street was becoming deafening, but still the house ahead of her was silent. *Shit! The bloody wench was wrong about where Gnetz has run to.* But then, at last, the front door thrown ajar; a man peering out warily, like a mouse emerging from its hole. Seeing nothing. Bolder now, stepping into the open. Then order vanishing as a group of his cronies start tumbling out behind him, jostling him aside.

Reen stayed hidden where she was as the Vermin stumbled past. She had no objection to letting them go. The fewer of them that were left here to be tempted into last-minute heroics, the better. She could hear Kursten, as ordered, beginning to retreat now that several of the occupants of nearby houses had taken over the task of screaming from her.

The room behind the window that Reen had smashed

was now quite merrily ablaze. In the flickering light she could see surprisingly opulent furnishings catching fire. An oil painting on the wall gave a low, breathy whoop as it suddenly became a sheet of flame.

None of the faces that had so far hurried past had been Gnetz's. Assuming he'd been here in the first place – which now seemed pretty likely, as otherwise why would the rest of the Vermin have congregated here? – he must still be inside. With how many others? She'd counted eight going past her, but in the fitful light and the confusion it had been hard to keep an accurate tally. Would Gnetz have been able to gather many more than that? She'd no way of knowing. The best she could do was hope not. Say there were a couple of loyal stalwarts still left. Just one, if it was another giant like Egroeg, might be enough to defend the little swine. She sucked in cold air through pursed lips, not liking the odds. Still, nothing better to do than see if she could get it over with . . .

As she stepped out of the shadows' protection she tried to recapture some of the blind fury that had smothered her when she'd assaulted Giorran, but it just wouldn't come. She could remember something of what it had felt like, but couldn't find the right emotional switches to click. Then her wrath had been directed primarily not at the Ellonia, however much she loathed them, but at Alyss, for letting her friends die. But she didn't have that sort of a target for anger now. Indeed, she realized, she didn't feel angry at all: just morose, reluctant. *A hell of a way to go into battle, my girl*, she thought ruefully.

The partitioning wall against which she pressed once inside the door was hot, thanks to the blaze on its other side. Creeping forward, she reached out her hand and threw open the door leading into the burning room. There was a sudden invasion of crackling noise and murderous light into the hallway. She could see ahead of her a broad flight of stairs leading up to the next storey; surely Gnetz wouldn't be fool enough to hide up there, letting himself get trapped by the flames beneath. No, he must be down here somewhere.

She threw herself across the open hall and crashed up against the opposite wall. It was unlikely that Gnetz would be in the room next to her; much more probable that he'd fled into one of the darkened rooms at the back. Still, he might be waiting until she'd gone past before sneaking out to stab her from behind and then scuttle out the front.

Warily she opened the door and checked. Nothing.

'Gnetz!' she shouted, stepping back into the hallway, hoping that her voice wouldn't be lost in the clamour of the flames. A chandelier crashed down somewhere in the middle of the inferno to her right, drowning any reply that the little Vermin might have made.

She cursed, then yelled his name again.

Still no reply.

Either he was already gone from the house, perhaps struggling with Rehan, or he was determined to stay concealed for as long as he could, ready to spring out at her when she least expected it.

Play it your own way, buster, she thought. *You're dead meat anyway.*

Then she paused. *Or are you? I've been assuming it, because Rehan wants you dead and, by all the lights in the sky, so does his little trollop, but who's the one with the swordhand here? If I don't particularly want to end the night with a killing, what right have the other two to contradict me? If you could hear my thoughts now, Gnetz, you fool, you'd be out here begging to be allowed to surrender to me . . .*

He'd been upstairs after all.

Out of the side of her eye she just saw a glimpse of movement as a black shape threw itself over the banister at her.

She took a quick, instinctive stumble sideways, so that he didn't land quite centrally on her back, but still she was thrown brutally to the floor. Her sword went flying from her grasp as the air was crushed out of her. She was aware that her attacker had jarred his elbow numbingly against the hard boards as they'd fallen. He was shouting with pain as his left hand grabbed her by the hair, pulling her head backwards to expose her throat. She wriggled and twisted, knowing that it was futile, that any moment now his dagger would be slicing across her taut flesh. Then she saw the weapon falling in front of her eyes as his senseless fingers finally lost their grip on it. Inspired by the sight, ignoring the screaming protests of her stretched neck, she clamped her forearms down on the floor and jerked upwards violently with her hips, forcing herself to her hands and knees, so that he was riding astride her. Suddenly his hand had left her hair, so that relief from the pain came singing into her through her scalp, but almost at once both of his hands were at her throat, the sharp nails of his fingers gouging into her adam's apple. Again she bucked, this time off to one side, hoping to dislodge him. He removed his powerless right hand from her throat and brought his forearm down like a club on the back of her head. There was an instant of darkness, when everything seemed to be very far away, but luckily she didn't lose consciousness. She jerked her torso in a complicated twist, upwards and sideways, trying to dash him against the wall. The clamp on her throat weakened, and so she did it again. This time there was a yell of protest as his head met brick. The squeezing grip of his thighs on her waist eased, and with a final spurt of strength she threw him clear of her.

Even in the darkness she could see her sword a couple of metres away, where it had come to rest at the far end of the corridor. She ignored it. It'd be useless for close fighting in the confined space. As Gnetz slid across the floor, shrieking in fury as he crashed against a couple of occasional tables, she dragged herself to her feet, feeling the muscles at the base of her back creak painfully. The dagger had gone from her belt, lost somewhere in the mêlée. Turning, she stooped rapidly and plucked the one from her boot.

Gnetz must have recovered more swiftly than she'd thought possible, because before she had a chance to straighten up he was on her again, flailing at her with his fists, driving her backwards with the force of his body. Off-balance, she groped out blindly with her unencumbered hand, hoping she could grab something to keep her on her feet.

No luck. She fell over backwards, and he fell uncontrollably with her. Rounding her back as she dropped, she stuck her hand into his open mouth, gripping him by the jagged front teeth of his lower jaw, her nails digging into the tender, slippery membrane under his tongue. Continuing her backward roll, curbing her agony as he bit down viciously on her fingers, she hauled him right over the top of her so that he performed an uncontrollable somersault and landed in an awkward, crashing sprawl of limbs against the door at the end of the corridor. He screamed again, and she snatched away her bleeding hand. She guessed he must have broken a bone or something: that had been a yell of pain, not of fury. She rolled over dazedly onto her front, surprised to find that she was still holding her dagger.

Groggily rising to a three-quarters position, she sprang towards the dark irregular blotch of his body, knife raised. She wanted to kill him, now; anything to end this torment.

She stamped a foot down ruthlessly on his exposed chest, feeling a couple of ribs crack. His face, inverted, was staring up at her in terror and anguish, and blood suddenly came jetting from his mouth. The unexpected sight halted her momentarily, and then she remembered that she wasn't supposed to finish the little shit just yet: first she was supposed to get some information out of him. She couldn't off-hand recall anything about what that information might be, but that wasn't the important thing.

She stayed the downward punch of her knife towards his throat and staggered wearily sideways to lean against the wall, gasping painfully. Now for the first time she felt the caustic pain of her hand, and she too gave vent to a yell. Through sheer force of will she kept tears of agony from her eyes. The bastard must have bitten right through to the bone.

The bastard was lying unnaturally still. In the light

from the blazing room she could dimly see the whites of his eyes.

'Rehan!' she bellowed. Why the fuck couldn't the bloody singer be here when she wanted him? 'Rehan!'

Now that she'd admitted the pain to her mind it was doing its best to rob her of her consciousness. She was aware that she was swaying on her feet, ready for collapse; she couldn't muster up enough rationality to care much about that. All she wanted was for Rehan to appear, to take over for her so that she could escape the pain.

And then he was with her. He knelt for a moment beside Gnetz, then stood and threw her undamaged arm around his shoulders. Together they staggered out through the splintered frames of the doors he'd barged down as he'd forced his way into the house on hearing her shouts. In a few moments he'd lain her on her back on cool, refreshing grass, so that she could stare at the moons and the stars and no longer feel like fainting. A very considerable distance away from her, Rehan muttered some sort of apology and left her side, soon to return dragging Gnetz, feet-first, so that the Vermin's head bounced on the stone-corners of the couple of steps that led down from the door.

She did lose consciousness then.

Very little had changed when she returned to her senses. Rehan was leaning over her concernedly, his head eclipsing Zoa's light. She smiled at him much more affectionately than if she'd been fully in control of her faculties. Realizing this, she turned the expression into a frown.

'You haven't let that bugger escape, have you?' she growled.

'He's dead.'

'You've killed him! You stupid . . .'

'No. No I haven't. He was dead already. You killed him.'

'But I . . .'

She remembered stopping herself from delivering the fatal blow. Was her mind wiping out her memories of having changed intentions yet again and putting an end to the Vermin's life? No. She could recall everything quite clearly until the time that Rehan had come to her.

A sudden guess.

'Not Kursten?' she said. A vision of the girl somehow creeping in through the main door while the singer was helping Reen out here. A blade flashing in the firelight . . .

'I don't think so. I wasn't gone long enough.'

Perplexity was giving Reen strength. With a lurch she sat up. Grabbing Reen's arm for support, she got to her feet and stood there unsteadily. She heard the clamour from the street on the far side of the house, but paid it no heed. All her attention focused on the dark form of the man stretched on the ground in front of her.

'Have you got a lamp?' she said.

She felt him shrug. Stupid question. They'd have to make do with the moonlight.

Squatting painfully down by the corpse, she ran her hands over its tangled clothing, seeking a wound. There was shiny black blood around the mouth – not just Gnetz's blood but hers as well. Seeing it made her hand hurt again. But the throat was unmarked, and she could find no puncture in the chest.

She looked up at Rehan, but his face was as blank as her own must be.

They were in a smallish, walled yard. Around the edges were a number of different-shaped pots containing small shrubs and bushes that didn't seem to be thriving. The central area was grassed. On the opposite side from the house the wall was broken by a stout-looking door leading onto whatever lay behind – a back alley, to judge from the houses she could see beyond. Some of the windows were lit, but surprisingly few: even in the more salubrious suburbs the natives of the Anonymous City must be accustomed to nighttime commotions.

'What about his back?' said Rehan.

'Can't be,' said Reen promptly, remembering the way Gnetz had been lying. But, grunting, she bullied the light corpse over onto its front.

Beneath the shoulderblades there was a deep, ragged laceration cutting across the backbone. The area was sticky with blood. She winced, but put her fingers into the wound, feeling the ends of sundered vertebrae.

'You're right,' she said bluntly. 'I did kill him. Damn! Damn and blast! What a bloody nuisance!'

'Some epitaph,' commented Rehan mildly.

'More than he deserves.'

She could see it now. Her sword, lying there on the floor near to the doorway at the end of the corridor where they'd been struggling. A useless weapon in the circumstances, she'd thought – and she'd been correct about the blade at least. But not about the metal disc of the handguard, sticking up from the floor. No wonder Gnetz had shrieked when he'd landed on it: it must have been agony. And then, of course, along she'd come and stamped on his chest, driving the metal cruelly further into him . . .

There was a shuffling noise over at the wall, and her maimed hand leapt to her waist, to where a dagger should have been. Rehan, seeing her, turned as well, his sword snaking out in front of him.

'It's all right. It's me,' came Kursten's whisper.

She clambered over the high wall and walked towards them.

'There's a door,' said Reen sourly, pointing.

'It's locked.' A petulant toss of the head.

Reen's eyes narrowed. She'd killed two men tonight, and her hand was causing her seventeen different kinds of hell. She briefly flirted with the notion of making accidents come in threes.

'Gnetz is dead,' Rehan explained.

'Shit!' said Kursten, stamping her foot. 'I wanted to do that myself. Slowly. At leisure.'

'Pity you weren't around at the time,' said Reen, then caught herself. 'Sorry. That wasn't fair.' Embarrassed, she gave a rapid explanation of what had happened. 'The real irritation,' she concluded, 'is that now we can't ask him about how to deal with the ffarg. You wouldn't have any bright ideas, would you, Kursten?'

The girl laughed briefly. 'I've hardly had much more experience of the monsters than you have,' she said, 'unless you can count being bounced around on the back of one of them for a few kilometres on a dark night.'

'Is there anyone else who might be able to help?' said Syor, over-riding Rehan's voice. 'You must have picked up a lot about the Vermin when you were waiting on them at table and . . .'

'When servicing them,' said Kursten, clearly confused by the change in Rehan's voice, but ignoring it as an irrelevance. 'Yes. But I don't think there's anything useful I can tell you. Not all that many of the Vermin knew about Gnetz's dealings with the creatures – he was good at keeping things close to his chest when he wanted to. And those that did know – well, they were good at keeping things quiet as well, because if they hadn't been they'd have been dead by then. I hated the little bastard, but I had to respect him for the way he kept his people under his thumb.'

Reen began to tap on her teeth with her fingernails. A few speculations were beginning to go through her head, and she didn't much like the feel of them.

'We could continue this conversation somewhere else,' she said. 'No need to hang around here any longer, waiting for the Vermin to come back and see what's happened, hmmm?'

'Yes,' Syor agreed, and Reen could almost hear her mind at work. 'Will you be wanting to come with us, Kursten? Now that Gnetz is dead, there's no one to stop you leaving this godforsaken city for ever. We're going on to Albion, in the end, and we'd be glad to have your company. You could start up a new life there, if you wanted.'

'Leave the Anonymous City?' said Kursten. *She's a bloody awful actress*, Reen thought with some satisfaction: it looked as if her speculations were proving to be justified. 'Whatever makes you think I would want to do that? This is the place where all my friends are. I've got a successful business here. The city may not look too fine to outsiders like yourselves, but if you've grown up in it you see it . . . differently.'

Kursten's attempted winsomeness was clashing with the gleam in her eyes. Quietly Reen purloined a dagger she'd discovered in a scabbard at the back of the dead Gnetz's belt. She could see the face of her companion writhing, as Rehan fought to regain control of his voice and his mind from Syor. Syor was resisting – successfully, as far as Reen could make out.

'I think we should leave as quickly as possible,' Reen said to Syor/Rehan. 'I have the feeling that in a few hours' time our lives won't be worth a sparrow's fart anywhere in the Anonymous City.'

Surprisingly, Rehan had won the battle with Syor.

'What do you mean?' he said furiously. 'We can't think of leaving without Kursten, dammit!'

'She's just said she doesn't want to come with us,' said Reen patiently.

'Rehan,' said the girl softly, slipping her arm through his. 'Can't you stop this creature bullying me so?'

'Get your filthy paws off him, you whore!' snarled Reen. Dagger in hand, she advanced towards them; one look at her face was enough to cow Kursten, who shrank away. 'Be thankful that you've not yet given me a quite good enough excuse to kill you,' Reen continued, ignoring the consternation on the singer's face, 'because slitting your treacherous little throat would be the first thing I'd enjoyed all night. And, by the stars, I'll do it still if you keep delaying us like this. Fuck off – no, not through the house: back over the wall. If you're not out of my sight by the time I count to five . . .'

'What are you doing?' wailed Rehan. 'Reen, stop this madness!'

Kursten wasn't fleeing. She looked at Reen's blade with contempt, her eyes flashing hatred. 'You wouldn't dare touch a hair on my head,' she spat. 'Rehan wouldn't let you.'

'Try me,' said Reen calmly. 'He's known me a lot longer than he's known you. Also, he's not the suicidal type. Go.'

Kursten glanced at Rehan's face. There she saw that the older woman was speaking the truth. The singer was obviously tormented by indecision as to what he should be doing, but it was obvious that one of his options wasn't harming Reen, however little he was able to understand what was happening.

Kursten's shoulders slumped, but almost immediately she pulled herself erect again.

'I should have known better than to rely on a milksop singer,' she said scornfully, 'a man who still trots around after his mummy's apron-strings. I'd have kept you here and given you everything your heart desired – but no, that's not what you want, is it. You'd rather have a warty old hag like this. Not my smooth body by your side each night and each morning; not all the luxuries I'd be able to buy you, so that you'd be waited on hand and foot, everything you wanted brought to you.'

'Have you taken leave of your senses?' said Rehan concernedly. 'How could you promise any of these things? Here? In the Anonymous City? And you a . . . a serving girl?'

'Oh, she can make the promises, all right,' said Reen, 'and for as long as it amused her to keep you alive I've no doubt she'd keep them. Gnetz is dead, you see.'

'Yes,' barked Kursten. 'You've killed Gnetz. For that at least I can thank you.'

'With Gnetz dead,' Reen continued, unperturbed, 'the Vermin have lost their most ruthless leader. There's a vacancy for the job at the top. And who's the most ruthless person left behind? Why, your sweet little charmer here, that's who. Especially once she's had a chance to tell the Vermin that she killed Gnetz herself – that should really have them all in awe of her. I don't know what she was like when you were last here, old friend, but she's had time to change – change a lot.'

'Yes,' the girl hissed. 'I've been used. But now it's my turn to do a little of the using. I've got the chance of ruling the roost around here – d'you think I'm just going to chuck it away for the sake of the life of a dandyman like you? A dandyman and his aged relative? A dandyman who's probably about as good at pleasuring a woman as a . . .'

'Actually,' Reen interrupted calmly, 'don't tell him I told you or – oh, forget it. We must go, Rehan, leave this tart behind to take command of her own personal cesspit. The biggest turds do float to the top, as they say . . .'

Kursten leapt forward, a small blade in her hand. Oddly, it wasn't at Reen that she flew but at Rehan. He had just time to throw up his arms in front of himself before she was upon him, exultant, her teeth bared.

Reen, with a shrug, knifed her in the back before she could do the singer any damage.

With a vast exhalation, the girl's body flopped heavily to the ground.

Rehan was too stunned to speak a word.

Reen wiped Gnetz's knife on her thigh, looked at it critically, approved of its edge and heft, and slipped it into her belt.

'Time we got going,' she said, turning towards the rear door of the yard.

Silently, with one last look back at Kursten's crumpled form, his mouth open, tears in his eyes, he followed her.

'You can thank me later, when you feel up to it,' said Reen brusquely. 'For the moment, give me a hand getting this bloody door open.'

5

'Thank you,' said Rehan, shivering.

They were standing outside the wall of the Anonymous City. At their backs was a cliff of stone and mud; ahead of them they could see very little through the coiling mists that shrouded the Broken Marshes. The only problem they'd had had been persuading the sentry on the sidegate to let them pass through: it wasn't that he'd wanted to keep them inside the Anonymous City, more that he'd been incredulous that anyone should deliberately choose to venture out into the treacherous mists and marshes, and had kindly attempted to convince them of the folly of their decision. Then Rehan had reminded the man of the time when the ffarg had attempted to come through this very gate, and the sentry had given way, palely: obviously, although he hadn't been a witness himself, he'd heard about the exploits of the mysterious stranger who could leap from rooftop to rooftop, or break a man in half with a slash of his hand. The woman with him didn't look quite like the golden-tressed princess of the stories, but . . .

'Thank you,' Rehan repeated as they huddled together outside the wall. They were standing in what was like a cordon of clear air cut away around the city by the cold moonlight from above: behind them the wall, ahead of them a great bank of dark, roiling mist that filled all of the rest of the World. Its margins seemed to be trying to reach out towards them, as if to grab them with insubstantial fingers and draw them into the mist's maw.

'That's all right,' said Reen, grinning. 'You'd warned us all she was an innocent.'

'Barra 'ap Rteniadoli Me'gli'minter Rehan,' whispered a familiar voice from the mist's obscurity.

Chapter Six
The Mistdom

1

'Barra 'ap Rteniadoli Me'gli'minter Rehan,' the voice repeated insistently. It was warm, yet to the two of them it seemed as cold and as dank as the mist.

Reen's sword was drawn again. 'This is like some kind of nightmare,' she muttered to herself.

'Don't be afraid,' said the voice. 'There's nothing to be afraid of.'

'Tell me that you can hear it too,' Reen snapped. 'That it's not just the mist playing tricks on us.'

'I . . . I hear it too.' Belatedly, Rehan had managed to wrestle his sword from his belt. He was unpleasantly aware of the way the blade shook.

'It's an enchantment,' Reen hissed.

'I'm no enchantment,' said the voice.

And now she was stepping into the open, so that they could see the light of Struan picking out the curls of her fair hair. Her face was in shadow, but Reen imagined that there were tiny grey points of light in it for eyes. She was dressed in a single long garment that covered her palely from the shoulders to the ankles; over it there was a lacy shawl of darkness. She was turning her hands outwards, more in supplication than as if she were showing them that she was unarmed.

'Kursten,' said Rehan, lowering his sword.

'Shut up, you arsehole!' Reen growled, gesturing him back with her free hand. 'This can't be your doxy – she's dead, dammit. Have you forgotten already?'

'But . . .'

'Shut up, I said.'

Reen looked at the motionless figure, seeing beyond it the shifting walls of the mist. She was as sure as anyone could be that Kursten had died, back in the Anonymous City – had she not felt the dead flesh with her own hands? – and then there was nothing of the immaterial about the form standing in front of them now. The woman's shape was Kursten's, and so was her voice . . . if it *was* her voice.

'It is indeed my voice,' said the figure, as if reading Reen's thoughts.

This time there was no mistaking where the words had come from. Momentary notions about twin sisters flitted into her mind, only to be expelled again with impatient immediacy.

'Let us see your face,' she said harshly, her sword unwavering. Rehan was saying something, but it was irrelevant and she ignored it.

The woman took a small pace forwards, but halted as she saw the blade twitch. She raised her shoulders expressively. Then, moving very deliberately, she raised her hands and pushed back the shawl, so that it fell to her shoulders. To make sure, she pulled her hair back behind her ears to reveal her face. Even in the stark whites and blacks of Struan's light it was easy to make out the features.

'Kursten!' Rehan exclaimed again, this time with more conviction. He looked with a smile towards Reen.

'Maybe,' she said. 'Then who was it we killed – back there?'

'An impostor! She'd changed so much since last I saw her . . .'

'Or this could be the impostor,' said Reen, gesturing.

'Rehan,' said the figure.

'I tell you, blast it, Reen,' said Rehan angrily, 'this is the Kursten I remember from the first time I was in the Anonymous City. The raddled old bag who was pretending to be her – she was the one that died. She didn't even *look* like the Kursten I remembered. We just took her word for it that she was – her word and Gnetz's, and

Gnetz's wasn't exactly worth a lot. Kursten must have escaped from the place a while ago . . . or maybe the ffarg finally got her, and she's been living with . . . well, which'd mean, I guess, that they can't be as bad as . . . but then it was mainly Gnetz who told me *that* as well, so . . .'

'Stop burbling, friend,' said Reen. Her voice wasn't totally unsympathetic, but it was final. 'I'm pretty certain it was the real Kursten we killed – you were convinced it was her, remember, even though her face had changed a lot. So this one must be a simulacrum. Right? The only question that remains is: is she a friendly simulacrum or a hostile one? Unless she's something else entirely – a dream weaselled into our minds by some necromancer, maybe . . .'

'It *was* the real Kursten you killed,' said the woman unexpectedly. 'But I'm the real Kursten *as well*. It's . . . difficult to explain.'

'Too bloody right it is,' said Reen, 'but you'd better get started and try explaining it to us anyway.'

Rehan opened his mouth to say something, but then found he'd nothing to say. He made a great play of tucking his sword away, as if to tell Reen that he thought she was being a bit harsh without actually using any words that might be quoted back at him later.

'It's difficult,' said the woman, motioning with her hands, 'when we're just standing here like this. I could take you somewhere warm where we could . . .'

'I'm not that stupid,' said Reen. '*He* might be, but he's got low-slung brains. Here's perfectly good enough for me.'

The smooth, pure face twisted in thought.

'Well, at least let *me* sit down.'

'Granted.'

The woman lowered herself to the damp ground and sat with her back straight and her legs bent, so that she could tuck her feet under their opposite thighs. She brushed away a clinging strand of grass from her knee and then put her hands in her lap; she looked nervously backwards and forwards a few times between Rehan – now likewise seated, seemingly in a gesture of solidarity – and Reen, finally settling her gaze on the standing woman.

'My name is Kursten,' she recited quietly, as if speaking the words of an old song that had been lost and was now rediscovered, as fresh as ever, 'and I have lived all of my life until very recently in the Anonymous City. My father – I *think* he was my real father – was a man who'd lost a leg; his name was Tom. I can't remember anything about my mother, although he always said fine things about her. My father was a cook by trade: he ran the most popular of the taverns in the poor quarter of the city. When I was a child I used to know many of his customers by name, because often enough I'd come down and move among them while they were eating; sometimes I'd bring my clarsach down from my room and play for them, and they'd admire me as much for my determination in getting the heavy instrument down the rickety stairs as they did for my playing. When I became a woman it grew a little more . . . difficult. My father gave me a shield he'd built, and insisted that I carried it around everywhere with me. He would only let me help him out serving the customers sometimes, because he didn't like the way that too many of them were beginning to look at me. He hardly ever let me leave the house on my own, because he didn't trust the knotted alleyways and the gaping doors, or the eyes that looked out from them. And he all but banished my harp to my bedroom, which meant that very often he'd banished me as well. He was right in a way to be so protective of me, because they were dangerous men, and cruel ones, that had become my sort of friends; yet his jealousy of me made him build my shield too large, so that I could only see over the top of it if I stood on tiptoes, which I hardly ever had the sense to see fit to try to do. And, the few times I did try, I didn't try very hard, and so I saw nothing.'

She sighed deeply.

'And then there came a time,' she said, 'when someone came into my life who was like a glowing, welcoming, embracing furnace. The flames of his being lit up all the shadows; its warmth caressed me, and gave me strength and – and curiosity. For the first time I really *looked* at the top of the shield that my father had constructed for me, and I stood up as tall as I could stand, and I was just raising my head so that my eyes could see over it . . . when strange creatures, ugly one-eyed creatures, came to the pantry at the back of my father's kitchen. He wasn't there – there was no one else there – and I screamed for fear, and then I was just about to scream again because of their ugliness – which was a stupid reason to scream, on its own, but I did a lot of things without very good reasons in those days – I was just about to scream, I say, when I felt the lace of their thoughts touching my mind.

'I stopped wanting to scream, then, because I could feel from their thoughts what good . . . *people* they were. I was very quiet, because that was the way that they wanted me to be. They told me – no, that's not right: let's say that I "gained the impression from them" that the life I'd always known was just about to change, and not for the better, as I'd thought when . . . when' – she glanced at Rehan, whose face was blank – '*you*'d come into the kitchen that night. No, it was suddenly evident to me, because now some of the thoughts I was thinking were theirs, not mine, that there was a very great . . . a very great *darkness*, a sort of nothingness . . . Oh, it's so hard to describe it in words! I can see it in pictures easily enough, the way I could see it then, when I was just discovering what it was like to think using other people's thoughts, but when I try to say it out loud in words it all gets so confused. It was like the Anonymous City was a sandcastle, and there was a steadily increasing flow of fouled water pooling around it, and the more water there was and the faster the flow, the more the sand around the edges of the castle was being eroded away – bits of it toppling off and splashing into nonexistence – and I knew it couldn't be all that long before there was enough of the vile water to cover over the sandcastle completely, so that afterwards, even when the water had gone, there'd be no sign of the Anonymous City left at all, except maybe some almost invisible, low, smooth, rounded shapes that you wouldn't notice unless you were looking for them.

'As I say, I got all this in pictures through the thoughts I was thinking – the thoughts of the ugly people, the ffarg. And I sort-of-said to them, "Look, it's all right, nothing to worry about. There's this man who came in this evening who's got eyes that brighten the colours of my dress, and he's got a sword and he'll be able to save me from the villains because that's what the heroes in the ballads do." And they just . . . *sounded* . . . sad, and they said that you' – another glance, a nervous one, at Rehan – 'that you were a part of the water, only you didn't know it, and that my father had already been drowned, but that he didn't know it, either. So that's why I went with them when they said they wanted to take me away to somewhere safe. They led me all through the city – peacefully enough, because nobody seemed to be able to see us, and a couple of men who were a bit drunk actually walked right through us without noticing. And they took me to live with them safely in the Mistdom, which is where I've been ever since.'

She stopped.

Reen looked warily at Rehan, but he said nothing.

'That sounds quite a lot like the version of it you've told me,' said Reen to him, 'but not enough of a lot for it to be the same story.'

Still Rehan had no words.

'What she's telling us – and it could be a lie – is, I think, that the painted harlot we've just done the World a good turn by ushering off into whatever afterlife'll have her was really a substitute, put in her place, when you thought she was being kidnapped by the ffarg. Maybe they ran a diversion, young friend, and you fell for it. Or maybe you just misunderstood what was going on, and killed a couple of her rescuers while she was being helped to escape from that sewer of a city.'

'*No!*' said Rehan. Then his body froze again, as if the single syllable had provided a complete explanation.

251

'No need to keep pretending . . .' Reen began.

'But he's right,' interrupted Kursten. 'You see, what I've just told you was the absolute truth. That's exactly what happened. Only – it's not the *only* truth of what happened. Because I can remember the other truth as well, and it's equally real. We – you might as well carry on calling us the ffarg, the way that the people of the Anonymous City do – we tried to kidnap the beautiful human-woman that Gnetz had told us about, because as everybody knows, just as everybody knows that the World is flat, we ffarg require human females for breeding purposes. What we do is we kidnap them – which isn't difficult because, even though every human in the city knows that we're an omnipresent threat and that women shouldn't ever wander outside the gates alone, they still do so whenever we need fresh breeding-stock – what we do is, once we've got them, we subject them to unutterably disgusting sexual perversions, enslave their minds and, once they've been reduced to gibbering husks both by our obscenities and by the physical strain of bearing dozens of malformed monstrous offspring, we torture 'em to death for fun and eat 'em. That's what we wanted to do with this Kursten child, because even though she doesn't look in the slightest like one of us, the various convexities and concavities of her body drive us ffarg into a sexual frenzy. We crept through the streets, our passage assisted by the money that Gnetz had spent bribing people to look the other way, and we seized the girl and made off with her. If it hadn't been for her gallant young romantic hero dashing to the rescue with his glittering blade, we'd have been picking the last bits of her gristle out of our teeth . . . oh, round about now, at a guess.'

The woman shrugged.

'And that's the other truth I remember,' she added.

Reen was grinning. Her sword had drifted aimlessly off to one side. 'You're pulling my leg,' she said. 'That's ridiculous. I never heard such crap.'

'No,' said the woman sombrely. 'It's drawn directly from my other memory, and neither of my memories can tell me anything but the truth. I swear to you that that's so. I swear it to both of you.'

Both of them were looking at Rehan now. His body had slumped down further into the shadows of the wall, so that all that they could distinguish clearly in the murk were his battered boots and a torn trouser-leg.

'Which *are* you?' he said, his voice ice-bleak.

'What do you mean?' said the woman.

'Are you the real Kursten – or the other?'

'I've told you, I'm the real Kursten. So was the other one. It's all in my memories that . . .'

'Stop weaving words into tapestries that you can blindfold me with,' he snapped, leaning forward into the moonlight. 'Either you're a one-eyed fiend taking on the form of someone I – loved – because it amuses you to tease me in that way, or you're the woman herself, and what we killed back there' – an angry jerk of the thumb towards the wall behind him – 'was the counterfeit. All I'm asking you is to be honest with me, to stop farting around with reality like this!'

Reen looked at him, puzzled. Surely Kursten had made it perfectly clear, by the sarcastic way she'd told her second tale, with all its implausibilities, that she was indeed the real Kursten, that the rest of it had all been illusion? Illusion brought about in some way that Reen hadn't as yet guessed, but illusion nevertheless. A trick. Maybe something moulded out of a bradz-dream. Kursten would doubtless explain it all to them more clearly later.

'I am not,' said the woman fastidiously, pursing her lips, ' "farting around with reality", as you put it. I'm telling you the truth. It's reality that's' – again the tightened lips – ' "farting" around with us. Yet again, I'm telling you the truth – the truths – and you don't like it, so you reject it . . . them. Isn't it blazingly obvious to you by now that the past isn't a fixed entity – that the past contains millions of possible realities, just in the same way that the future does? And that all of those realities are *true*? Usually we pick only one of them, and decide that it's the single reality of the past. But that's arbitrary. All I've been doing is telling you about two equally valid past realities, rather than only one. I've *always*, until recently, been a ffarg; and I've *always* been a human being.'

'Show us what you really look like,' hissed Rehan, ignoring her words. 'Go on. If you're the one that's so keen on honesty, let's see if you can do that.'

'I am as you see me,' said the woman simply, spreading her hands. 'I could take off my clothes and show myself to you naked, if you wished, but for the moment the garments are part of my real appearance, too, so in a way that'd be a dishonesty.'

'Kursten would never have said some of the things you've been saying to us,' said Rehan. 'She hadn't the . . .'

'Brains,' supplied Reen tartly. 'Good point. Except you're talking about the Kursten who hadn't yet – what was the way she put it? – peered over the top of the shield.'

He looked at her speculatively. 'No,' he said at last. 'Even if she'd . . .'

'You're making something complicated out of something that's really very simple,' said the woman, waving loosely at the air in front of her as if she were trying to dissuade an over-inquisitive fly. 'I've told you, I have two memories. One of them corresponds to the past reality of what happened to the Kursten-me, who is the real me. It goes all the way back to my infancy, and it's true in every detail. It was designed to be that way. The other – the other memory's different in kind from the Kursten one. It can remember all the braided realities there have been in that time, all of which are just as true – were just as real – as each other. It, too, has been designed to be what it is. The two thickest strands in the braid are the ones that I've told you.'

Reen stuck her sword in the ground exasperatedly. The weapon swayed to and fro for a moment, finding its balance.

'Then what are you?' said Rehan. 'No' – he raised his

254

right hand as a barrier – 'don't tell us all over again that you're really Kursten and that you're also really a simulacrum of her. What are you behind all the disguises you're creating for yourself?'

She got to her feet, looking warily at Reen. Seeing that the old woman was making no movement towards her still-moving sword, she raised her skirt clear of the grass and walked in small steps to where Rehan sat. 'Look,' she said, reaching out a thin hand to him. 'Feel my fingers. Touch me. Take me in your arms if you wish. Test my realness. I'm a human being, just like you are – I always have been. If you were able somehow to travel backwards along the line of time, you could follow me all the way until you saw me being absorbed into my mother's womb. That's how real I am. That's how real you've designed me to be.'

Understanding came into Rehan's eyes. Syor's understanding.

'And if Reen and I weren't here to design you?' said Rehan's voice. He made no move to touch her. 'What would you look like then? Who would you *be* then?'

'The matter of you and Reen not being here is an unreality,' said the woman primly. 'Your questions have no meaning.'

'*Imagine* that we weren't here,' said Reen from behind her. 'Pretend that we weren't – make a game out of it. What would you be, in the game?'

'If the two of you . . .' The woman flinched, and darted a quick look at Rehan. 'If the *three* of you weren't here,' she began again, 'I'd be one of the selves of the Mistdom, of course. And if only *you* were here,' she added thoughtfully, turning to stare at Reen, 'I'd be the other two of you.'

'Both of them?' said Reen drily. She was beginning, at last, to understand what the pseudo-Kursten – as Reen now thought of her, despite any protestations of genuineness – had been trying to explain to them. Reen could imagine that there were creatures – 'creatures' wasn't the right word, she admitted to herself, but it would have to do for now – that lived hidden away in the shrouds of the mist. They were discrete from each other, these creatures – 'selves' – and yet they had no forms of their own, and perhaps no personalities, either. No forms or personalities, until they encountered a sentient creature, such as a human being, and then they became . . .

'You become what people need you to be!' she exclaimed.

'Yes,' said Kursten, her face grave, as if she were a schoolteacher trying not to flatter an unusually bright pupil by displaying any signs of enthusiasm. 'But when that happens, we really *are* the beings that we're needed to be. We're not just illusions, or marionettes, or imitations of any kind: we come complete with flesh and blood and mind, and with true memories.'

'Your memories,' said Rehan's voice in Syor's cadences, 'are constructions, of course – at least in part.'

'The same could be said of anyone's,' Kursten pointed out.

'Indeed,' Syor agreed. Then she continued: 'Most of your life, Kursten, you can remember exactly the way that everybody else would agree that it had really happened. But then there's a disruption – isn't that it? You're the person that Rehan – my body-mate, as it were – needed to be here, the only person who was really in his mind when we arrived here, yet it seems impossible that you can be present, because Rehan remembers only too clearly – as do Reen and myself – the way that . . . that Kursten died, just a couple of hours ago. Your Kursten-memory might try to design itself so as to make the two events compatible with each other, but that's not feasible, so it has to go back further to find a place where it can anchor its mooring for the other end of the bridge that leads to here. And it's found one. A reality that can be superimposed on top of all the rest of the realities that otherwise might have come into being . . . including the one that *did* come into being, except that you cancelled it out. Am I right?'

Again Kursten nodded. 'Except,' she said, 'that, though my Kursten-memory is an artifice, that doesn't mean it isn't real. Just because something has been constructed doesn't mean that it's false.'

'Agreed,' said Syor. 'Your other memory, however, is a bit different. We could say that it's the overarching memory possessed by your "ffarg" self – and it contains the recollections not only of what has happened to you as an entity, as experienced by yourself, but also the same overall succession of events in the versions that other participants might consider to be the truth. We humans have the same sort of memory system as your "ffarg" self's, only we don't recognize it as such: instead we do things like have fun speculating about what might have happened if events had been just a little different – the ancient game of "what if?" What we don't realize is that all the "what ifs" were actually tried out – that what we think of as speculations are actually fading memories of events that don't fit in with the scheme that's been consensually derived by ourselves and all our fellows. We don't notice that we're constantly going through this process of *agreeing* what happened in the past, of imposing on past events a single reality that has been designed to be as it is by common consent. The only difference between that and what your Kursten-memory does is that you do it consciously – and unilaterally.'

'That's right.'

'You're very dangerous, you know. You and your kind.'

'I hope not,' said the woman, still crouching down beside Rehan, looking directly into Syor's eyes. 'We're lucky enough that our minds never experience getting old, and so we never feel that we can pretend to wisdom. It's wisdom that makes people dangerous.'

'No – you *are* dangerous nevertheless,' Syor insisted. 'Already Rehan is beginning to doubt his memories – his own *real* memories – of what happened when the monsters abducted you and he rescued you from their clutches. He's beginning to wonder if, somehow, inexplicably, he got it all wrong. That way lies human madness, you know.'

'Well, *I*'m not mad,' said Reen stolidly. She was quietly

returning her sword to its sheath, having come to the conclusion that, if the woman did represent a danger, it wasn't any sort of danger that could be combated using swords. 'Maybe I'd go nuts, like you suggest, if I were back in the past at the moment, watching reality being changed all around me. But I'm not. I'm here in the present. These creatures from the mist are busy changing the past, you say. Well, that's all right by me. The past is in a distant country, so far as I'm concerned – just like the future is. So long as they don't start mucking about with *now* I'll be OK.'

'But changing the past can create an impossible "now",' argued Syor. 'It has done.'

'What's impossible about it?'

'Kursten's still alive. Yet you know she's dead. You saw her die.' Syor spoke the words wearily, repeating the obvious.

'The Kursten that's dead is dead. The Kursten that's alive is alive. There are two Kurstens – always were – the one that's dead now and the one that's still alive. I can cope with that. I think you're thinking too much, Syor.' Reen patted her thighs comfortably and stood erect, looking pleased with herself. Then she looked startled. The smack of her bitten hand on her clothing hadn't hurt her. She stared dumbly at the whole flesh of her fingers; when she continued speaking the words came more slowly. 'Life's easier if you accept that things are the way they are, and then try to find out why that's so, than if you keep trying to find reasons why things *shouldn't* be the way they are. And I'm hungry.'

Syor faded from Rehan's eyes, and the singer's body sat upright. Reen noticed with interest that he showed no signs of repugnance as he instinctively took Kursten's outstretched hand to help himself to his feet. At some stage during Kursten's conversation with Syor he must have decided that she was as real as she claimed to be.

Which means, Reen mused, *that he must also accept that the ffarg he battled were likewise real. But who would require the existence of vicious, man-eating monsters?* She glanced at him: he was smiling now, looking with genuine affection into Kursten's eyes. In a way, Rehan himself had needed the monsters: it was through rescuing her from the clutches of the ffarg that he'd won the fair lady's heart, just the way it was supposed to be. Yet it was unlikely that for Rehan's trivial benefit alone the selves of the Mistdom would have performed such a wholesale reconstruction of the past as to make all of the occupants of the Anonymous City accept the existence of the creatures.

She looked up at the city's wall, towering above them. *Ah . . . yes*, she thought. *But Rehan wasn't the only one who needed the existence of the bogles. All the misbegotten citizens of the rathole needed them as well. Otherwise, who would they be able to build defensive walls against? They need the threat. They need to feel that they're victims fighting off a persecutor.*

She grinned.

Silly buggers. Making life complicated for themselves.

Arm in arm, Kursten and Rehan were walking calmly into the folds of the mist. Shrugging lightly, still holding her healed hand suspiciously, Reen followed them. She felt curiously secure. Maybe it was because Syor had been talking.

2

The mist was cold and clammy, yet it didn't seem so. With Kursten's arm in his, and the sound of her breathing in his ears, Rehan felt as if his eyes were being washed by the enveloping greyness; although he could discern no features other than occasional lighter or darker whorls in the mist that pressed around them, it seemed as if he could see as far as the invisible horizon. He could remember experiencing this sensation only a few times before, when he was creating a new song and had suddenly, after all sorts of trials and reverses, discovered with absolute clarity the single perfect way that the chords and notes could be blended with the words and phrasing, so that the image he sought was revealed completely to him. It was as if, in order to see it in its nakedness, he had himself to be naked, yet had spent hours fighting with recalcitrant buttons and hooks until suddenly the clothes had fallen from him.

He turned and smiled at Kursten, who smiled back at him as if she had been reading his thoughts. For a moment he assumed that she probably had, and was surprised to find that he didn't much care; then he recalled that by definition she could no more read his thoughts than the Kursten of One-Legged Tom's Kitchen could have . . . but, of course, she *was* the Kursten of One-Legged Tom's Kitchen . . . He gave up wondering about it. Reen had been right when she'd said to Syor that some things were just made more complicated if you thought about them too much.

Nearby Reen coughed unhappily.

Rehan paused, and Kursten with him.

'What's the matter?'

'Look,' Reen said, pointing.

A section of the mist had thickened. Rehan found that it was hard to tell how he knew this, because there seemed to be no detectable alteration of it – it was as grey and featureless as all the rest, without any line of demarcation to separate it off. Yet he knew that it had a form, as if he possessed some mass-detecting sense that he'd never noticed before. The form was human, he discovered; and as soon as he'd done so his eyes were able to observe its outline. As he watched it was washed with wan colours – a drained pink for the flesh of face and arms, a faded dun for clothing, a dull silver for hair. Only the figure's eyes were a full colour: they were green.

Reen's cheeks were puffed, as if she wanted to let out a shout but didn't know whether it should be of joy or of horror. The transformation in her was ironic: only moments before he'd been admiring her matter-of-fact acceptance of the Mistdom and its denizens, and yet now she was more dislocated at the sight of this new figure than he had been when Kursten had first stepped into the moonlight. He reached out to lay his hand comfortably on her shoulder, but she shrugged him away.

The woman standing ahead of them was a stranger to

him, yet her eyes brushed over him as if she knew him well. And then he had the most uncomfortable feeling that in fact he, likewise, knew her very well, better than he'd ever known anyone else – even though he'd never seen her before.

There was the sound of departing laughter in his mind.

'You!' he said to the newly emerged figure, astonished. For a few moments he forgot the shock of re-encountering Kursten – forgot, even, that now her hand was in his. 'You're – Syor!'

His mention of the name snapped Reen out of her petrification.

'Of course it's Syor,' she said harshly. 'Who else'd you expect it to be? The selves didn't bring your fancy lady into existence for *my* benefit, did they?'

'So Syor's the person whom *you* need to be here?' said Rehan. He was slightly disappointed that it hadn't been himself, except, of course, that he was already here, so it hardly mattered if . . .

'Yes – from every point of view,' said Reen. 'Not just personal preference. Think about it. If I'd been thinking straight a little while ago I'd have realized this was inevitable.'

He was aware that Kursten was looking at him worriedly, so he made his lips smile. He let Reen's last words echo around in his mind, and then realized that they were doing exactly that: echoing. It was not as if his mind had become an empty room; more that he was adjusting to the fact that a living-space that had until very recently been just the right size for two was now his alone. Syor. Yes, Reen needed Syor because, whatever she might normally say in her noncommittal, studiedly bluff fashion, Syor was probably the most important person ever to have been in her life – Marja and Qinefer, and Rehan himself, notwithstanding. But, of course, Rehan had needed Syor to be here as well, because he couldn't forever play host, no matter how welcome his tenant might have become. Most of all, *Syor* needed Syor to be here . . .

'You seem to be at the end of everybody's quest,' he

said a little breathlessly, trying to appear calm. 'Alyss found you inside me, at the heart of the seven ReLMS. You were their architect, the architect of all Starveling – the real Starveling, not the stones in Albion that represent it to our reality. And now Reen and I find you here.'

Syor laughed, the sound seeming to make the colours of her face more defined. Rehan knew it to be impossible: here in the Mistdom, all colours could be no more than tinted grey. Yet her eyes were brightly green . . .

Now Syor's face was sombre again. 'I'm sorry,' she said. 'You spoke truer than you knew, friend Rehan. I was embarrassed. It wasn't funny.'

'It isn't funny,' said Kursten, startling them all with her forcefulness. 'Syor is at the end of more quests than you two know about. Aren't you, Syor?'

Now Syor's face was clouding into sorrow.

'Yes,' she said. 'I am.'

Reen appeared to have come to a decision. She took a couple of steps forward and threw her arms around Syor's neck, kissing her on the cheek and ear. There were tears in her eyes as she pushed herself back from Syor, holding her at arm's-length, looking into her face.

'I'm still hungry,' she said, other words having fled.

3

The sunlight had played on them while they were eating; now, as he played a light nonce-melody on his flute, Rehan felt well filled, although he had no recollection of exactly what it was they had eaten. Syor had snapped her fingers and stated that she required that the sky be clear and the Sun be high in it; and the Mistdom had obediently opened up a space within itself. She had required, in exactly similar fashion, that there be food for them and a fire on which to cook it (and, more importantly, to be sat around). She had also – for was this not a celebratory feast, a ritual marking of the reunion of old friends? – required that there be other companions to join them, and so the party had become one of a score or more, with much laughter and noise, although now, much as with the delicacies he had consumed, Rehan couldn't recall any of the faces of the guests who'd so entertained him with their wit. There'd been an obscenely fat man who'd dominated the proceedings with his hilariously funny jokes, and then he'd called for his dog, who'd done some astonishing tricks in exchange for titbits of food. And then there'd been . . .

His mind was a little hazy as a consequence of forgotten wine, but he was still aware enough, even as he played, to notice that Kursten alone among them had been sour and miserable throughout. She was squatting now with her legs crossed and her hands in her lap, looking up at him as he stood with his flute to his lips; the attitude of her body indicated that she was a person listening perhaps a little too seriously to a tune that pleased her while at the same time showing a proper degree of respect for the musician, and yet her body language as a whole was telling him, just like the expression on her face, that she was distressed – doubly distressed, because she wanted to speak with him about it and couldn't, not within earshot of Syor and Reen, who were sitting with their arms around each other's shoulders, grinning like imbeciles, assuredly present. Rehan was becoming confused as to whether his melody should express his happiness or his concern, and the notes petered out in a series of breathy mis-blows.

'Carry on,' said Reen. 'That was getting good. Rubbish, of course, but good rubbish, if you know what I mean.'

Syor giggled at her. The two women were just about old enough to be his mother, yet they were behaving like two children sharing a secret. Rehan found it all somehow nauseating; although, if it hadn't been for Kursten's foul mood, he might have been doing much the same thing himself . . .

He wiped off his flute carefully and tucked it into his belt, then squatted down on the brown grass beside her.

'What's the matter?' he said. He touched her elbow lightly with the back of his hand.

She turned her head and buried her face under his chin. At first he thought that she was going to cry; in fact she was simply making sure that she could speak to him without being heard.

'I wish she weren't here,' Kursten whispered.

'Reen? She may call you "trollop" and stuff, but that's just because she likes . . .'

'No. Not her. Syor.'

'But you've never met her before – have you?'

'I don't have to have met her.'

He stroked her hair absentmindedly. It was something he'd forgotten to do when he was being a gallant hero. It was something he'd been wanting to do ever since. He was slightly surprised to find that it felt just like hair.

'It's silly to hate someone on sight,' he said.

'I'm not a child!' The words were spoken so forcefully that it was as if she had shouted, yet her voice was still no louder than a whisper. 'Maybe I was, when you first met me,' she added more quietly, 'but that was a lifetime ago. No, I'm not so stupid as to judge people I don't know. It's not that – quite the opposite. I know her far too well. I'm a bit of her, really.'

'I don't understand you.' And then he thought he did.

'Come with me,' she said, withdrawing herself and scrambling to her feet. 'Come with me,' she repeated, more loudly this time so that the others could hear.

Reen guffawed. Syor smiled benignly, blinking her green eyes at them. Rehan blushed, aware that Kursten had created exactly the effect that she'd intended.

As the two of them walked towards the encircling mist it shifted in outline, drawing back from them. As he followed her insistent tugging on his arm the mist closed again behind them, so that they were enclosed in their own small pocket of sunshine. As soon as they were sealed off from the other two, Rehan explained that he understood why she felt the way she did but . . .

'You have it wrong,' he finally allowed her to say.

'Oh.'

'Most of the time we selves are barely aware of each other's existence.'

'Oh.'

'But we're all aware of *her* existence. We're all aspects of her. And we resent it.'

'Oh. Why?'

'Don't you resent your gods for having brought you into the World?'

'I have no gods.'

'Your parents, then.'

'I can't remember very much about my parents. They were all right to me, I think.'

'No – I mean, don't you resent your parents for having given birth to you without ever asking your permission beforehand? Condemning you to a life here in the World, with all its hardships, for a crime you never committed?'

'How could they have asked me my permission before I was even born?' He grinned at her.

'Stop patronizing me, Rehan! Even though it wasn't their fault that you were born, don't you *anyway* resent them for making it happen?'

'Well . . . no, not really. I don't think about it much, to tell you the truth. If I ever do, I suppose I'm sort of dimly grateful to them, because if they hadn't given me the gift of life . . .'

'Some gift.'

'Well . . . yes. How can you be like that? Do you hate living so much? Even the happy times?'

'I've known very few of them. A prisoner in a cage can be happy if he's never known anything *but* the cage. He might even get upset if his gaolers forgot to give him his daily flogging. When I was a child, living with my father, I thought I was happy then – I *was* happy then – but it was the stupid, ignorant, blind happiness of the prisoner who's just had his lashing to remind him that all's right with the World. Call *that* happiness? *Real* happiness? Can you? Honestly?'

'Yes. You've got to judge happiness in terms of itself, at the time, not against some sort of sliding scale.' He looked at his hands; she was holding one of them. 'But what has that got to do with you resenting Syor?' he asked.

'Everything.' She let go of his hand and turned away from him. The bank of mist retreated a little, mimicking her movement. 'Sometimes I might love her, but all the time I also hate her – all the time since I became a part of the Mistdom.'

'Then you were captured? Not by monsters but by Syor?'

'I'm not talking from my Kursten-memory. I'm talking from my other. Always I've been one of the selves of the Mistdom; becoming a part of it was my . . . birth, you could say. When the Mistdom came into existence, I was created as a part of it, whether I liked it or not.'

'But what did that have to do with Syor? She was born herself only a few decades ago. The people of the city have been defending themselves against the ffarg ever since they got here, centuries ago.'

'The Mistdom constructs its own past,' she said gently. 'Had you forgotten?'

'Then . . . you mean . . . what you're trying to say is that Syor created the Mistdom, and what she created was a Mistdom that had always existed? But how could that happen? She's not some kind of god, you know – she's just a human being like the rest of us.'

'She was a human being, once. Now she's becoming something that's very like a god. She's not totally aware of it yet – or, at least, she is, because I wouldn't be if she weren't, but she's not allowing herself to be. It wasn't just the Mistdom or we selves that she created. Haven't you noticed the way that the World is changing? Wasn't it you yourself that said she seemed to be at the end of everybody's quest?'

'Yes,' he said warily. 'And *you* said that she was at the end of more quests than any of us knew about. And she admitted that she was, but she didn't say any more than that.'

'Well, this bit of her can say more than that.'

He looked at her. She still had her back to him. Her shoulders were hunched.

' "This bit of her," ' he echoed.

'That's what I am,' she said, almost defiant, turning towards him once more. The tears in her eyes were like crystals of ice. 'I've said so before, but you seem incapable of hearing the words I say. That's what all of the selves are: bits of her. It's not just that she created the Mistdom: the Mistdom *is her*.'

'She is the Mistdom, you mean?'

'No. That's not the same thing at all. She's much more than just the Mistdom. Just like she's so much more than the her who was inside your head, ignorant of her greater self.'

'You're trying to say that she's changing the World.'

'Yes.'

'And that she's at the end of everybody's quest.'

'Yes.'

'That she's a god, even.'

'Yes. Not quite a god, I said. Not yet. She's getting there.'

'But she used to be just a woman. Oh – I don't mean the reification that was born out of the Mistdom for the benefit of Reen and myself. I mean *her*, the *real* . . . the . . . original Syor.'

'That's right. She was a woman who was born and grew up and had a child, and then she died. All of that happened in Albion. But Albion wasn't finished with her – or maybe it was she who wasn't finished with Albion, I'm not sure – and so now she's in the process of coming back again, or maybe being brought back again. And this time she's *everywhere*. She wants to go to Albion, soon, because that's where her natural focus is, but really it hardly matters. All of the World is becoming her. She's everywhere.'

'At the end of everybody's quest,' he whispered. He pulled Kursten into his arms. The hair of her head was a soft cushion against his ear. Over her shoulder he could see the face of the mist. Nothing else.

The mist was like the future, he thought. As yet it was completely formless, with no ordering in it at all. Patterns could be imposed upon it; and in the case of the future they soon would be, as part of the continual process whereby the advance of time rapidly gobbled up its remaining allocation of the World's duration. The patterns that would be imposed on the future were like those of the mist: in a sense, they were already there, latent, as the selves were.

But the past should be different. The past should be like the ground beneath his feet: solid, unalterable, defined. The presence of Syor in the World was changing that truism, along with all the others: now the past, too, was a mist of latent patterns, waiting for a designer to come along and decide that *this* pattern would represent the true course of reality, and that *these* patterns should be left as they were, mere unchosen possibilities. And that was how it would stay until, maybe, another designer came along. Right now, Syor was the new designer.

Only she wasn't fully aware of it yet.

Or wouldn't let herself become so. This was the heart of it, the one thing that she didn't want to have to admit to herself. All the rest were subsidiary corollaries of it.

The fact that she was a designer: the new designer of the World.

And she wants to go to Albion soon, because that's where her natural focus is . . .

PART TWO
A Rent in the Fabric

> Now Salome was a dancer
> and she danced the hootchie-cootch.
> She did it for King 'erod,
> but she did a *bit too mootch*.
> 'Oi!' cried King 'erod.
> 'You can't do that there 'ere!'
> But Salome said 'Baloney!'
> and she kicked the chandelier.
>
> Children's skipping rhyme

Elsewhere & Elsewhen

two

Ah, you're slowly returning into yourself. The sounds are disappearing and the colours are fading fast. Well, now that you've flexed your mental muscles, as it were, in this scrying game, perhaps you're prepared to take on something a little more adventurous.

Your first adventures have been confined to our own reality – to the World – but now we're going to venture far out of it. No, not to a faraway planet, still less to one of the galaxies at the furthest end of the Universe – even those remote objects, so distant from us that the light of their stars has yet to reach us, are merely in the next room by comparison with our destination.

We're referring, of course, to one of the potential afterlives.

For many centuries the notion of an afterlife – even just a single one of them – was rejected by the mass of the World's population as just another of the ravings of the Holies. But that was foolish. Afterlives exist in plenty.

And there are portals within the mind of each and every one of us which permit us to gaze upon the worlds that await our occupation after we have left this one. We cannot control which window it is that we open, of course, or what the conditions will be like on the far side of the glass, but, every time we close our eyes in sleep or smoke the weeds sold by the cutthroats in the less reputable bazaars, our inner eyes are granted access to *somewhere* – some other reality – that is no part of the World.

Now, level your eyes as before and rotate your pyramid so that the next face to the left is directed towards you.

Concentrate upon its featurelessness until, once more, coloured images begin to move across it, and infant cacophonies to resonate in the bath of air surrounding you . . .

Chapter One
How I Slept with the Queen of China

1

There are the five of us down at the Prospect, by the river, and Hump is running a book. Each of us puts in a fiver and the winner is the first person to pull a bird, which should not be difficult for someone because it is summer and a Saturday night and so the place is crawling with all these French and Italian nubiles across for the English-as-a-foreign-language schools, only Hump then makes the mistake of chatting up a girl with a small vocabulary and a large boyfriend so we decide suddenly to leave the Prospect. Hump and the others say they want to go down to the Double Locks but I say no, I am tired, I want to get away from noise for a while, and Hump says I can't have my fiver back.

I like the walk back up from the river. The night air is cool and gentle on me, which is nice after the hotness of today, and the receding sound of all the people in the Prospect talking and laughing makes me feel rested, so that by the time I get to Mount Pleasant I am in the mood for sitting down somewhere quiet with a drink.

I go into the Grapes because that is a pub that no one hardly ever goes into except Ben and Cecil, these two old guys who spend all the time there just sitting side by side, not talking, looking at the dartboard opposite that no one ever uses. I guess that when the pub is shut they sit somewhere else, not moving, just waiting for it to open.

There is someone else in there aside from Ben and Cecil tonight, though, a smallish guy with a snake tattooed in blue on the side of his face, and he is talking with the barmaid, who is the Queen of China. She is not Chinese and she is not a queen, but she is the Queen of China because that is the name Hump once gave her when pissed because of the way she looks. Her face is very pale and it never shows what she is feeling at all; you could swear at her and she would not seem to get angry, or you could tell her a joke and she would not smile, but no one bothers because there is not any point. Hump said if she ever really smiled her face would crack up like china, and so that is how she got her name. Dave once said that if anyone ever pulled her we would have to double the stakes, but Hump said no one would want to because it would be like laying something that was not really human. I remember him saying this as I look at her tonight and I think he is probably right but it seems very odd because she has got a pretty face and a skinny sexy figure in faded blue jeans and a white blouse. Her hair is long and neat and a sort of muddy red-yellow-brown.

She turns away from the wanker – Snakeface – so I go to the bar. Her face does not try to smile at me but the corners of her mouth turn up to show that she is good at her job. I ask her for a pint of Flowers because it is the best they have got, even if not very, and she pours it in silence. I look around the bar and Cecil lights a cigarette. I get the idea that maybe the Queen and Snakeface have been arguing, because his silence tells me so. I give her money and she gives me change and I take my pint and go over to sit in the opposite corner from Ben and Cecil because I don't want to not have a conversation with them.

Snakeface and the Queen start arguing again – or, at least, he does the arguing in a little tight voice and every time he stops she tells him patiently to go away, which he does not. Clearly he is an old friend of hers. They stop for a while when Cecil comes up to buy a pint each for him and Ben, and then they carry on again, which is distressing because I want to think. Not about anything important: just to enjoy the thoughts drifting along across my mind. I realize that I do not like Snakeface very much. I wish he would do what the Queen says and go away. Then his words become like muzak so I do not hear him any longer, and I start wondering who if anyone is going to win the twenty-five quid and I discover how little I care.

It is a while later and I have almost finished my pint when Snakeface starts shouting.

'You cheap shit!' he is yelling at her. 'There must be lots in the till. You give me some of it or by Christ your face is not going to look too pretty.'

I turn to watch him and I see that he has got a razor in his hand. Without the razor he would not be much which I suppose is why he has it. His hair is dirty with grease and it runs down over the back of his collar, which is likewise dirty with grease. He is wearing an old grey suit with a shiny bottom and dandruff on the shoulders, and he has got a little sharp face that looks like a rodent's. I decide I very much do not like him.

'Put the razor away and get out of here,' I say and at first he does not hear me.

So I say it again and louder.

This time he hears and he looks at me and he spits on the floor so I stand up. I am pretty big and I know how to look bigger, and he sees the empty glass in my hand, and he sees the way it would be easy for me to hit it against the table so that I am holding a ring of sharp edges. I am watching his mind working behind those nasty little eyes of his. He thinks for a few moments and then he shuts the razor with a click and he sticks it into his shiny jacket pocket.

'I will be back, you mark my words you bitch,' he says in a steaming piss-stream to the Queen of China and then he walks out of the pub very fast, slamming the door behind him as he leaves.

I go to the bar again and I find my breath is a bit heavy but not too heavy and I ask the Queen for another pint before she says thank you to me, because that sort of thing embarrasses me. But I let her not take any money for the drink while Cecil lights another cigarette and does not look at Ben.

'He may hang around out there,' I say, 'whoever he is.

Let me get a bike and I will take you home after the pub closes.'

She shakes her head.

'I can take care of him without no difficulty,' she says. 'Anyway, Nadar, I know where you get your bikes. You borrow them from other people and you forget to take them back afterwards. I do not want to have anything to do with that sort of thing.'

I say something about how I always look after the bikes and the people get them back soon because the police find them, but she says nothing about that and says that there is no need anyway, she lives just a walk away, she does not need me with her, and I guess she thinks I might want to go into her home with her when I take her there, so it is end of discussion.

I go back to my ripped seat with my pint and I worry a lot because I do not like Snakeface and he looked as if he really meant to use the razor on her, so I decide that I will follow her when she goes home in case he tries anything on. Besides I have got nothing much else I want to do tonight and it is not worth going home yet because I already know that England lost the cricket and so why should I bother watching the highlights.

The landlord who has never had a name appears and looks newted and tells me and Ben and Cecil that it is nearly time for us to go, so I finish my beer and leave the Grapes and on the other side of the road I find a shadow that I can wrap around my shoulders.

2

It is nearly midnight when the landlord who has never had a name lets the Queen of China out and locks the door behind her. She looks around, probably to check that Snakeface is not there, but she does not see me, and then she turns away to the left, walking up Mount Pleasant Road. She is wearing a light coat now, and it is easy for me to follow her shape in the orange half-darkness. I stay on the other side of the road and move very quietly, so that she will not hear me. If she turns around I am just another person walking home, but she does not turn around.

We go left again, onto Elmside, and then I see that one of the other shadows is moving just a little too fast, and that is when I run across the road and sure enough it is Snakeface and he has got the razor out and he is waving it in the air.

I knock him sideways with my shoulder and he staggers. He is a bit heavier than he should be for his size, and the muscles inside his clothes are surprisingly hard, but he stumbles away sideways the way I knocked him, losing his balance. He drops the razor and it scuttles away into the gutter and I pick him up and throw him against the wall of somebody's house. I get ready to hit him, but his head hits the bricks hard instead and he just collapses in a heap. I stand there waiting but he does not move.

The Queen is shaking and in the dirty streetlight I see that there are tears running down her porcelain cheeks, and it is fascinating because I had never thought of her as being able to cry.

Some helpful neighbour must have called our friends in blue because in a minute or so which is quick even for them there are flashing lights and sirens wailing and a couple of voices, who come over and look at Snakeface and look at me and look at the Queen, and she tells them what happened and they stop sizing me up. So Snakeface is thrown into an ambulance that turns up and the two policemen go with us to the Queen's place, which is a neat little two-room flat with faded curtains and I have a slash and then they take our statements and by the time it is all over and they have telephoned the hospital to discover that Snakeface will live it is three o'clock in the morning and the Queen looks as if she is going to fall asleep standing up. They offer me a lift home but I see her looking almost frightened at that and anyway what would my neighbours say, so I say no to them.

When they have gone I say as soft as I can: 'Does that little bastard with the blue tattoo of a snake on his face know where you live?'

And she says yes, obviously he does, and I say that that

is bad because they might not keep him in hospital all night, and again her face shows something and very certainly this time it is fear. So I say I will sleep on the sofa if she likes and besides it is very late and I am tired, too, and I do not want to walk the rest of the way home now, and other things, and she gets the idea that I really mean it and that she is not in a fire-after-frying-pan situation.

So she fetches a pillow and a couple of blankets while I have another slash because of the beer and rub some toothpaste on my teeth with my finger, and as I get out of my clothes I hear her in the toilet and that surprises me again, because it is news to me that she might have to slash as well.

3

The minutes pass and I turn out the light and wriggle down under the blankets she has given me while she moves around in the bedroom making small female noises. There is a full moon tonight and a line of silver stretches across the dark carpet from the gap between the curtains. I watch it for a time and then I hear new sounds from the bedroom and after a while I realize that the Queen is crying and I do not know what to do.

So a little later when I cannot stand the sound of it any longer I go and I knock on her door and I ask her if she is all right, and she opens the door and she puts her arms round me and the hair on my chest gets wet for a few minutes as her shoulders jump and shake under my hands. It is then that I remember that I have not got any clothes on and peel her off me for long enough to go and get into my jeans.

When I go back she is sitting on her bed with her face in her hands but she is a lot calmer now, so the tears do not erupt the way they were doing earlier. I sit down beside her and I put an arm around her shoulders and just squeeze her against me, feeling the slithery cloth of her nightdress on the inside of my elbow and still wondering what I should do.

When she stops crying she begins to talk, and I let her

because the words are just the same as the tears, things she has to get out of her before she can feel all right again. What she tells me makes me glad I did not like Snakeface.

She and him have known each other for quite a while, she says to me. A couple of years ago, she says, she moved in to live with him. Her first love and all that and she thought it was for life but it was only for three weeks because that is how long it took for him to knock her around a second time and for her broken eyes to open to how long life can be. We all make our own messes but some of us make them for other people too, and now she had discovered that Snakeface was a latter. Rapid exit of the Queen of China from his life in search of pastures new – or at least to this little flat which is as tidy as her hair normally is. Since then she has been living on her own and working in the Grapes, and every few weeks he appears to fuck up her life a little more and get some money from her, and tonight is the first time she has decided she has got enough courage not to give him any. And now she is terrified because when they let him out in a few hours or a few days or a few weeks he is going to come and cut her open, she knows that for a fact.

All this time I am just sitting and listening but then she says she wants me to stay beside her for what is left of the night, and for once I do not reach for my flies but instead climb in under the covers in my jeans and I reach out a hand and pull her in beside me and rest her head on my arm and in the moonlight, which is brighter in this room, I watch her hair on the pillow and the way that her face melts and changes as she falls asleep. She becomes something else from the person she was when she was awake; older, it looks like a lot older, but it does not bother me. It is a trick that the pale light can play when clouds pass across the front of the bright full moon, I guess. And I lie there for a while wondering why it is that I am lying there in bed with a woman and not unhappy about the fact that we have not screwed, and then I fall asleep too because a few moments later the room is full of yellow and it is the middle of the morning.

I put some water and four eggs in a pan and work out which is the right knob on the cooker to turn while she gets to work with the electric toaster. She is in a dressing-gown with blue flowers on it and I am still in my jeans, which feel dirty on my thighs. As she squats down in front of a cupboard with her hair all ruffled from sleeping I look at her and see again how pretty she is and so I tell her so.

She says a thankyou very formally and she smiles at me. So the Queen does know how to smile as well. It is not the empty thing I have always seen her use in the Grapes because her whole face changes and I see her smiling with her eyes as well. I ask her her name and she tells me it is Syor, and I say that that is a nice name and that I have not heard it before but if it is OK with her I would like to carry on calling her the Queen, and she asks me why and I tell her what Hump said about her face cracking up if ever she really smiled, and I am just beginning to realize this maybe is not too tactful of me when I see that she has started laughing, so that is all right.

'It seems funny that we did not, you know, make it last night,' I say because now I think I know her well enough not to worry about saying things like that.

'It could have been fun maybe,' she says and she says it so easily that I can't believe my ears. She puts a stainless-steel spoon carefully beside each egg-cup. They are white egg-cups with pictures of Peter Rabbit on them.

'It is not too late,' I say because I expect it of myself, and she just shakes her head but she does not look angry at all, so we eat our toast and eggs and we talk about other things, and then after a bit things get less happy because the subject of what to do about Snakeface comes up. I say that it is a Sunday, it is her day off and I have got nothing else to do anyway, so if she likes I will stick around with her. She looks reluctant at this so I quickly say that it is a nice day and we could go out together, maybe down to the beach because I have got enough money for the bus fares, and she relaxes again and we finish eating and then get dressed in separate rooms.

She picks up the red plastic telephone and calls the police station and asks about Snakeface, only she calls him Lion or something. As she listens I see the angles of her body gradually become more rounded and when she puts the telephone down she comes across to me and kisses me hard on the lips for a second or less before she tells me that it seems as if a guy with a blue tattoo of a snake on his face has been a bit too generous with his razor a couple of times before and so the gents in blue are truly delighted to have got their hands on him at last and it could be a long time like months maybe longer before he goes back to the Grapes again.

And so we go down to the beach and eat ice-cream and build a sandcastle.

5

These days I do not see much of Hump and Dave and the others and no I never did get that fiver back. When I am with the Queen I feel I can talk about anything I want to, and she says the same about me, even those times when she seems to be somewhere else completely. Sometimes we kiss and maybe one day we will sleep together again but that is in the future and I am not very good at thinking about the future. At the moment she is just the best friend I ever had and life is rounded at the edges and I feel like I am a whole lot older than I was then.

Chapter Two
Down to a Sinless Sea

1

And so he discovers himself back *here* again . . .

Joli first began to wonder if perhaps he were turning into an alcoholic when the top drawer of the filing cabinet got so full that he could no longer close it, and had to start on the second. There they were, in their dozens, the gleaming green testimonies to all the mornings when he had told himself, told himself, told himself on the way to the office that *this* morning he wasn't going to drop in at the Thresher's round the corner and pick up a little something to get rid of the sweats and the dizziness, the dregs of last night's contented muzzy drunkenness. *Correction*, he thought. *They're markers of all the times I walked past Thresher's and then, about ten yards further on, slowed up and finally went back.*

He drained the last of this morning's quarter-bottle of Gordon's and swept it into the filing cabinet's second drawer, Export Invoices, which he closed with a careful slowness lest the bearings squeal. As always, he jumped up and down once or twice, making the office floor vibrate and listening carefully in case there was any tell-tale clinking. Satisfied, he went to his studiedly tidy desk, with its frowning white blotter that he never used and its wholesome sheen of buffedly honest oak veneer. If the expected promotion came through at the end of the month he could hope to graduate to a solid-wood desk; at the moment he was in something of a limbo, marked off as superior to his assistants, whose desks were of mere utilitarian metal, yet still not among the exalted demigods of upper management, with their broadly grinning expanses of solid rosewood and gold-trimmed insets of grey-green leather.

Bright sunshine reflected off the grey wall opposite his window and created an illusion of daylight. Outside it was one of those paradoxically bright late-October days that seem to be trying to remind you that it really hasn't been all that many weeks since it was summer. But the light was modified as it came in through his picture window, so that the fluorescent tubes in the office ceiling seemed to shine warmly by comparison.

Joli frowned. At times like this he sometimes found his mind filled with images of a land where there was perpetual sunlight. The experience was a curious one: he felt as if he'd lived there for quite a long time once, and yet somehow had forgotten about it. Perhaps it had been in an unusually vivid dream which his conscious mind had rejected, yet which still remained somewhere hidden in his unconscious; or perhaps there was some truth in this reincarnation business the tabloids sometimes chuntered on about. He'd once mentioned the latter possibility to Leonora, and she'd looked at him oddly and started talking about a holiday.

He took a packet of Tunes from his left-hand second drawer and expertly flipped the top one out with his thumbnail. Soon his breath smelled of heady menthol – menthol and something else, but in the warm cocoon that the gin had wrapped around him he was superbly confident that no one would be able to detect the something else.

Dragging his thoughts together with a conscious effort, he pressed the buzzer on his desk, summoning Ilse with her burden of the morning's post, little realizing that his own summoning was just about to begin.

2

. . . and let us tread here and there among the clusters, my Earth-bound love, see the stars being born and the worlds slowly dancing as this aspect of the polycosmos progresses inexorably towards its inevitable heat-death. I will show you the filigrees that rim the bright gas clouds where the stars are young, and the multiple coloured suns of faraway systems, and the great disc of the Galaxy towering like a wall of white flame above us . . . Let us be together where the two ends of time touch, as if shyly. I can take you away from here to live for the rest of eternity in a bodiless murmuring of spirits conjoined. Only reach out your hand to skim mine . . .

3

Joli shook his head to oust the intruding voice and looked up as Ilse opened the door.

She was handsome rather than beautiful, and yet her efficient movements generated an overall effect of warm sensuality – if only because there was nothing of sensuality in them, so that the mind noticed its absence. She had broad cheek-bones and a brush of near-blonde hair. He hadn't slept with her, even though she occasionally intruded into his fantasies, because he'd met her husband and liked the man; the double standards involved troubled him when he allowed them to. Another contributor to his hands-off policy so far as Ilse was concerned was that he suspected she knew about the contents of the filing cabinet, even though it was supposed to be for his use only, and so regarded him as being beneath her contempt. Thank God he could trust her not to prattle to other people about it all.

'Only a few letters today, Julian,' she said, settling herself into the chair opposite him, shorthand notebook at the ready. She smiled at him, but her dark-brown eyes were incongruously cold. He was irritated as always by the fact that, unlike everyone else except Leonora, who thought 'Joli' wasn't sufficiently dignified, she insisted on using his full name. 'Mr McPhee of Henderson Fergus probably needs a reply today – he sounds as if he's getting pretty hot under the collar about the missing software – but the rest can wait. Unless you want to get them out of the way, that is.'

She was in pale blue jeans today. Women in blue jeans always turned him on – to be more accurate, women turned him on full stop, but women in blue jeans even more so – except for Ilse, because he thought her husband was a good bloke. His hormones were incomprehensible.

'Let's see what we have here,' he said, ruffling through the small pile of correspondence she'd put on the desk in front of him.

McPhee of Henderson Fergus was indeed annoyed, and had every right to be. The company had supplied him with the most up-to-date laser-scanning hardware without informing him that the compatible software for his particular computer system had yet to be developed. There was a version of it available in Australia which, while as yet imperfect, would at least make the system usable until something better came along. The trouble was that the Australian stuff was in considerable demand, for exactly this reason, and Joli was having difficulty getting hold of a copy.

He looked through the window at the grey wall opposite, and as always it and the gin inspired him. Plausible excuses for the delay came sparkling to his lips, and Ilse's pencil moved swiftly.

4

At lunchtime in the pub he chatted superficially with his colleagues in the lower echelons of senior management, but he wasn't really concentrating on the standard round of blue jokes, interdepartmental bitchery and speculation as to the availability or otherwise of the female clerical staff. In the end he pulled himself away from the others and settled himself in a gloomy corner alcove.

To his surprise, he found that he wasn't alone there.

'Sorry,' he said. 'I should have asked if I could join you.'

'Feel free,' said a woman's voice. A pale hand gestured at the table. In the darkness the long, polished fingernails seemed to be independently mobile black gleams.

He lit a cigarette and then, as an afterthought, offered the pack across the dark to his invisible companion.

Again the pale hand moved, this time to delicately extract one of his cigarettes from the pack.

In the flame of his lighter, as she leaned forwards, he could see her face. There was the tiniest down of fine dark hair on an upper lip that creased elegantly up towards a proud, strong nose. Her face was perhaps a little narrow, but it had a sort of sweetness and innocence that called out to him. Her left hand cupped the flame, and he noticed there was no ring on it.

He felt as if his mind had been kicked.

This is ridiculous, he thought to himself waspishly. *I'm too old to be falling instantly in love with women in pubs. That sort of thing just doesn't happen – not so quickly as this, whatever the Mills'n'Boon novels might say. When you're in your mid-thirties you're supposed to letch after women, dammit, not . . . not want just to be with them for a long time, to be sixteen with them and show them your shell collection and watch as their fingertips trace along the rounded ridges of mother-of-pearl inside the treasured abalone shell that your aunt brought back from sunny California, or listen in the dark to the sad slow strains of your favourite albums – the ones that'll embarrass you when you drag them out and play them for old times' sake a decade later – or kiss softly, just once, on the nose as you say goodnight and go home dancing in the deliciously warm rain knowing that God must be up there somewhere in His Heaven, because otherwise how could such a fine world as this one ever have come into existence? And then of course what really happened was that you'd go and louse up your relationship with this very special girl because you'd discover that fat Sophia down the road would let you feel her tits for a Mars Bar. Years later you'd think of her, that very special girl, and you'd wonder where she was now, and you'd guess that she was locked up in some featureless box of a life just the way you are.*

He heard the synthetic leather of the padded pub seat creak and exhale as she relaxed back into the darkness, and saw the tip of her cigarette glow a hot yellow-orange.

'My name's Julian,' he said, slightly surprised that the words were leaving his tongue in the right order. 'My friends all call me Joli.'

She said nothing, but the cigarette tip glowed again, this time briefly and nervously.

'I got the nickname as a child,' he explained, his lips rubbery, 'because when I was an infant that was the nearest I could get to saying "Julian", and my parents thought it was cute.'

A pause.

He sat there feeling the embarrassment washing wetly over him. He took a deep draught of his lager, but the stuff wasn't strong enough. He coughed violently once, and felt the customary sharp pain in his stomach. The shakes were beginning to return, as they always did at about this time of day, once the effects of 'breakfast' started to wear off, and he knew that the only cure was to slip around into the other bar, where his colleagues never went, and order himself two double gins, one after the other. He felt the viscous sweat begin to form under his vest and pants and especially on the insides of his thighs, little rivulets of it trickling erratically down the backs of his calves.

'I'm Lisa,' she said abruptly, grinding her half-smoked cigarette viciously into the ashtray between them. The words and the action were so unexpected, so discrepant, that for a moment he could make no sense of them – the sound and the sight were interlopers in the little self-contained universe that had enveloped him.

'Oh . . . eh . . . oh, hello, Lisa.'

There was an unstable silence. He filled it by drinking back his lager as swiftly as he could. He forced – *forced* – his hand not to shake as he held the glass to his mouth. If he could finish it soon enough, before she'd had the chance to flee, then he could offer to buy her a drink. And while he was up at the bar he'd have the chance to load up with something a bit stronger.

He could feel her smile in the gloom. He started when she put her cool hand over his sweaty one.

'You're trembling, Joli,' she said. 'Why?'

What could he tell her? *I'm trembling because I'll carry on trembling until I get something to numb all the pain of the day – the work that's so undemanding I could do it in my sleep, and sometimes do, and the home that's nothing more than a sanitized children's play-house where the Sindy dolls that are myself and my family are moved into one rigidly unnatural position before the pudgy hands of the Great Child in the Sky move us into the next: Leonora with her wide unblinking blue eyes and her seven complete sets of matching clothing and her pony, me with my pipe although I never smoke a pipe and my tweed suit that falls apart if I raise my arm too high and my checked cowboy shirt and designer jeans for wear at weekends, and Sam with his bed-time by eight o'clock prompt except it's always nine before we can get him to go. Oh, yes, pretty-stranger-lady, I have all the reason in the world to tremble, and there's only one thing in the world that I've yet discovered that will stop it for a while.*

Instead, he said: 'I'm sorry. I don't make too much of a habit of striking up conversations with people I've never met before. Especially . . .' A wave of his free hand to explain to her.

He could feel through the touch of her palm against the back of his knuckles that she was taking his words for the lie they were. He was a salesman, for God's sake: his profession was embroidered into the crease of his trousers and the taut lapels of his jacket. It was his *job* to be instantly friendly, quasi-intimate, with people he'd just met: that was what he was *for*.

'May I have another cigarette, please, Joli?' she said, gently. Her voice was shaded by some accent he couldn't identify. He hazarded a guess at Cornish, but he couldn't be sure. She might even be from somewhere the other side of the Atlantic – New Jersey, maybe. A friend of his had once emigrated to rural New Jersey and, during the months until the letters had eventually stopped, Joli had gained a picture of the place as an impossible idyll, a jewel in the navel of the world. Leonora had told him that his friend was probably lying because he didn't want to admit that he'd emigrated to some vast garbage tip.

'Of course you may,' he muttered. 'No need to ask. Just feel free to help yourself.'

He put the open packet on the gummy tabletop between them.

'May I fetch you a drink, ah . . . Lisa?'

'Yes, please. That would be very kind of you, Joli. An unsweetened orange juice, please. They sell it here.'

As he got to his feet she added in a low voice: 'I think I'm going to like you, Joli.'

After the darkness, the garish lights of the main bar stuck into his eyes like sharp points – retinal acupuncture – and for a moment he was disorientated. Another moment later and vision had returned. He took care not to look at the raucous knot of his colleagues around the bar, on the principle that if he didn't look at them they wouldn't look at him, as he made his way furtively through the connecting arch into the lounge at the back. ('. . . and so,' Reggie was shouting, 'the tart looks up from her bag of chips and she says to him' – exaggerated wheeze, the punchline is surely coming – 'she says to him, "Sorry to expose myself, hossifer. I didn't realize he'd gone." She *didn't realize he'd gone!*')

5

. . . along the broad violet of the space-lanes we will dance, just you and I, and upon our brows there will be gleaming coronets of fresh spring flowers, each flower a soundless gathering of suns. And we shall talk between ourselves without words, sipping together at the dew-soft liquor of the Universe, kneading time between our fingers and watching as its irregular tatters spread twisting out across the gentle black fabric of emptiness. In a galaxy's heart, with all the ancient stars gazing eyelessly on, we shall consummate our love and feel all the Universe's million billion sensations passing through our aethereal veins. Our kisses will spark supernovae into being and the running of my parsecs-long fingers through the glistening veil of your hair will . . .

'What'll it be?' repeated the barmaid, looking bored.

'I'm . . . I'm sorry. I was thinking of something else. Er . . . a double gin,' said Joli. 'No – make that two. And a pint of lager. And an orange juice – yes, with ice.' He remembered the chink of the cubes in Lisa's glass.

He left the drinks on the bar briefly to go to the gents. After he'd peed – copiously, satisfyingly, looking down affectionately on the wrinkled little gnarl of flesh that was so important to him – he straightened his tie in the mirror and then, with unexpected decisiveness, pulled it askew. He didn't want to carry on looking like just another executive clone. With a smile at his reflected self, he deliberately ruffled his hair, hoping that the air of casual untidiness would conjure up in Lisa's eyes some aura of unselfconscious youth. He stuffed his handkerchief ruthlessly down into his top jacket pocket, so that the carefully folded inverted V of its tip no longer showed.

Back at the bar he noticed that his hands weren't shaking nearly as much as they had been before, but nevertheless he tossed back first one gin and then the other, just to be on the safe side. He took a mouthful of lager and swished it through his teeth to drown the betraying fumes of the gin.

On his way to the alcove, holding the drinks carefully, he felt as if he were half his normal weight. But the whole thing was ridiculous. He knew it was and he told himself so repeatedly, but today he seemed to be incapable of listening to himself. She must be at least ten years younger than he was, and she was beautiful, whereas he had the kind of face that middle-aged women describe as 'interesting'. Around Lisa there was a cloud of loveliness. She was probably just waiting for her boyfriend to turn up, and was too polite to tell this boring old fart to piss off.

He inched around the humming, popping, grinding, barking fruit machine and its mesmerized patron. As he went by it struck up the first few bars of *La Marseillaise*.

But he'd felt something pass between himself and Lisa. He couldn't tell what it had been, but he knew for a fact that it had been there. He was sure that she had felt it, too. There had been her nervousness. Her sudden switch into close understanding. The way that she'd let her hand rest so gently on his. He'd never sensed anything of this with Leonora, not even in the months before their marriage when, had anyone thought to ask him, he would have been able to swear with all sincerity that yes, of course he was deeply in love with Leonora. No: his meeting with Lisa must have been somehow preordained.

As soon as he was back in the dimness of the alcove he was aware that she had gone.

Obviously she's just popped off to the ladies, he thought, but he knew that wasn't true. The emptiness was a permanent one, not a temporary one.

He put the drinks down on the table and collapsed onto the padded bench. Very softly he pounded the sugary surface of the table with the edge of his tightly clenched fist. He waited for the breath to come. Of its own volition his hand crept forward, starting to shake again, and groped around for his lager.

The hairs on the back of his little finger brushed something.

He started. Then he felt for whatever it was.

His lighter.

His cigarettes had gone – she must have taken them with her, but that was all right, there were only a few left in the packet anyway – and maybe, in a curious way, the petty theft was some type of expression on her part of affection for him: 'I love you, but it can never be' – that sort of cliché.

And there was something else there, under his lighter. It was a flat rectangle, perhaps five inches by three, like an index card.

He picked it up, took it out into the light, and squeezed his eyes to look at what was written on the card.

First there was her name, Lisa, and it was followed by her telephone number.

It was only when he turned the card over that he discovered her price-list.

7

... and have you ever felt the dreaming caress, my love, of the shoals of silvery fishes that flicker mindlessly between the stars, the arcs of their fanned tails tracing out the parsecs in long unhurried ripples as they move their insubstantial forms across the oceans of the interstellar spaces? Have you held a planet in your palm, as if it were a warmly perfect pearl? Have you ever felt the Universe's kiss upon your brow, Joli, or its soft breath against your cheek? Be with me soon, my love, so that I may take you there ...

8

Once his head had cleared of the uninvited images, Joli told Reggie that he was feeling unwell and had decided to go home for the afternoon. 'You *are* looking a bit off-colour,' said Reggie with a poor imitation of concern, his rheumy eyes moving smoothly into compassion mode. He promised to pass the message on. A moment later his shout was filling the pub again. ('... "Oh, *I'm* all right," he says. "Mine's lipstick." *Mine's lipstick!*')

It was good to be away from there.

He'd left Lisa's card on the bar, vengefully hoping that it would be picked up by some really loathsome drunk who'd throw up in her bed. Reggie would be ideal – the two of them deserved each other. The sordidness of the wish, and of the emotion underlying it, seemed to accord well with the world inside the pub, inhabited by imitation people who forged between each other bonds of tissue paper held in place by dabs of spittle and synthetic bonhomie.

The cars in the road ahead of him shouted angry insults backwards and forwards to one another, each trying to shoulder the next aside, shoving and barging through the fray. Joli smiled at them. *Man made the automobile in his own image*, he thought, *and he's never noticed how accurate the likeness is*.

Somebody bumped into him, and he swayed. There was a strong whiff of what he recognized from his polytechnic days as marijuana. In this part of town it had to be Qinefer.

'Watch where yo' goin', honky trash,' the tall black woman said in an accent that would have been considered too exaggerated for a remake of *Gone With the Wind*.

'Damn' uppity no-good nigger,' said Joli automatically, his heart not really in it. 'You ever think you need a whuppin', you jus' give a ring, d'you hear?'

Qinefer was a systems analyst. They met sometimes during the course of work. Years ago she'd rejected the pass he'd made at her, but told him that it didn't matter because she liked him anyway. Since then, having nothing whatsoever in common, they'd got on very well together.

'How're things going?' he asked.

'So so,' she said. 'Some dummy in programming has . . . ah, hell, you don't want to hear about my problems. How about you? Say, Joli' – peering at him – 'are you OK?'

'Bit under the weather, Qinefer, that's all.' He mustered a smile and turned away. 'Decided to go home, put my feet up, hope I feel better in the morning. You know the sort of thing.'

'You sure you'll be all right?' Qinefer glanced at the watch on her wrist. 'I could drive you home, if you'd like.'

'No thanks. I'll be OK. Thanks, though.'

They shook hands – *how long is it since the last time I've shaken someone's hand because I wanted to, not just to clinch a deal?* – and he left her on the pavement. She stood there a while, looking after him. Then she walked off in the other direction, shaking her head.

It seemed to take him forever to walk the hundred yards to Thresher's, where he bought himself a litre bottle of Gordon's, forty Dunhill – 'No, make that sixty' – and a piercingly yellow carrier bag. He paid by Barclaycard, hoping that the jerky scrawl he made on the sales invoice bore some resemblance to his signature. He smiled at the young assistant, who knew him too well, and she smiled back in the same way that she always did.

'You look after yourself now, Mr Perriman,' she said, and then she turned her smile towards the next customer in line.

With difficulty he stripped open a packet of cigarettes, letting the wind take the wrappings, and lit up in the shelter of a shop doorway. As usual, he coughed after he'd taken the first drag and there was the familiar stomach pang; as usual, he cursed it silently and impotently, and then waited for the pain to go away.

Which it eventually did.

It always did, in the end.

9

. . . touch me, and feel my touch, feel the thrill of my touch on your chest and your back and your thighs and your loins. Feel the warmth of me embracing you as we recline at the core of a sun, the plasma insinuating itself into our bodies as we move entwined, a light too bright for vision in our eyes. Ah, the heat and the ecstasy, my poor little Earth-bound love, which could be ours if only you would come to me . . .

10

He was on the river bank, and the sun had set. He had no clear idea of how he had come to be here: it was as if someone else had been operating his mind for him. The only true gauges of the fact that he had somehow lived through the afternoon were the level in the bottle and the number of cigarettes that he'd got left, except that he couldn't now recall whether he'd bought three packs or settled for two. He unscrewed the top of the Gordon's and took a deep, refreshing draught. The rough ground was cold through his thin trousers, and he shuffled his bottom, trying to make himself more comfortable. A couple of people trudged by him a little distance away: an elderly woman and a rather younger man. The man glanced towards him and seemed for a moment about to stop and say something, but then changed his mind, and the two of them went on their way.

Joli's mind was filled with serenity. He thought of Lisa, and the cruelty of the way in which she had manipulated his emotions – and so simply, so economically: that had been the real refinement of the torture. But now he could think of Lisa without any feeling of pain. She was just something that had been there briefly and now had gone, like a cabbage white on a summery day. *Let's drink to the memory of Lisa, dear friends!*

And his head went back.

And to you, whoever you are, who's been filling my head with images culled from a pubescent schoolgirl's love letters the day after she saw a Star Trek *movie. I guess this must be really a toast to myself but, what the fuck, there isn't no one else going to raise a glass for me, so . . .*

The practised rocking back of the head.

Wait a minute, wait a minute. Now – just – you – wait – a – fucking – minute, do you hear? There's Leonora and Sam, too, the lights of my life, bless them, the little darlings.

The bottle was half-way to his lips when it stopped.

On second thoughts, no – no toast for them. Can do without a toast. Don't want to drink to them. Have another drink to myself instead . . .

He did so, but the refusal had had a slightly sobering effect on him. He often grumbled to himself about the sterility of his home life, but he'd always assumed that in his own tetchy way he really loved his wife and son, deep down, where it was important. Of course, he wasn't any longer as passionately in love with Leonora as once he'd been, but then, well, that was just the way love worked, wasn't it? Now the truth had come into him, as cold as the night air in which his breath steamed whitely in the lights from a nearby building yard. A lot of the things he'd been thinking while talking with Lisa had been adolescent claptrap, the product of one of those sudden infatuations that snared him every few weeks, but one part of it had been for real. Whatever he'd once felt for Leonora hadn't just been diluted with the years: it had gone completely, and now there was something utterly different in its place. A mixture of dimly felt obligation, numbed acceptance, a thin veneer of tolerance straining at the seams as it tried to cover over a bulge of resentment and . . . and . . .

Hatred.

This time the thought really shocked him.

He took another gulp of the gin as he toyed with the concept, turned it this way and that, looking at it from all possible angles. It was like the wreckage of a crashed vehicle: angular, spiteful and ugly, yet oddly attractive.

Yes. His mind was moving very slowly and cautiously now. *It's true. It's not just that I don't love Leonora any more: it's that I've learnt to hate her. Hate her mannerisms and her coyness and her artificialities and her prissy standards and her overbearingness and perhaps most of all the way she leaves half-uncoiled tubes of cardboard floating in the lavatory. I hate the way that the dreams I had when hitching round Europe during the long vacs – dreams of creating fire from the ice of the world and rain forests from its aridnesses – have been destroyed by her and her fucking stainless-steel parties . . . The tone of her voice as she explains oh so cogently why I can't go out with the few friends I have left.*

The bottle took a little more punishment, bravely, and he examined its level with a tear forming in his eye. Three-quarters of it gone already, and he'd no clear memory of drinking most of that. What a waste. He assumed he must have been enjoying it while the chilly-fiery liquid had been going down his gullet. He usually did.

And then there's Sam. A man's supposed to love his son. I've loathed the self-centred little shit ever since he spat out of his mother, a mass of crumpled protoplasm and stale-looking blood. Eight years old and a practised thief – I can't leave my wallet anywhere in case his fat little fingers pry out the odd fiver he thinks I'll never notice has gone missing.

Glug, went the bottle.

There was a floating light in the misty sky ahead of him, low on the horizon, skipping along above the fuzzed cut-out two-dimensional shapes of the city's skyline, apparently growing brighter as it seemed to approach him across the river's midnight-inky waters. He held up the bottle and looked at the brilliance through the lens of its neck, so that the light became bigger and paler and more amorphous and green. At first he watched it with only a single eye, the other folded tightly shut, but then its radiance grew so great that he had to disperse the brightness through both eyes, which watered in the cold, fragmenting the image into a thousand shards.

The light wasn't an aeroplane, of that he was sure. And, come to that, it wasn't a bird and it wasn't Superman™. He lifted the bottle higher, and the greenness exploded through the new lens of glass and gin. *And my job?* he thought. *I can remember the day that they recruited me, and me all eager and sparkle-eyed from the polytechnic, and the way that I went home to mum, because dad was dead by then, and told her that all of her scrimpings and seemingly piffling meannesses had at last come to something, that I was going to be a part of the cutting edge of technology. That was back in the days when I remembered what the company was there for. I used to know everything it sold and why those things sold so well, but now I've forgotten, and it doesn't seem to make any difference because I'm still selling the products well enough and the half-term figures are good the way they always are.*

The glow in the sky seemed to float down towards him and touch the ground near where he was sitting. He got to his feet and finished the bottle defiantly, forcing himself not to choke. He threw its emptiness into the river's oily dark.

As he walked towards the light on the frost-crusted ridges of hardened mud he knew that he was swithering from side to side, but he didn't care what kind of a fool this stranger he'd become was making of himself. He'd seen something that was more than just a light in the sky.

I have to get away from here. Somewhere that I can leave behind the life I'm living, it isn't any more than half a life. Take me with you, whoever you are.

11

Ah, you are my love and at last we are together. I can feel the framework of your thoughts interacting with mine, I know that we interpenetrate each other, so that the electric spark of a whim of mine is at once incorporated into and continued by the ganglions of your once-upon-a-time nervous system. I know the richness of your lusts and your longings, the surging of things that you have left behind with the shell of your sadly inadequate body.

Now we leave this place. Now we soar into the places where a nova is nothing more than a twinkling jewel on a young girl's ring. Touch my hand within your own and feel the clumsy warmth of its coldness as we pull apart the distance like cotton wool and watch the incessant blazing of the forthcoming death of reality.

They sparkle in the twilight do the sunsets, do.

12

No! he cried.

His voice echoing back through the past for eternity and into the future until the heat-death swallowed all.

No, I cannot do this thing!

From millions of parsecs away he was returned to the cold riverside.

Unaware that now the coding that Alyss had been implanting in his mind all day had been completed.

The coding that would take him all the way through the farness to the World.

13

Joli looked in his wallet and found that he owned exactly £37.48, which was exactly enough for him to go a long way away. Although his limbs weren't obeying him quite as they should, his brain seemed to him to be fully functional. He had vague memories of having travelled somewhere, but he didn't know where that could have been.

He saw the river and its slow but powerful urge towards the sea, and he saw the stars in the night sky looking down on him cynically.

£37.48.

Ah, yes, £37.48.

It wouldn't take him far enough on the train, but he could go almost to the far end of the country if he took the bus – or the coach, as the bus company preferred to call it. Perhaps it was too late to catch one?

He waved a hand shakily, and found himself sitting on one of the greasy benches in the bus station. They'd sold him a ticket that had cost precisely £37.48, so that he no longer had to worry about the irritation of having loose change jangling in his pocket. The next bus from Bay 14 was his, and the sign on the front of it said

THE WORLD

He could change his name, perhaps sleep rough for a while, find a new selfness in a city he'd never seen, leave the company and Reggie and Leonora and Sam and Ilse and the slightly acidic taste of what he'd thought Lisa might have been and even McPhee of Henderson Fergus (and it struck him as odd that the only one he'd really miss would be Qinefer, whom he didn't know all that well) and discover instead the wonder of lying in a frost-delineated field and watching as the stars performed their eternal arcs of love above his head.

The bus station stank of old vomit. Someone was peeing against a wall, looking anxiously back over his shoulder in case an inspector would spot what he was up to and throw him out. The someone, Joli was surprised to realize, was himself.

And finally the bus driver came to open up the big pivoted doors of his vehicle. He affected friendliness, his curious accent sounding to Joli as if the man came from Cornwall, perhaps, or maybe New Jersey. The driver looked at the tickets and joked with the two middle-aged women who were going to visit their grandchildren. When

Joli presented his ticket the driver's eyes changed from soft friendly brown to a penetrating feline green.

'I've seen you before,' he said.

'Yes,' Joli agreed. 'You travel in the farness.'

'Ay, and that'll be right,' said the driver.

14

The engine roared into life, and Joli nuzzled his neck back into the clammy sleek plastic of the headrest-cover. At most there were a dozen passengers on board, so all of them had plenty of room to spread out; even so, a young couple who'd got on at the very last minute had chosen to come and sit directly behind him. The man was scruffy, with long oilstains on his jeans; the woman was too-perfectly neat, her mousy hair arranged to form a flawless sculpture, her face immobile and yet not without life. They called each other Nadar and Syor, and the names seemed familiar to Joli but he couldn't recall ever having heard them before and he was too tired of everything to want to think about it. He looked at the newspaper he'd half-heartedly bought at the all-night newsstand; his exhausted mind was deaf even to the shouting headlines.

Soon they were in the suburbs, and he watched the lighted windows whipping by. Behind each of them there was a life, he knew, or more likely a nexus of lives. Each of the windows hid a story that he would never be told, a saga of love and hatred, joy and suffering, ecstasy and *angst*.

He, for his part, was on his way to the farness.

The voices of the couple in the seats behind him droned on, but now their sound was lost in the hum of the tyres.

The coach gathered speed, impossible speed, and the windows began to rush past ever more swiftly until they became almost a blur of soon-forgotten brightness, a line of lamplight.

He shut his eyes, but even through the lids he saw the rapid flickerings of pink-yellow brightness. He heard the rhythm of the accelerating flashes: *pok-pok*, *pok-pok*, *pokka-pokka, pokka-pokka, pokka-pokka-pokka, pokka-pokka-pokka, pokka-pokka-pokka, pokkapokkapokkapokkapokkapokka* . . .

And he knew that he'd been here before.

The windows into other people's lives were the brilliance of stars as Alyss drove him out through the cosmos into the interstices between the universes, moving swiftly and ever more swiftly, the lights scattering past them on either side as she and he sought out the heart of a galaxy.

Chapter Three
A Rent in the Fabric

1

It was another in a long succession of blindingly hot days, and the whole city of Ernestrad stank of rotting vegetables and horse and ordure. In the market stalls, crates of fish from Qazar were stacked crazily, customers and traders alike reluctant to open them because of what they might find in there. Flies were everywhere, but most of all in the butcher shops. Children were falling sick from drinking unboiled water, even though the wells were so deep that they seemed to lead down to some far distant cool world. Rats, never uncommon in Ernestrad even at the best of times, now seemed to be scuttling everywhere. There was little that anyone could think to do to find relief from the problem except, illegally, to revive the old religion and pray to the Sun to show mercy.

Even up here in Starveling, whose white walls normally ensured that the worst of the summer's heat could be barred from the innermost halls, it was unpleasantly hot. The brilliance of the sunlight through the stained windows made the interior of the chapel seem as if it had been bathed in blood, which parts of it were. Anya, seated in a wooden throne that servants had brought here to the central aisle, raised a glass of lemonade to her lips and found the liquid tepid and brackish-tasting. She swallowed nevertheless. Her hair stuck in hard ringlets to her forehead. Sweat ran down her face and dripped onto the embroidered robe she wore as a matter of policy: today was not a day for her to appear in her warrior's uniform, to remind her people that it was for this stinking, parching existence that so many of them had died under her leadership.

The day's executions were done. As usual, there had been about a dozen of them. She had expected that the heat might have reduced the number, with men and women and children grown too lethargic to commit deeds of villainy; but it seemed that this was countered by the wrath with which victims responded to even the most trivial of offences. She herself would perhaps not have disembowelled that woman for presumed adultery, but it was the will of her people that this be done, or worse, and above all Anya was a servant of her people. The people accepted their own wisdom in having as their ruler someone who was wiser than themselves, someone with sufficient steel in her soul to put aside her personal feelings and do whatever was necessary to make Albion not just one of the community of nations in the World but, in the due course of time, the greatest of them all. Then, perhaps, its citizens luxuriating in the riches that her determination had brought for them, she could move aside to let a less resolute leader occupy her throne.

But it was going to be a long time – an indefinitely long time – before everyone would be able to live happily ever after.

The executions were over, but yet again they had left her feeling impotent. For weeks now her militia had been searching the land without success for the one person who, she deemed, represented the greatest danger of all to the well-being of her nation. Staring into vacancy, she wondered what he must look like now.

Of his identity she was certain. The night that they had cast the freshly blinded Ngur out of the citadel of Starveling, the blood still drying on his face beneath the cauterized sockets of his eyes – those eyes that had once blasphemed by holding mocking impiety when they saw the painted image of her mother, that had so obviously doubted the wisdom of the 'magic' that had returned Joli to death – cast him out to find whatever death he could in the wastes of Albion, he had left them with more than the memories of his silence (*Why, why, why couldn't the bastard have screamed? Just the once?*): there had also been his promise to serve her well for the rest of his life by bringing her people into the embrace of Syor. Standing far above him on the battlements, trying to be as far away as possible from his pain, her cloak of sky a living thing around her in the night-winds, Anya had heard his pledge and had silently rained curses on his head. If he had shouted insults or oaths of vengeance upon her, she would have slept easy that night. But no: subtle as always, Ngur had chosen instead to undermine her more insidiously, by telling all who would hear that, despite the righteous punishment she had wrought upon his body, his fidelity to her was still intact.

And now the marks of that fidelity were strewn all across Albion. The Painter, the common folk called the blind man who wandered among them, the blind man with only a pig for permanent companion. He had few possessions, but he needed few, for the bumpkins were only too ready to take pity on his state and feed him and lodge him while he went through his ritual: the construction of a totem to her mother, the mother of all. On the rare occasions when Anya rode out from Ernestrad to be among her people – the people who loved her so overpoweringly – it seemed to her that every hillside, every roadside cliff, every cairn bore one of his daubings. The green eyes – sometimes in a face, sometimes scarifyingly solitary – those crude parodies of those her mother had gazed through in the days when her mother had walked Albion in human form, now stared at Anya wherever she went. There were even some on the walls of the houses within Ernestrad itself, and her subjects seemed curiously reluctant to remove them until driven to do so by the whips of her soldiers. To others the painted eyes seemed blank and sightless, but Anya could see the accusation so carefully crafted into them. That they were debasing and vulgarizing the eternal, omnipresent beneficence of her mother was blasphemy enough; that they should also seek to erode Anya's position as her mother's sole true representative in the World was a yet greater blasphemy; but that those eyes should so persistently keep *accusing* Anya, Syor's true avatar, of crimes – of *any* crime – that was surely the greatest offence against Syor of all.

She raised the lemonade to her lips again. It tasted no better. The victim being tortured in front of the altar, beneath Syor's earnest gaze, was withstanding the agony in silence, as Ngur had done.

It was growing hard to believe that the Painter himself was any longer a normal mortal. This was a reflection that Anya only rarely permitted to come to the surface of her thoughts. All of the villagers who had been brought here for questioning about the Painter's activities had claimed that he had worked on his own, without any assistance except, sometimes, from the children, whose chores of fetching and carrying seemed more demanding than otherwise on the man's time. Each of the great images that he had painted had taken him at least several days, and he had never seemed in much of a hurry, once his task had been done, to leave one place in quest of another, yet now there must be hundreds of them, if not thousands, strewn across Albion's landscape. Surely no mortal person could have done all this; an army would have been hard pressed to equal the feat. And yet the villagers, especially the children, were unanimous in their testimony to his bearing at least the normal trappings of mortality, for they had heard his stomach rumble when he was hungry and seen him empty his bladder in the fields; in one village he had even got drunk, and had had to be ejected from a spinster's house.

Anya had asked Syor's voice many times if indeed some evil spirit of magic had come to occupy Ngur's body, or to create a thousand replicas of him so that each could wander the countryside on its own, raising the signs of rebellion against her own temporal rule and the spiritual supremacy of her mother, but Syor was responding to her less and less often these days – a partial desertion that must surely again be attributable to the Painter's activities. But Anya was wondering if perhaps her mother had determined upon some more subtle means of communicating with her than through direct speech, for now she found that, more and more, convictions were growing inside her that she did not recognize as her own. And one of these convictions was that the World was a product of counterbalancing forces, that the spirit of Good, which was the soul of her mother, was constantly weighed against another spirit, that of Evil; the balance was a precarious one, the two opposing spirits being of almost exactly equal strengths, and it could be affected by even the smallest of human actions. Just as the spirit of Good had determined to act in the World through Anya, the spirit of Evil had selected Ngur to be its representative, giving him the powers of the wicked magic that had once enslaved the Ellonia. How else could a blind man paint pictures?

How else could a blind man paint *so many* pictures?

How else could a blind man so successfully evade the searches of her warriors? They had come tantalizingly close to him several times now – on some occasions, when they raided a village, it was to find that he had left there only a few hours before – and yet they had never seen hide nor hair of the man himself. And so bound were the villagers by the spirit of Evil that he had brought into their hearts that, even under the most stringent of ordeals, they would tell her warriors nothing more than that the Painter had indeed been among them but that now he had left again, without giving them any indications as to where he might be going.

But now, at last, her warriors had captured his accessory in Evil – the animal her spies had learned about – and brought it here to her.

They had nailed the pig's trotters to a board, dislocating its joints at shoulder and hip and stretching the plump flesh there so that it seemed it must burst as the weight of the body dragged against its limbs. The beast's exposed belly was a network of slashes and cuts; the eyes had been burnt out. They had propped the board up in front of the altar, so that Anya could watch them as they worked and so that Syor, too, could see the labours that were being undertaken to assist her Good to triumph over Ngur's Evil. Streaks of blood covered the cloaks of her priestesses, and rivers of it ran from the base of the board and the pile of shit that the pig had deposited there as a gesture of defiance as the first nails had been driven home. It had been screaming then, of course – high whines and shrieks of mockery interspersed with harsh brayings that made the windows shake and seemed to conjure obscenities from the air. But then the animal had fallen stubbornly silent, the Evil of its spirit keeping it mute to taunt even their most extreme efforts. The pig had made no movement even when the branding-irons had flashed into its flesh and the stench of burning had filled the place; had shown no reaction even when its ears had been sheared off, one after the other, and placed in its mouth.

Anya set down her glass very carefully on the little table beside her, exercising a firm control over her hand so that it didn't shake. Her eyes felt hot and wet. She was filled with virtuous wrath that the beast should so defy the will of Syor, the spirit of Good who spoke to the World through the mouth of her sole mortal representative.

'Talk!' screamed Anya suddenly, sweeping the glass from its table so that it shattered among the blood-lit pews. 'Talk to us, Devil!'

She was shouting at the immolated pig, and not at the portrait of her mother behind it.

2

I am meeting Hump in the Turk's Head and he is telling me it is odd the way we do not get together so often the way we used to with the lads and go bird-pulling or maybe riding the wings of joy in someone's car, but Nick the Hat's got this cunt he drools over so he is not interested any more and even Big Dave has got himself tangled up with some divorcee-and-mother-of-two who must have funny tastes, and I am the worst of all of them because now I live thirty miles away with a woman old enough to be my mother for God's sake and she does not even fuck.

I do not like to hear the Queen talked about like that so I do not tell him that as a matter of fact she does these days, but I get him another drink because there is not much else I can think of doing for half an hour before my bus goes and anyway it gets me away from him for a few minutes so that I can feel sorry for him without him noticing. The barman is a dickhead who looks at me like I was a wimp because all I want is a half again, and in the old days that would have been enough for me to have a pint instead even though I would have needed to slash on the bus, and might well have done so, but now I ignore him and pay my money and count the change and take the drinks back to the table where Hump is sitting looking at the pictures on the machine of Michael Jackson shooting people on the moon as if there are not enough people down here on Earth for him to shoot if he wants to, with his money.

As Hump goes on talking and I go on listening just enough so that I say 'yes' at the right times I wonder if I would feel just the same if it was not Hump I was sitting opposite but me the way I was before I met the Queen. I think probably yes, but I do not remember those times all that well because it seems in an odd way that I did not really live through them so much as just be there. Hump is still like that, I think as he sucks at the edge of his glass and wipes his lips with the back of a sleeve that has wiped other things too many times. He is alive at the moment, of course, because you can tell that by the way he moves himself around and talks the whole fucking time, but it is hard to imagine that he was alive a few minutes ago and that he will still be alive in a few minutes' time, and I think he would find it just as hard to imagine those things except that it would never occur to him to try. I light a cigarette and most of me thinks about the Queen instead of what Hump is saying because I like thinking about the Queen and do it a lot and it does not begin to seem like it is the same old boring thought again and again the way it does if you really *listen* to Hump. Which again makes me wonder if Hump is like me the way I was.

The time passes quickly thinking about the Queen. I did not tell her this morning that I was catching the bus into town to come and see Hump for old times' sake because you cannot just dump people who used to be your friends, but she knew all that anyway, I could see it in her smile as she put on her fawn coat and did up the buckle of her fawn belt, and I knew it was all right by her, and even if I had not then I would have guessed it from the way that the bed still smelled warm as I straightened it before going out myself. It is funny to look at my fingers, wrapped around a cold and sticky glass the way they are now, and think that only a few hours ago those were the same fingers that were running themselves all over the Queen's shoulders and pulling her close to me, and somehow I cannot believe, even, that those were the same fingers, and yet I know that if I put them up to my face and breathed deep I would still be able to smell the way the tiny hairs on her smooth skin were stroking them. Maybe I should have had a shower before I came out but I did not want to wash away the drying wetness of her, and Hump thinks that I am smiling because of some megafuck he has been telling and telling me about with two girls he met in the Timepiece one of whom was not really bad to look at, and I wonder what magazines he has been reading.

Time flies for no man as the saying has it but at least it keeps on crawling along, and I wonder if the Queen is thinking the same thing right at this moment because it will soon be time for her to finish typing the last letter of the day and go home, and there is just a chance that I will be there before her if I am lucky with the buses which means that she will get there first and oh shit I have just remembered that it is my turn to get supper and I forgot to shop and we cannot have fish and chips, not again, so I will have to pick up some crap from one of the late shops which will be expensive and maybe take me a while to cook, which means we will have less time together before I have to put on my tough-guy costume and go out to work making sure pissed kids do not hurt each other at least not on the premises, by order of the management, and look it is only my job and why do you not make things easy for all of us and just fuck off out into the night before I smear your head all over a wall, and thank God I will be out of there at one.

The second-hand on the clock behind the bar seems to almost have stopped, so that you have to hold your breath waiting for it to pass each of the numbers, but it will get there in the end I think and I can get out of here and into a bus that will not have Hump talking on it, and I discover that I have got oil on my jeans that I must have got there when I was on the bus into town, which is one of the disadvantages of buses over bikes because it is perfectly fair if you get grease stains riding bikes.

The Queen and I have started living on another planet. I would like to tell him that and watch his face, but he would probably just shit all over it the way he does most things, the way he would if I told him how good it feels when the Queen is asleep and her breath tickles the hair on my chest, or how you can be talking sometimes and not notice you have not got any clothes on. So I do not tell him anything about Albion, which is the planet that the Queen tells me both she and I lived in before we were born here, and how I was a great general and she was just a peasant woman, and how I fell in love with her even then but I did not know it so all I could think of doing was fucking her and how I never did. And I do not tell him the way that sometimes when she and I are alone together in the darkness of the flat and there are not any cars going by outside and the dickhead upstairs is not playing his country'n'western records I too can hear the trumpets blaring as I ride into town at the head of my cavalry, or feel the push against our faces of air that has not been farted out the back of a lorry. It is not often that I can see Albion as clear as that, but I think that the Queen does a lot of the time because more and more often these days I find that she is sad when she does not know I am watching and when I ask her if there is something wrong, if it is maybe something to do with me that is making her sad, she says no, it is not, it is the way things are on Albion and there is a lot to be sad about there. And then later maybe if I am lucky she tells me more in the darkness and I can see the sun of Albion, which is brighter than the one here, lighting up the bedroom so I could read the titles of her books on the shelves except I know them all already. And when I say to her that maybe the two of us could go to Albion, really go there properly, and help things get better and all that, because if I am a great general I could fight the forces of Evil – when I say this to her she just breathes even sadder than before and tells me that even she cannot make things better for the people there yet even though she is almost a god there, and then I say that if she is a god it is not fair and I want to be a god too and is not there such a thing as this equality of the sexes you hear about on the box and she starts giggling and maybe we make love and I think maybe that is a way of making things better in Albion, too.

So I tell Hump nothing at all of the things I think, right up until at last the clock behind the bar tells me that it is time for the cell door to open and I have got to hurry if I am going to be sure and catch my bus, and I carry on not telling him anything even after I have left him there because Hump would not be able to understand, never having been to Albion even the once.

3

Syor had wanted simply to tell the Mistdom that she required to be in Albion – more specifically, on the standing-stage above Ernestrad so that she could look out over the city – but Reen had managed to dissuade her, explaining that it was all very well for Syor to insist that it was the *real* Albion that the Mistdom would create for them, but that nevertheless, so far as she, Reen, was concerned, it would be no more than a replica, and she was damned if she was going to risk her life being in the wrong reality when Alyss returned from wherever she currently was to keep her appointment with them. Rehan had sided with Reen, and for much the same reasons, plus the fact that he was in love and wanted to have a few weeks' grace in which to explore that happy state. Kursten, being a part of Syor, was not asked for her opinion.

So Syor packed the Mistdom, which was also herself, into a small stone vial which she put on a leather thong around her neck so that it would rest safely between her breasts. In the resulting chaos, as the people of the Anonymous City discovered that their cordon had vanished, leaving them exposed to the eyes of the World, it was easy enough for Reen, assisted by Rehan, to steal five horses, one for baggage. They spent the next fortnight or so trekking in easy stages up the coast, paying their way with gold coins that Syor manufactured for the purpose. Eventually they came to the fabled port of Llandeer, which looked much like fabled ports anywhere, and were lucky enough to be able to book passage on a rather seedy trading vessel that was sailing for Qazar on the morrow for unstated but doubtless illicit reasons; there was even room for the horses, which pleased Kursten, who had become very fond of the animals, and Reen, whose relationship with her own animal had become close enough that they frequently held conversations with each other.

Rehan was seasick for most of the two-day crossing, and Kursten tended him solicitously except when she didn't.

4

The pig was dead. The priestesses had thought that they were risking her wrath by telling her so, but in fact they had been only confirming her suspicions. Anya watched them leaden-eyed as they carried off the board with its gruesome burden, destined for the kitchens; its fate seemed somehow cannibalistic, but Anya hadn't been able to think up any logical reason for letting the good meat go to waste. Now the women were swashing away the blood with buckets of water and mops and scrubbing brushes, and still Anya was sitting on her makeshift demi-throne, running her hands along the gilded carvings of its arms, feeling them slowly cool as the evening itself had. The air was still oppressively hot in here, and it would be days before the stink of spilt blood and the last of the flies could be completely dispersed.

Hardly the atmosphere to grace a god, Anya breathed to herself, gazing into her mother's cool green eyes.

It was rare for Anya to worry about purposes and the means of achieving them. When she had been younger it had been easier, for there had been a single, concrete foe to hate and destroy. The Ellonia had been powerful, but it had required no thought to establish how they should be striven against: you took up arms, and you trusted that your weapons and your courage would be more effective than theirs, and it didn't matter if the opposite was true because at least, then, you'd have died in glory and be out of it. She had been almost irritated when other forces had joined themselves to her own, forces she hadn't really comprehended: the filthy little vagabond Joli, with his dreams that slew; the effeminate-seeming Rehan, who'd cajoled her into becoming his lover for a while before she'd tired of him and the pictures he painted with his music; the Wind that had obeyed no one's commands but its own; and Alyss, inscrutable behind her masks. Anya had driven them all from her, after the Ellonia had been vanquished, and had never regretted having done so except on rare occasions like this one, when events were conspiring to thwart her. She refused to permit herself the luxury of thinking, even momentarily, the almost heretical thought that perhaps, just at this moment, she might have benefited from having them still beside her. For the foes of today weren't the simple, clear-cut foes of old. Instead her enemies were manifold, intangible, insidious, unquantifiable: you couldn't point crossbows at them.

A priestess drew shyly near and Anya got to her feet and backhanded the woman across the face, so that she staggered and fell between two pews. *Introspection's all right as long as you don't think too much about it*, thought Anya wryly as she sucked her knuckles, welcoming their pain. The priestess was whimpering – the blow had probably broken a tooth – and Anya's soul revelled in the noise: at least it was a manifest consequence of her having performed an action. Too often these days she was having to satisfy herself with the approval of her mother for the deeds she did, rather than seeing any direct and tangible benefit from them.

Her mother had approved, for example, of her efforts to force the pig to tell them of Ngur's whereabouts. Syor hadn't whispered this in so many words, but she had encouraged the growth of Anya's inner conviction that this was the case. And Anya knew, for the same reason, that her mother had approved of the executions that had been held earlier in the day, and that they hadn't just been a futile waste of her executioners' time – and Anya's own, for that matter, for the people required her to be present to enhance the spectacle. But she was becoming weary of having nothing more than these wordless convictions as a reward for her actions. Even though she always held before her in her mind's eye a picture of a prosperous and tranquil Albion, with herself as its adored ruler, she was aware that that picture was hung at the far end of an implausibly long corridor, down which she had as yet taken only the first few steps.

Leaving the weeping woman, Anya took one last glance into her mother's immobile eyes and then strode from the chapel, tugging her robe around her as if the night air were cold. Although the Sun had long since set, the thick foggy covering of cloud above Ernestrad was still dimly lit by the lanterns and fires of the city. Anya had a sudden irrational itch to see the stars – or even just a single star – but she knew that it was hopeless: the heat of the days kept the night skies obscured. She snapped viciously at a pair of sentries who hadn't been holding themselves quite erect enough, and left them quaking.

As she crossed the courtyard towards the doorway that

would lead her to her own quarters, she saw that there was a hooded figure waiting for her. Her first thought was of assassination, and her hand went to the pommel of the short sword she carried at her waist; but then the light of the torch in the niche above the doorway flickered, and she saw that the man was Darl 'ap Haptan: a friend, so long as he was well enough paid.

'Make yourself useful, scum!' she said to him, loudly enough that others could see that he was just some minor servant. 'Albion will not thrive if its people dally in doorways! If you've got nothing better to do, bring some hot water to my chambers. At once.'

He winked at her and moved off towards the kitchens.

A few minutes later he was watching her as she sat on the edge of her richly quilted bed, washing her feet in a basinful of warm, soapy water. She had drawn her robe up almost to her waist, and not for the first time he admired the smooth curve of her thigh and the long, well muscled lines of her legs. She was aware of the stare, but paid it no attention. One of Haptan's duties in her employ was to serve as an occasional lover, when her rebellious body demanded that she bed someone; since the contract was purely mercenary between them, she had no objections to his looking at her body as if it were nothing more than a well designed erotic object.

'What news has brought you here?' she said, pushing a finger between two toes. Haptan was by profession a petty spy. Clad in the attire of one of the peripatetic singers who had once upon a time traversed Albion in numbers, bringing light to the peasants' gloom, he wandered among them as if he were the last of the bards, playing and singing to them tunes and songs that they were too courteous to mention were poorly done. His purpose, of course, was not to entertain or even to educate, but instead to find out what he could – things no soldier could – about what the common people knew. He and others like him were Anya's main sources of information about the mood of the land, and she paid them well for their services.

'It may be nothing of importance, ma'am,' he said

politely, 'but I thought it would be best to let you decide its merits.'

This was the way he always began. He did so in order to convey respect, but she had become tired of the convention.

'Have you caught any whiff of the Painter?' she said angrily. Then she relented and smiled sweetly at him. It had, after all, been thanks to Haptan that they had captured the pig, and it was no fault of his that the pig had refused to divulge anything of its master's whereabouts. Assuming – and her eyes fleetingly narrowed – that it was the correct pig that he'd informed on, and not just some poor innocuous villager's beast. But no: no ordinary pig would have kept its silence once the torment had begun in earnest.

'It seems not,' said Haptan thoughtfully, 'and yet . . . perhaps I have. It was because of my own perplexity in the matter that I thought it best to consult directly with your majesty.'

'Oh, forget the ceremony, Haptan,' said Anya impatiently. 'You're not so bloody formal in bed. Tell me what you want to tell me, and get it over with.'

'There is a soothsayer . . .' he began.

'Report him. Or her. You need not watch the punishment being exacted.'

'Anya, Anya. Stop being so impetuous. I know that you are our wisest possible leader, but haven't you yet realized that it is in your own interests to condone certain illegalities in order to attain a greater good? Poxy old peasant women with casts in their eyes can be killed later on, when they're no longer of any use to you.'

'Soothsaying is just a false belief, a deception practised upon the people in order to enslave them.'

He grinned. 'Then I have brought you false information,' he said. 'I pray your benign forgiveness, and I shall leave now.'

Despite herself, she matched his smile. 'Don't act the clown.'

'Well, Anya, here are some of the lies the soothsayer

told me.' Haptan's face had become sterner now. He would really be quite a handsome man, with his prominent nose and his deeply engraved eye-lines, were it not for the way that his eyes always avoided looking directly into one's own. 'She told me that Albion was a ship sailing rudderless upon a tempestuous sea, and that the waves were higher than the mainmast. But then they all say that, don't they? There was quite a lot more of this window-dressing – all doom-laden portents that you find don't actually mean much once you start thinking about them – but then she got around to the main burden of her prophecy. For which I had, I should remind you, to pay.'

'Indent for it as a justifiable expense,' she muttered peevishly. 'Get on with it, man.'

'She talked of the ship battling through the storms until eventually it came into a harbour. The dock there was almost empty – no porters scurrying about their business or stevedores cursing, only a few people standing watching as the ship inched towards the quay. She couldn't draw any of their names from her inner darkness, or whatever her hocus pocus was, but she was able to describe their faces for me. One of them was a tall man, although his shoulders were bent over as if he were bearing a great weight, the weight of the World; he was naked, and in place of eyes he had only the blackness of night, and there was a pig sitting by his legs. It struck me that that was as good a description as any of the Painter.'

'But his pig is dead. You caught it,' murmured Anya. 'And I saw it die myself.'

'Some are more dangerous dead than alive,' Haptan reminded her. 'Your father, Lian, was one of those.'

'I had no father,' said Anya bleakly. 'The receptacle from which my mother drew seed was nameless.'

'As you wish it.'

There was silence between them except for the soft splashing of water as Anya moved her feet.

'This man was not alone on the dock, you say.' He was startled by the abrupt sound of her voice. 'Tell me who his companions were.'

'They weren't his companions, according to the soothsayer,' said Haptan. 'They stood separately from him.'

'No matter.' She waved her hand crossly, spattering the counterpane with grey water. 'Forget the elaborations and qualifications. Just tell me what I ask. Who were they?'

'There was a small man, capering and spitting. His face and body were filthy and his mind even more so. She told me enough that I was able to recognize him as that interloper you had me . . . um . . . terminate so grotesquely some months ago.'

'Joli.'

'That's the one. The one your treacherous husband believed you had destroyed yourself using magic-of-night. Anyway, he was there on the jetty, swearing and cackling like an irate gosling. And alongside him there was a minstrel like myself – only not, so the soothsayer said, quite half so good-looking as myself – who had his lank arm draped around the shoulders of a somewhat toothsome wench. At first, Anya, I thought that she might be you yourself, not only because of her beauty but also because of her hair, which was golden fine, like yours, and shining with curls, also like yours. But the soothsayer was insistent that the singer's doxy was still barely more than a girl. A little distant from these two there was another girl, this one still more like a child than an adult – although here the soothsayer's brow grew lined.'

He paused. Anya looked at him sharply.

'The soothsayer said that this slip of a child was also by far the eldest of the people there, that it was through her very youthfulness that you could guess her real antiquity, that she was as old as the World itself, or older. I think the woman was blathering about this, to tell you the truth, Anya, but you asked me to report everything.'

'No, Haptan, you did right; and the woman wasn't blathering, as you say.' Anya was now looking directly towards an empty space of wall. Haptan felt as if she were simultaneously beside him and in another country; he shifted his stance uneasily, began to speak and then thought better of it.

'I recognize some of these people she told you about,' said Anya wearily. 'They were friends of mine in the days when I was foolish enough to think that I could have friends. One of them wrote songs that I have heard you sing yourself – surely you must know him by repute, even if you never met him?'

'Barra 'ap Rteniadoli Me'gli'minter Rehan,' said Haptan, looking apprehensive. 'Yet the ballads say that he was far more good-looking than I.'

'The ballads also say that he had the strength of ten,' said Anya succinctly. 'But ignore that. The ancient child I knew well, also. I had thought that she was long gone from the World, never to return – at least, not in our own lifetimes. Did the soothsayer talk to you of her small, catlike face and the way she was constantly preening and titivating herself?'

'Yes, she did. And she said that her hair was cut almost like a boy's, and looked as if it had been spun from copper strands.'

'Then that was Alyss. She was as undeserving of my trust as were all the rest, and by far the most dangerous because she possessed great power – greater, almost, than that my mother has grown to have.'

Haptan stared at her slack-jawed. He had no time for Anya's primitive ancestor worship himself, but he realized that, in its terms, Anya had spoken something close to heresy – Anya of all people. How would she react when she heard of all the rest he had to tell her? With an easy atheistic laugh? He thought not.

'And tell me,' she continued in the same distanced voice, 'was there also present an ageing woman dressed in a warrior's garb, her hair as silver-grey as a winter's sea?'

'There were two of those,' he said grudgingly.

'Two?'

'Aye. One was indeed clearly a warrior: the soothsayer could see it in the woman's bearing. She was old, and yet she was light upon her feet: her eyes were the midnight, and her arms were those of a young man.'

'Reen. I had expected her, if the others were there. I

had hoped that she was dead. But no matter: if she ventures back to Albion she soon will be. She speaks poison of my mother, and cannot be allowed to live.'

Haptan gulped. The door was still a little open, he noted with relief out of the corner of his eye. Flight would not necessarily extend his existence for very long, but it would still give him some hope. If only he had thought through what his message might mean before he had come here to Starveling to convey it to Anya. If only he had swiftly dispatched the soothsayer and made himself forget all that she had told him. Too late. And perhaps too late, now, to lie . . .

'She had her arms around the other woman, the last of those on the pier,' he said unwillingly.

'Describe this last one to me,' said Anya.

'She was about your height, ma'am, and of your build, though clearly not so strong. That's . . . that's all I can remember the peasant woman telling me of her: that she was about the same height and build as you, but that she was old and grown flabby. I wish there were more I could say, but you know how patchy my memory is becoming these days . . .'

Anya turned to stare at him. He could see sharp knives in her eyes.

'Don't lie to me, Haptan,' she hissed, 'or you will wish that I had merely thrown you to the mercy of my torturers.'

The spy spoke reluctantly. 'She said that this woman had hair of a mousy brown, and that she was dressed in robes of white.'

'There must be a million women who look like that in the World! I can tell by your face that you have more to tell.'

'She is not fair, like you.'

'Don't waste your breath with compliments. Her eyes, dammit, her eyes!'

'They are green, and wide open, unblinking, as they watch the ship coming into harbour.'

'My mother! It must be her! Haptan – why didn't you

tell me this at the outset?' Leaping to her feet, tipping over the basin so that oily water flooded across the floor, Anya began to pace up and down, rubbing her hands together, her wet feet nearly dancing, her face vivacious with joy. On impulse, she turned and embraced the man, then realized that he had remained silent and motionless, his eyes downcast. 'Why aren't you rejoicing? Surely this is the best news there could possibly be? My mother is to come into Albion, to reign here with me, so that all of us shall know the blessing of her presence! With her by my side, I care not a fig for the others being here: should they rebel against my mother and the will of the people, they'll be torn limb from limb. I'll be safe on the throne, at last! I'll have no *need* for a throne, since Syor will be here! So rejoice, man, rejoice – like me! Rejoice or I'll . . . But no, no, there'll be no need for such threats in Albion now. Tell me, Haptan: did the soothsayer – who shall of course be publicly pardoned for all her crimes of necromancy, shall be raised, indeed, to an exalted position, shall be . . . but did she tell you anything about *when* Syor would be walking here among us? Will it be soon? Speak, man, speak!'

'It'll be soon,' he said, barely audibly. 'But you haven't heard the rest of the soothsayer's vision.'

'Was I there? Did she see me hand-in-hand with my mother?'

'She saw you, yes. But you were not holding your mother's hand.'

'A detail! Were we embracing?'

'No. Sit down, please. I want to tell you this in the right order.'

As she sat on the edge of the bed once more, composing herself with petty formality, like a small child who's been told that she'll be getting a present but not until she's settled down, Haptan glanced at the doorway again. Then he wondered about his priorities. He was not by nature a man much given to concern for the feelings of others, so he was confused to discover that, mixed in with his genuine fear for the consequences when Anya heard the rest of the soothsayer's dream, there was a feeling of sympathy for her. He wanted to put his arm around her shoulders and hold her tight to him, and then to tell her the ill news as gently as he could. But he knew that she'd begin by resenting his presumption – he could have sex with her, but it would be impertinent for him to show her any affection – and that she'd end by . . . and his gaze flickered yet again to the open door. Moving casually, as if merely easing his legs, he negotiated his way a few extra paces towards his chance of safety.

'The ship bumps against the dockside, and some of the crew leap ashore with hawsers, which they wrap around bollards to hold the craft steady. But others who jump onto the dock with them have their swords drawn to guard their fellows; clearly they're expecting the people standing there to try to attack them. The captain of the vessel is shouting orders to them – "Hold steady, my boys!" and "Kill the scum if they threaten you!" and so on. It's clear that the captain hates and fears the people who've been waiting for the ship to pull in, and it's clear, too, that the crewmen didn't know this before, because they're looking backwards and forwards perplexedly among each other, even the ones who're standing there with their swords unsheathed. But they're obedient – at least for the moment – because they're terrified of their captain.'

Anya's face had lost all its smiles and become icy.

'And tell me,' she said quietly, 'who is this captain?'

'You.'

'You lie!'

'The soothsayer may have lied, ma'am. Not I. I have told you exactly what the old woman told me.'

'And you let her live?'

'There was no compelling reason to kill her.'

'Her treason was surely enough.'

'She can be killed later, should you so desire, ma'am,' he said, thinking: *And should you remember*.

Anya blew out her cheeks. Haptan could see that her display of fury was her attempt to cover up something else, which he guessed was fear.

'And is this all the old witch told you?' snapped Anya a few minutes later.

'No, ma'am. There was more.'

'Tell me. Ignore my wrath. It isn't directed at you, friend.'

Haptan plunged on.

'The people on the dock don't make any movement, no movement at all. They just keep watching what's going on. And the crewmen with the swords are now becoming openly restless, glancing back at the ship and at the figure of their captain – er, you – on the deck, and they're talking to each other, their swords drooping and forgotten. All of which goes to make . . . you even more outraged than you were before, the target of your loathing seeming to be your mother most of all, because she's the one whose name sounds most often in your curses. You're distracted for a few moments when the pansy man starts playing on his flute, but it doesn't last long; then you're back foul-mouthing Syor again.'

'But I love her!' said Anya uncontrolledly. 'I . . .' She put her fingers to her mouth to silence herself. 'Go on,' she mumbled through them.

'Soon your temper can tolerate the situation no longer,' said Haptan, his eyes glazed as if he were no longer merely telling her of the soothsayer's vision but was living a part of himself. 'You turn towards a few of your astonished officers and, before they can think to deny you, you've snatched the crossbow away from one of them and are loading it with a bolt. The weapon's already charged, so it's only a couple of seconds later that you have it levelled on your mother's face, on her eyes . . .'

'Why would I seek to hurt someone I love beyond my own being?'

'You squeeze the weapon's trigger and the bolt flies true. And then . . . and then . . .'

'Then what? Look at me when you speak! Then what?'

'Where your mother was standing there is nothing but a featureless column of grey mist swirling. The bolt passes through it, beneath the arc of the other woman's arm that was around your mother's shoulders, and shatters harmlessly on a warehouse wall behind.'

'Thank her beingness. She saw my folly and saved herself. And now, all-forgiving, she will have mercy on my moment's madness . . .'

'The column of mist grows taller and taller,' Haptan continued as if she'd said nothing, 'curving as it grows so that it becomes like a vastly undulating serpent. And still it grows, so that now it is pressing against the ceiling of the sky, and spreading out there, so that the Sun itself becomes the grey of the mist. And now the other people that were waiting for you on the dock are moving. They've drawn each their different weapon, and they're advancing across the paving-slabs towards where the ship is moored. Your crewmen are shouting between each other, and now they're throwing down their swords, and one or two of them have dropped onto their knees to worship the column of mist, which is still growing, and the others are welcoming the strangers aboard, ushering them up the gangplank as if they were honoured guests – not like foreign potentates, more like old, close friends. But the faces of the visitors are grim, as if they've got something unpleasant that they must accomplish.'

'And what of me? What am I doing all this time? Defying them like a warrior, I trust.' Anya's fingernails were drawing blood from her palms.

'No, ma'am,' he said, his voice very weak. 'Having tried to command your officers to support you and found them unwilling to do so – indeed, some of them are looking at you as if for the first time they'd seen you were their bitterest enemy – you're retreating back along the deck. You cast the crossbow over the side, so that it flies in a great tumbling curve until it splashes into the water. Then you're pushing further away from the strangers, shoving aside members of your crew, who are just standing there numbly, as if they're incapable of doing anything either to help or to hinder you. You scream curses at them for their impotence, until finally one of them moves to help you. The soothsayer saw his face quite clearly, and it was because of that that she was willing to tell me of her vision.'

'You?' said Anya with as much of an imperious sneer as she could muster. 'You are my sole friend in my time of utmost adversity? I have fine friends, do I not?'

'You choose the friend who chooses you as a friend,' said Haptan sadly.

'I see the soothsayer decided to flatter you in her vision,' said Anya, misreading his thoughts. 'But do not pay the honour too much heed: dreams seldom bear much relation to reality. Continue.'

'The two of you – of us – carry on retreating towards the stern of the ship. You have a dagger between your teeth, and I'm armed with a cutlass. You're still screaming, now not in wrath but in terror for your life; you've wet yourself in dread, and so have I, so that we're slipping in our own fresh piss as we scrabble back across the planking.'

'Do you cast doubts on my courage, turd? Can you even for a moment conceive the possibility of your warrior-queen betraying cowardice like this? Would I not stand and fight – yes, and probably overcome them? Would I not?'

'Ma'am,' he said, an apologetic smile incongruous on his face, 'I mentioned that I'd pissed myself as well.'

'You are *allowed* to. It is in keeping with your lowly status. But *I* am . . . Carry on with your tasteless little fable. It will pass the time until I call my guards and demand recompense for your impertinence. Tell me of the strangers' quaking as they approach me, of their terror in their knowledge that surely some of them must die at my hand.'

'I cannot, ma'am. They show no fear. Only reluctance and determination mixed, like a farmer that is setting out to put down an old and much loved dog that has gone mad and become a danger to the children.'

'You die,' she hissed. Slowly she drew herself to her feet, uncoiling herself like a cobra, her fingers clawed. Then she shouted it: 'You die! No – on further thought, take your lies and begone! Be thankful that I do not think it worth my breath to call my soldiers and have you killed – stepped on like an insect scuttling across my marble floor. Go! Go!'

The last word was a scream. It passed over the shoulders of the fleeing Haptan, past groups of guards and soldiers and courtiers who shiftily pretended not to hear it, along corridors and down flights of stone stairs, and finally into the heat and steaminess of the great kitchen, where it blended with the scream of one of the cooks, who had been just about to plunge her heavy cleaver into the mutilated flesh of a pig when the carcase had disappeared.

5

The bus station has a notice in a glass box with dead flies in it which says that it once won an award for the best-dressed bus station of 1963 or some time but I am not looking at it when I go in and check by the clock that is lit up in the dark sky that there is still eight minutes before my going time is come, excetera, which is just about long enough for me to go and have a pee, not that I really need one but it is good to feel confident, when I see this blue anorak and the funny coloured hair above it and a pair of blue jeans, and I am just telling myself that if I did not know she is wearing a fawn belted coat I would think this was the Queen when she turns around as if she was expecting me and she smiles and I see that in fact it is the Queen, and I think that this is all wrong because the Queen should be finishing work right now in the bumhead's office thirty miles away but she is here instead, which cannot be right, especially since she did not officially know I was going to be here. I have just about got all the bits of that thought in the right order in my head when she is taking me by the hand and telling me to hurry because if we are not careful we are going to miss our bus, and I am saying that we have got plenty of time, look, eight, no now it is seven minutes, and she is saying it is not that bus she is talking about, that it is a different bus, that we are never going back home again, and I ask her about the hamster and she says it is all right, that the lady next door has agreed to take in the hamster because she has been lonely ever since her cat died which was called Furry Boy.

If it was anyone else but the Queen I think I would be pulling away from her, telling her to fuck off, not be so fucking crazy, of course we were going back home, but because she is her I do not do that. I think maybe Snakeface has been let out and he has tracked us down though God knows how he would be able to do that but criminals have all sorts of ways of doing these things, I mean real criminals and not just people who are very stupid and steal the occasional bike and leave it somewhere that the owner can get it back because that is not the way to get some holy joe to write a book about you. I think lots of other things as well, like how I am pissed off being a bouncer because the pay is OK but the job does not do much to broaden your mind's horizons, but most of all I guess I am thinking that I would rather be in hell with the Queen than back at the flat without her, so I do as she tells me to which means that she is not tugging my sleeve any longer but instead she is running along beside me, and the next thing I know we are climbing up the steps into a bus and she is waving a pair of tickets that she has already bought at the driver, whose eyes change colour as he sees the tickets. Maybe all the bus drivers' eyes do that when they see tickets and I have just never noticed before. He tells us that we are going to Far Ness, wherever that is, and the Queen just says yes yes yes and waves the tickets at me and calls the guy Alice which I think is just about enough to get us thrown off again before we have properly got on, but he does not seem to mind because he just smiles and nods and his eyes do the colouring trick again, which I remind myself I must ask him how he does it if we get talking to him later because it would be something that would make a big impact with the nubiles down by the river only then I remember that I do not go down by the river any longer, but still it would be a neat trick to learn in case I ever did.

There is not all that many people on the bus so I cannot understand why the Queen says we must sit down near some pissed old fart with a smell of gin a distiller would give his soul for. She smiles and says hello to the aforementioned fart as we go by him but he does not seem to recognize her or even to hear her say anything because his red eyes just stay fixed on something out the window. And we sit down and I pull out my cigarettes which the Queen has mashed more than a little because they were in my pocket and the seats are too narrow, all right, all right, it was me that mashed them because I sat down too close to her but what the hell, and I pull the ashtray out of the seat back and the whole sodding lot comes away in my hand so that fag-butts and an empty condom foil go everywhere and the Queen giggles at me so I kiss her on the nose because there was once a time she never used to giggle and I get the ashtray back in its slot somehow and I get black ash under my nails and I do not care because we are wondering how someone came to be unwrapping a condom in a bus and what did they do with it when they had used it, stuffed it down the back of the cushions maybe, and I pretend I am going to look and see which makes the Queen giggle again and the bus is moving and the noise of the wheels makes it difficult for us to hear each other so we just look out the window.

And then there is a strangeness because the wheels stop thundering and we cannot even hear the sound of the engine any more and I look at the Queen and she looks back at me.

'Where did you say this bus was going to?' I ask her.

'We are to Albion going,' she says. 'To Albion as I always said we one day would, but you did not believe me.'

And I say to her: 'It was not that I did not believe you exactly, because I do not think you ever lie to me, but though I thought Albion was real I did not think it was the same sort of real as we are and here is, and I did not think that you could go on a bus to it.'

And she says: 'I think maybe it is realer, in a way.'

And I say: 'This is all a bit above me. Wake me up when we get there because being talked at by Hump was tiring,' and I ease myself down so that I am comfortable with my ear feeling her shoulder move up and down as she breathes, and she says: 'No, Nadar, do not waste the experience. Look out of the window and you can see us going there.' And I do as she says because I cannot think of any reason for not doing as she says, and I see out of the side of my eye that the pissed old fart who does not seem quite so pissed as he was is also now sitting up in his seat and looking out of the window as if there is something interesting that he can see there, and I start wondering again why the bus is so quiet because the silence makes it seem as if we are not going anywhere, which of course we are because you can tell by the street lights and the house lights going by us that we are going at a high speed. Only the street lights and the house lights is looking funny now because they are not square and they do not look as if they are very close to us but instead a long way away, most of them. And I have my arm around the Queen and it is not just to keep her warm, and she is making herself comfortable under my jacket against my jersey that my mother made for me with the arms too short, and she is looking out the window as if there is something very exciting there.

And all that I can see is that we are slowing down again and coming to a motorway service station, which is wrong because it is only five minutes since we were leaving the bus station, and just what the fuck is going on here. But I am just about to express my views to the Queen when the bus comes to a stop with a jolt and the doors at the front whoosh open like it was something they had been wanting to do a long time only the driver would not let them, and the driver himself is coming back up the middle towards us except now I can see that the driver is a herself, so maybe the Queen knows her and that is why she called her Alice without getting us thrown off, but the eyes are still doing their stuff so I know that it is the same person all right, only the driver seems to be hardly more than a child, no real tits yet.

But we do as she says we should which is get off the bus and the Queen and I go and slash in our separate neon-lit boxes of privacy that some kind person has built by the road side especially for us and complete with smells, and then we meet back by the bus and tell each other how we are not really hungry but if the Queen is I will have a burger if she has the money so that she does not feel like a greedy pig eating on her own when I am not, or maybe it is the other way around, and we are walking across the tarmac towards some bright windows and a smell of grease and a sign that says

LITLe CHeFF

when I notice that there is something very wrong, again, and I pull the Queen up short and tell her so and she asks me what it is I mean and I point out all around us and above us and even beneath our feet, and she says: 'Is that not what you expected to see?' and I say: 'No it is fucking not', because there are no other cars or noises of cars and there are no motorway lights and no house lights, but just whichever way you look a lot of tiny glistening lights like they were the stars, and maybe they are the stars above us, but I do not see how it is possible I can see stars in the ground beneath me as well, a point I put to the Queen with some cogency, but she just smiles and tells me we are both going home and not to worry if some things seem a little strange on the way there, and come on because she has decided she really is hungry after all and she would like a burger even though it will be vile.

So we carry on walking towards the LITLe CHeFF sign which someone cannot spell right and it feels like we are walking on air a zillion miles above anywhere like in the Spielberg movies maybe but I do not feel dizzy. Inside the place, which has swing doors that do not swing properly, there is again the silence like there seems to be a lot of right now, which is because there is nearly no one inside except the fart who was pissed and the driver who is sitting beside him and the other passengers of which there was not that many to begin with and who are looking frightened. There is not all the tired young thickos in uniforms with plastic smiles like you would normally expect to get thrown in for free with your Toilers of the Deep fish-style fishburger, so people are all plucking up their courage to just grab for themselves, and the Queen takes a packet of crisps and I take some nuts and then I find I am putting down some coins on top of one of the boxes like I had got a bad case of honesty or something. The Queen pulls me over to where the driver and the fart are sitting, and it is weird about the fart because he still stinks of gin and his eyes are still red but he is as sober as you could be although he talks filthy like I expect the Queen to blush, only instead she kisses him on the cheek and tells him he is jolly, which he is not.

I sit down while the Queen talks to the driver who is still called Alice and I look at the fart and see he does not want to talk to me which is all right by me because I do not want to talk to him, so I just sit there thinking for the hundredth time today, if it still is today, that I wish I knew what the fuck was up.

After a bit I go round the back of one of the counters and fill a LITLe CHeFF carrier with fags because I do not know when the Queen and I will next find a shop, and I leave some money for them as well but I still feel guilty because it is not enough money for the fags I am taking because I do not have enough with me, but I leave all I have and the odd thing is that before I met the Queen I would of not left any.

6

The Sun had been just rising when they arrived at Qazar. The horses had forgotten that they'd been safe enough climbing the gangplank to come aboard, and so it had taken Reen a long time to coax them down over the narrow strip of wood and onto the dock. Rehan had looked pale and not terribly interesting as Kursten had helped him across the gangplank; if anything, he'd been just as much of a bother as the horses. Syor had followed behind them, paying them no attention but instead seeming to be devouring all the sights and the smells and the sounds of the harbour, as if she had been trying to make Albion be the air in her lungs and the blood in her veins.

Kursten had said a curious thing to Rehan as she and Reen were checking the horses' tackle; he had been leaning against a bollard wishing the ground would stop moving.

'Harbours,' she had said, 'are the only places in the World which seem to be in two places at once, or maybe not in any place at all. I noticed that when we were booking our passage.'

'What do you mean?' he had said, not really listening. His stomach had been making strange protesting noises, and they were tending to drown out anything else.

'Well, if you think about it, as far as the land's concerned, the harbour's a gateway to the sea, even though it belongs to the land. But, as far as the sea's concerned, the harbour's a gateway to the land, but it's a part of the sea. So the harbour isn't really a part of either of them. We could think of ourselves as having come across the sea to get to the nearest harbour, so that we could set out from here on a voyage – a voyage across the land.'

He had groaned, only partly because of his stomach. 'So you want us to turn things arsy-versy in our heads, so that Albion is really the sea?' he had said leadenly.

'Something like that,' she had brightly replied. 'Here, your ship is safely saddled now. Climb aboard.'

Now they were riding at a good speed along the busy road from Qazar to Ernestrad. There were wagons going in both directions; only occasionally were there people on horseback like themselves. The whole scene evoked feelings of honest toil and moderate prosperity; there was, Rehan reflected, something very comfortable about it. Certainly it was like nothing he could ever have imagined during his youth in Albion, when the life of a peasant had been short and often enough savage, and fortunately little remembered. He found that the placidity of it all – the smell of dung, the sound of hoarse shouting – was lulling him into the desire that things could always be like this, that Albion's manifest contentedness with itself would endure forever. Yet surely that would be a fate almost as bad, in its way, as if the island had continued under the lash of the Ellonia.

He wondered why Syor had wanted so much to come here. Of course, her plans had melded well with Reen's and his own – rather too well, he now began to think. Alyss had perhaps been a little too off-handed in her manner when she'd suggested that the two of them might like to go to Albion by way of the Anonymous City, and in her request that they find out some more for her about the ffarg. Reen had said: 'You want us to bring you a monster.' Alyss's voice had been suspiciously ingenuous when she'd retorted with a smile: 'I'd like you to bring me a ffarg as well.' Rehan glanced at Kursten, riding demurely beside him, and grinned: she was no monster, but she might be a reason for that smile of Alyss's. But in that case so might Syor – except that Syor wasn't so much *a* ffarg as *the* ffarg, collectively. Had Alyss realized that this was the case? Was this the reason that she'd set up the rendezvous in this way? Already knowing it was going to happen?

And she'd failed to fulfil her half-promise to visit one or both of their silent-minds to tell them when they should meet her, or that they should go somewhere else. Was this because she had already looked into Syor's intentions, and knew that there was no need to tell them anything more, that they'd be reaching Starveling-stage at the appointed time without any further intervention by herself?

Rehan stopped worrying about it. He found that thinking through issues of cause and effect and intention made his head hurt, especially when he was trying to double-guess a person to whom past and future were only loosely differentiated. Instead he chatted with Kursten, which he enjoyed doing much more. And, anyway, his stomach had settled down.

There was nothing to slow them, and so it was only a short while after noon when they saw Starveling-stage – the truncated peak that floated in the sky over Ernestrad.

7

'It is time,' says the driver, 'for all of us to get back on board that bus out there and carry on with our journey to the World, which is more than just Albion whatever you might think, Syor, so finish eating your goodies like nice cooperative children and get a finger out.'

Me and the Queen have already finished our goodies and have even put our crumpled wrappers in the conveniently positioned litter bins set at various sites around the cafeteria for the benefit of our valued clientele, so we pick ourselves up and check that we have not left anything behind the way you always do even if you have not brought anything that you could leave behind in the first place, and the Queen puts her hand in mine and tickles my palm where no one can see her doing it so that as we are going out the swing doors that still have not learned to swing properly I am grinning like something out of the muppets. As we are getting back on the bus, which we are the last of all to do except the driver herself and a Japanese tourist, who should of thought to have his slash earlier like the rest of us, the Queen stops us and says to the driver who is standing beside the steps:

'Alice,' she says: 'Is it the right thing that we are doing, this going back to Albion biz?'

'Syor,' says the driver, 'it is a very important thing that you are doing. Even if it were not a very important thing that you were doing, it would come about that you would do it anyway, and there would be nothing neither me nor any other godling, if there was any, could do to stop you, even *you* could not stop you, because you are essential to the ongoing happiness of all of the World. It will not be a functional mechanism until you are joined with your other fass ets to make one integral hole, which will be not only a part of the World but also the World itself, and also something much greater than the World.'

The Queen looks as blank as I feel on hearing this, and I wonder if she is made discontented by the prospect of becoming a hole, which is maybe a rude thing for the driver to be thinking of calling her, but she must of understood something of it because she says:

'So you mean that I am not the only myself? There are others of me?'

'Yes,' says the driver. 'You have hit the nail right on the button, and are not such a bimbo, whatever everyone else says. You are a part of a greater hole that is Syor, and once you are joined up with all the other parts you will discover that this is what you needed to be all along, because you never really belonged in this afterlife that you have been living in and into which chance rather foolishly cast you. Your transformation will be a bit upsetting for your male friend, of course, but he seems a bit of a thicko anyway and probably will not notice.'

I am wondering whether to pulp the driver's head into the middle of her chest for saying this, but the Queen clamps her fingers round my arm, so I know she does not want me to, which she never does even that time someone in the pub called her a trollop, though I did not notice her objecting too much when it was Snakeface I was dissuading from conscious activity, as us bouncers call it in the trade. Before I can put any of this into words, the Queen is saying:

'You misjudge him, Alice. He may seem to you at the moment as if, if you described him accurately, you would of got angry letters from short planks, but that is just the frame that his soul has been locked into for the purposes of his life in this particular otherness what we have just left behind us. Inside him there is an intelligent person and I think a nice one too, although he has never known it, especially not when I first met him in Albion and sometimes hated him.'

The driver's eyes become like letterboxes into neighbouring houses, one with a brown hall-carpet and the other with a green hall-carpet.

The driver says: 'I did not realize you had met this bozo in Albion. That was not in the plans. What is his name?'

I say my own name, because it is not right that the Queen should do all the talking for both of us, I'm not dumb or anything, so I say: 'My name is Nadar, which is a bit of an odd name but I think my great-grandfather was Turkish, or that is what my mother used to say.'

And the driver says: 'Oh shit. I forgot.'

Which is discourteous of her unless she is a teacher, as they taught us at school. I look at the Queen and her face has got little pink patches where the bone pushes up from under the skin, and she says: 'Tough-o, Alice. I am taking him with me to Albion, whether you like it or not, and if you say that I must just dump him then you can have another think. Perhaps I know something about all this that you do not know, but from the first time I saw him I knew that he was an essential part of me, that we were complimentary to each other.'

That seems an odd thing to say but Alice knows what it means because she nods, even though her eyes are still letterboxes.

'Maybe you are right, Syor,' she said. 'If I had of thought it through a bit harder I would of recognized that. I am still not sure it is a good thing, and also I think it is something you may regret over the next thousands of billions of years, but there is an old saying among us eternals, or would be if there were more than one of me, to the effect that there is no mucking about with the dictates of supreme beings, which latter move in ways that are either mysterious or a pain in the butt, depending upon viewpoint.'

Says the Queen: 'I did not realize I was a supreme being, Alice. I had thought that was more your bag.'

Says the driver: 'You have not seen nothing yet, bub.'

So we get aboard and go and sit down where we were before and the old fart in front of us does not seem any friendlier than he was before, even though the Queen is being as nice to him as she knows how, which is pretty goddam nice as I am the first to know, and we wait a minute longer until the Japanese tourist gets on with us, and then the doors whoosh shut again, and the only sign that we are off again is that the lights of the empty LITLe CHeFF are left behind us and the lights like stars are all around us now and I turn to ask the Queen if *she* has any idea what the fuck is up but she seems to have fallen asleep so I do not ask her but instead find out how my fingernails taste, which is full of stale fag ash from before.

I am glad that Hump is not with us, but that is just about all I am glad about.

8

The courtyard of Starveling was barely half-full when Anya walked out the next morning to seat herself on the throne placed for her on the royal dais. This had been demolished when the Ellonia had been expelled – it had been blackened and cracked by the heat of the conflagration – but during the winter Anya had seen fit to have it replaced, rebuilt as nearly as possible in the original position. There were stone-faced warriors on duty at intervals all around the walls of the courtyard, and a contingent of half a dozen at the great gate. The executioners were on their own long platform, from which yesterday's blood had been but poorly cleansed; they were sharpening their blades and puffing bellows at the charcoals of the braziers. The condemned had yet to be brought forth, but already the people in the courtyard could hear the screams of some of them.

Anya shifted uneasily in her throne. Only a few months ago and the place would have been packed; her own entrance would have been cheered echoingly by the crowd, come to see her enact justice upon the sinners in the name of all the people of Albion. Now they were a sorry lot, most of them looking sullen and resentful, as if they'd been dragged in off the streets by her soldiers and told to watch the spectacle in an orderly fashion or participate more directly in its sequel on the morrow. Some were disreputable-looking enough that she guessed they were only there on the promise of the free meal that the guards gave out afterwards. And there were a few who were looking eager: they were here to enjoy themselves gloating over others' agonies, and Anya despised them for it.

She always experienced each of the individual torments of the condemned as they died. She had to steel herself to come here each day. Had it not been in the interests of her people that she witness the administration of the nation's revenge, she would have certainly stayed away.

The prisoners were being brought up from Starveling's depths now, and she turned her regal head to watch their slow, shuffling, tear-stained progress. Those who had been screaming just a little while ago had been cudgelled into silence; one had been clubbed viciously across the mouth, so that all the noise he could now make was a straining gurgle. Others were trying to struggle against their bonds, which was good; the crowd enjoyed best watching the deaths of those who had come to meet their fates with still a bit of life left in them. One or two had fainted away completely, and were having to be carried up the stone steps; they would be awoken in time for their anguish to begin.

9

The fart in front of us seems to decide that it is time he started to be nice to us, or maybe just to the Queen I do not know, but he turns round in his seat and looks over the back of it like a kilroy with his long nose and red eyes and he says to her: 'Hi there, good looking,' which I suppose is his idea of cute, it makes me want to vomit, boring old suit.

But the Queen just smiles as if he has buttered her up with the kind of art I once thought I had. She says: 'Hello jolly, you have not changed much you temper mental old grump you.' He says: 'How is it that you know that, not that I admit any of it, you understand, but what makes you think that, and how did you know my name back there in the LITLe CHeFF?' She says: 'Are you not starting at least to remember how it was in Albion?' And he says: 'I am beginning to I think, but I cannot be sure. If I am right in what I am thinking, you must be Syor, although you do not look very like her, because your face does not have many smile-lines and hers always had a lot.' She says: 'I can smile, you ratbitten old bag of bones,' and she smiles, and he smiles as well, and I am the only one that is not smiling because I have decided I do not like him much. So the next thing is that he wants to sit beside her and she looks at me as if she is asking if that would be OK and I tell him to fuck off because I can see the way he is looking in the front of her anorak and she tells me that I am over reacting and he is just an old friend, and I tell her he is certainly old, and the end result is that he does not sit beside her but has to stay kneeling up on his seat looking backwards at us.

I think they are friends though. I think if she said she would do one of the things he sometimes asks her to do as they are talking he would run a mile. I think it is because they are good friends that she likes it when he says those things and he likes it because he knows she will not do them. I hold her hand and I see she is not angry with me any more, so I put a smile over my mind so that she cannot see I would still like to stick his head up his bum hole.

He is telling her about his dreams, which is very boring, especially when he says they can come true. I look out the window.

The driver comes past us to go to the lavatory at the back of the bus. The bus is still going on as usual, even though there is no one driving it. The jolly fart pats her on the bottom as she goes by and she almost hits him but he calls her Lisa and she does not seem to mind that, the same way she did not mind the Queen calling her Alice, so perhaps she has more than one name.

I wish I could understand what is going on. By now I should be at work watching the England versus West Indies highlights on BBC2 in Oliver's back room before the club fills up. It is the last day of the game, and I am wondering who won. I ask the suit but he does not know. If the Queen is right and we are going to Albion and will never come back again I will never know who won the England v. West Indies match.

10

The first of the condemned had died before disembowelling, and the enthusiasts among the crowd were grumbling, although not quite loudly enough for the guards to be able to identify the potential troublemakers. The executioner cut the carcase open anyway, but it wasn't the same: just the revelation of what one could see any day in the butcher shop.

Anya sent up a mental prayer of gratitude to Syor for having shown mercy to the man, although even she felt strangely unfulfilled.

Her attention was distracted by the arrival of a messenger at her side.

'Yes,' she said coolly to the woman.

'A man came to the sentries earlier this morning with news he felt ought to be imparted to you, ma'am,' the messenger said. Her face was going pale as she tried not to look across at the platform where an executioner was beginning to flay the next of the condemned.

'And the nature of this news?' said Anya.

'This morning, not long after dawn, he saw a naked, blinded man and a pig.'

'But the pig is . . .' And then Anya remembered the report she had received from the kitchen. 'Go on.'

'They were heading purposefully, the pig leading the blinded man, for the lower slopes of Starveling-stage. The peasant thought it might be the Painter, and that you would pay him well for the intelligence. He was congratulated on having performed his patriotic duty, and was sent on his way.'

'Did he have any more to tell?'

'Not so far as the sentries could ascertain.'

Anya put her chin in her hands and turned away from the messenger, who began to wonder if she had been dismissed. But then her leader spoke again.

'Has a search party been organized?'

'No. The sentries didn't know what to do at first. They're not very bright. It took them until only a few minutes ago, when they came off duty, to decide they'd better pass the information on to their commanding officer.'

That's the trouble with loyal soldiers, thought Anya ruefully as blade sliced through flesh and blood flowed. *Loyalty and intelligence seem somehow incompatible*.

'Then I shall raise one now,' she said. 'I shall lead it myself. It's imperative that we seize the Painter, and I would like to be there myself when he is taken. You may occupy this throne in my stead until my return, or until the last of the condemned has met his fate, whichever comes earlier.'

She got to her feet and smoothed her robe around her hips. She smiled graciously. 'You may serve as my consul for a while, may you not?'

'I . . .' The woman looked sick. 'It is an honour.' She half-knelt.

'This is a duty for which a substitute is acceptable,' said Anya rather wistfully as the messenger settled herself. 'I should have learned long ago that the same is not possible for others of my duties, most especially leading my troops forth from Giorran.'

It was only after Anya had left her in a swirl of richly embroidered cloth that the messenger realized that her ruler had used the old name.

11

'It's a nice enough place for a picnic, I suppose,' said Rehan, throwing himself down on Kursten's outspread cloak. 'A bit windy, but that's OK on a day this hot. And the view's magnificent. Funny the way those painted eyes on the lower slopes seem to be watching you wherever you go, isn't it? Still, they're no doubt looking at me sympathetically, wondering how a single human being of my slight build could perform such a feat of endurance. Oh, I feel *so* happy.'

'Shut up,' said Reen, looking down at him with affection. 'You've never been very good at sarcasm, my friend. Why not dig out your flute or your bodhran from the baggage and play us a tune to pass the time?'

'Wait,' said Rehan, 'until I get my breath back.' He groaned histrionically. 'I may have broken my own spirit, you know, carrying all that weight.'

'You ever get fed up with him?' said Reen to Kursten, who was standing nearby, grinning at them both.

'I'm learning fast.'

They had brought the horses as far up through the lower slopes as possible, keeping the bulk of the mountain between themselves and Starveling. For the last couple of hundred metres, however, it had been a question of tethering the animals to the edges of a scrubby patch of shrubbery and scrabbling onwards on hands and knees and feet. Kursten had shown a remarkable agility, leaping from rock to rock with the sure-footedness of a mountain goat, but she had been able to carry only one of the panniers plus Rehan's flute and bodhran. Although Syor had seemed to float up the steep mountainside, there had somehow been no question of asking her to bear anything. And so it had fallen to Reen and Rehan, in equal measure, to drag the bulk of their provisions up with them. Rehan, on seeing the size of the task, had argued in favour of leaving the baggage with the horses, but Reen had pointed out that they didn't know how long they might have to camp out on Starveling-stage before Alyss arrived, and, although she, Reen, had no objections to him, Rehan, having to climb back down here and up again every meal-time . . . So amid much cursing the singer had knuckled down to it. Now he was almost as exhausted as he was claiming to be.

'Bring me,' he said to Kursten, rolling over onto his

back, 'a bottle of something cool and preferably alcoholic. Bring me a pillow for my head. Bring me sleep, and the sweetness of dreams. Bring me . . .'

'Here.'

He sat up in surprise. He took the wine-bottle in one hand, and then squirmed around to help Kursten remove his jacket. His blouse was sticking to his arms and back, and the wind blowing across it cooled him. She bundled up the jacket and put it down behind him.

'There,' she said, 'oh mighty master. A pillow for thy head and a bottle for thy belly. The sleep and dreams you'll have to organize for yourself.'

'You'll make someone a good mistress one day, Kursten,' he sighed, then took a deep swig on the lukewarm but tartly dry white wine. They had bought three bottles of the stuff in Qazar, and this was the last of them. There was a spring within easy reach of the summit, so they wouldn't die of thirst; it was good to be able to drink as much as he wanted of the wine without feeling guilty about it. He'd earned it, after all.

So had Reen. He wiped the neck and passed the bottle to her. Then he lowered himself back downwards onto his pillow.

The Sun was now far enough away from the zenith that he could look at the sky. Even though at a conscious level he'd become accustomed to the fact that the Sun could shift from the centre of the heavens, he still found it faintly disturbing to be able to lie here like this and stare directly upwards. The sky itself wasn't much to look at today: it was cloudless but so filled with haze that the effect was the same as that of clouds. There was a bird of some sort – a curlew, he thought, but he had never been very good at recognizing birds – circling around, far above him, and he fancied that it might be a spy sent by Anya to observe them, but after a while it turned and caught a new air-current and drifted off to one side. His eyes were too lazy to bother following its course.

Reen sat down beside him. He didn't have to turn his head to know who it was: the familiar and much loved smell of leather and woman and sweat was identification enough. If it had been Kursten there would have been a different smell altogether: much fainter, and slightly more acid, yet not at all unpleasing. He wondered how he himself smelled, because of course he was so accustomed to it that he didn't know, and he made a mental note to ask Reen or Kursten some time, knowing as he did so that he'd probably forget. It was odd, though, the way that nature had seen fit to tag everyone with their own individual odour. Most people never noticed the fact, probably thinking that it was rude or something to pay any attention to the evidence of their senses, but animals must be aware of it the whole time – must revel in it.

Rehan wrinkled his brow. Try as he might, he couldn't think what Syor smelled like. Another thing to ask Reen one day, some day, except that he knew that he wouldn't . . .

12

Syor was likewise gazing up at the sky, her fingers fondling the small vial at her throat. Through the stone she could feel the vital force of the contained Mistdom, as if it were agitating itself just enough to remind her that it was there. As if she could forget! She not only felt the agitation as a movement within a dissociated part of herself but also was its conscious inspiration.

She didn't see the hazy blueness that filled Rehan's vision. Instead the sky was clear as coldness. It was black, but here and there tinged with a faint rust-red. Scattered everywhere across it were hard points of cold light in many different shades of white and yellow and orange and red and blue; some were bathing in irregular pools of luminescence, fringed by asymmetrical tendrils that stretched out across the ebony arch as if trying to touch their neighbours; others were gathered in clusters to form brightly sparkling diamond islands; others were regal in their solitary austerity. And most distant of all were dim fogs of light that she knew had been formed from the same stuff as the contents of the crude vial in her fingers. It would not be long now before the Mistdom could be released to mingle with its siblings in the sky.

She sensed the closeness of the occasion in the same way that she sensed the Sun's heat on her skin, which was in itself only an improbable membrane, for there was no longer anything but the most tenuous division in kind between herself and the World and, beyond the World, the Universe. She was coextensive and coeternal with them – almost. She had formed the Mistdom and the Mistdom had formed this body for her. She had taken from its home within Rehan the shard of herself that she had long ago lodged there – before either she or the singer had been born – and she had brought it into her own temporary frame. The one who had called another aspect of her from the soul-stuff of the Universe would soon be here, and he would give up to her his precious burden, making her even more nearly whole. And the part of her that was human would arrive last of all.

No, not quite last of all.

For there was a final facet of herself that she had once deceived herself could be lost forever within the ocean of the Universe's soul-stuff, diluted to such thinness that it would no longer have any presence. It had been a fool's delusion, she realized; she had known that at the time, but had carried on with it anyway. The child whose body – but, alas, not whose soul – she had brought into the World had assiduously swept together all the vestiges of this final element, and would be bringing it here also.

Syor did not want it back.

She had taken measures, moreover, to ensure that she did not have to take it back. She was not proud of those measures, for she was fully aware of their cruelty, but she was able to justify them within herself.

She permitted herself a moment's sorrow that the child would have to die – sorrow not for the child, nor for any closeness that the human aspect of Syor might once have shared with her, but for Reen and Rehan, who had once upon a time, each in their individual but identically misguided way, loved that child.

She stretched out her arms, and across the intergalactic voids the seas of the Mistdom saw her, and stretched out their own arms to share the embrace.

13

Anya shrilled to her soldiers to halt their horses and dismount, which they did with a clattering of harnesses and weaponry. They were in a narrow defile which a long-vanished stream had carved out of the rock; winds and rains had etched the exposed shales differentially, so there were places to tether the beasts. Once the soldiers had seen to it that this was done, they gathered around her expectantly, strangely quiet, as if they knew that the mission their ruler was leading them on was more than just a matter of capturing a man and slaying a pig.

She slung the loop of a crossbow over her shoulders, feeling the comfortingly uncomfortable weight of the weapon against her shoulders and spine; it would chafe as she climbed, she knew, but she wasn't frightened of the petty pain. Far above her, perhaps half a kilometre away, she caught a glimpse of the silhouettes of the Painter and his frighteningly undead pig as they surmounted the lip of the plateau. Why they should be going to Starveling-stage she couldn't imagine; she refused to countenance the possibility that they might merely cross the tabletop and descend the mountain on the far side, so that they would be long gone by the time that Anya and her party reached the summit. No, she was convinced that within at most an hour or two the Painter – the treacherous husband whom she had divorced and cast from her – would be hers to dispose of as she wished. And this time he would not live to perpetuate his heresies.

In the corner of her eye a high-flying bird moved against the foggy backdrop of the sky; she ignored the distraction.

In doing so she was alone among the soldiers, for they saw the slow, purposive way in which the curlew was now circling the mountaintop. Had they been less well trained they might have spoken of it among each other, and perhaps even deserted her there, for the curlew had been a cursed bird among the Ellonia, and the superstition had not died. As it was, each of them kept his or her silence, and suffered a solitary dread.

'Follow me!' she cried abruptly. 'Follow me, for the glory of all Albion!'

She ran as far as she could up the course of the defile, and they followed her. Then, as one, they began to scramble up over the rough rocks and rougher heather.

14

The bird was definitely coming closer.

Reen had been watching it spiralling through the sky for some minutes now, at first simply because she couldn't think of anything better to do – Rehan, by whose head she was hunkering, having fallen into a light sleep, Kursten having drifted off primly for lavatorial purposes and Syor quite evidently being in a different universe – but now because it was evident to Reen that the bird was not simply moving at random. It was coming nearer and nearer to them with each succeeding circle of its long downward glide. She glanced to one side, looking for something that might be the focus of its descent, and saw the ancient, disorganized cairn that stood at the centre of Starveling-stage. Near to the cairn Syor was standing, her arms out towards the sky – towards the sky, but not towards the bird . . . although that did not mean that it was not towards her that the bird was flying.

There was a commotion near the edge of the table, and Reen looked over towards it idly, assuming that it was being caused by Kursten's return. When she saw that it was not, she punched downwards with one fist onto Rehan's shoulder, jolting him into wakefulness; her sword was in her other hand before she had time to think of drawing it.

On their feet beside each other, the two of them stared at the newcomers.

The pig seemed to be of little interest, although it was bizarre that a farmyard animal could have been able to negotiate its way up the steep inclines and jagged rock faces to reach this place.

But that was as nothing compared with the impossibility of the man getting here. He should have been dead. Where his eyes should have been there were only cakes of dried blood. His face was a patchwork of cuts and bruises. Blood was still dripping from the holes that had been punched through his wrists and, as Reen and Rehan could now see as they squinted at him, his ankles. Raw flesh and a gleam of yellow bone showed where his genitals had been. The rest of his torso had been cut and slashed repeatedly; one breast had been sheared off completely, and the other had lost its nipple. His arms hung limply from bulging dislocated shoulders; his hips displayed the same grotesque wrongness, so that it was clearly impossible for him to walk.

And yet walk he did, in a curious half-collapsing way that he seemed to accept as perfectly natural; Reen, Rehan and now Kursten, who had joined them unnoticed from somewhere, could see no indication that he felt any discomfort as he manoeuvred himself along on rubbery legs across the short grass towards the cairn, the pig dancing around him and nudging his calves whenever he seemed uncertain.

He walked towards Syor, who was turning to face him, her arms still outstretched, as if he were a part of the sky that had come down to earth to be closer to her. Her green eyes seemed to be larger than they could possibly be.

As the man approached her, his strides became more assured and the obscene bulges of his hips shrank. That was the first change that Reen noticed – the sympathetic agony she felt as she watched him walk was ebbing swiftly away. Then she saw that the deep cuts were melting from his back, that his ankles were becoming whole. As if aware that she and Kursten and Rehan were watching him, he paused and turned part-way towards them, and they could see that his chest was whole and hairy, that the incisions were gone from his belly, that his genitals were dangling jauntily between his thighs. His cheeks were now glowing with something more than mere well-being, as if there were a lantern behind the mask of his face.

Still there were only scabs in the sockets of his face, but it did not seem to the three of them as if he were any longer sightless.

The pig, satisfied that its master had been guided as far as he needed to be, trotted towards them in a couldn't-care-less fashion, as if they were only one of many destinations to which its whim might take it. But, for all that, it reached them soon enough, and sat down in front of them, its bright, intelligent little eyes glancing backwards and forwards between their three upraised swords, as if politely hinting that they were perhaps being a trifle discourteous. As they sheathed the weapons, childishly embarrassed, the pig lowered one ear over an eye, as if winking approvingly at them. Then it raised itself to its feet, turned, and with a final twitch of its heavy bottom at them trotted back to rejoin its master.

The man was kneeling now, not in humility but as if he were the bearer of a gift which he wished to present with full ceremony.

Syor licked one of her thumbs, and reached out to press it against his forehead.

Reen narrowed her eyes. There was a flurry of coloured movement in the air all round the two frozen figures, the kneeling naked man and the standing robed woman. There were glimpses of blue dresses and dirty black hair and darkly bruised knees, far too many to distinguish from each other, swirling rapidly around the tableau, and she swore that she could hear faintly the strains of laughter and song, as well as the shouts and tears of trivial wrath. Reen was reminded of the time, once, indefinitely long ago, when Anya had scampered like this around Syor's knees – Syor's and Reen's own – and she found to her annoyance that there was a mistiness in her eyes.

The rush of glimpses was becoming ever more swift, as

if they were coalescing together to form a vortex into which they were themselves disappearing. Watching, Reen felt a touch of vertigo, as if she were standing only just far enough away not herself to be swept into the imploding current of the colours.

And then the motion was gone.

Syor and the kneeling man at her feet remained frozen, her arm still reaching out to him, her thumb still pressed to his forehead.

The pig was snuffling inquisitively at the objects that lay on the grass between them.

An open-topped canvas bag, from which the pig was now snouting, contained cloth pouches. As the pouches fell to the ground they spilled haphazardly, so that powdered pigments scattered across the close-cropped grass, mixing with each other as they fell. There were the colour of amber seen in candlelight, the colour of the blue wraiths that play around glowing coals, the colour of the sky in the moment before dawn, when the stars are still bravely shining, the colour of the ends of fresh straw, the colour of a moist young cheese, the colour that eyes have in the darkness . . .

The naked man slowly lowered his hands to this sea of pigment. He picked up the powders in his fingers and idly let them fall again, so that rainbow tails of dust flew away from him into invisibility. Again he scooped up the powders, mixing them further, but this time they did not leave his hands when he splayed his fingers. Instead, his hands became piercing lights of countless filmy hues all shifting and flowing together like the skin of a soap-bubble as his arms moved. Now, once again, Reen could hear the sounds of children – all the hundreds of Halgiad's daughters – dancing and fighting and playing, while behind them there was the sprightly piping of a piccolo or flageolet, as if Starveling-stage were the scene of a glorious party which the adults had forgotten to supervise.

The naked man was standing now, washing his body with his hands so that all of his skin became an ever-changing patchwork of all the colours of the World.

He moved to the cairn and stood in front of it, then turned to look back over his shoulder at Syor, who nodded her approval.

With a single broad sweep of his incandescent arm he painted, right across the countless crumbling stones of the cairn's face, a solitary, stylized green eye, which was focused on where the three of them stood and was clearly watching them – not uncongenially.

The children's voices were raised in ear-shattering cheer after ear-shattering cheer, as if they were set to send cracks through the ceiling of the sky. The Painter stepped slowly back from the cairn, the colours and the light slowly seeping from his body to drain off into the earth beneath his feet. There was a smile on his face as he looked towards Syor now; and she, with her head slightly bowed as a mark of respect, was smiling back at him.

The cheers of the children continued to grow louder and louder as a curlew circled out of the sky towards the cairn's peak.

15

Anya heard the noise and looked back over her shoulder furiously to see which of her soldiers had so lost their discipline that they had begun to scream.

None of them had. They too were looking behind them at the source of the screaming that seemed to be filling the World.

Spread out below them was the toy city of Ernestrad and beyond that were the fields and lanes of Albion, their patterns distorted to form the tongue and throat and teeth and uvula of a lividly many-coloured mouth which was screaming its hatred at them.

Anya turned stoically back to the rock face directly in front of her. Dark red blood was seeping from three of her fingers where the nails had been torn away.

16

With one last dainty pirouette in the air, its head poised as if it were smiling at Reen and Kursten and Rehan, the curlew flew in to land on the cairn's topmost stone.

17

I am sitting in the bus and wondering how it is that I am smoking the last of my cigarettes when I had boxes and boxes of them only half an hour ago, and I wonder if maybe the Queen or more likely the jolly fart has been nicking them but no, I can see the empty packets lying all around me like flotsam the sea washed in and there are fag-butts thick on the floor around my ankles so I guess the journey must be taking longer than I had thought or maybe I am smoking a lot faster than I usually do but surely it is not possible to smoke that fast. There is certainly a lot of smoke in the air so that I find it difficult to see the Queen or the elderly suit, although I can still hear their voices. Also I can see the driver as she passes close to us again and this time her flashing eyes like a traffic sign are so narrowed down that I tell her she might as well just shut the things but she tells me to get stuffed because she is very busy right now and has a lot on her mind and if she had known who I was she would not have allowed me to buy a ticket to go on her bus, which I am about to say is a bit fucking much of her but she has gone by then.

The voices of the Queen and of the old guy are getting more excited now, so maybe at last something is . . .

18

The noise of the cheering stopped as if a door had been slammed on it. The echoes drifted slowly away until they were lost in the sky.

Beside her Reen could hear terrified whimpering, so she put her arm around Kursten's shoulders, realized her mistake, and put her other arm around Rehan.

Then there was the most almighty explosion of air, and all of them were thrown flat on their faces.

By the time they had climbed to their feet again, Starveling-stage had changed. Shockingly so.

19

. . . going to happen, but my throat is . . .

Suddenly we are in the brightest of daylight, so that for a moment I can see nothing at all, just the light beating against my instinctively closed eyelids. I reach out to one side and feel the Queen reassuringly taking my hand, squeezing my fingers between her own. Even the old guy with the suit – whose name is Joli, of course, not jolly; the Queen once told me about him – is shocked by the abrupt transition, because he swears as if someone had just hit him.

As I open my eyes I can see through the windows that we've come to rest at the top of a mountain, or something, because for miles around us, on every side, there are different-coloured fields and forests laid out across the landforms as if they were painted onto a hearthmat. The sky is still painful to look at, but it is hazy with heat – the same heat that seems to be pummelling my body, even though the treated perspex of the window is darkening rapidly to compensate for the sudden increase in brightness. I drop the Queen's hand and stand up as much as I'm able without banging my head on the underside of the storage rack. I check quickly up and down the bus to assess the situation.

It isn't very good. I'm trapped in here next to the window by the Queen's body, so I bark at her to move it out of the way fast!, dammit, fast! Joli looks at me like I've gone mad, but I chop his face out of the way, jam my hands down on the backs of the Queen's seat and his, and haul myself over the Queen's thighs. She yells something at me but I pay her no attention.

The Japanese prat is likewise half-standing, photographic equipment dropping off him like scales, his mouth forming a nearly perfect circle – right now he's being goddam uninscrutable – so I tell him to get fucking sat down just as I'm landing in the aisle. The floor of the bus is on a crazy cant, as if the whole bloody vehicle had been thrown like a javelin and dug its front end into the ground at an angle. A couple of the other passengers have got bleeding noses from where the impact hammered their faces into the backs of the seats in front; a pair of adolescents who must have been smooching in the back seat have faces that look like someone let rip on them with a chain saw, or something, and the girl shrieks like a banshee until I bawl at her that unless she shuts the fuck up I'll make her pick her lover's tongue back up and swallow the thing.

I'm not really too worried about the rest of the passengers, of course – not even the Queen and Joli, because neither of them's strong enough to cause me too much problem. The one that's nearly making me piss myself is the fucking driver, who I hope has decided which sex he or she wants to be. Either way, I recognize in the driver what I was too slow-thinking to recognize until now: a sort of power that's fucking terrifying because it's so great that it doesn't need to dress itself up in any kind of imposing outfit.

Sure enough, the driver's the only one apart from me that's fully aware of what's going on. She – yeah, definitely a she – is climbing out of the driving compartment, not bothering to open the little gate that separates it off from us plebs. I see a flash of thin leg and then she's standing looking at me down the aisle, patting a sort of rust-coloured tunic she's got on; it comes to half-way down her thighs and is ragged along the edges, like she decided one night she didn't like the hem and ripped it off. She's still got her peaked uniform cap on, though; she notices me noticing it, shrugs and smiles like she wasn't at all nervous (why should she be? I'm only about six times her size and have been brought up to know how to fight), then pulls it off her head and throws it away to one side, where it disappears in thin air. So the little turd's got magic powers, has she? Just as I half-suspected. Pretty little turd, though.

I move down the aisle towards her, going not too quickly, just quickly enough that she'll realize that she's not going to stop me merely by standing her ground.

Which she does.

Which she is perfectly within her rights to do, because I discover she's thrown some kind of invisible net around me, so that it's like I'm trying to fight my way through treacle.

'Passengers are requested to resume their seats,' she says coolly. I don't know how she does it, but her voice sounds like it's coming through one of those loudspeaker systems that hasn't been tuned quite right. 'Universal panaceas to cure all your injuries will be distributed among you as soon as the staff have decided that it is safe to do so.'

'Fu . . .' I start.

'Please resume your seat, you foolish child. I have no intention of having to fight my way past you in order to give these pills to the people at the back, who most certainly require them rather more than you do.'

The air doesn't drag on me like treacle as I turn and sit down on the nearest seat.

'That's better,' she says in that mechanical voice of hers. 'Most of our honoured clients find out, sooner or later, that it's best to do just exactly what our staff-members ask them to do.'

She smiles sweetly.

'Makes ya want to puke, doesn't it?' Joli hisses from somewhere nearby me. I begin to wonder if perhaps I've misjudged this guy.

I give him a hard grin and then look back beyond him to see that the Queen's OK. She's not looking at me but instead is staring out of the window on the far side of the aisle. She moves her head to one side as Alyss goes by, doling out free pills wrapped in tearaway foil packets; it's like the Queen hasn't even noticed the interruption. Her face has drained itself of all its colour, which it didn't have much of in the first place.

I turn my head to follow what she's looking at, but there's an upright between two windows in my way, so that I have to crouch forwards, getting my head between the seat-backs in front of me.

Then I can see what the Queen's been looking at, and why she's so horrified to see it.

We're at this crazy angle on a sort of tabletop mountain, you see, and we aren't the only ones there. There's a guy strutting around without any clothes on, but it's not him that the Queen's looking at. Nor is she looking at a little group of three people off to one side – an old bat with a younger guy and a much younger girl. So far as the Queen's concerned, the pig that's sitting beside a pile of rocks, looking at us, just might as well not be there, and the same goes for the pile of rocks itself and some dumb bird that's sitting on top of it.

No, the person that the Queen's staring at is herself. I kid you not.

Now, it's not exactly the same self as *her*self, if you see what I mean, but it's perfectly obvious that the two people are one and the same. Oh, I could give you a whole list of differences between them, I guess, from the pretty goddam unimportant – like this other Syor's dressed in long robes, like you've got her out of bed to come and answer the door or something, whereas my Syor's still in her blue jeans and blue anorak – to the somewhat less superficial – like no one's exactly going to get a hard-on in the bath thinking about the version in the robe, but then the real Syor's face doesn't radiate brightness like that except when we're making love, which sounds a bit contradictory but you'd know what I mean if you'd been there. But, as I say, there's no question but that they're both the same person. Really. Sort of down-under really.

I guess I know now why the Queen's so fucking shitless because I think I would be, too, in the same circs. What I want to do is to get back beside her, so that she can have someone to cling onto until she's got over the worst of it, but at the same time it's not going to do any of us much good if all that happens is that Alyss dumps another of her fucking drums of invisible glue over my head; so, in a fit of decisive indecision, I keep my arse firmly locked in place.

'Right,' says Alyss, who has been having understandable difficulty getting the juvenile Don Juan at the back to swallow his pill, 'now that we're all a bit calmer, there's no reason, so long as we do it in an orderly fashion, why we shouldn't all get off this vehicle. Which,' she adds in a voice like ice, her eyes shooting around the upholstery like it should want to curl up and die, 'was not expected to accompany us on this very final stage of our excursion. Still, if I got everything absolutely perfectly right every single time, I wouldn't be able to charm you with my rare fallibility, now would I?'

'You wouldn't believe it, would you?' says Joli in a whisper to me. 'For a little while, back in the afterlife, she disguised herself well enough that I quite fancied her.'

'She'd be just about OK if she kept her gob shut,' I retort, with similar quietness. 'For a paedophile,' I add, just to show him that it's all right for us to hold a civilized conversation but that I don't trust him yet.

Even though I kept my voice so low, she must of heard me, because she gives me a smile like it was solid aspartame and says, right out loud so that my Syor could hear if she weren't totally fixated on her doppelgänger on the plateau outside – no, let's skip what Alyss says, you wouldn't be interested anyway. Joli giggles, but some people will giggle at anything.

The Japanese tourist manages to be the first off the bus, which is OK by me because I want a few moments to think things over and, besides, I want to be with the Queen when she has to step outside and see her double without a layer of light-sensitive perspex to shield herself from . . . herself, I guess. To my surprise, Alyss puts her head on one side and looks at me as if to say that she quite understands, and won't push me to behave in an orderly fashion like all the other kids. Joli's none too keen on rushing for the door either, but she tries to persuade him for about one millisecond and then, losing her patience, crooks her little finger at him so that the next thing he knows he's out on the turf with the rest of them. Dragging his feet like he's on the way to see the bank manager, he moves across to where the old dame's standing with her arms round the high-strung-looking fucker and the girl – who, I now notice, being an expert first-sight man, is worth at least half an hour's discussion of politics and a couple of halves of lager – and the old bat looks about as glad to see him as anyone ever can have, which is mildly tolerant.

Now there's only me and the Queen and Alyss still left on the bus, and Alyss is signalling that it's time for it to be only herself, so I go and take the Queen's arm. That seems to wake her up, or something, because she smiles up at me with her eyes as well as her mouth, just like she does when I give her a bunch of flowers or some crap like that, and she stands up willingly enough. We make our way, hand in hand, me going first, down the narrow central aisle of the bus to the door.

If it was hot inside it's like a furnace out here. I think one of the other passengers is going to faint, but then he shouldn't have been wearing a thick Shetland jumper and a woolly ski cap in the first place. I put my arm around the Queen's waist and give her a squeeze and she smiles at me again, which is somewhat pleasing to me, since now I'm the one who's beginning to feel nervous. I'm beginning to get memories about some of these people, just dribs and drabs, you understand, but enough to make me think that perhaps they'll forgo the red carpet when they meet me.

Like, I get this sudden cameo that the woman with the grey-white hair who looks like she can use the sword that's at her waist is a lot younger and she's in a swords-and-arrows battle somewhere, and so am I, and from the way she's screaming at me through all the racket it doesn't take an Einstein to work out that we are not on the same side. Not in the slightest on the same side.

Like again, Syor – the Queen – is staked out on the ground, with her hands and her feet tied, and I'm standing there with a dick like it was reinforced concrete and I'm chuckling because there's nothing she can do to stop me from doing what I'm just about to do to her.

Like for the third (and last) time, there's this guy being cut up so bad that I can – now – feel the puke coming up my throat, and the thing that I'm gladdest about is that they've just cut off his cock and I know that he was the man the Queen loved.

You will thus appreciate the reasons for my timorousness, as a guy I once knew used to say just before running like fuck. If the other kids out there are beginning to get the same memories – the Queen especially – I had better be on my bike. Only thing is, if that was really me that was doing those things to the Queen, I'm not sure that I exactly want to bother getting out of there, so I look at her and I can see in her eyes that she has yes indeedy had that very same recollection of our joint eventful past, and that it's OK, you know, because it was all such a long time ago that we were different people then. That makes me feel so good that I bend down and I kiss the Queen on the lips, which are very warm and smooth and a little salty against mine, and they could have killed me then and I probably wouldn't even have noticed.

20

Joli came up and said something to Reen. She found herself oddly unsurprised to see him. Already this was a time of miracles, so that it seemed almost natural that old friends should begin to appear out of the monster's maw. Clearly whoever had told her that Joli had died at Anya's hand had got it wrong; she'd half-expected as much, having known him die once already and seen him returned to life. He seemed as offended as he would ever allow himself to be by her lack of response to his greetings, but then he saw the concentration on her face, and quietened down, turning to watch along with her.

She wasn't certain, but she thought that one of the few remaining shapes moving around behind the many darkened eyes of the monster that had come out of the thunderclap was probably Alyss. There was something about the angle of the head . . .

At first she hardly noticed the two people who descended from the monster's mouth a little after the others; she just assumed that they'd be uninteresting strangers, like most of the rest, or at best uninteresting old acquaintances, like Joli. It was only when the taller of the two figures bent to kiss the smaller one that she gave them more than the most cursory of glances.

Then her whole body stiffened.

'Shit,' she said.

'What's the matter?' said Rehan, who had recovered much of his customary cockiness.

'I have someone to kill,' she muttered, more to herself than in reply to him.

She took her arms off their shoulders and checked automatically that her belt was fully equipped with dirk and sword; she wished that she'd thought to sling a crossbow over her back, but she hadn't really expected there to be any danger of a kind that could be fought with weapons. The big bastard was most definitely Nadar, the sadist who'd been directly or indirectly responsible for the deaths – many of them sickeningly violent – of almost all of those whom she'd allowed to come close to her in her youth, including He Who Leads, of course, but more importantly Marja, whom she'd loved with such an intensity that it still astonished her that it had been the figure of Syor, not Marja or Qinefer, who had greeted her in the Mistdom.

'I have someone to kill,' she repeated, just a little more loudly than before.

Rehan, watching her face, saw it register who was the woman being kissed by Nadar.

'She seems to be at the end of everybody's quest,' he murmured to her.

Reen felt as if she'd just been kicked in the stomach.

That there should be yet another aspect of Syor at large in the World was emotionally confusing but, as with the emergence of Joli, not entirely unexpected. But that Syor should be willing not only to stand equably in the presence of the bastard who'd beaten her and tried to rape her, and who had destroyed her mate so cruelly, but to accept his embrace . . .

Reen's eyes no longer seemed to be transmitting to her full information about the scene around her. All she could see was an ashen blur with, at its very centre, a tiny circular frame in which two miniature figures were picked out in brilliant colours and knife-edged detail. There seemed to be a gale blowing past her ears, drowning out every other noise, so that the two people were moving and talking in total silence. Aside from them, all she was fully conscious of was the roughness in her hand of her sword's pommel.

Then there was a shout in her mind.

No! Reen! No!

She halted, the sword half drawn from its scabbard. The voice had been Syor's, but she didn't know which Syor it had been – the real one, whom she was beginning to realize she was knowing less and less, or the creature in Syor's guise that had stepped from the gargoylish mouth of the monster. Was the latter some spirit of Evil, disguising itself as Good in order to deceive even Syor's loyalest friends?

The creature must have heard her thought, because it glanced up at her. Its involuntary movement of recognition confirmed to her that indeed it had been this tool of Evil that had shouted at her to stay her hand. She pulled her sword fully free.

Reen, you are wrong. Put your weapon away again. This is no time to be making a fool of yourself, old friend, old love. In a very short time it'll all become plain to you, and you'll start laughing at yourself the way you've always been so good at doing.

It's incumbent on a person to laugh at herself when everyone else is doing so, sneered Reen. *I'm pissed off with creatures like you inveigling their way into my head and . . .*

Reen, look at me. I shall hold up three fingers as a sign.

Reluctantly, Reen looked at the creature of Evil. It seemed bewildered, as if it were unable to understand what it was doing, but it was holding up a hand with the central three fingers splayed.

So you are indeed the tongue of Evil, snarled Reen.

Look further.

She turned her head towards where the real Syor was standing, near the cairn, the naked Painter a few paces from her. And the real Syor was likewise holding up a hand with three fingers.

You are both the same? said Reen humbly. *There is no deception?*

No deception except what I am now about to practise both on my facet from the afterlife and on poor Nadar.

'Poor!' said Reen out loud.

Kursten cowered away from her.

Yes, 'poor', continued the voice in Reen's mind. *He was as much a victim of his place and time as both He Who Leads and I were. The torture to which he was put during his last lifetime in Albion just wasn't so obvious, that's all.*

You can repeat that it wasn't so obvious, grumbled Reen, but she slowly returned her sword to its case.

And 'poor' also because, for those very trivial, long-ago crimes, he's about to be punished for the rest of this eternity . . . although at least he won't be aware of his own suffering, just like he was unaware of it the last time.

What do you mean? said Reen.

You saw one aspect of my wholeness descending from the . . . the monster's maw, replied Syor, *and for a time you were speculating that perhaps it was the embodiment of some sort of spirit of Evil. Well, in a way, you weren't so far wrong, my old friend – you've always been far more perceptive than the people around you have been prepared to grant. There is a spirit of Evil in all of us, just as there is a spirit of Good. When the two are in a state of complete imbalance, you find you have a saint or a devil, but you mortals are very fortunate that either extreme is a rare occurrence . . . saints being every bit as dangerous and destructive, you know, as devils. It is not given, luckily, to any mortal to be completely lacking in either of the two components: if that were possible, it is unlikely that there would be any mortals left. But gods, on the other hand . . . ah, yes, gods are a different matter . . .*

Reen found that she was becoming furious with the smugness of her lover's voice. *Are you setting yourself up as a god, now?* her thought raged.

I'm not 'setting myself up' as one, dear Reen. It was something that became inevitable as soon as all the disparate aspects began to be drawn together, each for a different reason. Alyss has helped matters along, of course, but only when she herself recognized that the result was inevitable, whatever she did; her aim now is simply to try to control the process, to limit the damage, as it were . . .

But why should there be any damage? Tell me that, Syor. Explain it to me so that even an elderly warrior's narrow mind can understand it!

You have never been narrow-minded, Reen: quite the opposite. Look around you at the friends who are still gathered here, and realize by how much you are the odd one out. Joli through his dreaming, Ngur through his knowledge of Anya and his prayers, Rehan through his music, Kursten through her origins in the Mistdom, Alyss through being Alyss and likewise myself through the fact that I am My Self – all of us have had gateways into the World that lies behind this World, all of us have been prepared in some way for our encounter, our collision, with the polycosmos. All but you, Reen, the only mortal among us and yet the most trusted and valuable and loved of us all. You've seen things that would have driven most ordinary mortals into madness, but they haven't driven you mad. How can you, then, describe yourself as narrow-minded?

You have a heavy hand with the sugar, Syor, thought Reen crossly.

I don't know that I have. But, if that's the case, it's because of what I'm about to do to poor Nadar – I'm feeling guilty about it, and that makes me sentimental. Besides, you and I, we're not going to be lovers any longer in the sense that we used to be. Even though we'll be closer than ever we were before, in a way I'm saying goodbye to you, oldest and dearest friend. My love.

Reen looked around her hotly. Rehan and Kursten were still staring at her. Nadar and the Queen were still embracing. If it hadn't been that the curlew was preening itself and the pig was trotting around snuffling the ground, she'd have thought that time had stopped.

Why is what is happening so inevitable, then? she demanded.

It began through the merest coincidence. The aspect of myself that was living in one of the many othernesses that co-exist with this one – the places that you would call afterlives or dreamlands – began to dream herself back into this World. That wouldn't have been too damaging in itself – I would simply have wondered about the vividness and consistency of my dreams – but then I, or rather that aspect of my being, encountered the aspect of Nadar that was also dwelling in that otherness. Although he never realized it, he was the catalyst for my discovery that Albion was more than just a place of dreams: he was the proof my silent-mind needed that Albion was just as much a real, concrete, existing place as the otherness in which I was living and which I had always been told was the sole reality. At first I clung to him because I needed him – he was, quite literally, the key to my existence – and then I grew to see how, even during our lifetimes in Albion before, had circumstances been different we would most assuredly have been lovers. I wouldn't have given He Who Leads a second glance, and that would have changed the World's history. I wouldn't – maybe I wouldn't have given even you, Reen, a second glance, even though I know that that would have been a very great loss to my life. And when I came to realize this, I also came to love Nadar.

And yet, thought Reen, *you are about to deceive him? You were always much crueller at heart than I was, Syor, always much more devious, were you not, even when sometimes you seemed to be so much more tender-hearted?*

Yes. Much more selfish. And now I am going to be the most selfish I have ever been, and give Nadar, my loved one, a gift which he will treasure beyond all others that I could ever give him . . . I shall give him eternity, just as I shall give eternity to all of you here. But in his case he shall have powers that will almost match mine. I shall give him the very part of my essence that allows me to be so cruel and duplicitous as to make this gift to him.

He shall be your spirit of Evil? thought Reen.

That is as good a way of expressing it as any. The aspect of myself that dwelt in the otherness has drawn these two othernesses too close together for them to be separated ever again. To avoid chaos in the matrix of the polycosmos as a whole, for the othernesses are not granted ever to be fully aware of each other, Alyss has tried to minimize the damage by punching a hole, a gateway, between the two of them, to speed up the process of assimilation of each by the other. The mutual destruction of the two othernesses was inevitable, in the long term; it is Alyss's aim to let their destruction be so fiery that from the ashes we – she and I – will be able to create a new universe, a new otherness.

'Fiery'? thought Reen anxiously. *We shall be devoured by flames? All of the World will be consumed by the furnace . . . ?*

No. Not flames that will char your flesh, Reen. Rather, a fire that will singe your souls.

Now, the voice of the almost-god continued smoothly, *I must turn to other matters. I shall have one last favour to beg of you, as you shall soon discover. But now I must make myself entire, and I must give Nadar my poisoned gift, and then I must embroider both his essence and my essence into the fabric of the new otherness that for the rest of your days you shall watch me creating . . .*

21

Her soldiers had deserted Anya some while ago. Two of them had fallen to their deaths, and the remainder had seen the flaring colours and heard the colossal sounds that were emanating from Starveling-stage above them. That, and the sight of the land screaming its loathing, had sapped their souls; she hardly blamed them for having fled.

Were it not for her own hatred, she too would have fled.

She'd abandoned the crossbow, of course. It was obvious that no bolt would kill the Painter, or even his pig. She wasn't sure exactly what would, but trusted to the providence that had always smiled upon her to hand her the necessary weapon at the right moment during the confrontation. Most certainly it would not expect her to use her bare hands, for these were now raw and bleeding, so that agony shot through her entire body each time she touched the hillside.

But carry on touching it she did. She was faint from exhaustion and from loss of blood, but her spirit still drove her body onward. Another five metres and she would be at the place where she had seen the Painter and his pig silhouetted against the sky, a forever ago. She had no idea what she might see, and she was terrified of that ignorance, yet the thought of giving in to her fear and descending the hillside in the path of her soldiers never occurred to her.

Five metres . . .

. . . becoming four metres . . .

. . . which is soon three metres . . .

. . . and then only two . . .

. . . and then she is there.

The first thing that she saw was that no one had seen her. She tried to make herself look as inconspicuous as possible, but there was really no necessity: all eyes were upon the scene that was being enacted close by the cairn at the centre of the plateau.

Syor, her mother, robed, was still standing there, beckoning towards her a woman that was also Syor, but strangely attired, and a man whom Anya didn't recognize but whose garb matched that of the second Syor. The two of them were linked by their hands and, Anya sensed, by much more than that. They were slowly advancing upon her mother.

And then Anya took in other details of the scene, and understood at once that it was no stranger to her. There was the naked, blinded man, and there was the pig. There was the weaselly dreamer whom she had had Haptan slaughter, and whose corpse she had touched with her own hands. There was the singer whom she had once foolishly permitted to roam her body as if it were his own, and beside him there was the child-woman, as the soothsayer had described. And near to them both was Reen. Other human figures, bizarre ones, were randomly scattered around the tabletop, mostly looking ill, but Anya hardly saw them.

Central to all was the figure of her mother, whose green eyes now fastened upon Anya's own, and who nodded almost imperceptibly in sad acknowledgement of the fact that she, Anya, was a witness to all this, that she had driven herself to this appointment, exactly as the soothsayer had foreseen.

Stay there for the moment, Anya, said her mother's voice inside her. *Hide like a rat from the sight of these people – hide as you will have to hide for the rest of your life.*

Anya felt her hatred growing to an ever greater intensity. Her mother, to whom she had sacrificed all of her love, was now content just to let her skulk here, away from her, while all of those she had made into her enemies were allowed close, almost intimate association with the god. And was it not she, Anya, who had created the god? Had it not been for her devotion, her servitude, would not her mother have been just another long-dead, long-forgotten peasant woman? Whoever remembers a hero's *mother*?

But she had the sense to do as she had been told, and stay hidden.

The two Syors had now reached out one hand towards the other, so that their fingertips were lightly in contact. The one in the blue trousers had shaken away the hand of her male companion; he stood watching the two women as they stood for a long moment, only just touching.

With her free hand, the robed Syor drew a small stone bottle from between her breasts. She clutched it in front of her, between the two of her selves.

They were blending, those two. Mortal eyes could not follow what was happening, although perhaps Ngur could comprehend it through the medium of his inner sight, and certainly the curlew was watching the whole process with seeming comprehension. To Anya it was as if space were folding in upon itself, making creases along the edges of dimensions that should not have been visible. It was impossible now to perceive the form of either woman, yet it was shoutingly obvious that the indefinable shape was Syor's. Perhaps Anya had witnessed something similar to this in her dreams, for in a curious way it was not totally unfamiliar to her; or perhaps it was simply that her mind was pretending to her that this had been the case, so that she did not revolt against the evidence of her consciousness.

And then it was over.

There was only the robed Syor standing there, with the vial in her hand.

She had changed, however, in a way that was undetectable and yet very plain. She had about her presence something of the god that Anya had both created and worshipped, but at the same time she was the absolute negation of that. She possessed might and power and a terrifying vastness; yet a child would have run to her and buried its face in her lap.

The curlew made a hoarse noise, and lifted itself into the air.

Syor put the cork of the vial to her teeth and plucked it from the tight stone neck.

From the vial, slowly at first, the Mistdom began to curl.

Smiling sorrowfully, Syor took a piece of it on her palm and blew it towards the stranger in blue. He took one astonished pace backwards, and involuntarily caught his breath, so that the tiny cloudlet of darkness was drawn in through his nose and mouth.

Nadar, hissed Syor's voice in everyone's mind, *I give you my gift.*

Both of them were beginning to change. Their figures were fraying at the edges, small wisps of them swirling away to join the greater clouds of the Mistdom that were pouring from the vial and encircling them. Soon all that Anya could see of her mother was a column of coiling greyness from which protruded one single, seemingly disembodied, supplicatory hand. Of the man, who had screamed once, shrilly, briefly, there was nothing she could see except a lesser blue pillar.

The heat of the day had vanished. Anya was shivering as she watched. All the hot energy of the sky seemed to be being drawn into the two rapidly increasing shafts of cloud. Now their bases were almost contiguous, only a thin line of the tabletop's grass showing between them. There they paused, at least so far as their breadth was concerned; but, as Anya had known they would from Haptan's incomplete description of that anonymous soothsayer's vision, they were growing in height rapidly and ever more rapidly, intertwining with each other to form a helix that plunged towards the haze-shrouded sky.

Reen, said Syor's voice, now very faint but still clear enough for all to hear, *I said that I would have one last favour to beg of you. Grant it to me, for I can trust no one else. For the sake of the peace of the World that is being made afresh all around you, you must destroy Anya, my daughter – my poor misbegotten, misguided daughter . . .*

And then the pillars of the Mistdom, with the curlew incongruously circling them, smote the lowermost stratum of the sky's own haze, and spread out across it like a jet of steam against a wall, so that the two darknesses – the greater grey and the lesser blue – began to arch across the ceiling of all the World, changing its colours subtly so that it seemed hardly altered and yet was quite different from the way it had been before. Even the Sun of the World allowed its own light to be subjugated by this spread of fresh pigment, its hot yellow fading to a cool green, as if it were a single round green eye painted upon the canvas of the sky by the brushes of a blind man.

23

Anya saw little of this.

Nor did she see Alyss climb down at last from the door of the bus and look around at the others, her hands on her hips, the beginnings of an impatient smile on her face.

Anya had heard her mother pass down a death sentence.

She was scrabbling down the mountainside, her breath loud in her own ears, sweat pouring from her face and arms and breast to join the great wetness that was spreading across her military tunic.

Like a rat, her mother had said. Anya, as she fled, wondered if she was going to learn to glory in that description.

PART THREE
The Seven ReLMS

> If we shadows have offended,
> Think but this – and all is mended –
> That you have but slumbered here
> While these visions did appear.
> And this weak and idle theme,
> No more yielding but a dream,
> Gentles, do not reprehend:
> If you pardon, we will mend.
>
> – *A Midsummer Night's Dream*

Elsewhere & Elsewhen

three

Congratulations! You have successfully scryed into an afterlife, and you have returned safely to the reality of the World. Already it must be clear to you, however, that there are profound changes afoot.

At first it may seem a little tame to you, now that you have ventured so far into one of the potential afterlives, that your next expedition will take you no further than to the remoter areas of the World. But don't be so cynical! Do you *really* think we could be so cavalier with your expectations that we would force you to walk after you had learnt to run? No – of course not! True, during the last of these preliminary exercises you will remain confined within the spatial boundaries of the World, but you will discover how to push back the temporal restrictions that constrain your conscious mind.

In short, you will journey into one of the World's many potential futures.

Yes, but *which* future? That all depends on how much the past is being tampered with! And, as you discovered when you initially encountered the Mistdom, during your first scrying exercise – assuming your first scrying exercise is still a part of your past by the time you read these words – the trouble with the past being altered is that here, in the 'now', you've no way of telling that it's been done. In the future you're going to, Ngur's pig might fly (although it probably won't), and you'd have no way of knowing that that hadn't always been a normal way for pigs to behave. All *sorts* of realities might jumble themselves, and still you would know nothing.

Now:
Turn the pyramid once more, and prepare to find yourself wherever – whenever – you will find yourself . . .

Chapter One
I NeVeR SAD IT WUOLD Be eASY

1

Thog the tavern-keeper looked up suspiciously as the new customers pushed open the swing door that had

NO DOGS

on it, and came jangling into the Grapes. He didn't like new customers much and wasn't particularly keen on old customers either, but, as business had gone unaccountably slack since he'd taken over what he'd been assured was one of the most thriving establishments in Qazar, he was getting to the stage where he was glad to see anybody.

Even new customers.

Thog was just about to take a breath to say that, even so, he drew the line at customers who were not only bristling with weaponry but were also – not to put too fine a point on it – scruffy, not to mention dripping wet, when he stopped himself. It was nearing midday, and with luck the travellers would be hungry. The home-baked pies that he'd placed temptingly on the counter would be good for at best another day or two, so this might be their last chance.

He eyed them suspiciously and gave them what he hoped was an ingratiating smile.

'A bite to eat, sire and ma'am?' he coaxed.

'Two tankards of mead,' snapped the woman. She was of about average height but held herself so that she gave the impression of being tall. Her fair hair had been recently and badly cut into a boyish style. She was dressed in an ill-fitting brown leather tunic and brown leggings; her boots had seen considerable wear, but had obviously at one time been of the best quality – stolen from some roadside unfortunate, Thog decided. Her clear eyes raked him as if she were memorizing his face in case she should ever need to recognize him again. It was not an appreciation that Thog much enjoyed, and he turned hastily to dig among the clattering tankards.

The mead poured, the woman paid him with three pound coins from the pouch at her belt; stooping behind the shelter of the bar as if he'd just noticed something small he must have dropped earlier, Thog covertly tested them with his teeth and discovered to his surprise and faint disappointment that they seemed to be genuine. He made change and gave it to her; her fingers looked as if she'd stuck them in a mincer and they'd barely started to heal.

The two went to a table that was as far as possible from both the doorway and the jukebox and settled themselves down wearily. Bastards. To think that he'd given up a perfectly good life as a soldier of fortune in order to fetch and carry for the likes of them.

He looked up fondly at the wall where hung his old horned helmet. The leather-and-metal dome was much battered and one of the horns had been broken half-way up, but still the sight brought a rush of warm memories to him. And it was Thog the Mighty who sank into those memories, allowing his eyes to be filled with carnage and his ears to be filled with the din of battle.

Flies buzzed unnoticed.

2

Her horse bathed in sweat and spittle, Anya had ridden in through the main gates of Ernestrad as swiftly as the beast would carry her and headed straight for Starveling, carelessly knocking children and market barrows aside as she went. Nobody had dared to stop her for, even with her hands bleeding and her face stained with dust and tears, she was easily recognizable: better a broken arm than a death sentence.

She had pelted straight into the courtyard of Starveling and thrown the reins to a nearby soldier even before she had touched the ground. She had sprinted in through the door that led to her own quarters and up both flights of stairs and along several corridors until she was alone in her chambers. She had shrieked to one of the bemused attendants she'd passed to fetch Darl 'ap Haptan to her rooms, and as soon as he'd been brought to her she'd tersely described what had happened at Starveling-stage.

'Just like the soothsayer said it would be,' Haptan had summarized after her hasty recital. 'Which is, of course, why you've sent for me. If, in the vision, I was the only ally prepared to stand by you, you think the same will necessarily be true in real life.'

'Yes,' she'd said, sudden doubt assailing her.

'Well, you may be right,' he'd said, the beginnings of a smile touching his face. 'There are enough people in this rotten little country who'd be glad enough to profit from the chaos of your overthrow and quietly stick a dagger in my back when the militia have plenty of more important things on their minds. We might as well be allies, after all, at least until we're well clear of Albion.'

'You think we should leave Albion?' she'd said, her eyebrows raised as if she wished to rebuke him. 'I have to bear in mind the responsibilities of my throne, you realize: I would be in dereliction of duty if I simply abandoned my nation and its people to their fate.'

'Anya,' he'd snapped, 'right now your first priority is to make sure your beloved people don't catch you and *nail* you to your throne. Maybe once we're abroad you can allow yourself the luxury of plotting your return to power – maybe the whole thing's just a storm in a tea-cup and you'll be back here in a few weeks sentencing more innocents to protracted deaths. But right now is not the time to start thinking of your future plans. Right now you should be trying to save your skin!'

'It's not a storm in a tea-cup,' she'd said wistfully,

crossing to one of the windows. 'Have you taken a look at the sky recently?'

He had followed her raised finger and seen that outside it was raining heavily. The long heat-spell had finished at last, and the sky had been trying to put out the fires it had started. Even through the rain, however, he had been able to discern that the sullen clouds had a strange bluish tinge to their greyness that he'd never seen before; the texture of the air itself seemed subtly to have altered.

'I take your point,' he'd said. 'How long do you think we've got?'

'Certainly an hour, maybe as long as two, before they reach the gates of Ernestrad. I can give orders that the sentries detain them there . . .'

'Orders that might be disobeyed. Ngur's bound to be recognized, if he's with them. You shattered a lot of people's loyalties when you treated him the way you did. And it's likely that someone will remember Reen or Rehan as well; they'll be so awed by being in the presence of a living legend that they'll forget the commands of their rightful ruler. Best to say nothing to the sentries – then Reen and the rest won't say anything to them.'

'You seem very confident of yourself, Haptan,' she'd remarked coldly. 'I haven't heard you dare speak to me like this before.'

'Right now, Anya, we're no longer sovereign and subject, we're just two people trying to live a little longer. If you start pulling any of your majesty on me, I'll dump you where you stand. Understood?'

She'd nodded. For the first time since she'd started her pell-mell flight down the mountainside she'd felt the true force of her loneliness.

'Then go and do something about your hair. That great shock of curls can be seen a kilometre off. Cut it short, like a boy's. Do the best you can – it won't matter if it's a bit of a mess. We're going to be a couple of itinerant travellers until we're on the continent, so the less well heeled we look the better. Talking of well heeled, though . . .'

As she'd watched him, frozen, he'd put his head round the door and calmly told one of her personal guards that the Lady Anya desired two full pouches of gold coins to be brought to her here from the treasury, urgently. That done, he'd turned to her with a furious curse and she'd scampered through to her dressing-room to grab the little cosmetic scissors that lay there on the chest of drawers. A few minutes later, feeling like someone prepared for the stocks, she'd returned to her main chamber to find Haptan stooping over the body of one of the guards, stripping off the clothing.

'These things'll do for me,' he'd said, tossing a heavy purse to her. 'They're far too big for you. Are any of the other warriors out there about your size?'

She'd nodded and given him the name of Kylon. On his appearance at the door, Haptan had swiftly slaughtered dainty Kylon in the same way as he had done his predecessor, by raising the rear of the man's coarse jacket and plunging in his dagger to the hilt. The back of Kylon's shirt had been uncomfortably wet and sticky on her spine once she had pulled it on in place of her own, but the rest of his well-worn clothing had not obviously been marked. She herself had pulled the boots off the corpse, finding to her relief that they weren't too ridiculously large on her own feet.

'Is there a back way out of here?' Haptan had said, tugging at a lace. 'We can't go past all your sentries and servants out the front there – word'd spread like wildfire.'

'Yes,' she'd said. She'd led him into her privy where she'd pressed firmly against a small square panel behind the bath. A moment later they'd been clattering along a black, completely enclosed corridor, Anya looking nervously around among the twitching shadows, terrified that the ghost of one of the Despots' discarded mistresses – many of whom had made their terminal departures by this route – might suddenly advance out of the darkness towards them.

Nothing of the kind happened, of course. They'd emerged behind one of the feeding-boxes in the stables and, after they'd despatched a pair of inquisitive ostlers, they'd appropriated two of the finest steeds.

No one had paid any attention in the continuing rain to the two slumped, uncommunicative, nondescript riders who'd left Ernestrad by one of the little-used side-gates, and soon they'd been on the road to Qazar, the hooves of their horses kicking up clots of mud into the faces of the wagoners whom they'd overtaken. Anya had felt roused in a way that she hadn't been for years, it seemed: it was as if she'd been for a long time unconsciously yearning to throw off the shackles of rulership, and now at last had been given the excuse to do so with a clear conscience. She'd grinned across at Haptan, riding alongside her, but he hadn't noticed. When she'd caught on the tip of her tongue some of the rainwater that had been dripping from the end of her nose, it had tasted finer than the finest wine that she had ever been served in the halls of Starveling.

By the time they'd reached the outskirts of Qazar it had been too late to enter the town without possibly arousing some unwanted interest among the inhabitants. Haptan had vetoed their using one of the tatty caravanserais that dotted the roadside on the basis that, even though – gloriously – news of the developments in Ernestrad had manifestly not reached the sleepy wayfarers to whom they'd talked, the situation might change dramatically before the morning. Accordingly, they'd put themselves up in the outlying barn of a small farm and there, among the hay and the rats, Anya had leapt upon Haptan and virtually raped him, repeatedly. She'd been unable to recall any time when she'd ever felt so invigorated, so full of vitality; it had been as if she'd shed the past twenty years. In the morning, the storms of the night already receding into their memories, they'd made love with a slow affectionate tranquillity that had likewise been a rediscovery for her.

Then Anya had stolen some vegetables – escaping detection by only the luckiest of chances – and they'd devoured them on horseback as they'd picked their way cautiously through the streets of Qazar until they'd come to this ill begotten tavern, where they sat breathing air that smelled of the tavern-keeper's breath.

3

After a while, Haptan left Anya with the tankards of mead and strolled down the crooked lanes that led towards the docks. The town hadn't as yet fully adapted to the fact that it was expected to be a centre of importing and exporting rather than a sleepy fishing port, and as yet, although plans had been agreed, there was no reasonably sized thoroughfare leading out to the Ernestrad highway. All the house- and shop-fronts he passed had suffered damage at one time or another from the collisions of overlarge vehicles making their haphazard way around the corners and up the steep cobbled hills; on one occasion he had to step into a shop's recessed doorway to make room for a large wagon, ridiculously overloaded, and the straining oxen that were drawing it. He tapped his forelock amicably at the wagon-driver, but the woman made no response beyond a sour glance.

He was glad to be away from Anya for a while. It was the first opportunity he'd had since their dash from Ernestrad yesterday afternoon to be alone to do some thinking about the situation he had found himself in. His decision to flee with his deposed tyrant had been a spur-of-the-moment affair, born not only from the quite genuine fear for his own neck should he be without her protection but also – and this surprised him – from a sudden, renewed upwelling of sympathy for her: she had momentarily seemed to him like a child who had landed itself in a scrape through committing all sorts of follies, so that his sense of 'serves you right' had been coloured by a sort of protective instinct. The whole business worried him: he was concerned that he might have been guilty of a considerable error of judgement, one that might yet cost him his life. And one such mistake could so easily lead to another.

He made a mental note to review the circumstances

once they were in Llandeer and, if necessary, to take their money and unceremoniously jettison her – which was almost certainly, the more he thought about it, what he should have done in the first place.

The small harbour itself, when he came to it, had berths for only three vessels at a time, and all were occupied; he could see a further two little ships moored a couple of hundred metres out from the shore, quietly waiting their turn. Fishing had not entirely given over to commerce, and from one of the craft at the dockside baskets of mackerel and eels were being unloaded. The air smelled pleasantly of freshly caught fish; the rain must have washed away most of the stench of the detritus of earlier catches. There was a deal of good-natured abuse being shouted both between the ships and, the sea-folk uniting against a common enemy, between the crews and the dockers. In a semicircle around the docks was a broken terrace of warehouses, shops and a couple of taverns that looked a lot more fun than the Grapes.

He tried a chandler's first, from where he was directed to one of the taverns. Soon, over a glass of ale that tasted if anything stronger than the rich mead that he and Anya had been supping, he was negotiating their passage on one of the tramp ships that was sailing for Llandeer that evening. The skipper with whom he was arguing terms seemed more drunk than alive; Haptan was reassured by the fact that the mate, even though he was drinking as much as his master, appeared completely sober. The weather, he was told, was set fair for the night; they should be in Llandeer not long after dawn.

And from Llandeer, he reflected as he left the two seamen, the road was open to wherever in the World they wanted to go.

Correction: to wherever in the World *he* wanted to go. Whether or not Anya came with him, he reminded himself, was something yet to be decided. Last night and this morning he'd discovered that, stripped of the trappings of state, she was at least an adequately imaginative lover, rather than the cold fish he'd dutifully bedded in the past; but he told himself firmly that he shouldn't take this into account. What was rather more worrying was that he'd found himself enjoying their lovemaking not just at a physical level – Anya still had a long way to go before she could match some of the peasant women he'd casually romped with – but also at an emotional one. Might it be that her fall from power had divested her of more than just her inhibitions and affectations? Could it be that, now she was allowing chinks to appear in the walls she'd built around herself, he was in danger of actually becoming fond of her? If so, he recognized, this was a pressing reason for ditching her at Llandeer: the last thing he wanted were any emotional complications. On the other hand, it was always good to have someone loyally guarding your back . . .

She seemed not to have moved at all in his absence, although the level of mead in her tankard had gone down a few centimetres. The dour, hefty bruiser behind the bar seemed not to have moved either. Haptan wondered if the man had tried to strike up a conversation with Anya and been told to get lost. No: Haptan had briefed her very carefully before they'd ventured into Qazar to do nothing to offend anyone, lest in so doing she made herself unduly memorable.

He grinned at the tavern-keeper, who didn't grin back.

Rapidly, in low tones, Haptan explained the arrangements with her while drinking the rest of his mead. She nodded a few times, but otherwise said nothing. He looked at her concernedly – she'd been dangerously vivacious earlier – and he saw that her eyes were dull.

'What's the matter?' he said.

'It's over,' she said slowly, wonderingly. 'It really is over.'

'What is?'

'My leadership of my people. By now Ngur and the others will be ensconced in Giorran – Starveling. They'll have sent out search parties to try to track me down. It's just as if I were a criminal on the run, whereas yesterday I was the ruler of as far as the eye could see.'

'You're rather rich for a common criminal,' Haptan reminded her, clinking his purse.

She waved his words away apathetically.

He took her hand, and began to speak to her very earnestly.

'Anya, you've got to stop thinking like that. You've got to forget about your past lifetime, as if you'd shut a door on it, and concentrate instead on the new one that you've just started living. At the moment all you're thinking about is what it used to be like, and of how now compares with then. That's a futile way of going about it. If you'd spent all of your last lifetime living in a shitty-smelling farmyard and somehow things had changed so that you found yourself where you are now, you'd be thinking how lucky you were to be footloose and fancy free, with a reasonably attractive man by your side and a well filled purse at your belt. Wouldn't you?'

'I suppose so.'

He took her chin and lifted her face towards him, so that he could look her directly in the eyes. 'It doesn't matter what you were in your previous lifetime: it's what this current lifetime is like that's the important thing. All in all, it's not too bad a lifetime, is it? There must be a lot of people who'd envy it. Think of it in isolation, not in the context of what's gone before; take it for what it is.'

'That's easy enough to say.' There was a little spirit in her words now, and he was glad of it.

'It's easy enough to *do*, as well,' he affirmed, and out of the corner of his eye he saw the tavern-keeper glance up. 'Look,' he continued, lowering his voice, 'I'm not just telling you the theory: it's something I've learnt from experience. If I hadn't have discovered how to partition off my existence this way, I'd have died of depression years ago. Life isn't a logical, steady progression from one state of existence to the next, whatever people say. Rather, it's a series of disjointed episodes, few of which are a rational consequence of any of their predecessors. It's like you were given a number of different lifetimes to lead during a single life, one after the other, some of them good and some of them, well, not so good. Imagine to yourself that the Anya who was ruler of all Albion has died; the mourning ceremonies are not quite the grief-stricken affair that you might have anticipated, but that doesn't matter to the regal Anya, because she's dead.'

He took a glug of her mead.

'There is, however, a woman of the same name and of remarkably similar personal appearance who's a wandering adventurer and who just happens to be sitting in a pretty dowdy Qazar tavern at the moment, feeling maudlin. She's got no reason to feel maudlin, of course, because she's got plenty of money and a good companion, and soon she's going to be climbing aboard a ship that will take her across the sea to the World, which is somewhere very exciting because she's never been there before. The old Anya – the one that died, remember her? – could never have gone to explore the World at all. Oh, sure, she could have set out in a fleet and travelled in state to hold formal meetings with some fat foreign emperor who'd have been bored by her presence and might well have showed it, because as far as the World is concerned Albion is just an irrelevant little offshore island – interesting past, of course, but after you've done the history what else is left? The dead Anya would have come home having seen nothing at all of the World. *This* Anya, on the other hand – the lucky Anya who happens to be living in *this* lifetime – she's got the freedom to actually see the place: to buy crap in the marketplaces or preferably steal it, to get pissed in the taverns and to swim off her hangovers in streams whose waters taste different for some reason she'll never be able to understand. She's allowed to get a bit sad from time to time if she wants, of course, thinking about that poor, miserable, fenced-in Anya who used to be alive and who could never have done any of these things.'

He put his fingertips on his lower eyelids and pulled them down to produce a monstrous caricature of a doleful face.

She was beginning to smile in spite of herself.

'There *was* an Anya like that,' she said. 'Only she lived a long time ago.'

'Hey,' he drawled, gazing exaggeratedly around the

dusty tavern, 'it's always fascinating to meet folks like you who claim that they can remember their previous incarnations. Like, they sure make you think, you know? I guess maybe they're right, that life's really just an endless parade, and the soul's immortal only it doesn't realize it. I saw a housefly the other day looked just like my grandmother.'

'You're as irrational as those others you were guying,' she said. 'I've seen people still alive whom I'd earlier seen killed. For example . . .'

She paused. For example there was Joli. He'd died, but Alyss had returned him to life again – with difficulty, if Alyss's account of it all was to be believed, but still . . . And Joli had been killed again, and brought to life again, and she'd seen him there yesterday on Starveling-stage, which was also where she'd seen Rehan, who'd died years ago during the siege of Giorran but who'd been returned to life . . .

'Stop thinking about yesterday,' hissed Haptan, correctly guessing the tenor of her thoughts. 'That didn't happen to you, remember? It was something that happened to the Anya that's dead and gone. Maybe that's why there's no such thing as reincarnation – so that we don't get all hung up over dismal memories of the rotten things that never really happened to *us*. Eh?'

She smiled again, at first with some difficulty.

'Yes,' she said. 'All right. You've convinced me.'

Haptan breathed more easily.

'Good,' he said. 'Now, as it happens, we've got a few hours to kill before we need to be down at the dock. We can either sit them out here, in this oh-so-excellent hostelry, or we can go and have a look around at the tourist hotspots of Qazar.'

'OK,' she said, grinning. 'This place sucks – right?'

'Drink up, then.'

'We could always find ourselves another barn,' she murmured a few moments later as they were pushing their way through the swing door that still said

NO DOGS

'I think not,' he said firmly, dragging her out into the street.

4

A little over an hour later, Thog the tavern-keeper looked up angrily as another customer came in.

'I'm not stopping,' said the blind man hastily, 'and besides, this isn't a dog.'

'You're improperly dressed,' snarled Thog.

'I told you, I'm not stopping. All I want to know is whether or not a pair of wayfarers have been here. One of them's a tallish, thin man, with a most memorable nose. The other's a woman, very pretty, with lots of yellow hair, although it may be that she's cut that off. Have you seen them?'

'Haven't had a customer all day,' said Thog as a matter of principle. 'Now bog off out of here before I have to throw you out.'

'Thank you,' said the blinded man, retreating as the tavern-keeper rose ponderously to his feet. 'Thank you most kindly.'

Soon Thog was once more lost in a world where men were men and women were loose, and he'd worn his glory in the form of blood smeared all over his chest. He could smell the grease of the big engines revving . . .

He shook his head. At some time during the afternoon he must have dozed off. People didn't wander around the streets of Qazar stark naked, did they?

You could see the most curious things in dreams.

5

'There was some'un looking for you,' said the skipper thickly after they'd hauled themselves up over the bulwark and onto the fetid-smelling deck of the good ship *Ten Per Cent Extra Free*.

'Who?' said Haptan anxiously. 'What did you tell them?'

'I jus' tol' 'em to . . .'

'He sent them away,' the mate explained, winking. 'They were a bunch of soldiers here from Ernestrad. Seemed bored, like they didn't expect to find anything. Routine. You know.'

Anya was looking at the man with undisguised fascination, and he grinned at her and held out a hand for her to look at. She bent forward for a closer look, but didn't touch it.

'How did that happen?' she said.

'Just the way I was born, lady,' said the mate. 'Perfectly natural. You never been off Albion afore?'

'No. Never.'

'Well, you're going to see a lot of people like me, so you might as well get used to it.'

'Talking of seeing a lot of people,' said Haptan, 'd'you think we might go below-decks? Lit up like this, we must be the biggest centre of attraction in the dock.'

'Lit up?' said the skipper aggressively. 'Who're ya sayin's . . . ?'

'Good idea,' said the mate. 'Those militiamen might take it into their heads to call back.'

He led them through a dirty doorway, down a dirty wooden companionway, along a short but dirty passage and into a cramped but dirty cabin. 'It doesn't look like much,' he explained, 'but that's because it isn't.'

Anya laughed. Even the information about the soldiers hadn't troubled her. After Haptan had succeeded in selling their horses – something which they'd done reluctantly, but there was no way they could have hoped to take the animals aboard the *Ten Per Cent Extra Free* – they'd spent the rest of the afternoon drifting around Qazar, looking in the shop windows and browsing among the market-stalls. The rain of yesterday had constantly threatened to return, but had never quite done so. Anya had bought herself the most exquisitely crafted rose, seemingly woven out of finely spun threads of crystal, and had a little while later, much to Haptan's relief, accidentally dropped it. They'd eaten bread and cheese as they walked; the bread had been a little stale, the baker recognizing tourists when he saw them, but the cheese had been full and filling. Throughout, Haptan had kept her spirits buoyant with a constantly diverting commentary on everything they saw and everywhere they went. Once or twice she'd thought back to their conversation in the tavern and acknowledged to herself that yes, he'd been right, she was doing things that the old Anya could never have done . . . would never have realized that she might have *wanted* to do.

'Don't pay any attention to Baylli,' said the mate. 'Our skipper.'

'He's a bit . . .' began Haptan.

'He always is,' said the mate. 'But we still get there. You people eaten?'

'Not for a few hours,' said Anya, 'but we're OK.'

'We'll be having a meal once we've cleared port,' said the mate. 'Nothing special. Don't know what. Not my turn to cook. Welcome to join us. See what you get.'

He left them.

Immediately Haptan allowed worry-lines to come to his face. He sat down on the single bunk and clenched his hands together.

'Those soldiers,' he said. 'I wonder how widely our friends have spread out the search parties – and how many search parties they've actually sent out. It sounded to me as if there might be quite a lot of them.'

'Explain,' she said.

'According to the mate, the soldiers were looking bored. Small parties tend not to get bored: they're enthusiastic, too enthusiastic if anything, because there's always the chance that they're going to be the lucky ones. No, the bunch who came to the boat must have been just a small part of a larger operation. Or maybe they were just counterfeiting boredom. Thank the heavens we'll be leaving port soon.'

Anya hesitated a few moments, then said rather

nervously: 'I wonder how many other passengers there might be aboard the *Ten Per Cent Extra Free?*'

'A good point. I should have thought to ask the mate.'

'So should I,' she said pointedly.

He glanced up at her. 'Yes. Sorry. You're right. I forget.'

'Please don't, OK?'

'OK.'

'I could see if I can attract the mate back here, and then we could simply ask him,' she said. 'He seems friendly enough.'

'Leave it for the moment. With any luck, there'll be some good reason for him to come back here of his own accord – or maybe one of the other crew will.'

He bit his lower lip. If no one came to check that all was going well with them, the next decision would be whether or not it would be better to skip the probably vile meal to which they'd been invited or to risk allowing themselves to be scrutinized by their hypothetical fellow-passengers. Their very absence might be noticeable. There was a good excuse he might have been tempted to use in other circumstances, but people tend to gossip about young couples who're so much in love that they can't even be bothered with meals. He shrugged. Apart from anything else, he was beginning to get hungry.

A few minutes later there were shouts from outside the porthole, and Anya hurried to look through it.

'It's OK,' she said, smiling. 'It's just that we're casting off.'

Then she took a short pace back.

'Uh oh.'

'What is it?' Already Haptan had his sword out.

'There's a bit of a commotion going on at the back of the dock. It may be nothing to do with us. Some fighting going on just outside the chandler's.'

There was a loud crash of shattering glass, audible even through the porthole.

'The chandler just lost his window,' said Haptan flatly.

'Got it in one.'

The porthole was very small, its glass was dirty and it was only about half a metre above the level of the jetty. Anya was finding it frustratingly difficult to work out exactly what was happening. About thirty or forty people seemed to have spilled out into the enclosed dock area from the narrow streets that led there from the upper parts of town. Some of them at least were armed. A similar number, attracted by the first sounds of the disturbance, had emerged from the two taverns, which had been doing a busy trade all afternoon. It was almost inevitable that what might start as a good-natured brawl would soon deteriorate into something a great deal nastier, and Anya reached instinctively for her dagger, wishing she could be there to join the fray. The old Anya – the one that had lived many years ago – had been a fine street-fighter, had she not?

'Get away from there and let me have a look,' said Haptan impatiently. He shoved her aside and squinted through the smeared glass. Overhead they could hear the tempo of the crew's movements increase; clearly the men were keen to put a stretch of cold choppy water between themselves and any possibility of trouble. The gangplank came aboard with a screech like a cat that's been stepped on.

Some kind of wheeled vehicle came shooting out of a side street and pulled to a halt in the middle of the mêlée. The façades of the buildings around the dock's semicircular terrace were lit up by flashes of vivid blue light; there was the macabre ululation of a siren.

The *Ten Per Cent Extra Free* was drawing away now. As Haptan watched, the side of the dock slowly retreated from him, seemingly at the same level as his face. At the edge of his field of vision he could see the end of a boathook pushing insistently against the wet stones, turning the *Ten Per Cent Extra Free*'s bow away from the land. Even with this encouragement, progress was desperately slow. The skipper of a larger or a much smaller craft might have been able to call upon oarsmen to speed things up, but the *Ten Per Cent Extra Free* was just the wrong size: she would have to wait until the first useful gust of wind took her sails, and that might not be for quite a number of long minutes yet. In the meantime, the strip of water separating them from the land was still narrow enough for a determined person to leap across it . . .

'There's nothing we can do,' said Anya calmly, 'so we might as well just settle down.'

'We should get clear of this cabin,' said Haptan briskly. 'If it proves that it's us the people are after, our friendly old blotto skipper might just decide that it would be safer to put us back ashore. Much better we weren't here should he send someone to come look for us.'

'Agreed,' she said. Then: 'Just a few seconds.'

Her hands moving with speed, she gathered together the pitifully worn bedclothes on the bunk and plumped them up together into a single long cylindrical form. She grabbed the chamberpot from beneath the bunk and added it to one end of the cylinder, covering it over with a loose edge of blanket so that it vaguely resembled the bulge of a head.

Haptan nodded approval to her and blew out the light. The deception was a crude one, but it would at least mean that someone merely glancing in from the passageway might assume that one or both of them had settled in for the night and leave them undisturbed.

'Now what?' he said, addressing the question as much to himself as to her.

'The other direction from the way we came in,' she said decisively. 'We can either try to lose ourselves in the bowels of the ship or, with luck, we'll find a companionway that comes up at some less used part of the deck. I'll go first; attackers always pause a moment at first when they see it's a woman.'

She cackled softly.

He followed her as she snaked along the passageway. He'd never known that anyone could move so swiftly and so efficiently; he'd heard some rumours, during the lifetime that he'd very definitely since slammed the door on – the one in which he'd been a captain in the army of the Ellonia, though by lucky coincidence never anywhere near the action – that the warriors in the army of the peasantry could manipulate their weapons with supernatural speed, but at the time he'd just dismissed it as the kind of exaggerated scare story that soldiers have always made up to frighten each other in the barracks. Now he understood what those long-forgotten comrades had been trying to describe. He almost had to run to keep up with her, and yet she herself seemed to be moving at no faster a rate than a casual amble.

As she went she was checking each of the doors with her ear and then throwing it open to check inside. So far all the cabins – and a couple of lockers – had been empty. Haptan wasn't sure what Anya planned they should do if they came across anyone living. He hoped it wouldn't happen.

Hopes dashed.

There was a wail of protest, cut off almost immediately and with a clinical finality. When Anya emerged into the lighted passageway, an instant later, the blade of her dagger was dripping blood. She put a red finger to her lips to warn Haptan to keep his silence.

They must have come almost the full length of the ship. Ahead of them there was a bare metal wall, painted off-green. The passageway they'd come down formed the upright of a capital T, with two smaller, shorter passageways going off it, one to each side. Anya glanced briefly down them and turned determinedly towards the right. Haptan, hastening after her, could see over her shoulder the base of a companionway, although it looked disused and dangerously dilapidated. Just what they were after.

He hardly heard the man who stepped into the corridor behind him.

He felt rather than saw Anya spin around and pounce through the air like a leaping cat. There was a high, soft yell of anguish and then the sound of a heavy body falling.

'Quickly,' she gasped into his ear.

Within a few paces they were at the base of the companionway they'd seen, Anya looking up at it apprehensively. Haptan followed her gaze and saw, at the top, a hatch. Closed. From here, beneath it, there were no signs of any fastenings, but that was no indication that there might not be a ton of freight stacked on the deck on top of it.

She shrugged at him and then, signing him to keep back, she shinned lightly up the rotten-looking steps, allowing her feet never to rest long enough on any one rung for it to have the time to give way under her weight. Haptan, not taking his gaze away from her rump above him, reached out and felt the rung nearest to him; although the wood was crumbly at the edges, the rung seemed reasonably sound as a whole.

Anya, taking her entire weight on her arms, which she'd wrapped around the companionway's two uprights, was straining her shoulders against the underside of the hatch-cover.

All of a sudden, just as it seemed as if the uprights were about to collapse inwards towards each other, the cover gave way. Haptan heard it crack back onto the invisible deck.

Anya, bloody dagger between her teeth, sweat shining on her face and neck, grinned down at him.

'Bingo,' she hissed; and then she'd vanished through into the darkness beyond in one silky movement.

Haptan tried to emulate her trick of alighting for such a brief moment on each rung that it wouldn't have time to break, but he was clumsy at it and lost his footing entirely. Fortune smiled at him: the rungs held. A few seconds later he was beside Anya on the deck, contrasting his own hoarse panting with the even, almost silent sound of her breathing.

He looked around.

They were right up at the stern of the ship in an area of the decking which had clearly been used as a dumping ground for years. Broken crates, empty cable-drums and bits of twisted, unidentifiable machinery lay all about them in total confusion. Clearly the skipper of the *Ten Per Cent Extra Free* wasn't one of those old sea-dogs who believed that a tidy vessel was the sign of true seamanship. There was a fair amount of oil swilling about, and Anya whispered in his ear that they'd both have to watch their footing.

There was also quite a lot of light. Struan was three-quarters full and almost directly overhead; more threatening, however, were the lights from the dock, no more than ten or fifteen metres away from them. There now seemed to be two cycles of the powerful blue lights circling around the tops of the buildings and catching the foremast above where they crouched. There was also a deal of torchlight, and someone had rigged up a powerful searchlight whose beam was currently probing the waves but which any second would be got under control and directed onto the ship.

Anya tapped his shoulder and pointed deliberately towards a blacker splodge of black that lay directly beneath the stern bulwark. From here, even with the help of the intermittent light, it was impossible for Haptan to make out what was there. Anya's eyes must have been keener than his, because she obviously saw it as a potential hiding-place. Resting her fingers one moment longer on his collar, she was suddenly off across the deck, crouching low, once more moving like a cat, every movement executed with supreme confidence.

She vanished into the anonymous black maw.

She hissed at him to hurry.

Doing his best not to slither on the oily deck, he went in her direction as nimbly as he could. Almost immediately his feet slid out from under him, and he went the rest of the way on his hands and knees.

Out of the darkness Anya's hand leapt to grab him by the arm and haul him to safety.

They were lying together in a foul-smelling cavity formed fortuitously by a pair of tea-chests shoved up against the stern rail; thrown against the chests and covering the top and part of the front of the gap between them was a roll of rubber matting. For the moment at least they were well concealed, but Haptan was only too urgently aware of the broad track they had left behind them: two corpses and an open hatch-cover would lead any pursuers directly to them. He wondered, as his rasping breath filled the space, if it wouldn't be a good idea to get out of here as soon as possible and to make their way along the deck towards the bows, looking for somewhere less obvious to hide themselves.

He gasped as much to Anya, and she whispered an agreement, but told him to wait a few seconds longer.

He peered out through the thin gap between the side of one of the chests and the hanging flap of matting, and in a moment saw what she'd been waiting for. Some of the people on the dock must have thrown a line aboard the *Ten Per Cent Extra Free*, and someone at the bow had grabbed it and made it secure. Now the craft was slowly swinging around, its stern still moving away from the dock. Soon the whole of the stern area would be shielded by the ship's superstructure from the worst of the light from the shore.

The moments seemed to pass very slowly.

Then Anya gave a small cough to show that she was satisfied the time was right. Again she was moving away across the deck with that incredible, easy speed. He lost sight of her almost at once; just before it vanished, the pale reflection of her head showed him that she'd taken a path that curved towards their left. After a second's hesitation he decided that it would be better to follow her that way than to split off from her and go for the right-hand side of the castle.

Just as he was about to spring forth he saw a glow appear at the level of the deck. Clearly someone was climbing up the dilapidated companionway with a torch or a lantern. Haptan cursed both himself and Anya for not having had the wit to shut the cover behind them.

A dark object appeared at the centre of the glow. Squinting at it painfully, Haptan could just make out that it was a human head and shoulders. Someone was silently scanning the garbage-littered deck for any sign of them.

He held his breath, keeping himself absolutely frozen. He was certain that it was impossible for the observer to see him here. He wondered if Anya had noticed this new development, or if she were waiting vexedly up somewhere in the shelter of the castle, trying to guess what the hell it might be that was keeping him so long.

'Hey, you there!' said a quiet voice.

Haptan forced himself to become even stiller.

'I know you're there. I can see your foot sticking out. Don't mean you any harm. Nobody else has thought to look for you yet, just me.'

Haptan recognized the mate's voice. The man was either genuinely on their side – for reasons that Haptan couldn't even begin to guess at – or a complete fool. If Anya had heard him, and she almost certainly would have, she'd have been quick enough to pick up on the fact that so far only the mate had any idea where they'd fled to. Haptan half-expected to see a slender arm snake out of the darkness into the aura of light and deftly slit the man's throat.

To forestall this, Haptan pushed himself clear of the curtain of matting.

'What brings you here?' he whispered, trying to keep his tone light, as if the two of them had bumped into each other in the tavern.

'I've got no great love for Albionian soldiers, whatever they say their allegiance is,' said the mate quickly. 'Bunch of those shits – or others very much like them – got hold of my brother a few years back. Apparently they'd never had a black guy to play with before, so they spent a while trying to find out if we hurt in the same places as they did. There wasn't much of him left to bury. You enemies of them, you friends of mine.'

Smothering the irony that it had almost certainly been Anya's own soldiers who'd killed the mate's brother, Haptan said: 'Then we're fortunate to be able to welcome you as our friend.'

'Got a couple of bodies back here,' said the mate. 'Given me an idea. Grab some cord and a couple heavy things from the deck. Get the woman to help you, if she's there. Back here in half a minute.'

His head and shoulders disappeared.

Haptan hissed to Anya, but already she was beside him.

'I heard,' she said. 'We do as he says.'

Soon they were again beside the open hatch. Anya had found a few metres of fraying rope, and Haptan had with difficulty – now blessing the slipperiness of the deck – manoeuvred there a broken hand-printing press and a rusty object of unknown purpose and a hundred sharp edges.

'What's his plan?' said Haptan.

'I think I've guessed,' said Anya, hacking the length of rope in half with her dagger. In the light coming up from below Haptan could see that her eyes were shiny with excitement. He could imagine that they must have been like this lots of other times, when a much younger Anya – a different Anya – was stalking enemies through the night forest or planning around a campfire the sneak attack that her guerrillas would launch at dawn the next day. He found himself shivering.

'Lower an end of the rope,' called the mate softly.

Anya fed one of the pieces down through the hatch. Haptan, peeping over the edge, could see that the big man was swiftly tying a loop around the chest of a small, foppish man whose head had been nearly severed from the body. Clearly Anya didn't cut throats by halves.

'OK,' said the mate, not bothering to look up. 'Heave. I get the other one.'

A moment later the corpse was beside them. Anya, fingers moving surely even though the light was poor, undid the mate's knot and dangled the rope back down again.

Another of those quiet yells, another great haul on the rope, and there was a second corpse to lay beside the first. Soon the mate had clambered lithely up the companionway to join them. Gently he lowered the cover.

'Still a hell of a lot of blood down there,' he said. 'With luck, be yet a while before anyone goes below. The soldiers telling things about you make all the crew too shit-scared to go down. C'mon. Get those things tied onto the dead guys.'

As they worked he explained to them what they should do. He himself was going to have come around the stern of the ship, ready to prevent the fugitives escaping. Suddenly he'd give a shout, and the watchers on the shore would see a body leaping overboard, followed almost immediately by another. In the dancing lights they wouldn't be able to make anything out too clearly, and by the time the first of the crew reached the starboard gunwale where the mate would now be standing, babbling how the criminals had made a jump for it, the bodies would have disappeared.

'OK,' he concluded. 'As soon as you've chucked the second stiff, get round the back of the castle as fast as you can, then down the port side where you'll find a lifeboat hanging. Get in under the tarpaulin and don't make a sound until I come see you. Got it?'

Some clown on shore had now started firing bullets overhead. A couple of them pinged uselessly off the mainmast.

'If you pay taxes in Albion,' said the mate, 'you ought to write and complain about that bumswipe wasting your money.'

'Might just do that,' whispered Anya.

She kissed him impulsively on the cheek.

Then he was gone.

They bent to tackle the first of the corpses.

6

It must have been five minutes after that, though it felt like no time at all had passed, when they were jumbled together at the bottom of a swaying lifeboat. The inside smelled of tarpaulin and dead fish, and there was a corner of wood pressing into the groove beneath Haptan's ear, but he felt relatively secure for the first time that night since Anya had peered out of the porthole.

They maintained silence while the shouting on board the ship rose in a new crescendo, and then diminished until finally it petered out altogether. Soon after that they could tell from the way that the *Ten Per Cent Extra Free*'s plates were taking up a longer, more regular pattern of creaks that the ship was making way out into the open sea.

Haptan kept quiet for a further half-hour or so. It seemed that those of the crew who were not involved in keeping the boat on course had settled in for the night. He'd heard no one come anywhere near them.

'What's the plan for the morning?' he said.

'Same idea the mate had, only for real and on the other side of the sea,' said Anya, settling herself more easily on top of him. 'As soon as we get sight of Llandeer, we slip over the side and swim for the shore. Unless we're very unlucky, no one will spot us. You can swim, can't you?'

'Of course. You?'

'I've swum rivers before. I guess swimming at sea's much the same.'

'It'll be a lot further than you've gone before.'

'Then I'll just have to keep swimming for a lot longer, won't I?'

Quite a while after that he said to her: 'I'm surprised the mate hasn't sneaked around here to see that we made it OK.'

'He won't be coming,' she said casually.

'Oh. How d'you know that?'

'He was the only witness, wasn't he? Besides, you told me never to trust people too much just because they seemed friendly.'

'Shit, Anya, but you're a cold-hearted . . .'

'What was it you said? My primary responsibility is to save my neck. I thought you'd admire my efficiency. As soon as the others had dashed off towards the bow again to get torches, it was in with the knife and over the side with him. He can't have felt a thing.'

Soon afterwards, Anya fell into a light sleep.

Haptan didn't.

* * *

7

Later that night, after the last customers – Ben and Cecil, as usual – had been pitched out into the rain, Thog the tavern-keeper scratched his head lazily and looked back over the events of the day. This was his favourite time, when the only sounds were those of the tavern settling itself down for the night – little comfortable sounds, like a person makes in bed when they're just checking in the darkness that the blankets aren't falling off.

There hadn't been many customers since that first pair, the ones who hadn't eaten any of his Finest Meat Pies, but had just had the two tankards of . . .

He began to scratch his head in earnest. He could have sworn that he'd served them from an old oaken barrel, but that couldn't be right. The pub didn't feature wooden barrels, just steel-ringed cans in the basement from which little electric motors pumped up the carbonated beer to the bar. And he most certainly never sold drinks in pewter tankards, like the ones that he could now see so clearly in his mind's eye. On top of all that, there wasn't any such thing as draught mead these days, was there? Surely it all came as mixers in those prissy little bottles that cost you three times the number you first thought of?

He bent over and switched off the jukebox at the mains. Time he got the rep to put in some new records.

Still the memories lingered of the curious pair, sitting in the dusty light from the window, their tankards on the table between them. Come to think of it, hadn't they been a bit oddly dressed? Maybe they were shooting some tv serial nearby, or something, though it seemed odd to be filming Robin Hood in the middle of a city. Or maybe they were participants in one of those live-action role-playing wargames that sucked the moral fibre out of you and led inevitably to satanic orgies.

A sudden dread pierced his heart.

Fingers fumbling in terror, he opened the cash register and sorted through the coins in the one-pound tray. Sure enough, there were three that were just a bit larger and a lot heavier than they should have been. Now that he looked at them more carefully, he could see that their edges weren't milled and didn't have PLEIDIOL WYF I'M GWLAD, whatever that meant, written round them. Their metal felt almost soapy against his fingers, and he knew even before he raised one of them to his mouth what the result would be.

Frustrated, he threw the counterfeits down on the counter and looked at them. How could he have been so blitheringly stupid as to have accepted such crude, obvious fakes? Hadn't he checked them, the way he always did? In no way at all did they resemble the real things – they were even the wrong colour of gold. A quarter of the day's takings gone down the tubes. What could he have been thinking of?

He picked one up and examined it more carefully. The design on one side showed nothing but a pair of eyes; on the other, partly obliterated by a tooth-mark, there was the stylized face of a woman, who looked slightly familiar to him but most certainly wasn't the queen.

'Well, bugger me right down dead,' he said to the empty room in a voice thick with emotion.

He tossed the heavy coin down among its equally valueless fellows. In the morning, if he was passing by there, he'd take them into the coin shop and see if they weren't perhaps worth something, after all. For the rest of the night, though, he had a berserker warlord to fight.

Chapter Two
THe MUNKeY HOUOSe

1

Anya looked back down the road and saw, behind Haptan, a great expanse of not-quite-right-blue sky that denoted the sea.

'Hurry up,' she said.

'What's the hurry for?'

She stared at him.

'We're in a different country now,' he said. 'We can take things a bit easier, if we want to. There aren't any patrols of Albionian soldiers likely to leap out at us from behind the bushes, you know.'

'The soldiers were never the main threat,' she explained angrily, spacing the words as if addressing a peculiarly backward child. 'It wasn't to the soldiers that Syor gave her orders that I should be slain, remember? It was to Reen. You don't know her. She's unlikely to regard the boundaries of nations as much of an obstacle in her search. And she won't give up that search easily – she's dogged, and she's immensely loyal to those she loves.'

'I thought she loved you.'

'Once. And even then she knew me better than my own mother does – did. Better even than myself, maybe. I can see her thinking that she was killing me because it was in my own best interests that I be dead. That she was doing me a favour, sort of.'

'She's an old woman, Anya. If she found you, you could slay her where she stood. I saw what you were like back on the . . .'

'You were impressed, huh?' She laughed bitterly.

'Well – yes.'

She took his arm. 'Reen taught me how to move like that. She never told me so, but I think she gave up teaching me when she realized that I was as good as I was ever going to get – good enough to know what she was doing when she made deliberate errors so as not to be embarrassed by the ease with which she was able to defeat me in mock combat. She may be old now, Haptan, but if anything that'll have made her wilier, and I doubt if she'll have allowed age to sap her strength.'

'You may be undervaluing yourself,' he said uneasily.

This time there was no rancour in her laughter. 'No court in the World would ever find me guilty of that! Not even my own.'

'You have no courts,' he said, changing the subject. 'It was a long-dead Anya who used to have courts.'

'A long-dead and unlamented Anya,' she agreed. Letting go of him, she danced a few twirling paces down the centre of the stony road, her arms stretched out at her sides. 'Now there's only a vagrant, her past history as obscure as a vagrant's always is. But' – she stopped midstep – 'a vagrant who wishes very profoundly to keep alive. So let's get as far as we can as quickly as we can from Llandeer, OK? It's not going to be long before news gets back to Reen of the shooting-match last night at Qazar. And when the *Ten Per Cent Extra Free*'s found drifting, she'll put two and two together, all right. She'll have an army of spies over here by tomorrow's dawn. We don't want them to find two itinerants curled up asleep in a field, within the very sight of Llandeer, laid out as if specially prepared for capture. Do we?'

'No, but . . . No.'

They'd already been in a field. He'd been exhausted after their early morning rise, sneaking around the *Ten Per Cent Extra Free*, quietly dealing with what Anya had described as 'untidy bits of evidence', and then by the long, draining swim for the shore. In a way, he'd found the cutting of sleeping throats quite relaxing, cathartic almost, as if his mind were taking a well earned rest while watching his hands perform the familiar chores. Then there had been the cold, gagging water. He always forgot how slow swimming was by comparison with walking, the way that it always took you five times as long and ten times as much effort to cover a distance as you'd thought it would when first you'd eyed it up. He'd been fit for nothing when he'd flopped onto the beach, and had been muzzily delighted to see that Anya was in no better condition. Unfortunately, that hadn't lasted long. Within minutes she'd been chivvying him to pull himself together, to get to his feet, to start walking, and wasn't it a glorious morning? Certainly she'd seemed quite genuinely to think it was. They'd gone only about a kilometre, though, when they'd seen a platoon of mounted men in unfamiliar uniforms heading their way; that the cavalrymen would have had any interest in them was remotely unlikely, but anyway they'd dived into a field of barley. Once the hooves had gone, Anya had smiled at him mischievously and begun tugging at his laces – aroused by the killing or the swim or simply the shedding of responsibilities, he still wasn't certain which. He'd protested fatigue, but then the shining of the cool white globes of her buttocks among the green shadows of the stalks had inflamed him, and he'd mounted her like a dog. Moments later, face straining as he spent himself within her, he'd thrown his head back so that it had emerged like that of a deep-sea creature above the waving surface of the unripe cobs, and had seen the startled eyes of a small boy, who'd promptly fled. Reminding each other that it would probably be a long time before he told an adult what he'd seen, they'd nevertheless straightened their clothing up rapidly and made good speed away from the place.

'Not in a field,' he said wearily.

She laughed at him and once more took his arm.

'Then let's keep moving,' she said.

2

Mid-afternoon, and both their stomachs grumbling. Away from the port, this region of Intheria seemed to be sparsely populated. Since the soldiers of the morning they'd had the road almost entirely to themselves, all the traffic to and from Llandeer and Arnas, the capital, presumably going by the new six-lane highway that the Intherians had been so proud of when they'd opened it just a few years back. Here, by contrast, there were broad expanses of sky and the uninhibited chants of the birds. They saw people working in the fields and dozy-looking sheep and cows in the pastures sometimes glanced up at them uninterestedly; once or twice there was a distant farm building. Otherwise, however, it was as if they had the World to themselves.

They were surprised to come across the wall.

It was fully four metres high, and looked from the outside as if it might be equally thick: elsewhere they might have assumed it to be some monumental fortification, but in this remote area it was hard to guess what there might be to fortify. The palace of a nobleman, perhaps, unchanged since an earlier and more dangerous age when civil war had riven Intheria? Or perhaps a repository of the nation's wealth, secured behind the great red stones from the greed of criminals? None of these explanations seemed very satisfactory.

Their interest in the puzzle slowly ebbed as they strolled along the wall's featureless length and began to talk of other things, primarily where they could get hold of some food. They could easily have purloined vegetables from the fields, but as yet they weren't hungry enough to regard the prospect of raw potatoes or turnips with much relish. It would have been only a little more difficult to kill a sheep, but they were reluctant to make a fire and, although both of them had eaten raw meat in the past when there had been no option, they'd decided silently that this would be very much a last resort.

Suddenly there was a break in the wall. Between two sturdy columns topped by carved figures of minstrels there was a heavy oak gate, its black paint peeling. On the gate, neatly printed in faded blue letters on a discoloured white background, was a sign:

McGRUDER INSTITUTION
FOR THE CRIMINALLY SANE
Top Security Area – No Visitors Except by Permit
BEWARE
(*The Playing of Ball Games on these Premises is Prohibited*)
Greater Llandeer District Council

Belying the grimness of the notice, one wing of the heavy gate stood invitingly half-open.

Anya and Haptan looked at each other inquisitively and, in unison, nodded. They strolled through the opening.

Inside there was a broad expanse of neatly kept lawn spotted with oval and crescent-shaped flower beds and small, well kempt trees and shrubs. Over to the left there was a fair-sized pond with weeping willows dotted around it; on the calm water swam ducks and a solitary swan. A winding drive, surfaced in compacted pink stone, led easily through the gardens to a house that looked like a château built to a smaller scale; the white stone, catching the afternoon sunlight, seemed to glow opalescently. Haptan noticed that the tall windows on the lowest storey were secured by thick black metal bars. Some of the upper windows were open, and from one of them the trailing edge of a thin blue-and-white curtain was flapping.

'A house that size must have kitchens,' observed Anya.

'And kitchens must have food,' agreed Haptan. 'Great greasy joints of cold roast meat, perhaps, or plump poultry . . .'

There was a noise like a swarm of angry bees with indigestion spilling from their hive, and the two of them froze. Then, a split second later, they were crouching in the shelter of a puffy round bush with pink-purple flowers and dense, dark green foliage.

Over a slight rise of the lawns came a large diesel lawnmower, on top of which perched a broad, red-faced man with a straw hat and a missing arm. With his remaining hand he clutched the handlebars of his vehicle, wrestling with them like a rider trying to tame a wild horse.

His legs, dressed in torn blue jeans, stuck out crazily on either side, completing the illusion.

Anya grinned. The rider was weaponless.

She stood up, followed a few seconds later by Haptan.

It was several moments before the man on the lawn-mower caught sight of them. As soon as he did so, he did something clumsily with the right-hand handlebar and the engine sputtered a last few times before expiring. He stayed astride it for some seconds longer, holding himself tense as if expecting it to give one final eruptive burst of energy, and then, seemingly satisfied that it was truly quiescent, clambered down to meet them. The machine cooled with a host of muted crackles and clanks.

'No trespassers allowed 'n here,' he said in a broad accent. He was grinning as he spoke, taking the sting out of the words. 'Unless you be voluntary admissions, that be.' The grin broadened. 'Not 's we get 'uns too often, 's you might say.'

This seemed to be a great joke, for he huffed and puffed, and tears came speeding to his eyes. Haptan felt an irrational sense of worry that the man's body might explode, spattering them with bits of gore, as it struggled to contain the laughter which for some reason he seemed unwilling to let escape.

'We're voluntary admissions,' said Anya calmly once the wheezing had died down to tolerable levels.

Haptan glanced at her in astonishment but nevertheless said smoothly: 'Yes, that's right. Voluntary admissions.'

The man looked at them strangely.

'Don't seem nothin' missin' from 'ee to me,' he said dubiously. 'You sure 'n you're lackwits?'

'Very sure,' said Anya, smiling easily. 'Can't you tell by the odd way I speak? We thought we might as well come here and give ourselves up for treatment before we had to be committed. Saves so much fuddy-duddy paperwork, don't you see, and in an odd sort of way it's a whole lot less embarrassing. Ah, well, say goodbye to your freedom, Haptan: it looks like padded cells for us for the rest of our lives.'

She shrugged and grinned at him.

'Urgle urgle urgle,' he said solemnly, playing along with her.

'My companion,' she explained to the sweating man, who was now standing with his hands on his hips, eyeing them with open suspicion, 'doesn't talk very much. Well, in fact he talks quite a lot but, as you'll have . . . Need I say more? He's never been quite the same since he started having this recurring dream about wolves peering in through his bedroom window.'

'Yogorto!' said Haptan emphatically, nodding with vigour.

'What's so wrong with having dreams about wol . . . ?' began the gardener. Then he made a great show of scratching the back of his head, so that his straw hat tilted down over his nose. 'Well, if things is as bad 'n you say with 'ee two,' he drawled, 'nothin' better 'n you go right on up to th' Big House.'

'Why,' said Anya, 'to think that it could be so simple as that. Come along, Haptan. We don't want to be late.'

With a small mock curtsey to the red-faced man, she took Haptan's elbow and guided him back onto the drive.

'What in the bright bard's breakfast do you think you're playing at?' he hissed as soon as they were out of earshot. 'This is a joint for fruitcakes. As soon as we go through that front door they're going to lock us up and throw the keys away.'

'Except that you and I are clever enough to get the keys back any time we choose,' said Anya complacently. 'Don't you see that this is the perfect hiding-place for us for the next few weeks? Reen and her spies will never think of looking for us in a nut-house, will they? We can give them a month or so to have given up hunting for us around here, and then we'll be free to move exactly as we choose. Besides, I seem to remember you licking your lips at the prospect of a decent meal: much better to have one put in front of us than to have to go to all the effort of stealing it, surely?'

'Hmmm,' said Haptan, unconvinced. Nevertheless,

with the gardener still watching their backs, now was hardly the time to provoke a full-scale argument. Besides, since they'd fled from Starveling Anya had consistently been surprising him with her mental versatility and resources; it was about time he gave up the repeated error of underestimating her. She more than probably knew exactly what she was doing. After all, she must possess no little cunning to have succeeded in deposing the Ellonia Mob from the top-dog position, all those years ago, so that she could control the entire booze-running operation into and out of Ernestrad.

The front door of what the gardener had called the Big House had been not long ago repainted in reassuring white. It was casually half-open, as if to dispel any notions that anyone might have that this was a place of incarceration. Out of the corners of his eyes, though, Haptan noticed as they entered the big locks with their press-button action and the dead-man mechanisms that would presumably drop bars down over the portal like a latter-day portcullis. The careful precaution pleased him professionally: he would have installed exactly the same safeguards himself.

A burly nurse dressed in smart uncured skins sat behind a long table covered in papers and books and quill pens.

He looked up at them.

'Who are you?'

'We have come to commit ourselves voluntarily,' Anya said.

'You have reason for your decision?'

'Most certainly. Very good reason.'

'Then it sounds as if you could do with our help. I must ask you both to sign here, please, and to surrender any offensive weapons you might be carrying.' He nodded at their swords and daggers.

'But what,' said Anya, staring at the ledger he'd placed in front of her but making no move to pick up a pen, 'if we should be attacked by one of the other patients?'

'Clients,' the nurse corrected automatically. 'Even if

that did happen, we cannot have you killing your attackers.'

'But,' said Haptan, 'if we were bearing our weapons, none of your other . . . clients would think of attacking us, would they? Much better that we keep them with us.'

The nurse rubbed his chin, his face never losing the vague, focusless smile it had been bearing when first they'd entered. 'Hmmm. The concept of deterrence. Not terminally logical, but potentially so. You two *are* in bad need of care, aren't you? In that case, you'd better keep your weapons with you.'

'I knew you'd see sense,' said Anya, signing a false name with a flourish.

The nurse winced.

Haptan slid the book away from her and added a signature beneath hers. 'We're very hungry,' he said to the watching nurse.

'This isn't a scheduled meal-time,' said the man, squinting at the ledger. 'But if you'll come with me, Mr Duck and . . . er, Miss Boop, I'll see if I can't get the kitchen to rustle you up something cold.'

They followed him across a spotless carpet of bureaucratic grey and through a door into a long white corridor down which doors were set at regular intervals on either side.

'I'll put you in the common room for the moment,' he said, 'while I check with our catering staff.'

He opened one of the doors, and a warm gust of tobacco smoke seeped out. 'Your fellow-clients will doubtless introduce themselves,' he said. 'Don't worry, none of them have been known to be violent. They're a very friendly bunch, really, as they'll be the first to tell you.'

He ushered them in and shut the door behind them.

Hand on dagger, Haptan surveyed the room. It was reasonably spacious without giving the impression of being particularly large. Down one side there were four tall barred windows through which he could see a narrow veranda which was obviously hardly ever used; beyond its small stone balcony there was a tract of lawn with, in the distance, the high wall that presumably encircled the establishment completely. Inside the room there was a profusion of overstuffed armchairs, their woolly fabrics decorated in faded patterns, most of them showing wide streaks of greasy ingrained grey down their inner backs. Some dozen or so of the chairs had been pulled into a rough circle around one of several low tables; the table's surface was cluttered with half-empty tankards and brimming ashtrays. These chairs were occupied by an equal number of people, some slouched back so that they were almost lying horizontally, others sitting tensely upright on their seat's edge, as if in a state of perpetual expectation that at any moment the headmaster might walk in. One of these looked up and rapped her hand against the table to interrupt the flow of what had obviously been a long monologue from one of the slouchers.

'Pull yourselves some chairs over, duckies,' said the woman, who was of indeterminate age, seeming youthful in some of her attributes and quite astonishingly old in others. 'The name's Glassa. The rest can introduce themselves when they feel like it.'

'Which may be never,' said the interrupted sloucher with a hollow snigger. 'Your entrance has perchance rendered impotent and broken one of the most pivotal foundations of tomorrow's philosophy. Sad, of course, but never mind. I can always solve the World's problems all over again another day.'

'Pay him no attention,' said Glassa, frowning at him reprovingly as she'd clearly done a thousand times before. 'Jonem's just a stodgy old grump who doesn't know how properly to welcome newcomers and make them feel at home.'

They felt amused eyes on them as they hauled a couple of the bulbous armchairs up to join the circle, which shifted and adjusted to make room for them. The chairs proved to be hideously uncomfortable on first contact, before becoming almost seductively yielding as soon as the body was properly settled into them; it was hardly surprising, Haptan reflected, that some of the clients had slid down so far.

'You can ring this for some tea or coffee,' said Glassa, passing a small brass hand-bell to Anya, 'but no one'll come.'

'I'll just leave it unrung, then,' said Anya, finding space on the table to put it down. 'But thank you, anyway, for the thought.'

The nurse who had greeted them at the door came in, bearing a tray. His morningstar swinging dangerously at his side, he came over and insouciantly swept most of the contents of the table onto the floor, depositing the sandwiches.

'Spam,' he said apologetically. 'It was all they had.'

3

Anya and Haptan stayed in the McGruder Institution for some weeks, enjoying the food and the softness of the bed they shared, swimming in the heated basement swimming pool, practising both armed and unarmed combat daily, engaging in philosophical debates most afternoons, and walking in the grounds most mornings. The only difficulty, they found, was preserving their own insanity.

Outside the massive stone wall, unknown to them, the World as always kept on changing.

4

They were playing badminton one morning when Anya suddenly stopped, just as she was reaching for what would have been a winning shot. The shuttlecock spindled on, tumbling on the grass.

'What's the matter?' said Haptan anxiously, forcing himself not to look behind him.

'Nothing like that,' said Anya. She dropped her racquet, clearly having lost all interest in it. 'There's no immediate danger. You can relax.' She walked up to the net.

'Then why did you stop? Just when I was winning.'

'Because we're growing soft, you and I, my friend.'

'Not I.' He tapped his taut stomach confidently. 'Nor

you,' he added, prodding hers under the net. 'We get enough exercise here. We're as fit as we have any need to be.'

'But we don't have much need to be, here.'

'That is one of the many great charms of this place, Anya,' he said, stretching his arms lazily and grinning at her. 'Each night before I go to bed I offer up a little prayer to the nonexistent gods of the World to thank them for having created such a bounteous benefactor as the late McGruder, wherever he lies. I'm well fed and relaxed, and I don't have to worry about where my next coin is coming from or about whether or not we'll be able to find somewhere warm to sleep by nightfall. I can relax.'

'That's what I mean about us getting soft,' said Anya, staring reflectively at some daisies and scratching at the side of her nose. She was dressed in a short white tunic and, when the angle of the sunlight was kind, looked about nineteen. Her hair had grown a little, so that the cut appeared less gamin-like. Haptan had the horrible feeling that he was possibly in love with her; it was strange to associate such a gentle emotion as love with a woman as steely and ruthless as Anya. And certainly she'd never expressed anything of the like to him, never calling him anything more intimate than 'friend'. Even their lovemaking, after that long-ago morning in the barn near Qazar, tended to be more exhilarating and adventurous than companionable and sharing: he wondered if someday soon he might tire of relentless ecstasy. Someone had once remarked to him in a quite different context that a life of banquets was fine, but that sometimes a meal of bread and soup is good, too.

'We can't stay here indefinitely,' she said. 'Oh, we could, I suppose. They wouldn't stop us. We could live out the rest of our lives in peace and quiet, if we wanted, courtesy of the Intherian Government and its scheme of nullifying intellectual troublemakers by isolating them here and surrounding them with sufficient comfort that they never quite bother to want to leave again. Look at someone like Jonem or Glassa! They've got fine minds, even if they do both talk bullshit nine-tenths of the time. The other one-tenth, though – ah. Most people would count themselves lucky if they had as many good ideas in a lifetime as there are in Jonem's or Glassa's one-tenth of the time. Yet all that fruitful thinking is just being wasted in here, so that it stagnates, so that it's never all put together to make something useful. We're different, I know, but the same sort of thing is likely to happen to us if we stay here much longer. I want to be out in the World, seeing things, doing things, but I have this terrible feeling that if I put off doing that much longer I'll find myself putting it off forever.'

He looked at her angrily. She was right. That was what was making him angry.

'We could leave right now,' he said bitterly. 'The gate's open. It always is.'

'It's open if you're wanting to come in,' Anya said. 'I suspect that it's never open to people who're wanting to go out. You've seen the kind of equipment they've got in the Big House – photoelectric detectors and all – so that if you ever made too much trouble the staff could, as a last resort, press a button and fill you with crossbow bolts until you looked like a hedgehog. I'll bet you that they've got similar devices rigged up for the gate.'

'Is that what you'd have set up, back when you were running the Organization in Ernestrad?'

'The Anya who headed up the Mob,' she said, making a show of choosing her words fastidiously, 'would have done exactly that, yes. It was you who taught me to think of my life that way, Haptan: you shouldn't look so irritated when I follow your advice.' A quick grin. 'She wouldn't have had quite the same sort of sophisticated gadgetry, of course, and she'd have been better pleased if the malcontents were dead rather than rusticated, but yes, if she'd had them in the situation that we're in now, that'd have been the way she'd have thought. Keep everything all seemingly open and free, right up to the moment that someone took advantage of the ever-open gate, and then *chonk*!' She slammed the edge of her hand downwards into the other palm, making a thump that caused a moment's consternation among the birds of the nearby bushes. 'I think I probably made a mistake when I decided we should come in here – it just seemed such a good, infallible idea at the time.'

'Hey, now,' he said, reaching out to touch her. 'Don't forget that I thought so too. I came in here along with you of my own free will.'

'Yes, but before you did so you said that they'd put us in a padded cell and throw away the keys. That's exactly what they've done – only they've disguised the padded cell very effectively.'

'But, as *you* pointed out, we can always get the keys back, and let ourselves out.'

'That may not prove to be as easy as I thought it would.'

'We could always try just asking for them.'

'Yes, I suppose we'd better, to start with. Then, when that fails . . .'

She let the sentence die away.

The badminton net digging into his adam's apple, he leaned across and kissed her lightly on the cheek. They both knew full well that the first stratagem would fail, but the protocol would have to be observed.

5

It failed.

That afternoon, changed back into their own garments, they announced to one of the nurses – Marc, the same one who had supervised the skimpy formalities of their admission – that they had both come to the conclusion that the rest and gentle, almost undetectable therapeutic treatment supplied by the staff of the McGruder Institution had effected a complete cure in both of their cases. They were ready to face the rigours of the World again and, since they were voluntary patients, presumably there would be nothing more to the matter of their leaving than that. He nodded, his face showing sympathetic understanding, and explained patiently that there was just a little bit more to it than that, but not to worry. They would have to have a final interview with one of the menticians, just to ensure that they were absolutely well again, but really that was nothing more than a formality: it was obvious to him, Marc – indeed, it had been discussed among the staff – that they were now perfectly capable of resuming their lives outside. He would see if he could find a free mentician right now – they'd yet to see one during their stay, it was true, but that didn't mean that there hadn't been any on the premises, observing them and directing their treatment – so if they could just wait for a few minutes in one of the offices? There was a pot of tea freshly brewed, so if they'd like to help themselves, biscuits in the tin, shouldn't be long to wait . . .

They woke in a room that was sealed, damp and pitch-dark. Haptan's head felt as if someone had been working on it with a meat tenderizer, and a low moaning in the darkness was enough to convince him that Anya was in no better condition.

'The tea,' he said, once he'd worked out how to synchronize his tongue, teeth and lips.

He heard Anya vomiting. He couldn't decide whether or not comforting words would be welcome, so he said nothing until she'd finished.

'You all right now?'

'Yes.' Her voice was quite crisp. 'I strongly advise you to do the same. We can't do anything about however much of that accursed drug's already got into our bloodstreams, of course, but at least we can stop any more from doing so.'

He had a suspicion that this was poor science, but it was better to take an unnecessary precaution than to discover later that it hadn't been so unnecessary after all. Although his wrists were bound together, he was able to thrust a couple of fingers into the back of his throat, and a moment later he was doubled over in the darkness, feeling as if someone were dragging out his entire digestive tract. Once he was finished, eyes streaming painfully, he wiped the back of his mouth on his sleeves.

'They didn't exactly stint on the black paint, did they?' he said, trying to sound lighter-spirited than he felt. There wasn't even a suspicion of grey about the echoing room they were in.

'No, they didn't. I've been trying to see if I could spot a chink of light anywhere, but there's nothing. How tightly are you bound?'

'Very. But only at the wrists and ankles, and they've left my arms in front of me. You?'

'The same. Maybe they didn't expect us to waken so quickly. Or maybe this time they've *really* done what you suggested – locked us in and thrown away the key. They've left me my weapons, which was . . . considerate of them.' He heard the control in her voice: she, too, was trying not to betray the slightest trace of gloom.

'Where do you think we are?' he said.

'In a basement,' she said. 'Probably the basement of the Big House. I heard something scuttle a little while ago and I'd guess it was a rat. Besides, underground dungeons are the traditional places to put awkward customers, aren't they?'

'Sort of makes you wish they'd show a trace of imagination for a change,' he said sarcastically.

It was enough. She laughed. 'Thanks, but no,' she said. 'If we can find each other, we should be able to get ourselves untied, at least. I'll start speaking steadily, and you snake your way towards the sound of my voice – all right?'

'I suppose so. You can't remember exactly where you puked, can you?'

'No. You'll find out for yourself soon enough, though.'

Again she laughed. Then she started reciting the alphabet in a long steady monotone.

Soon he was beside her. Their two heads bumped together, and he worked his face around until he found her mouth. They kissed briefly, upside-down, noses to chins, ignoring their mouths' sourness. He hadn't encountered her pool of vomit, for which small mercy he offered up silent gratitude to any passing deity who might want it.

Then they discovered something neither of them had realized before. Ropes led from the bundles of knots at their ankles, tethering them to moorings that were invisible in the obscurity. They had enough freedom of movement that their heads could overlap, but no more.

'Raise your hands up towards my mouth,' said Haptan resignedly. He hoped the knots hadn't been too well tied: as every warrior knew, a broken tooth could be more debilitating than many a more serious injury.

To his relief he discovered that, although the rope was tightly wound around her wrists, the knots themselves were fairly slipshod affairs, as if their captors hadn't expected them to be tested. He tried not to think about the possibility that the captors just didn't care that he and Anya would soon be unbound: that would mean that she had probably been right in her supposition that the locks on this prison were unbreakable – that the keys had indeed been thrown away.

As soon as her hands were free, Anya pulled herself away from him. In the darkness he could hear her wrestling with the bonds at her ankles. A minute or two later she was rubbing them, letting out a string of curses as the blood circulation returned to them – and, with it, pain.

'You do realize,' she gasped in between oaths, 'that you've been unutterably stupid, Haptan.'

He'd been thinking exactly the same thing himself. In working to free her first, he'd put himself in the position where his own freedom depended entirely on her deciding that she wanted him free. If, instead, she came to the conclusion that she'd have a better chance of escape on her own . . . He'd told her himself never to trust anyone, especially the friendly people, the people who seemed to be on her side. She was a fast learner, and experience had shown that she'd taken this lesson in particular to heart.

'You're lucky,' she remarked with a chuckle, 'that I'm the kind-hearted, gentle-spirited creature that I am.'

Then she was untying his wrists and, soon, his ankles. As soon as he could walk, the two of them followed their tethers back to the beams to which those had been tied and attacked the knots there. All the pieces of rope were carefully coiled up and distributed about their garments: both Anya and Haptan knew of old that something potentially so precious shouldn't just be discarded. All the time they kept reciting the alphabet, over and over again in a regular rhythm, so that at any moment each of them had a reasonably clear idea of the other's whereabouts. Finally, using this system, they shuffled slowly back towards each other and, meeting gently, embraced.

'Ever been laid when you've been locked up for life in a pitch-black cellar and the air is pneumonically damp and your breath smells bad and there're probably hungry rats around and someone might come charging in at any moment and want to kill you?' she inquired.

'No. And I don't propose to try it, right now.'

'Chicken.'

'Yes. I suggest we go all around the walls, feeling them, trying to find out if there's anything like a door.'

'Could be only a trapdoor in the ceiling,' she said.

'Probably is. However, let's check the place out in case we're lucky.'

'OK. Together or singly?'

He thought for half a second. The search would go more quickly if they split up, but it'd be easier to maintain some semblance of optimism if they didn't.

'Together,' he said, as if the answer had been obvious.

Ten minutes or an hour later – it was impossible to judge time down here with any degree of accuracy – their investigation of the walls was done. There hadn't been anything remotely resembling a door, but at least they'd established the size of the place they were in. The basement – they were now unanimous that it was indeed a basement – was about twenty-five metres long and about fifteen wide. At a guess it ran the full length of the Big House but only about one-third of the width. They had no way of knowing which part of the ground floor they might be under.

A less welcome discovery had been a skeleton. Fumbling through the bones and rotted garments, they'd been able to scavenge a dagger, its blade rough with rust, and a light mace. They tried to cheer themselves up with remarks about how it was good to be adding to their armoury, but both of them were wondering just how many other skeletons might be lying around on the great open area of unexplored floor. They'd been hardly reassured to find the dagger not at the skeleton's belt but wedged in under the jaw.

'Why didn't they just kill us?' said Haptan drearily. 'It'd have been simpler, surely, than going to all the effort of carrying us down here and tying us up.'

'Maybe they're sadists,' said Anya. 'Maybe they've got a secret peep-hole. Maybe they want to watch our reactions, like they might watch a rat in a maze, just to see what we do. Or maybe they're forcing the other "clients" to watch us, so that our fates serve as a deterrent in case anyone else is beginning to think of the attractions of home.' Anya shrugged, even though Haptan couldn't see her. The last idea made perfect sense to her.

'I can't see them making the others watch us,' said Haptan decisively. 'That just doesn't fit in with the whole practice of the place. The McGruder Institution continues to function only because it successfully maintains an illusion – the illusion that the inmates are free to come and go as they please. But the idea that *someone* might be watching us . . . that's more appealing.'

'We could disrupt the illusion,' Anya observed.

'How do you mean?'

'It'd be hard to sustain the pretence of complete normality if smoke started coming up out of the floor, wouldn't it?'

'The skeleton's clothes! But we don't have . . .'

'Flints? Of course we have. Well, I have, anyway. You don't think it's only money I keep in my money-pouch, do you?'

By the slow process of working their way around the walls again, they eventually located the skeleton. The garments felt cold to their fingers, but seemed to be dry.

'This may not work, you know,' he said conversationally as they were gathering the pathetically small bundle together. 'There's a good chance we're not under any of the places that the inmates are allowed to go. And we don't even know that it's not night-time. And' – he drew a breath – 'even if we're lucky about both those things, these clothes on their own aren't exactly going to make a colossal blaze.'

'They'll give us some light, though. Enough to see if there's anything else inflammable down here – other sets of clothes, just for starters. And enough to let us have a look to see if we can locate the trapdoor they must have brought us down through. Cheer up.'

'If you can get the cloth to light.'

'Thanks for the vote of confidence.'

There was a *click!* that seemed to ricochet around the unseen walls, and a few sparks of blue-yellow light; none of them landed on the bundle of clothing.

'Heigh ho, try again,' said Anya.

The second time she was luckier. A couple of the sparks landed on the rotten cloth. One of them vanished almost immediately, but the other caught, creating a tiny, uncertain red glow in the gloom.

Cautiously she blew on it. For a second it looked as if even this softest of breaths was going to extinguish the smoulder, but then it seemed to cheer up a little – rather like someone stepping out into a cold wind and then soon realizing how refreshing the gusts are. She puffed again, this time with rather more confidence.

Haptan suddenly ripped off one of the cuffs from his blouse, and passed her the piece of thin cloth. 'Here,' he said, 'this might be just that extra bit drier.'

She took it from him, and touched a corner of it to her small, precious ember. To her vast relief the cotton seemed eager to take up the flame, and within seconds it was glowing brightly. She dropped it under a layer of the old rotten material, and then pulled at her waist, tugging her own blouse free. Keeping a steady draught of air on the smouldering patch, she ruthlessly cut away a section of the blouse with her dagger.

Soon they were standing beside a somewhat tentative-seeming fire.

'Told you so,' she said.

'We've got plenty of fuel,' said Haptan emptily.

She turned, following his gaze. Piled up in the centre of the cellar were at least a score of tangled corpses, most but not all of them reduced to skeletons. One of them was still well enough preserved that Haptan could detect a likeness to one of the inmates whom he'd hardly noticed when alive – a self-effacing, depressed-seeming woman who had arrived not long after they had themselves and who hadn't exchanged more than a few dozen words with anyone before departing as unremarkably as she'd come. Evidently she'd chosen to kill herself by strangulation with a ligature. The results were ugly.

'Oh, good,' said Anya. 'They've all still got their clothes on.'

Chapter Three
BeYOND THe JADe GATe

1

Joli flicked back his watch-cover and checked the time. He was going to be several minutes late for his appointment with the Painter, but that didn't matter too much: the traffic in Whatever was so notoriously bad that arrival on time was seen by the locals as being almost a discourtesy. Outside the window of his hansom cab there seemed to be a solid mass of struggling pedestrians, creaking vehicles and weary-looking horses in well worn harness. It was one of those late days of summer when the Sun is bright and the sky clear, yet there is just a nip of coldness in the air to remind you that autumn is fast on its way.

He leaned back in the sweet-smelling leather and sighed. He had come to the conclusion, these past few weeks, that he loathed the Intherians. He loathed humanity as a whole, if the truth were told – which it frequently was – but he'd decided that he detested the Intherians even more than he detested the Albionians, himself included, who formed the only other large sample of the human species he could recall having known. And of all the Intherians whom he detested, the citizens of Whatever, taken either individually or collectively, were the ones who inspired him to new and most imaginatively vituperative loathing. Being forced to live among these descendants of anthropophages was . . . well, 'bliss' was the first word that sprang to Joli's mind.

He swore at the cabbie, telling him to get a move on. To his surprise, after the man had reeled off a stream of curses back at him, the carriage did indeed seem to pick up a little speed, attaining the rate of a brisk walk.

Joli gazed out at the packed streets again, his face set in deep lines of gloom. All of the men in Whatever were confirmed sodomites, he'd learnt as soon as he'd arrived here, most especially the physicians who examined dying people on first arrival and then cheerfully told them that they were suffering from nothing more than a mild bout of seasickness, the shopkeepers who kept harping on about the junk coinage that the Intherians pretended was money, the policemen dressed as if they were on the way to a drag ball, which they probably were, the . . . And all the women of Whatever were syphilitic tarts – you could tell it by the way they walked. Of course, as Joli had discovered during his long and eventful life, women were by definition syphilitic tarts anyway, with the possible exception of his long-dead mother (although even she had had leanings in that direction), but nowhere outside Whatever would you find women who were both quite so ostentatiously syphilitic *and* so brazenly tartish as here; it was a wonder, in fact, that they could walk at all.

He assumed that the children of Whatever had been placed in the city by some malignant demon.

And into this cesspit of humanity, where he had to keep both back and front to the wall at all times, Reen (who was a syphilitic tart only when at a very considerable distance) had sent him and the Painter with firm instructions to serve as her eyes and ears. Once a week the two of them were permitted to meet to report solemnly to each other that neither of them had made any progress – not a trace of a sighting, not a whiff of conversation – before, for half an hour at least, the Painter was allowed to enjoy the pleasure of listening to a reasoned discourse on the subjects of anal intercourse, venereal disease and prostitution. Then the Painter would be off to whatever fleabitten dump of a lodging he'd been able to procure for himself while Joli would sadly return to his vile, soulless, despicable five-star hotel, where the maids and waitresses refused either to serve him or even to speak to him. And to think that he'd told them all that he was prepared, just this once, to risk the syphilis.

Ah, well, maybe the Painter would have some news for him this week. Maybe. Otherwise, Joli had decided, it was time to send a telegram to Reen to tell her that this particular branch of the hunt should be closed down, or whatever it was you did to branches. She'd failed to reply to similar telegrams in the past, but one of these days she must realize the sense of what he was saying. The woman, Anya, wherever she might have fled to, certainly hadn't fled to Whatever – as Joli had tried to tell Reen right at the outset. This was the place from whose surrounding wetlands had come the bradz upon which Anya had built her empire, and so it was the very last place to which she might think of fleeing. The city must be crawling with people who knew Anya by sight, from supply bosses down to humble runners, and there were numerous reasons why they would be only too eager to assist in her capture, or more likely to kill her themselves – which Joli suspected they might well have already done. So long as she ran free they were in danger: she was completely unscrupulous and, if the rozzers had the sense to make her a suitably appealing offer, she would blab everything she knew about the routes of supply, the network of corruption within the Intherian customs department, the shippers . . . Or she might have decided that she had a few old scores of her own that she'd like to see settled: the Organization here had the ghastly example of what had happened aboard the *Ten Per Cent Extra Free* to contemplate any time they started to become complacent about Ernestrad 'ap Anya still being at large. No, it was obvious: Anya certainly wasn't in Whatever, and if she was she was so well hidden that nothing either Joli or the Painter could do would ever dig her out.

He looked at his watch again and saw it measuring the wasted time.

2

They'd dragged bits of burning cloth over to the pile of the dead and stuffed them around the base, not even cursing their scorched fingers in their exhilaration. Soon they'd been rewarded by the sight of confident flames beginning to leap up among the tangle of bones and withered flesh.

'We may not have a chance later,' said Haptan, his face red from both the exertion and the reflected light, 'so I just thought I'd say it's been nice knowing you.'

'Yes, yes, I'm sure it has been,' Anya replied offhandedly, not removing her stare from the outline of the trapdoor overhead. Even with her standing on Haptan's shoulders they hadn't been able quite to reach it. 'Why should you want to come out with that now?'

'Because there may not be a later.'

'True. So belt up.'

The blaze was growing ever more enthusiastic. Already it was becoming unpleasantly hot and smoky in the enclosed space. Haptan was uncomfortably aware that not all of the tightness in his chest was a product of nervous anticipation of carnage to come. It wouldn't be many minutes now before breathing started to become difficult.

He looked at the array of weaponry they'd laid out for themselves, scavenged from the skeletal heap. The pistols they'd found were useless, of course, without ammunition, and had been flung into far corners, as had a laser sabre from which the charge had long since ebbed; but there'd been more than enough by way of weapons – swords, daggers, axes, a couple of garottes and even a malevolent-looking morningstar – to compensate for that disappointment. Both he and Anya had opted to retain their own swords as their primary weapons, but it was reassuring to know that there were plenty of replacements to hand. They had more daggers than they properly knew what to do with, although Anya's eyes had glittered when she'd first surveyed the hoard: these were not throwing knives, she'd said, but they could certainly be thrown.

Haptan shivered, despite the heat. His whole body seemed to be aching for the trap to drop – *if* it was indeed going to drop. The clamour of battle would be a relief after this nerve-racking business of waiting.

He wiped sweat from his face with the back of his hand

and, without thinking, licked it, tasting the saltiness. His body felt gritty all over; he wondered if he smelled as badly as Anya did. Was it day or night outside? *Think of something else.* He recalled having sat by a river's edge in Albion, watching a little moorhen bravely struggling against a current that was so much bigger than she was. There was an amazingly fine feast he'd once attended in Starveling: he could taste the venison still . . .

The trap burst open, and Anya let out a scream of ecstasy. There was a heavy screeching crash as a flight of folding wooden stairs collapsed down from the ceiling to the floor.

In the confusion it seemed as if a hundred armed men and women were stumbling down the stairs. Haptan paused just long enough to reckon that in reality the figure was nearer to ten, then he let out a bloodcurdling war-whoop in imitation of Anya's.

Bright light shone among the attackers. Daylight.

Anya's arm flickered and the leader of the aggressors, Marc, suddenly had a rusty dagger in place of a throat. A spout of blood came from his mouth as he staggered; it drenched the floor ahead of him as he tumbled forwards down the last few steps. The black little revolver he'd been carrying skittered off across the floor. Haptan automatically memorized where it had gone.

Again that lethal flash of Anya's arm. More blood. A death scream. Haptan took in all this in a single confusion of sight and sound as he scampered around behind and beneath the folding stairway, punching brutally up between the treads with his sword, again and again. A burly woman dropped off the side of the stairway. As she struggled on her back to bring her clumsy tommy gun around to bear on him he dropped on her, stabbing her through the right eye. For a moment, as she died, he tugged at her weapon, but the strap was tangled around her shoulders and he couldn't afford to keep his back to the invaders for more than a second.

As he turned he saw that Anya was using her sword with her right hand and a double-bladed hand-axe with her left. There was a man kneeling, screaming, looking down stupidly as his intestines spilt out. A woman dressed in a brown tweed two-piece suit lay a metre away from her arm. Haptan's sword stabbed into living flesh and he saw eyes widen in a mixture of astonishment and offence. The sword lodged. Not pausing to tug at it a second time, he half-knelt and scooped up from their arsenal the first weapon that came to hand – the morningstar. Yelling like something out of a nightmare, he began to whirl the heavy weapon around his head. The remaining attackers were so astounded by the apparition that they froze momentarily. To compound the confusion, he simply threw the weapon at them. Its sharp spikes impaled one man fully in the chest, puncturing him as deep as the heart and lungs. His already dying body, struck backwards by the momentum, felled a couple of those pressed up tightly behind him. A bullet took Haptan in the shoulder, but luckily it was only his left shoulder.

The surviving attackers had all now cleared the stairs and were standing on the blood-greasy cellar floor. Two of them had lost their weapons somewhere in the mêlée; one of the others had an automatic that had apparently jammed, because he was fighting with it; the remaining two had tommy guns.

Anya was on the move. Again she was possessed of that supernatural speed that Haptan had first seen on the *Ten Per Cent Extra Free*. In the fitful illumination it was hard to make out exactly where she was at any one time, but he distinctly saw her bend down, without breaking her stride, and catch up three more of the antique daggers; then, twisting around the upper part of her body, she let them fly through the air – one, two, three, faster than he could count – so that two of the Institution staff, the two with the tommy guns, plummeted to the floor as if struck down from behind. The third dagger clattered uselessly off a wall.

A quick-thinking attacker had seized one of the tommy guns from the hands of a dying man and, gripping it like a pike, was bringing it to bear. He let off a burst of bullets.

Haptan dropped just in time, hearing the missiles zing only centimetres above his head. The man screamed, dropping the gun, the hand that he'd held over the perforated barrel burning him.

Haptan lay where he was, feigning death, lodged up against the woman he'd killed.

He glanced behind him, careful to move only his eyes, not his head, and could see through the deepening billows of smoke that Anya was at the far end of the cellar, too far from any source of further knives – and anyway too far for a throw.

It would only require one of the Institution people to have the wit to grab up the fallen tommy gun . . .

One of them was already leaning forwards to do so. Neither she nor her companion was looking in Haptan's direction, and the yelling man was looking nowhere except at his palm.

Swiftly Haptan, smoke in his eyes, reached his arm across the dead woman and swivelled her weapon around, using the taut strap now as a hinge, until he had it in roughly the right direction. Still he was unobserved, but that couldn't last for more than another fraction of a second. The woman with the gun was turning towards Anya with it, finger on the trigger; she, too, was going to burn her hand but that wasn't going to be much consolation to Anya who, though she was dancing elusively around now, trying to get nearer to the protection of the settling blaze, was unlikely to survive the first salvo. The other Institution person had spotted Haptan's movement and was shouting while trying to duck behind the stairs as Haptan squeezed the trigger and felt through the body of the dead woman the brutal repeated kicks of the discharging weapon.

The gun, held single-handed, was riding upwards. He couldn't grip it hard enough to stop it. The enemy who'd been about to fire at Anya was going down, though, a ragged line of bullet-wounds stitching her from groin to face. The one behind the stairs was unarmed still and Anya was streaking past Haptan in a blur of gold-topped brown and there was the squalid sound of a blade being sunk into flesh and a gurgle and Haptan wouldn't have heard either if he hadn't at some forgotten moment remembered to release the trigger.

His head slumped forward, using the dead woman's torso as a pillow. For the first time the pain of his shoulder hit him, and he felt consciousness beginning to ebb and flow. All that he wanted to do was to sink into sleep's inviting arms, to let the soft blackness at the edges of his vision wash right over him like a blanket, but he knew that he couldn't allow that to happen because, even though the trap was open, the smoke down here was now building up to suffocating levels and so if he lost consciousness where he was he would never wake up.

He forced himself to throw back the advancing quilt of oblivion and somehow managed to get his knees under him, so that he could push his body up a little from the ground. His left arm was near to useless and his right was shaking from nervous reaction. On hand and knees, he permitted himself to rest for a few seconds, trying to gather his energies for the next upward thrust, shaking his head stupidly. He wondered where Anya had got to. A sudden panic in case she were no longer alive. He'd assumed the sounds he'd heard had been of her killing the last of the enemy, but what if it had been the other way round?

He got his torso vertical, and collapsed back onto his haunches. He coughed twice, sharply, unexpectedly, and pain shot the length of his arm. No mere flesh wound could be hurting him this badly: the bullet must have hit the joint. His eyes streaming from the smoke and the agony, he tried to screw round his head to look at the damage directly, but this seemed only to increase the pain, so he gave the notion up.

Where the fuck has Anya gone? he thought, finding himself swaying on his feet with no clear idea of how he'd got there. *Either she or the Institution bitch should have been with me by now.*

He stared in the direction of the stairway, but all he

could see through the busy grey smoke and his own tears was a glow of white light at ceiling level. Talking inaudibly to himself, he stepped around the corpse that had been his shield and tottered in the direction of the light.

'Wait,' said a voice close beside him, to his right.

'Anya!' he gasped. 'Thank the Sun you're . . .'

He reached out in the direction of her words, but his hand found nothing. With difficulty he avoided losing his balance.

'I can't see you,' he mumbled.

'My mother placed this mist here,' said Anya's light voice. 'I saw her with my own eyes. She created the grey mist and she sent it out into the World, so that it could reappear wherever she wanted it to, and ensnare me at any moment of her choosing. It's all quite simple really, once you know the explanation.'

'Anya, what are you talking about?' he said, then coughed again. *No more coughing*, he commanded his body as the pain reluctantly ebbed. *That almost had me off my feet* . . . 'It's not mist,' he said finally. 'It's smoke from the fire. It's going to kill us soon if we don't get out of here. Grab my arm, won't you. Grab my arm!'

'You're wrong about that, you know.' Anya might have been having a conversation over a relaxed drink in a quiet tavern somewhere. 'It really is Syor's mist, and she really has sent it in an attempt to thwart me. She won't be successful, of course, because I'll be escaping from it very soon – escaping for this time, at any rate.'

'Anya, can we talk about this later? Once we're outside?'

He took another step towards the light, holding his right arm out in front of him both to fend off any obstacles and to grip them for support. Another step, and then another – but this last time the effort was almost too much for him.

'You were such a graceful bird,' said Anya blithely, 'but look, now you've got a broken wing and can't fly properly.'

Even if he hadn't been immobilized by the pain he'd

have stopped. His eyes combed the smoke, desperately hoping for a sight of her.

'I'll be flying higher than ever in a few weeks' time if only you'll help me get out of here.' His throat hurt as he spoke with a series of individual agonies, one for each syllable.

'No,' she said. 'It's kinder not to keep birds with broken wings alive.'

Then her arms were around his shoulders, and he felt her warmth pressing against him, her breath on his face. Her lips found his, and she forced a long kiss on him.

Then she slithered around behind him, whispered a 'goodbye' in his ear, and clinically cut his throat.

3

Another fortnight had passed since Joli had at last dared send Reen a telegram suggesting that it was pointless keeping himself and the Painter in Whatever any longer. Her promptly wired reply had been to the point:

JOLI GREETINGS STOP IF YOU MOVE FROM WHERE YOU ARE PERMISSIONLESS I SHALL EMASCULATE YOU REPEAT EMASCULATE REPEAT YOU STOP UNDERSTOOD QUERY THE WEATHER IS GOOD HERE STOP REEN

He'd shrugged helplessly while reading it in the little room off the hotel manager's office. Reen certainly had always had a way of stopping rational debates before they properly got started.

The carriage deposited him on the corner near the place where he and the Painter had their weekly assignations. Joli paid the cabbie the exact sum demanded, then walked away smiling in satisfaction as oaths peppered his back like tommy-gun bullets. The man would doubtless thank him later for the health-giving rush of adrenalin he'd induced.

The shop he was heading for had two large front

windows in which were displays of outstretched hands covered in rings and bangles with, behind them, rather disconcerting headless and armless torsos dressed in scuffed black velvet and adorned with brooches and necklaces. In curving lavish script across the top of each window were the words

THe HOUOSe OF JADeS

The pun always made Joli grin, for behind the respectable façade of its jewellery business the shop was the home of a strictly speaking illegal but nevertheless publicly well regarded bordello, all of which was ideal camouflage for the fact that, behind *that* façade, it was also the home of a number of strictly speaking legal but nevertheless distinctly non-public interview rooms which could be booked, for a large fee, by people such as himself and the Painter who wished no connection to be made between their overt and their covert preoccupations. Joli had no idea who else might make use of the facilities, or when, but he suspected that most of them were probably people like himself, here in Whatever on quasigovernmental business. Outside the privacy of his own head, he made a point of never guessing even that much; it had been spelt out to both himself and the Painter beforehand that this was the wisest course of action.

Today, as always, he walked in through the open plate-glass door, swaggering a little under the illusion that he looked like a well-to-do cosmopolitan businessman, here to spend a deal of money catering for the whims of one of his *de rigueur* string of mistresses. As soon as he was inside the shop, the roar of the traffic and the shouts of the drivers and pedestrians were cut off behind him, as cleanly as if by a knife; it was an acoustic trick which mystified him and which he secretly admired, since the door remained open as always. Of course, he allowed not a trace of his curiosity as to its workings to affect his strut.

A distinguished-looking gentleman in a frock coat came towards him with a courteous smile and a clothes brush.

'And how may I assist sire this morning?'

Joli scowled at the man.

'I would like to gain entrance to the Gate of Jade,' he said, according to the formula used by potential customers of the establishment's less mentioned business.

The floor manager, bowing, gestured to one of his assistants. 'I shall ask Karod to show you a range of the type of jewellery you desire, sire,' he said.

The assistant was a little man whose immaculate black suit and restrained bow tie did nothing to smother a certain air of seediness about him: Joli always half-expected Karod to throw back the superbly pressed flap of his jacket and ask which of his sisters the customer would like to purchase today, sire. Instead, as usual, Karod merely bowed sombrely and asked if the gentleman would like to follow him through to the display rooms at the rear of the shop.

As they retreated towards the back of the building, the aura of select gemster seemed slowly to become diluted by that of even more select host. The transition was not an abrupt one, and it was impossible to pick out any individual elements that accounted for the change of the feel of the surroundings, but by the time that Karod had led Joli through a small, unobtrusive door at the back of the shop, down a long, sumptuously decorated, gaslit corridor, and then through a succession of rooms whose walls were embellished with priceless paintings of pagan gods disporting themselves, there was no longer any possible doubt that they were in a house of pleasure. The last room they came into was larger than the others, and circular; from one side a broad flight of red-carpeted stairs led in a graceful arc towards the upper storeys. Elsewhere around the curving walls were freshly upholstered antique sofas and chairs; on some of these young men lounged, smoking through long cigarette-holders – as was currently the fashion, Joli had loudly observed on more than one occasion, among the very pansiest sodomites of Whatever – or pretending to read ephemeral magazines. The carpet was of a white that was almost silver, its pile several centimetres thick, so that one waded through it rather than walked across it to a big, kidney-shaped reception desk. This was a phenomenal piece of furniture, looking as if it must have been built *in situ*, because it was obviously far too massive ever to have been carried in through the door. Its cream-painted sides bulged as if they were having difficulty containing its brute bulk; they were decorated with imaginatively lewd carvings whose details were picked out in what Joli had once determined to his own satisfaction were genuine precious stones – opals, diamonds, pearls, sapphires . . . Unfortunately he'd never been able to prise one of them off.

Karod moved in his mincing way around to the back, so that he was standing in the inner curve of the kidney.

'Has sire decided upon any particular variety of . . . gem?' said Karod, his black eyes gleaming wickedly.

'Harrumph,' said Joli, looking furtively about him at the other clients. None of them seemed to be paying him the least bit of attention. 'Eye-catching,' he said. 'You know, er, fully rounded, yet with good angles. The, ah, usual attributes.'

'Thank you, sire. A most useful description.'

Karod ran his fingers swiftly along a rack of lantern-slides in a long box on a shelf that protruded out from the desk just below his waist-height. At one stage he paused, pursing his lips and shrugging before rejecting the slide concerned, but otherwise he seemed to expend no thought at all in making his selection of six. Touching a button at the side of a magic lantern, also on the shelf, he waited for a few moments while the machine heated up and then slid the first of the slides into the recess at the top. Immediately the wall behind him was filled with an exquisitely detailed watercolour painting of one of the most beautiful nudes that Joli had ever set eyes on.

'No. Not for me,' he said reluctantly. 'I don't like 'em with acne.'

Karod frowned but said nothing. Instead he replaced the slide with another. This time the woman had the face of an all-wise virgin and the sort of body that makes men dream immortal dreams.

'She looks as if she's got bad breath,' said Joli with agonized finality. If only he could afford to come here one day at his own expense . . .

The third woman was black, her face betraying a long history of aristocratic breeding in the fine planes of its . . .

'Strabismus,' said Joli with a painful wrench.

The next woman carried a baseball bat in her hand and a cigarette butt in her lips, was covered in tattoos and smallpox scars, and was built like a professional wrestler. She was grinning, which was a mistake.

'Yum,' said Joli with as much conviction as he could summon. 'She looks cute.'

'Certainly, sire,' said Karod, 'but' – he riffled rapidly through a card index – 'Miss Angeline is engaged at present. Perhaps . . .'

'With a big blind naked fellow and a pig?'

'That is, er, correct.'

'Well, count me in on it, eh?' said Joli in a rush. 'The man's an old friend of mine – we've done this sort of thing countless times before. He'll be glad to see me.'

'I shall call Miss Angeline and discuss the matter,' said Karod tersely. He gestured towards one of the sofas and its accompanying pile of glossy magazines. 'Perhaps if sire would like to wait a moment?'

While Karod went through a pantomime of winding up the telephone and speaking into it in courteous monosyllables, Joli sat and steamed. Why they had to go through this charade every time was something that he would never be able to understand. Surely it must be patently, blitheringly obvious to the other customers waiting here for more orthodox purposes that the whole business was just a pretence? No one in their right minds would ever choose . . . *Yes*, thought Joli suddenly, *but can you be sure that they're all in their right minds?*

'Sire,' said Karod. 'Miss Angeline has graciously acceded to your request. Perhaps if you could follow me?'

Forcing himself to walk with casual, lounging slowness, retaining as much of his swagger as he could, Joli followed the little man up the great loop of the staircase, feeling the cool polished marble of its banister running beneath his fingertips. He cast his eye back at the reception hall and saw to his dismay that a couple of the young men were breaking with the conventions of the establishment and staring at him, their faces twisted into mixtures of incredulity and contempt. Joli gulped ashamedly and hoped that he never encountered either of them outside these four walls. There was always a chance that one of them might even be staying at his hotel . . .

At the head of the stairs Karod turned to him, his demeanour changed from that of upper-crust pimp to that of hurried businessman – an impression somewhat marred by the imperfect soundproofing of the establishment's doors. 'Here,' he said, pressing a large gold key into Joli's hand. 'You know where you're going, of course. One or other of you should settle your account on the way out of the shop.'

Left on his own, Joli scurried up two further flights of stairs, the second of which had abandoned all pretence at opulence, being narrow, uncarpeted and poorly lit. Right at its very top there was a small landing, floored with pocked yellow linoleum, off which led a single door. On this Joli beat a little tattoo with his knuckles.

'Enter,' called the Painter.

The attic into which Joli emerged was a place of bright light. It was roughly triangular in shape, and taller than it was wide, most of its walls being occupied by uncurtained windows. There were several small upright chairs and an ashtray; otherwise there were no furnishings or decorations of any kind. Joli always expected to find an artist sitting here at an easel, with paints and brushes scattered all around. Instead he found something rather different, in the form of the Painter, naked as usual, seated astride a chair that looked as if it had been made for someone smaller. Somehow the pig had manoeuvred itself up onto one of the other chairs, where it perched unsteadily on its haunches, its flesh overlapping the hard wooden seat and hanging down in flabby folds all around it.

'You're late,' said the Painter resignedly. He gave Joli

an identical greeting each week.

'The traffic.' Again no variation in the established ritual.

'You've seen the newspapers, of course?'

Joli started. This was unexpected. The Painter's next line was supposed to be 'Might as well drag up a pew, then'.

'No,' said Joli. 'I haven't. All drivel, these Intherian gutter rags. I never . . .'

Wordlessly, the Painter drew out from behind him a folded newspaper and tossed it to Joli, who caught it at the second attempt. One side of it was still warm from the Painter's flesh, the other from the sunlight. He unfolded it, and found that it was dated three days earlier. The main article on the front page, ringed in red crayon, was devoted to the news of a

MASSIVE CONFLAGRATION AT McGRUDER INSTITUTION
No Survivors

Underneath this Joli rapidly read several closely printed columns to the effect that one of Intheria's foremost psychiatric centres for the criminally sane had been razed to the ground by a conflagration that had also devoured much of the surrounding estate. The only survivor had been the gardener, who had been taking his afternoon nap in an outhouse at the far end of the grounds. The blaze seemed to have been started in one of the main building's cellars, which had been discovered littered with the remains of the deceased. None of the Institution's clients outside the cellar had survived either – and here the language of the report waxed even more sensationalist. Although it was hard to be certain with those who had died on the ground floor, the flames having charred the remains so thoroughly, there was no doubt that most of the unfortunate inmates on the upper storeys had had their throats cut. The police were regarding the entire affair as a mystery, and had sent in not only a hand-picked disaster-investigation squad but also a team of witchfinders, whom the gardener was currently helping with their enquiries.

'Nasty accident,' said Joli after a while. 'Now – to business. I suppose there's been neither hide nor . . .'

He stopped. It was normally hard to read the Painter's facial expressions, but not now.

'Did I miss something?' said Joli nervously.

'That crime could hardly have been more clearly Anya's if she'd left a signed confession,' rumbled the Painter. 'It has all the characteristics of her work – the effrontery, the ruthlessness, the careless disregard for concealment. I begin to wonder if the reason that we have had so far no intelligence of her whereabouts is that the more mobile member of our partnership has been walking around Whatever with his eyes shut!'

'But this was many kilometres from here,' Joli protested, gesturing towards the newspaper on the floor.

'Yes. You're right, of course,' said the Painter, subsiding. 'I withdraw part of my remark – we have no evidence that she's been anywhere near here. But I stand by much of it, Joli. You have so firmly decided that you have no chance of catching sight of her activities that, even when evidence of them is laid directly in front of you, you choose to ignore it.'

'If this atrocity was indeed her work,' said Joli, speaking rapidly in an attempt to stifle the Painter's criticism before it became too cutting, 'I should think we have strong indicative evidence that in fact she has most certainly not been in Whatever.'

'Perhaps you could explain yourself.'

Joli pointed at the discarded newspaper again.

'What better hiding place could there be for someone on the run,' he said, 'than cooped up inside an institution? Even if anyone dreamt of looking for her there, there would still be so much bureaucracy to disentangle in order to get permission to check the names of the inmates that no one would bother. And even if they did there'd be no guarantee that they'd be any the wiser, because she'd have signed in under an assumed name. She must have seen the possibilities of the set-up immediately. No wonder none of Reen's other searchers came across any sign of her: all the time she was right under their noses, barely a score of kilometres away from Llandeer, three meals a day, all tucked up at nights in her nice warm bed, no problem . . .'

'Yes,' said the Painter unwillingly. 'You're right, of course. Reen will be very angry when she reads of this – angry with herself, I mean, for not having had the foresight to instruct that all such places be scoured.'

Joli picked up the newspaper, relieved that he'd satisfactorily deflected the Painter's complaints.

'Hmmm,' he said, rubbing his forefinger up and down the cleft of his chin. 'I see this rag's three days old. She could be anywhere by now.'

'Indeed,' said the Painter. 'Anywhere, including Whatever.'

'But equally likely anywhere else,' stressed Joli.

'I doubt it.' The Painter reached out to tickle his pig between the ears. The animal gazed at him lovingly, then returned its stare to Joli's face. 'I doubt it because of the very fact that we're here. Reen wouldn't have been so definite about stationing the two of us in Whatever if she hadn't had pretty good reason to believe that Anya would turn up at some point or other. We may appear to most people to be sorry spectacles, the weakest of all Reen's allies, yet we're two of the very few people who have the power to genuinely *frighten* Anya.'

'Yes! My dazzling swordplay, my . . .'

'You she's now seen die twice over, the second time under her direct instruction. Yet still you live. The first time she might be able to pass off as an aberration of circumstances, a matter of mistaken impressions as to what had really happened. It seemed as if you'd died and certainly, afterwards, you were keen enough to tell everybody that this was in fact the case. But then you're such a notorious liar that most people don't bother wasting the breath to contradict you. The second time, though, when she'd discovered that you were an undercover police informer and had you exterminated as messily as possible in order to make an example of you – that time she couldn't explain it all away to herself so easily. She'd seen the results of her assassins' work; she'd touched the evidence for herself. And yet, months later, there you were again, giving bad pennies a bad name . . .'

'But what makes you think she's seen me?'

'Don't you remember it? When we were all on Starveling-stage? When Syor metamorphosed?'

'I remember all that, yes. But Anya wasn't there.'

'Didn't you *feel* her presence?'

'No.'

'Ah. It is hard, sometimes, to remember that others do not possess the senses that were given to me in exchange for my eyes. No, she was there, all right. Just for a few minutes before Syor pronounced the sentence of death upon her, and charged Reen with carrying out the execution.'

'Then why didn't Syor simply smite her where she stood? It'd have been easy enough for her, surely? She was screwing up all the rest of the local meteorology, so a quick extra thunderbolt wouldn't have made much difference.'

The Painter smiled. 'I don't think either of us is in any position to try to second-guess a god,' he said. 'Who can tell? Perhaps Syor is like Alyss, who cannot herself kill us mortals – or will not, which is much the same thing when the will involved is a divine one. But if you were to ask me for my own, totally unfounded speculation, I'd tell you that I think that Syor was setting us some kind of a test of our fidelity – an utterly pointless exercise, of course. But such futile, childish demands seem to be part of the paraphernalia of all divinities, whether real or imagined. So my guess is that that was indeed her will: to test our loyalty.'

'Reen's most of all,' said Joli angrily. 'She specified that it was the responsibility of Reen to ensure that the task was carried out. Our beloved god' – he spat on the linoleum –

'must be a gratuitously heartless one, if your hypothesis is even remotely correct. She knew that of any of us it would be Reen who'd find the command most difficult to obey. Reen raised the child. Reen loved the child – not unquestioningly, but very deeply. She may recognize the monster that the child has become and may even accept that the monster must die, but that still doesn't mean that there isn't a lot of love left in her for the child she brought up.'

The Painter's head was held at a curious angle. The blankness of the scars where his eyes should have been seemed to be probing right in through all Joli's armoured outer layers to the core within.

'You're very fond of Reen, aren't you?' he said softly. 'You'd die for her if you had to.'

'That old bit of walking leather? Give me two fistfuls of Miss Angeline any day.'

The Painter waved the remark away. 'You'd incur the wrath of your god if it were for Reen's sake, wouldn't you?'

'I . . . Well, you sort of get used to her being around.'

Joli slumped in his chair and stared hard at the faded pattern of the linoleum. Originally it had showed baskets brimming with misshapen flowers, but now the colours and most of the shapes had gone, so that the overall effect was of a freckled skin seen in close-up.

'Enough about me,' he said suddenly. 'What about you? Why should Anya be supposed to be so terrified of you?'

'Because she sees in me her nemesis,' said the Painter, stretching easily and glancing sideways at nothing of interest on the rooftops of Whatever. 'She believes that I loathe her to her very soul, and that I will not rest until either I am dead or she is. She cannot understand her own hatred of me – her dread of me – so she tries to rationalize it. Back in Albion, when I was in my self-imposed exile in the wilderness, she persuaded herself that I was the embodiment of the Evil principle, its avatar, and that it was for this reason that she wanted to see me slain. But that wasn't it at all. Her fear of me was born from something far less metaphysical than that.'

'What?'

'I was her antithesis. I had forgiven her the crime that she had perpetrated upon my body. The thought that was too terrible for her mind to countenance was this: my forgiveness. It was something that she would never have been able to emulate herself, not in a million years – look at the way, even before she turned to orthodox crime, she drove Rehan and Reen away from her simply because they'd been right and she'd been wrong in some most trifling matters, and she couldn't stand the possibility that other people might be capable of something that she herself was not. You see, although Anya herself has not the capacity for forgiveness, she nevertheless considers it a virtue – a virtue that she detests, because it is unavailable to her. Whereas, of course, to most of the rest of us it comes fairly easily. With a little practice.'

'Speak for yourself,' muttered Joli. 'Prig.'

'The question remains,' said the Painter, clearing his throat as if he had heard nothing, 'as to why it should be that Reen decided that two of the people that Anya most fears should best be deployed here.'

'Perhaps to drive her away again, should she ever come to Whatever?'

'No. Had that been the case, Reen would have commanded us to make our activities as obvious as possible, so that Anya would hear about them and make a point of avoiding the place.'

'Because Alyss told her to?' said Joli off-handedly.

There was a pause.

'Joli,' said the Painter slowly, 'you do have the most admirable ability to see through to the perfectly obvious, when everyone else has been sidetracked by the surrounding complexities. Yes, of course, Reen must have been working with foresight granted to her by Alyss. Which would mean that Alyss must have known that, for whatever reason, it would simply *happen* that Anya would come here, eventually, and that we would play an important part in whatever then took place.'

'That doesn't explain very much to me,' said Joli dubiously.

'It explains enough,' said the Painter. 'We have no need to enquire further into reasons and possibilities. The outcome of the matter is already laid out quite definitively in the course of the future, so that all we must do is carry on in our preordained ways and see how it all pans out. There'll be time enough afterwards for us to discover the reasons.'

That, thought Joli, *is a very poor philosophy, in my 'umble opinion. The map of the future is never something clearly defined – not even for Alyss. We shape the future, to a greater or lesser extent, by our own actions and inactions. For the first time you have given me a reason for putting some effort into what up until now I'd been regarding as a waste of time. Pah! If we were to just wait and see what 'panned out', the chances are it would never happen. And the other thing that you haven't thought about is that Alyss's motives may not be anything like what you imagine them to be: it may be part of her great plan that we both suffer agonizing deaths. I've died quite often enough, thank you very much, to know that I don't want to do anything to hasten a repeat of the experience. But if I tried to tell you any of this, you self-satisfied lard-bucket, you wouldn't pay me too much attention and, if you did, it'd be only to argue with me. And I'm tired of the sound of your voice, my friend: just plain tired of it . . .*

'I must go,' he said. 'There are many things I have to do before the end of this day.'

'I'm glad we've talked,' said the Painter. He was smiling broadly. 'I'll ring you at your hotel if there are any developments – which I feel in my bones there soon will be. And you – you'd better have this.' He picked up the newspaper from the floor between them. He held out his hand. 'A pen, please.' A few moments later he tore off the relevant strip of paper from the newspaper's edge. 'My number – you can reach me on it always.'

Joli took the scrap and tucked it away in his chest pocket. He stood.

'Until we meet again,' he said. 'Next week – or perhaps before then.'

'Before then,' said the Painter. 'I'm certain.'

His whole face was glowing. Joli winced. If there was one class of people that he couldn't stand – beyond even sodomites and syphilitic tarts – it was enthusiasts. 'You'll not be leaving yourself yet?' he said.

'No,' said the Painter, looking puzzled. 'I never do.'

Now it was Joli's turn to look puzzled.

'Never?'

'No, of course not. How could I venture outside, when I have no clothes to wear?'

'You mean you *live* here?'

'Yes.'

'With . . . ?' And Joli's mind filled with the pictures that Karod had showed him downstairs, projected by the magic lantern. He felt as if something were going to burst inside him.

For the first time in more years than he could remember, he found that there were tears in his eyes.

'Of course,' said the Painter.

4

Anya nodded. She'd been right.

She could have sworn that it had been Joli she'd seen going into the big jewellery shop an hour ago, but she'd decided to wait here on the opposite pavement to confirm her suspicions – or, as she'd admitted to herself, preferably to confound them.

She saw him emerging now onto the pavement. His face was normally a pattern of lines and shapes that looked like a lump of clay a potter had put to one side for later use, but now it was more contorted than she would have believed possible. Something must have happened inside the shop to infuriate the man far beyond the bounds of even his customarily expansive fury.

She melted back into an alley as he hailed a carriage.

What to do? She could flee Whatever at once – that was

what her common sense told her to do, for Joli had proven before that he was indestructible, blessed with invulnerability through the graces of Alyss. Or she could follow Joli to wherever it was that he was going. Or, finally, she could find out what it was inside the jewellery shop that had inflamed him so much.

The jewellery shop was right there opposite her, its broad plate-glass windows and its lavish displays seeming to beckon her.

The jewellery shop it would be, then.

She settled back into the shadows and prepared to wait for nightfall.

There seemed for a moment to be someone waiting alongside her, but there was no one there when she looked and so she gave the matter no further attention.

Chapter Four
DRABSVILL

1

An electric clock was disturbing the darkness, ticking softly every few seconds and giving a laboured wheeze at the end of each minute. Anya could dimly make out its face in the gloom, watching her from the far side of a bare glass counter.

Other than the clock, there was stillness. At this time of night – it was four in the morning – there was barely any motorized traffic in the mercantile part of Whatever, and pedestrians were few. The recently installed electric street lighting cast a disgruntled orange-yellow glow through the windows into the interior of the HOUOSe OF JADeS. Motes of dust hung in the air, silently executing their private orbits. There was the scent of a mausoleum in the air.

Anya stood absolutely motionless, listening intently. She'd broken into the shop by a small side window fully twenty minutes ago, easily circumventing the burglar-alarm system, which was less sophisticated than most of its counterparts in Ernestrad, but since then she'd moved hardly at all, concentrating all her attention on listening in case there might be anyone else still awake in the building. As yet she'd heard nothing, except the clock.

She was certain that the HOUOSe OF JADeS must be more than it seemed to the casual passer-by. All afternoon she'd kept the front of the shop under surveillance, breaking from her observation only for food and to use a nearby public convenience, and she'd noticed that there were two quite distinct categories of customers coming in through the great plate-glass door. First there were those whom one might expect to frequent any expensive jewellery shop anywhere: well-to-do men, often with a veneer of finery in their dress and bearing which suggested that they were not quite as well-to-do as they wished the World to be told; middle-aged women who clearly believed that a new diamond at the throat would more than adequately compensate for a new wrinkle at the waist; married couples of all ages, who were using the displays as a species of free entertainment; and young men, nervous, their suits imperfectly pressed, who had brought the price of a fortnight's dinners to try to buy just one gem, no matter how small and no matter the metal of its setting. But in addition to these stereotypes there had also been a substantial minority of the clientele who fitted none of the patterns. Joli had been one of them: any jeweller would have taken one glance at him and assumed that he was a sneak-thief. There had been several men in their early thirties who had carried their superbly tailored bodies haughtily, the silver rings on their canes shining boldly; always they had paused on the step to glance, as if casually, up and down the crowded pavements before plunging into the shop's lesser light. There had been portly middle-aged men in brown tweed suits with shining seats; the chewed butts of their cigars had been picked up from the pavement by the urchins who had streaked past here on what was obviously a regular foraging mission. These and others had seemed to Anya to be unlikely customers for tiaras and rings, yet each had been met with grave solemnity by the eons-old floor manager and then, with only a couple of exceptions, led away to the unseen depths of the shop by one or other of two slippery-seeming minions.

Was there a treasure trove at the rear of the shop, a special display room where the best of the merchandise could be laid out for a private viewing? There might well be, of course, but Anya doubted if it was for this that the anomalous clients had come.

Did the secret have anything to do with what had so obviously upset Joli?

It was time to start moving.

Pausing just one further moment, for luck, she darted across the main showroom, her feet silent in the lush carpet. Again she froze; again she heard nothing but the clock.

Something soft brushed her leg.

Almost off-balance, she held herself as still as a statue.

Once more the soft touch.

Allowing herself to move her head, Anya glanced downwards. Looking back up at her, its mouth open in a silent miaow, was a small black-and-white cat. So that was why she hadn't been hearing the skittering noises of mice . . .

Letting out a great gust of relief, she squatted down beside it, ruffled it between the ears, ran her fingers along its arching little spine, tickled its chest until its eyes eased closed in luxury, and stabbed it through the heart so precisely that it made not a sound.

Staying hunched down so that her back was beneath the level of the counter-tops, she scuttled in a series of short dashes to the back of the showroom, where she stood up flat against the wall, running the palms of her hands over its flocked surface until she found the moulded frame of a door.

The painted door itself was contoured to give the impression it had been built of wood, but its coldness against her fingertips betrayed that it was metal. In the darkness her eyebrows rose briefly, but then she realized that of course such defences were only to be expected: whatever unknown transactions might be carried out beyond this door, certainly there must also be storage facilities for gems. It was then for the first time that it crossed her mind that, if circumstances worked out that way, she might have a chance of making a substantial profit out of this venture. *Haptan*, she thought, *why did you desert me, back at the Institute? You'd immediately have spotted the secondary benefit of breaking in here! But now it's all up to me to see the obvious . . .*

Like the alarms on the windows, the lock on the door proved under the blind examination of her fingertips to be only rudimentary. She fished in her pocket for one of the wallets she'd purloined earlier in the day, while waiting in the street, pulled a credit card from it, and cautiously set to work, aware that the simplicity of the lock might disguise the fact that it was more securely guarded in other, less obvious ways. Again she wished that Haptan were with her: he'd have thought of that earlier, and would have better known what precautions to take. When they'd done the airport job together, in the years before she'd graduated into politics, he'd managed to thwart a thermal-lance device that she still didn't fully understand . . .

The tab of the lock eased back. The door whispered open, its base rustling over the carpet's pile. She crept into the unknown. She had little idea of the size of the room that she was entering, although its twin trace-lights told her that at least the part closest to her was no more than two and a half metres wide. She hoped that it was merely a corridor, because a broader space seemed somehow more threatening. The blunt clicking of the electric clock was long since lost to the distance, but now she could hear the ponderous, smothered sound of subterranean machinery functioning – perhaps some kind of pumping system for the shop's primitive central-heating network, assuming that it had one. Otherwise . . . otherwise she couldn't guess what it might be, but filed away in her mind the note that, where there was operating machinery, there might also be attendants.

Left hand forward, left knee forward, right hand forward, right knee forward . . . She imagined herself to be like a brown bear, slender after its winter hibernation, padding hungrily through the forest . . .

The top of her head bumped into something solid.

She felt around in front of her and discovered that she had come to another door. Clued by this information, her eyes were able to detect the faintest of lines of light delineating the door's outline. She let her fingers walk up both sides of the door's face, guided by the pale vertical lines, until her left hand encountered a bulky metal construction. The lock.

Now she stood, curling around the protrusion as if it

were a secret object that she wanted no one else to see, cradling it in her hands, running her fingertips and fingernails all over it. The device was approximately cuboidal, about ten centimetres square and jutting about one centimetre from the surface of the door itself; the fact that it projected at all indicated that it was almost certainly not as advanced as some of the security devices she'd coped with during her criminal years in the rat runs of Ernestrad. The contraption had an integral lever that presumably served also as a handle; through cautious experiment she discovered that it pulled outwards, but there was no resistance in its motion, as there would have been if it had been connected to any bolting mechanism. Almost certainly the lock functioned on the basis that the key acted to engage the handle with the gadgetry that operated the bolt. This meant that only the correct key – or something crafted to deceive the tumblers – would make the required connection: this was no task for a credit card.

If she'd had any forethought at all, of course, she'd have bought herself a pencil-torch and a packet of hairpins – she'd seen both on sale during the afternoon in the local corner shops – but of course she'd been feeling too childishly venturesome to bother with the practical details. She was surprised – and vexed – that her training in much more difficult circumstances than these hadn't automatically cut in, taking over her mental processes so that she prepared herself adequately without having to spend too much time thinking about what she was doing. It was a good job that none of her old Ernestrad cronies could see her now: they'd have laughed their socks off at her hapless naïveté.

Enough of such negative thinking. She reviewed the route that she'd followed so far, and tried to imagine what it would be like if she were retreating along it at speed. In the outer shop, of course, there was enough light – coming from this complete gloom it would seem momentarily like daylight to her starved eyes – for her to see what she was doing. Shinning up and through the side window might delay her flight slightly, but not for long: she'd painstakingly removed all the treacherous shards of glass from its frame before making her entry.

It was worth the risk, she thought, to opt for the decidedly unsubtle approach.

Silently she counted two full minutes during which she remained completely still, listening for the slightest noise. Aside from the whumfing beneath her, she still couldn't hear anything. Then she pressed the tip of her dagger forcefully into the gap between door and frame, the wood squeaking slightly against the metal. Not pausing for thought, she jerked the body of the weapon savagely to the left, so that there was an almighty *crrrack!* as the wood splintered and the entire square section into which the locking device had been built shot out of its moorings and tumbled across the carpeted floor.

The door, deprived of its lock, opened smoothly enough.

Peering through the gap she saw a smallish reception room, perhaps a dozen metres long and four metres wide. In its roof was a domed skylight, through which moonlight was shining to give indistinct illumination to the paintings on the walls and to the occasional tables and upright chairs spread casually around.

And to the man who was sitting in one of those chairs, smoking a cigarette and looking directly back at her.

She dropped into a half-crouch, the muscles in her legs preparing for the spring, her knife up by her bared teeth . . .

'Wait!' he said coolly.

. . . but she was leaping before her brain had had the time to translate the word. Her dagger swung in a short, vicious arc, its blade a liquid smear in the moonlight as it sped towards his throat . . .

Except that he wasn't there any longer.

Instead, he was sitting on one of the other chairs, tapping off his cigarette ash into the pewter bowl at the top of an oaken smokers' companion.

She regained her balance almost instantly and spun on

the balls of her feet, adjusting her grip on her knife, so that her thumb was along the centre of its blade's flat, positioned for a harsh upwards stab into the belly.

'Please wait,' he repeated, holding his hand up to stay her. 'I wouldn't wish to have to harm you. I've been expecting you for some time now.'

'Who are you?' she hissed.

'The tender of the machine.'

She jerked the thumb of her free hand towards the floor and raised an eyebrow questioningly.

'No.' He smiled, as if at a child who has just made an obvious but understandable error. 'Nothing so mundane as the central-heating system. The machine that I look after is much more important and also much more subtle than that. I build it myself, you see, each night, so that it can serve my master's aesthetic sense – no, better I say that I *help* build it, for my clumsy mortal fingers are guided by the master himself, to ensure that the machine perfectly fulfils his requirements.'

She recognized him, now: he'd been one of the two assistants whose task it was to escort the atypical-seeming customers away from the front of the shop. It might be worth keeping him alive a little longer than was strictly necessary: although she couldn't risk the racket involved should she try to force him to tell her what the shop's secret was, he might nevertheless do so of his own accord. Clearly he was no ordinary staff-member, who'd have scurried to the nearest alarm bell as soon as he'd heard the din she'd made smashing open the lock. Besides, there was the curious confidence of the way that he'd said he'd been expecting her . . .

She pretended to relax, straightening up her stance and letting her right hand fall to her side, although she retained the killing grip on the knife.

'You must know that I haven't the first idea what you're talking about,' she said.

'Of course you haven't. To be honest with you, I understand only part of it myself. Suffice it to say that I know that my master believes that it will assist his purposes if I show you the machine, and he has required me to offer you every courtesy towards that end; in addition, he has supplied me with certain defences, one of which, as you've seen, has already demonstrated its usefulness. But as to the why of all this, then I'm as much in the dark as you are. Perhaps we shall find out together, if that is my master's wish.'

'Who is this "master" of yours?'

'You have felt his presence ever since he became a part of this World; you almost saw him earlier today, when you were lurking in the alleyway opposite, imagining yourself to be unobserved. He has given me no name for himself, yet . . .'

'I know his name,' said Anya with complete certainty. 'It's Nadar.' She recalled the scene at Starveling-stage, as well as the tales that Reen and her mother had told her in her youth of the man who had striven against her nominal father. Syor she had seen transforming herself into one of the principles underlying the World; she had 'given her gift' – the gift of being – to the man destined to be her balancing, complementary principle, and she had named him as Nadar. It was inevitable that Anya should come in some way to be associated with him – with the man who, in an earlier life, she'd begun to consider as her real father . . .

And then she shook her head confusedly. How had this conviction as to the 'master's' true identity established itself with such immediacy in her mind? This little man could have elected to serve any one of a number of masters, none of them known to her . . . or perhaps familiar to her, after all. Joli might have observed her at the same time as she'd been watching him: the little shit had often shown himself to be astonishingly more perceptive than he'd seemed. And then there was . . . but her heart refused to allow her mind to contemplate the name. Yet for all this logic she could find in herself not the slightest genuine doubt that it was Nadar of whom the little assistant was talking.

'I will take your word for it,' the man was saying. 'It

doesn't matter to me what he's called. In his own good time he will doubtless confirm his name to me. Or otherwise. It is . . . unwise to predict his decisions.'

'I can imagine. Where is this machine of yours?'

He got to his feet, regretfully stubbing out his cigarette in the bowl before it was half-way smoked. 'Perhaps you would be good enough to follow me,' he said, as if she were a respected customer. However, he added: 'Please do not attempt to stab me in the back. As you will have gathered, it would be a complete waste of your own time, and would harm me not at all. Nevertheless, a part of me would be offended by your betrayal of my trust in you.'

'I give you my promise,' said Anya formally, inconspicuously failing to return the dirk to her belt. Magical defences or no magical defences, she reckoned she could if need be get him with an uppercut punch in the base of the back, severing his spine and . . .

She touched him on the arm as he moved past her.

'But tell me,' she said. 'What is your own name?'

'Karod,' he replied. 'It's of no importance.'

'A name is always of importance,' she said tartly.

'As you say.'

He led her further towards the rear, shining a pocket flashlight ahead of them. Anya was amazed by how far there was to go. From the front the shop looked of little more than medium size, but clearly it ran back for the full depth of a city block. After they'd gone down a further corridor which she guessed was much like the one she'd crawled through in the blackness they came into another small reception room, this time circular, with curved couches in place of the upright chairs. Once again moonlight shone down from above. The pictures on the walls, she gathered from the partial glimpses she had of them, were here more overtly erotic, with people coupling in configurations distorted so that the genital organs could be more clearly visible. *It's a whorehouse!* she thought. *That's the secret of the HOUOSe OF JADeS! I should have guessed it from the name of the place!* Karod stepped to one of the paintings and, ignoring the curves of engorged flesh only centimetres from his nose, tilted the frame sideways by a carefully measured amount. There was a *click* of engaging machinery and then, with a complacent hum, a large rectangular section of the wall swivelled backwards. The light it revealed was crystal-bright, dazzling Anya for several seconds until her eyes accommodated to it – several seconds during which her sole thought was of how vulnerable she was. But when her vision finally returned properly to her she could see that Karod was ignoring her completely: his back towards her, he was at the foot of a short, shallow flight of stone steps beyond the wall, standing in front of a colossally massive door, spotlit from above, in whose centre was set a three-handled lock. This Karod was manipulating precisely, first an exact distance in one direction and then, after only a moment's hesitation, a different but again meticulously gauged distance the opposite way. As Anya came down the steps he moved back, turning to smile at her.

'There's always a short delay,' he said, 'before the safe will open itself.'

Not even a time-lock, Anya was thinking. *If I end up staying a while in Whatever I'm going to be able to have a field day.*

'My master alters perceptions,' said Karod while they were waiting. 'He does so in many ways, of course, some of which are more subtle than others: he is the god that comes to people's hearts when they seek reasons for the deeds they have done. You have doubtless spoken with him many times in your life, yet never known that you were doing so.'

Anya said nothing. It was a folly to seek explanations for one's actions.

'Here,' Karod continued after a moment, 'he has worked his powers to more tangible effect. Each night the most trusted members of the management strip the shelves and cases in the shop of their valuables and bring them back here for safe-keeping. They put them in neatly labelled boxes, and store them in this safe, all in perfect order for ease of withdrawal in the morning. Then they depart, secure in the knowledge of what they've done. Yet it's an ill placed confidence, for that's not what they've done at all. Instead, they've repositioned all of the jewels precisely in their proper places, reassembling the machine that I first created under my master's supervision.'

The door gave a twitch. The lock had disengaged itself.

Karod touched a finger to the door's lip. Hidden machinery strained and the door opened, pivoting on a central axis.

Anya gasped.

'You are welcome to enter,' said Karod demurely. 'My master instructed me to receive you in his name.'

The interior of the vast safe was made up of a radiant assemblage of more jewels than Anya could ever have believed there existed in all the World. They shone with a supernatural light of their own, a pulsing brilliance made up of more colours than the eye knows, a many-shafted beacon that was cold and yet shone with infinite power. The uncountable facets and knife-sharp edges of the gems blended to form an impossibly intricate pattern of gleams and lines that yet seemed perfectly united into a single, quite simple totality. There were stones of all different sizes and hues – from fist-large sapphires to tiny solitaires to egg-sized rubies – and yet it was hard to focus her eyes so that she could see them as such: instead they were just a single amorphous mass, so that her senses told her that she could reach out a hand and plunge it inward and feel the conglomerate close frigidly and smoothly around her flesh. And the mass was moving, all of its inseparable components performing precise staccato rotations, each meshing perfectly with its neighbours so that there was no sense of any intervening boundary between them.

'So this is your machine,' she breathed at last.

'My master's machine,' Karod corrected courteously. 'Yes.'

She gazed at it for several further minutes. She felt as if it were drawing her inwards towards it, as if it wished to absorb her into its completeness, and she knew that with all her soul she *wanted* to be drawn, wanted to unite herself with the moving crystals, so that through becoming one of them she would become the whole. Hesitantly she took a step forwards.

'As I said, my master bids you welcome.'

She paused.

'This machine,' she said, forcing the words between her lips. 'It has a function?'

'It serves my master's purpose,' said Karod. 'It is more than simply a machine, of course.'

'Then what is it?'

'Its full nature should not be of any importance to you: surely it is sufficient that it has been given to you to look on it.'

'That is *in*sufficient. Its full nature *is* of importance to me. The machine is seeking me, wooing me, unclothing me. It is telling me that I have spent all of my lifetime, conversely, seeking *it*, yet not knowing that this was so.' She looked sideways at Karod's face; half of it was in shadow and the other half was a throng of colours, as if the two were unrelated, belonging to different worlds. 'I do not know why your machine wishes to convince me of this, because I do not think that it is telling the truth. Or not the whole truth. So, you see, I already disbelieve it in part. If you fail to try to explain to me the nature of the machine, then I shall disbelieve it entirely.'

The half of Karod's face that still seemed to be human, the shaded half, twisted reluctantly.

'My master did not give me instruc . . .' he began.

'Then your master is not omniscient,' said Anya softly, feeling her ability to resist the call of the machine growing stronger. Her emotions and her senses were still urging her to accept its embrace, yet her intellect was coolly levering against them. 'But I am sure that he would wish you to try to reveal the machine's mysteries to me.'

With a sudden jolt Karod's face lost its indecision.

'Yes,' he said. 'You're right. My master has spoken within me. You're speaking the truth. Those are indeed his desires. Let me tell you.'

He pursed his lips and half-closed his eyes.

'The World,' he said, 'is only a part of a greater whole.'

'A large part,' said Anya.

'No, an infinitesimally small part – smaller than a grain of dust, or the mote in an ant's eye – far, far smaller than that.'

'But we are told that the World is huge,' she protested.

'It *is* huge. It stretches further even than from the north of Albion to the south of Intheria. I have travelled many of those kilometres in my time, and I know how long they are.'

'That is but a minute fraction of the World,' said Karod sadly. 'Your mind is unprepared for these things. You will not let me explain them to you, translate them into terms that might make sense to you.'

'Then tell me in your own terms,' she said stubbornly. 'I won't interrupt you any further. Perhaps your master will . . . alter my perceptions in such a way that I can understand what you're talking about.'

He breathed a sigh of relief.

Then he talked to her of how the World was only an eye into the Universe – one of countless similar eyes, all of which saw the same Universe and the same events, and yet all of which saw different things than did all the other eyes. And he told her of how the visions of the billions of eyes combined to form a single vision, a complete truth, and of how that was called the Universe. And he told her of how there were many complete truths, and that each of them was also called a universe, and that all of the myriad universes co-existed but were in eternal isolation from each other, because their complete truths could exist only when separated. And he told her of the way in which the complete truths could be viewed all at once by the original creators, whose own complete truth was so great that it could contain an infinity of others and yet not lose its own integrity. And he told her of how this greatest of all the complete truths was called the polycosmos, and that the machine in the safe which he had built under his master's tutelage was likewise the polycosmos.

'You mean it's a model,' said Anya, interrupting despite her promise.

He didn't seem offended by her interjection; instead he looked as if he'd been expecting it.

'No,' he said. 'It isn't a model. It *is* the polycosmos. All of its parts are connected precisely with all of their corresponding parts in the greater polycosmos, so that the two are in a state of complete identity. You can't disturb the polycosmos without also disturbing the machine, and the converse is equally true.'

'And where is the World in all this?' said Anya, gesturing towards the array of brilliance with something approaching disdain. She was no longer feeling the full power of its attraction.

'You can't see the World there, Anya,' replied Karod. 'Neither of us can. I can't see it because it's too small. And you – you cannot see it because it is too large.'

'These are merely jewels,' she said contemptuously. She'd never seen so many gemstones all together at once, and she was awed by the complexity of the hidden gadgetry that must have been constructed to keep them all moving like this, but she could no longer understand how it was that she'd been initially so humbled in the sight of them. The great disorganized heap of crystal possessed no radiance beyond the countless sparkling reflections of the light-bulbs overhead. It was the gems' movement and the brightness of the spotlights that created the illusion of life. There was a despot's ransom there, all the wealth that a mortal could imagine – but nothing more.

' "Merely"?' said Karod wryly.

'Look,' said Anya crisply. She reached out and plucked one of the stones, a blood-coloured ruby, from the pile, and held it up to him on her palm. 'In this model' – she spoke the word scornfully – 'that you've created of your wild fantasies, is this perhaps the World?'

'Yes,' he said, 'if that is what you would want it to be.'

'And this?' She seized another gem. 'And this? And this? And *this*?'

'All of them. Each of them is the World. If that is what you desire.'

The machine's movements were becoming disjointed, the rotating jewels grating against each other as they tried to compensate for the ones that Anya had yanked away. The entire pile of stones seemed to be heaving, as if it were trying to adopt some new configuration that would allow it to continue operating as smoothly and perfectly as before.

Trying but failing.

'And this? And this? And this?' Anya was repeating crazily, grabbing more and more of the stones, stashing them away in her pockets, scattering discarded wallets in a heap on the floor around her feet. 'And this? And this?'

The protesting noises of the machine were now becoming far too loud to ignore. The entire vast safe was rocking from side to side as it attempted to contain the stress of the disruption. The floor was creaking and straining beneath their feet. Smoke was pouring out of the safe's doorway. Anya was screaming at Karod, and yet he remained perfectly passive, his mouth curled very slightly in the beginnings of a smile.

When he eventually spoke, his voice was as quiet as a puff of air, and yet through the din she heard his words perfectly distinctly.

'Thank you,' he said. 'You have fulfilled my master's purpose. You may keep two of the gems if you wish – any two, because they will be the right two. The remainder you must return to me of your own free will – which you will find yourself unable to disobey. And then you must leave me and go about your own purposes, so that I may rebuild my master's machine in peace.'

2

Anya found herself standing in front of a huge kidney-shaped desk without any very clear idea of how she'd come to be there; there were bright lights in sconces around the walls. She recalled breaking into the HOUOSe OF JADeS, and of manipulating her way through a door and then down a corridor until she came to another door, the lock of which she'd had to shatter, but thereafter there was a hazy interruption in her memory, as if a bank of fog lay over a whole section of the map of her recent past. She knew without being able to picture the scene that she'd come across a vast hoard of precious stones, and that she'd seized scores of them; there was a hysterical joy associated with that knowledge, but the emotion was not attached to anything definable. She patted her pockets, knowing as she did so that all she'd find in them were strangers' wallets, as before, and . . .

Oh. What was this?

She turfed out a wallet from her right-hand breeches pocket and discovered, tangled into the loose ends of thread at the bottom, two small jewels, one a pale grey and the other a hazy blue. They seemed to be stuck together somehow, and for a couple of moments she wrestled with them, trying to wrench them apart.

Still holding the bonded stones, she looked around her. There was no one to be seen in the opulence of her surroundings. The large paintings on the wall were of such a pornographic explicitness that their effect on her was more scientific than erotic. A broad, curving flight of stairs led up from the room where she was to less brightly lit regions above.

She glanced back at the objects in her hand. Correction: object. The two stones had somehow managed to coalesce into a single gem, no larger than each of the other two had been. Startled, she held it up to the light to examine its colour: the grey and the sea-blue were streaked together, so that it was hard to tell which of them was the stone's primary shade.

A stone as marred as this was worthless, of course.

She chucked it carelessly to one side and headed for the stairs.

3

Snores were coming from behind some of the doors along the corridor, but from most there was silence. Anya, listening for a few seconds at each of them as she progressed quietly down the corridor, on two occasions heard the unmistakable sounds of sexual activity. At the far end of the passage there was a wall with a small square window near the ceiling that looked out on muted street lighting. Her back to the wall, the fingers of her free hand feeling the coarse linen of the covering, she looked along the length of the corridor down which she'd come. It was curved slightly, so that she couldn't quite make out the landing, the dim lights on which provided the main source of illumination here. The carpet was flecked cream. Plain wainscoting and pelmets were painted in gold; the walls' covering was of rough-woven bleached cloth. There were sconces here and there along the walls bearing artificial candles with bulbs shaped like stylized flames. The effect would be hideous when the bulbs were lit, but in the gloom it all looked rather splendid: cosily luxurious.

Still she'd seen nothing out of the ordinary, nothing that could have accounted for Joli's fury. It looked as if the entire endeavour of breaking in here had been a complete waste of time: she'd have been better off following Joli to wherever it was that he'd been going, and tormenting information out of the little man.

She was bracing herself to get moving, contemplating picking up a few of the paintings from the walls on her retreat so that at least she'd have something to show for the enterprise, when she heard an odd snuffling grunt. Then she saw, trotting around the corridor's curve towards her, the pig.

A shock ran all through her. If the pig was here, Ngur couldn't be far away. Ngur, the one whom she tried never to think too hard about, not since . . .

The animal stopped as soon as it caught sight of her. Showing no signs of fear, it plopped down onto its haunches and cocked its head to one side, looking at her as if it were laughing silently to itself.

Anya, instantly infuriated by its seeming complacency, caught herself in the act of throwing a dagger underhand at the beast: it would be insanity to waste a valuable weapon on a dumb animal when soon, surely, she must confront its master.

The two hesitated, gazing at each other, neither making the first move, for a couple of minutes. *I'm afraid of it, which is idiotic*, thought Anya. She pushed herself away from the wall, gave the pig a forced smile, and set off towards it.

The pig suddenly became alert. It shifted to one side, as if readying itself to cut her off.

Anya paused, the fear that she'd succeeded in quelling returning with a rush. 'What's the matter?' she said foolishly.

The pig gave no indication that it understood her words. It continued to hold itself half-tilted off its haunches, clearly ready to move to intercept her.

'Are you trying to keep me here?' She looked at the dagger in her hand. Perhaps, after all . . .

The pig got to its feet and stood facing directly towards her, its hindquarters swaying from side to side. She was abruptly conscious of how weighty the animal was: she recalled how, in an earlier lifetime of hers, the bulk of the pig had burdened the thick board to which the beast had been nailed. A trickle of cold fear ran down her spine as she suddenly wondered if the animal in front of her had any recollection of the doings of that day. Like Joli, the pig had met its death at her instruction, and yet, again like Joli, still it lived, defying her.

She must have spoken her thoughts aloud, because a voice responded to them: 'It was not my porcine friend that your priestesses tormented, Anya.'

Anya looked up, startled, dragging her eyes away from the pig's almost hypnotic gaze. A few metres away, not far behind the pig, the blind Painter was standing easily, rocking on the balls of his feet, his hands behind his back, so that he looked like a naked traffic policeman waiting for a response from a recalcitrant driver.

'I knew that, wherever this swine was, you couldn't be very far away,' she said, trying to inject an element of calmness into a voice that was in great danger of cracking.

'What brings the two of you so very far from Albion? Run out of rocks to deface?'

The Painter just smiled, moving his arms around to fold them in front of his chest. The darkened scabs where his eyes had been seemed, unnervingly, to be subjecting her to a close examination. She noticed that his hair had been cropped shorter than when last she'd seen him; he'd put on a little weight as well. *A case of the master growing to be more like his beast*, she thought acidly. *How fitting that he's naked.*

She took another half-pace forwards. Neither the Painter nor the pig made the slightest move, yet she felt as if they had – as if they were beginning to creep towards her, preparing for the kill. *This is silly*, she thought. *I'm armed with a dagger and a sword, and I can move twice as fast as either of them. I was always a better fighter than my husband – I could best him when I was blindfold, rather than the other way around. So what have I got to be so bloody frightened about?* And yet still she couldn't find it in herself to make the first commitment to a fray.

He startled her by speaking without warning.

'Your life has become very dull and drab, has it not, Anya?' he said conversationally. 'You've travelled a long way since the time every move that you made was accompanied by pageantry, by riotous colours, by brazen sounds. The Sun shines in the skies, but it doesn't seem to have any light to shed on you.'

She laughed. For a blind man to be speaking to her of sunshine! 'I see the World nowadays more vividly than I've done before in any of my previous incarnations,' she said at last. 'The colours of a person's life aren't measured in terms of the extravagance surrounding them. Since I left Albion I've felt as if the blood coursing through my veins were that of a sixteen-year-old.'

He raised his skimpy eyebrows at her.

'You misunderstand me,' he said. 'The pageantry I was referring to wasn't the stale pomp and celebration with which you surrounded yourself once you'd installed us both in Starveling and begun to impose your vengeful will on our people . . .'

'I did not impose my will on my people,' she snapped. 'They begged me to rule them. I was a servant of my people. There was nothing I would not have done to improve their lot.'

'Now is not the time for me to puncture your illusions,' said the Painter softly. 'Please let me continue with what I was saying.'

She felt chastened – and appalled at herself that she felt so. She nodded her acquiescence.

'I was talking rather of the natural pageantry that was within you when first I saw you,' he said. 'I don't know how long you'd been in the forests and the wildlands with your people – and they *were* your people then – when I met you, but I can remember the way that, grubby face and runny nose and filthy clothes and all, you appeared to be ringed by brightness, so that you seemed to leave a trail of wraithlike coloured afterimages behind you whenever you moved. Your eyes were alive, in a way that they soon stopped being. There was a grace in the way that your body moved – oh, I'm not saying that there isn't now, but it's not a grace born of internal dignity any longer. Now the grace that you have is sinister, every motion that you make seeming duplicitous, deceptive, underhand . . .'

'And I'm enjoying the most exciting time of any of my lives,' she said firmly.

'Are you? Are you indeed?' He sighed. 'You discovered that there was an exhilaration in battle, in endangering your life and those of others in the pursuit of an end that seemed sufficiently desirable to you to make the sacrifice worthwhile. In a way, I felt much of the same exuberance myself, when I was waging battle against you. But once both of us had won our different prizes, which were really the same prize – the peace and security of the country which we both in our opposing ways loved – I learnt to elicit the same exhilaration from other, less savage, things. That was something, alas, that you could never accustom yourself to, Anya.'

'I do not enjoy the sight of death or suffering,' she said stubbornly. 'I take measures to ensure desirable outcomes, that's all. I have learnt to steel myself against the consequences of some of the measures it is important that I take. It does not please me to spill blood.'

'It probably doesn't much, now,' he said, 'but still you keep on trying it, don't you? And it never, ever works any more, does it?'

'I'm alive,' she said. 'Despite all the odds against me, I'm still alive. How many people could boast that they had survived despite having had sentence of death passed on them by a god?'

'And how many are dead, for you to be alive?'

'They got in my way – I couldn't help it that they had to die. I wasn't the one who engineered the circumstances in which there was no choice left for me but to take their lives, was I? I didn't condemn myself to death, did I? All I did was take stern measures in the interests of my own self-preservation, which I considered to be paramount. Wouldn't you have done the same?'

'Once upon a time I might have,' he admitted. 'But not now. My own life simply isn't that important, I've come to realize – neither to me nor to my species as a whole.'

'And what makes you think that the lives I've taken were of any importance to their owners or to the rest of humankind? They were all trivial little people, who knew nothing of glory. The World will rub along very much as it always has without them, thank you very much! You trap yourself in your own words, old enemy: if *my* life is of such little importance, if *your* life is of such little importance, what precisely was so thunderingly important about *theirs*?'

'Choice.'

'You . . .'

'You gave them no choice. Without any knowledge of the rich colours they could see in their lives, you robbed them of those lives – and of the colours. But your acts of theft didn't bring you the colours for yourself, didn't add them to your own life: instead they were just wasted, lost to the World. Nowadays you don't leave multicoloured afterimages wherever you go: you cast a monochrome shadow.'

'Perhaps I see colours where you can't,' she said. 'I have my eyes, still.'

'I see more . . .' he began.

The dagger took him in the belly, the impact sending a jolt throughout his entire body, stiffening his limbs crazily. For a moment it looked as if he were going to topple over backwards, but an instinctive movement of his feet kept him upright. His face was looking down in astonishment and consternation at the obscene protrusion of the hilt from his flesh. His arm moving as if powered by clockwork, he caught hold of the dagger and tugged it out of himself, releasing a flood of blood. His face twitched from the pain, and a bright red droplet squirmed from the corner of his mouth.

'I had not expected this to be a part of the scheme,' he said with difficulty. He almost smiled, as if a novel thought had just struck him. 'Perhaps I was wrong about the importance of my being here. Perhaps my presence is merely ancillary to that of my dumb friend.'

'Scheme?' she said, sword drawn, its point directed unwaveringly towards the pig, although the animal was simply looking on with apparently mild interest, unperturbed by the agonies of its master. 'What scheme are you talking about?'

There was more blood coming from his mouth now. His whole body seemed somehow to have lost its purpose. He threw the bloodstained dagger, hilt-first, so that it landed on the carpet at her feet.

'What scheme?' she insisted, wondering whether to stoop for the weapon or if this was a trap.

'Everything we do, you and I, is surely a part of a scheme,' he said, his voice thick with blood. He had his hand over the wound in his belly, but it didn't seem to be doing much to assuage the bleeding. 'I can see only the tiniest portion of that scheme, and you can't see any. It's funny' – he shook his head with painful slowness – 'but whatever it is that was bequeathed to me by the love I once had for you wishes that I could help you see more of the scheme.' He was on his knees now. 'To see more of the colours.'

'You're drivelling,' she said scornfully. 'Drivelling your way to your death.'

'Perhaps I am,' he conceded mildly, 'and I'm making a filthy mess on this carpet for the housemaids to clean. I hope they can get the stains out, because it would be a shame . . . to waste . . . such a fine . . . carpet.'

She grabbed the dagger up from her ankles and threw it underarm at his face, at the accursed mouth that it seemed she could never silence. The blade shot between his teeth and into the back of his mouth.

He lurched and fell over sideways, his left arm falling in front of his face in a grotesque parody of an attempt to defend himself.

She sprang forwards and knelt beside him, both to retrieve the dagger and to check that he was indeed dead.

There were tears in her eyes.

Tears of fury, she told herself angrily.

She wiped the blade carefully on the thigh of her breeches, resigning herself to the stickiness of her fingers.

The pig came across and stood beside her, looking impassively at the wreckage of its master's face. Then it turned towards her, and still it seemed to be laughing at her.

She raised the dagger to stab at it, but the beast was gone.

4

Alyss, drifting among the glittering baubles of the universes that formed the polycosmos, saw the hard demarcation that suddenly sprang up around two of them, clearly defining them as separate from the others, isolated.

She had expected that this would happen – indeed, had known it with what came as close to certainty as the workings of the polycosmos would allow – and yet the confirmation of her knowledge still depressed her. She watched how the other bright existences jostled and shoved as they strove to shun the abnormal pairing.

So that was it. It was final, then. She had hoped that

somehow the impossibly improbable might have happened, that the effects of the fusion of the two othernesses might have been absorbed, damped down, by the other myriad quirks of chance that guided the polycosmos, so that little would have been changed by the unnatural union. It had been a foolish hope, of the type that she had often castigated mortals for sustaining.

From here on the new universe would be on its own, unaccompanied by othernesses. Unlike the rest, which were still infinitely interconnected through the polycosmos, it was a solitary.

She drew what passed for a sigh, and thought of what the future was going to be like for the mortals who dwelt in the place that Syor had brought into existence. There would be no afterlives, no havens for their souls, no rebirths in other universes; Syor's empire would be a closed system, where death would be a final punctuation mark rather than merely a pause in an infinite flow of the soul through the infinitude of different worlds; there would no longer be the possibility, even, of rebirth in the sense that she had always observed it, but instead only a reappearance in the same limited bubble of existence.

From what she had seen of the passage of souls through the polycosmos, however, she wasn't certain that this loss was necessarily any punishment – on the contrary, the new situation could be no worse than the old, and might well be better. What she did regret, on the mortals' behalf, was that they were also losing their dreamlands.

Since the development had now followed its predicted course, it was time for her to ensure that a certain series of incidents that might be important for the future history of Syor's universe was set in train. Statistically there was almost a complete certainty that those incidents would come to pass without any intervention on her part, but she had to make certain. Otherwise Anya would remain forever at large, and some of those whom Alyss loved most greatly (although 'love' was, of course, quite the wrong word to use) would be lost to existence altogether.

Spreading her wings – or the currents of abstract energy

that she'd decided for the moment to think of as wings, because she thought the notion a pretty one – she spoke directly into Anya's mind.

Remember the flawed jewel, she said, *the one that you cast away so lightly. It bears the future of the World. If you possess that jewel once more, then it will be the whole of the World that you'll have in your grasp.*

She felt Anya's response to her message, and she permitted herself a sly smile. It had been a lie, and she was always enchanted by her own skill in lying. The fact that the lie was an essential one, and that it had been told to assist a good purpose, detracted not one iota from her pleasure.

Turning away from the new universe for a moment, she looked out at all the other baubles of the polycosmos. There was one among them whose bright colour caught her eye, and on a whim she turned her thought-course towards it.

5

Joli sat bolt upright in bed, his head feeling as if there were a battle raging inside it. He looked around him at the crumpled sheets, the stained pillows (why wouldn't the sodomites and syphilitic tarts in this five-star dump even change his bedding these days?), the bottle that had fallen over and spilt purple-brown tarry rum into the pale-blue carpet, the half-open door leading into the en suite bathroom that it didn't do to think about too much, and the clothes piled in a heap on the floor, and wondered if it wasn't about time that he swallowed his pride and introduced a woman into his life. In his head he started to compose an advertisement that perhaps he might put in a newsagent's window, but the clangour of battle was too distracting and he lost his train of thought in the midst of an internal wrangle over the relative merits of nymphomania and domesticity.

He looked out of the window, screwing up his eyes. Dawn. His least favourite time of day. Worse, even, than morning, noon, afternoon, evening and night. He had always avoided dawn like the plague, convinced that the sickly greenish light of the rising sun afflicted the body with wasting diseases. Diseases like syphilis, for example. It was not so much hypothesis as a proven fact that the tarts of Whatever – indeed, of all Intheria – were so avaricious that they kept at it until well after dawn, taking on customer after customer.

He was too old for the Service, that was the trouble – too old even to remember precisely what the Service *was*, come to think of it. He should never have accepted this last assignment, but Reen herself had called him in. 'Joli, you fine fellow,' she'd said. 'Here's a challenge that all our younger agents – well, they just wouldn't be up to it. That's why I'm begging with you – pleading with you – to take it on. For the love of the Service. For the love of' – and here she'd given a particularly stomach-churning gratuitous simper, her eyelashes batting as if they were likely to take off – 'me.'

Well, it hadn't been exactly like that. But near enough.

The noise that had woken him came again.

Surprised, he looked towards the door. There seemed to be someone shuffling against it, as if they were trying to knock but had their hands full.

Joli looked again at his grease-stained pillowcases and a torrent of optimism came into his eyes.

'Just coming!' he cried, falling out of bed. Congratulating himself on the usefulness of his habit of retaining his socks and underclothes for sleep, he trotted towards the door. 'Welcome!' he said, throwing it open.

The pig lurched into the room. It looked exhausted, as if it had run a long way.

'Oh,' said Joli. 'You.'

The pig looked up at him with tired, reproachful eyes. It settled itself down on its side, its flanks heaving.

'Your master never pauses to think about other people's convenience when he picks his times for calling, does he?'

The pig said nothing.

Joli stuck his head out into the corridor and looked

briskly one way and the other. There was no sign of the Painter – only a chambermaid who, on seeing his grainy chin and his malevolent eyes, dropped her brushes and fled.

'Has he got stuck in the lift, or something?' he demanded, turning back into the room. After a few moments he added: 'I know you can talk freely when you want to. You just never do so when I'm around.'

Something different about the appearance of the pig caught his attention. Straining his muscles, he squatted down beside its panting form. There were browning stains on its two front trotters, and similar, lighter marks on its shoulder and snout, as if it had been in contact with . . .

'Blood!' snapped Joli. 'Your own? No, not your own' – grabbing a trotter and swiftly examining it – 'so it must be someone else's. Ah, the marvels of logic. And the only person I can think of right now is your master. Am I right?'

The pig didn't respond at all, but it seemed to Joli as if it had nodded confirmation to him.

'Your master is injured – no, more likely he's dead. Yes, certainly he's dead or, shagged out as you are, you'd be trying to drag me to wherever he is. But, if he's dead, what was the point in your coming here at all?'

While still speaking, Joli was now moving quickly round the room, stepping into one set of clothes while throwing the rest into a leather suitcase he'd dragged out from underneath the bed. 'You came here to warn me, that must be it. Did the Painter, noble in his dying hour – he always was a noble bastard, the smug old turd – did he say: "Prithee hearken close to me, o leal and stalwart pig. I command thee to go and give warning to the finest man it was ever my privilege to meet in the World"? Was that the gist of it, eh?'

The pig gave a cough.

'You're not going to upchuck on the carpet, are you? If so, the corner I always use is that one over there. So: your master, the late lamented Painter, may Syor bless his fertile memory, sent you here to tell me: "Joli, me old mate, time you was a flitting onward, 'cos I've been snuffed and Anya reckons it's your turn next." Was that . . . ? Ah.'

Half-way into a pair of trousers, Joli froze, staring at the animal.

'It *was* Anya, wasn't it? Must have been. Unless he finally had a heart attack taking on a couple of whores too many. No: that wouldn't explain the blood. So, seeing as it's Anya . . .'

He redoubled his speed of packing, again thanking his foresight in travelling light: no bloody toothbrush to worry about. 'Will you be coming with me?' he asked. 'I can't promise you a restful life, of course, nor necessarily a very long one, but it ought to be pretty adventurous – while it lasts. Ideal for a pig seeking to broaden its horizons through foreign travel, you know. See the World and die.'

Ready to go, he looked down at the pig.

'No, you'll be happier where you are, getting a bit of a rest after your ordeal. You just wait here until one of the bloody tarts that're supposed to clean this place comes along, and get your old hypnotic charms working, eh? I'm sure she'll give you a good home. Answer to a maiden's prayer, you are. Or whatever they have in this ratfart country that approximates to maidens. Word of advice for you, though, my old chum: don't turn your back on the blokes.'

The pig coughed again, and Joli bent down to look at it worriedly. 'Not sickening for anything, are you?'

By way of answer the animal spat out a single jewel.

Joli picked the stone up and wiped the saliva off it on his waistcoat. Holding it up to the light, he scrutinized it carefully with the air of someone who knew nothing whatsoever about lapidary work. 'A pretty enough gewgaw,' he said. 'I don't think the best precious stones are supposed to have mixed colours like this, but it still ought to be worth a few bob if ever I need it. Nicked it from the HOUOSe OF JADeS, did you? Just as a little present for your master's old bosom buddy? A poignant thought, my friend, and one that I'll treasure until the end of my days. Which will be a little too soon for my preference unless I bugger off out of here fast.'

Stuffing the gem into his pocket, he picked up his case and dashed out into the corridor. The lift – the lift might be a trap, but he wasn't about to tackle the stairs on an empty stomach. He pressed the 'call' button frenziedly, and watched as the illuminated numbers overhead danced.

With a whoosh the doors opened in front of him. The car was empty, and he hurled his case and himself into it and stabbed at the button for the basement. The underground car-park: that was his best bet. All the rich sodomites staying in this dump kept their limousines there (he mouthed the word 'limousine' with silent, relished loathing): better to ride for free than to try and get hold of a taxi, especially when you weren't certain how far your money would take you.

He pounded gently on the wall of the lift with the side of his fist. Come on, *come on*!

To his fury, the car slowed as it came to the ground floor. He leapt to the twin doors and pressed against their polished-steel surfaces with his palms, trying to keep them from opening. Anya was definitely waiting for him out there – v-e-r-y d-e-f-i-n-i-t-e-l-y.

A young man dressed in the dapper uniform of the hotel was standing outside the lift, looking at him in perplexity.

'I'm so sorry, sir,' he said hesitantly. 'They didn't tell me they'd 'phoned up to your suite to tell you it had arrived.'

'Tell me bloody *what* had arrived?' Joli half-screamed, throwing his eyes all over the lobby in search of Anya. 'You haven't seen any blonde females around, have you, covered in edged weapons and other people's blood?'

'Eh, no, sir,' said the man, holding out a hand to stop the doors, which were starting to attempt to close. 'No one like that. Would you like your telex now?'

'What effing telex?'

'The one that they 'phoned up to your room about, sir.'

'Give me, give me, give me!' Joli scrabbled at the air with his clawlike hand. 'If you don't give it to me at once you'll be wishing you still had balls left for me to hack off. Give!'

'Er – certainly sir.'

As soon as he had the sheet of paper in his hand, Joli shoved the man away and breathed with relief as the doors slid shut. He jabbed at the button for the basement again, but already the car was moving downwards.

The telex read:

JOLI GREETINGS STOP KEEP RUNNING AND KEEP RUNNING FAST BUT DO NOT FAIL TO KEEP US POSTED AS TO YOUR WHEREABOUTS STOP GOOD LUCK STOP YOU NEED IT STOP WEATHER NOT SO GOOD TODAY STOP LOVE REEN

It had all become a bit too bloody obvious, he thought as he scuttled out of the lift, dragging his leather suitcase behind him along the oily concrete. The painter and himself hadn't been sent here to Whatever to try to find Anya: they'd been sent here so that *she* could find *them*. Anya left plenty of signs, in the form of murder and mayhem, wherever she went, but they were always evidence that she was leaving *behind* her. They told Reen where Anya had *been*, dammit, not where she actually *was*.

No keys left in the first three lim-ou-sines. Bastard shits! Didn't they know that sometimes it was important to let people steal your car?

But once she'd got a sniff of Joli, it'd be a different story. She'd be after him like a ferret after a fieldmouse, she would. She wouldn't let up until she'd planted her greedy little dagger – in his mind, he now saw it as a very colossal dagger – right up to its hilt in his gizzard, or worse. And as long as Joli was still running he could be relied upon – the faithful servant, the noble sacrifice for the prestige of the Service – to keep 'phoning home to

Auntie Reen to tell her where he'd got to in his travels around the World. Since wherever Joli was, Anya couldn't be far behind . . .

He stared incredulously at a motorbike. Of all the bloody vehicles to be the one that harsh-hearted chance had chosen to leave the keys in! Not one of your eight-seater limos with built-in cocktail bar, sofa bed, condom machine and jacuzzi – oh, no, not something like that for a man who was going to give up his life for the sake of his Service. No luxury for him. Just an effing motorbike!

He kicked his suitcase a goodbye, and threw himself astride the great black machine. An attendant was shouting something to him, starting to run towards him, but Joli just blew a raspberry. He hadn't ridden a big bike in years – not since long before he'd joined the Service. He twisted the key and felt around with his foot.

The attendant was close to him now, but too late.

Hammering his foot down with the skilled ease that could only have been born from decades of practice, Secret Agent Joli brought the engine into roaringly virile life.

Then, with the machine bucking and heaving beneath him like a wild stallion, he careered across the underground car-park, bounced numbingly off one of the exit pillars, jerked spasmodically up the ramp and – with a final contemptuous burst of exhaust fumes – was speeding on his way.

Chapter Five
JAM TOMOROW

1

Joli fled first to Insalvar, the City of Spices, whose brazen domes seemed to touch the sky. The air was full of birdsong and the scent of sandalwood, and the people were kindly to him, taking him in when he arrived in their midst destitute, his body a mass of cuts and bruises. After reclining a few weeks in the home of a rich heiress – for the culture was matriarchal, inheritance passing down through the second-born of each pairing within a group marriage, paternity being established through runecasting and genotyping – he remembered to send a rather disgruntled fax to Reen, mentioning only in a footnote that he was at death's door.

The people of Insalvar had long ago decided to reject the use of the wheel, and so the streets were quiet; Joli's stolen motorbike had, with his enthusiastic acquiescence, on his arrival been cast into the harbour, from the bottom of which it could still be seen dimly gleaming when the light was right. Horses and camels were used for the carriage of lighter goods. For heavier freight and for longer overland journeys, huge snakes captured at considerable hazard in the surrounding jungle were trained to act as beasts of burden: travelling at speeds of up to one hundred kilometres per hour on the open road, they slithered efficiently to the other cities that lay in the vast basin of the river Insal. Collisions had been frequent and loss of life high because of the quietness with which the snakes moved until a clever Insalvarian inventor, using imported microelectronics, had devised an audio system which could be attached to the serpents' harnesses and programmed to broadcast a randomized noise pattern that sounded much like an express train going through a tunnel.

Joli stayed among the Insalvarians for several weeks, until his shared mistress's spies reported that there had been sightings in several locations along the banks of the Insal of a blonde woman, armed to the teeth and covered in bloodstains, who seemed to be questing for someone. He promptly stole whatever valuables he could lay hands on and bought the next passage out of Insalvar aboard one of the mighty snakes.

Despite the theft, which they had been expecting, the Insalvarians did Joli the favour of carefully misdirecting Anya when she arrived, hours later, in search of him.

2

The streets of the vast metropolis of Harmadree were paved with gold and the houses and other buildings constructed from it, the metal being common in the district and the soft local sandstone being of use only for temporary structures because of the virulent acid rains and fogs that poured over the Mountains of Hands from the smoke-factories of Barondia on the far side of that range. These factories had been in operation for millennia, and diplomatic efforts to persuade the Barondians to adopt adequate anti-pollution measures had come to naught. In the people of Harmadree and its hinterland the vocal cords had generations ago atrophied, their function being replaced, thanks to a quirk of evolution, by a thoracic cavity across which were stretched taut strings of cartilage. These the Harmadreeans learnt to pluck in infancy to produce melodies that could be strident or harmonious, depending upon their mood. To communicate with tourists, such as Joli, the Harmadreeans were prepared to accept approximations of their speech played on small wooden ukuleles issued by immigration control at the same time as visitors' passes.

Joli, having despatched a fax to Reen as before, settled

down to try to enjoy life as best he could among the Harmadreeans. Although it was impossible to venture outside for long without breathing equipment, he discovered that there were many enchantments brought to Harmadree by the atmospheric conditions, and that these, while they could not be said to outweigh the disbenefits, certainly did much to counter them. The greater density of the air had permitted the evolution of insects much vaster than anywhere else in the World; and intelligent bumble-bees plied a lucrative trade ferrying commuters hither and thither and taking tourists for flights around the more scenic venues on offer. The sunsets were of course spectacular, and Joli was assured that the dawns were even more so. He almost regretted it when one day he heard of a series of brutal murders that had recently started in the suburbs and were rapidly progressing towards the city centre.

Pausing only to wrench up a few cobblestones and stuff them into a sack, Joli bought a cheap mayfly for a song and put as much distance between himself and Harmadree as was possible within the span of a single day.

Before leaving the metropolis in hot pursuit, Anya was able to purchase on the black market a primitive form of needle-gun which was capable of firing, at speeds close to that of sound, stings harvested illegally from the local wasps.

3

When Joli first arrived in Juna he was dismayed to discover that he was treated as by definition an idiot; almost immediately, however, he realized that this assumption provided him with the perfect camouflage, and he settled down for a long and tranquil stay in the city, mixing easily among the other idiots of his age-group. Unlike the case anywhere else in the World, the citizens of Juna – who were confusingly called Kakadokians, the etymology of their language being even more baroque than most – were each born with a strictly limited reservoir of useful thought, more than which they could not use during their lifetime. Thus the new-born were easily the most intelligent and wisest among the society and, as soon as they had learnt how to control their bodily functions, were placed in offices of authority. Over time, naturally, their abilities decreased, and they were replaced at about the age of puberty by younger and brighter children. The system had represented a triumph of evolution for as long as history recorded, although now it was heading for the rocks, the supply of useful thought, which had once been sufficient to last an individual's lifetime, now proving totally inadequate to the hurly-burly of a hi-tech society. Crawling futurologists predicted moistly that the Kakadokian culture had less than a century to live before high-pitched chaos descended; their elders inevitably responded to the forecasts with the observation that the history books had been predicting exactly this sort of doom for generations, and yet Juna was still thriving. The futurologists, who still retained the ability actually to read the history books, could find no such references, but wisely kept their mouths shut, being small.

Despite his protests, Joli was immediately hustled into a creche where he was expected to play with brightly coloured alphabetical plastic building blocks all day and stay out of fights. This being a progressive creche, feeding was on demand – a practice which suited him just fine, as did, once he had got used to the taste, the local gripewater. The business of sending a message to Reen was not easily solved, but he was finally allowed to make a reverse-charge phonecall. That done, he relaxed and started to enjoy himself.

After some weeks, however, he began to grow uneasy: surely sufficient time had passed that Anya must have tracked him as far as the city, even though she would have difficulty locating him more precisely, since in Juna no one ever told the adults anything. Reluctantly he picked his golden cobblestones from their purloined-letter concealment in the building-block box and stole out of the creche, out of the building in which it was housed, and eventually out of Juna.

Anya had indeed managed to follow him as far as the city. She too had been consigned to a creche, and had discovered that life there was more pleasurable than she had ever imagined life could be. It was to be some months before she could bear to tear herself away from this merry sociopathic whirl and resume her quest.

4

The Brooding Borough of Silence proved, on Joli's arrival at the end of a long flight through the heart of the Great Southern Continent, to have been aptly named, for it seemed to brood beneath a gallery of dark, slaty hills, and it was most certainly as nearly silent as any human habitation could ever be. At first he thought it must be a ghost town: there was no sign of human activity, let alone of any people. He walked down the long streets, noticing that everything was spotlessly clean and in a state of perfect repair. Although there were pigeons and starlings everywhere, cooing and squabbling on bridges and window-ledges and public statuary, there was not a trace of bird-droppings anywhere; and there were many other similar signs that something – an invisible something – was controlling the environment. The something's purpose in so doing was obscure, until Joli, driven to desperation by the fact that all the shops were stripped of their contents, their shelves brightly polished, broke into a house in search of food. Trying to track down the source of a barely audible hum, he nervously descended unlit stairs to the basement where he discovered a mother, father and two children lying pale and motionless in coffin-like tanks. Plastic tubes that connected with the blood vessels at the people's elbows and knees contained a pale yellow fluid which Joli correctly guessed to be an intravenous feed. Implanted into the four skulls were wires that led to a central box on which there was a tiny red electric light; it was the hum of this that Joli had heard.

Discovering from his searches of a few other houses selected at random that this mode of existence appeared to be universal rather than idiosyncratic, he made his way to the public library where, muttering to himself despite the

SILENCE

signs, he discovered that years before, when humanity had lost the power to dream, clever scientists at the Brooding Borough of Silence Institute of Technology had devised what had at first been called a sleep enhancer. The function of this device was to play pre-recorded dramas directly into the user's right cerebral hemisphere. While the user was conscious, the activities of the left hemisphere effectively drowned the stimulation provided by the machine, so that the effect was at best subliminal; but during sleep the user was permitted to play a role (of his or her choice) in a drama (of his or her choice) in a manner very much like controlled dreaming. A side-effect was that the body automatically responded to the stimulation by producing dream-state-like rapid eye movements, thereby keeping the user's extrinsic optic muscles in athletic trim. For the cost of a week's average earnings, entire families could plug themselves into an infinitely mutable scenario, complete with cast of thousands, in which they could conquer worlds, travel between the stars, engage in improbable congress with an astonishing diversity of partners, make staggering scientific advances, improve their batting averages, change sex on whim and be revered as international heroes – in short, have a lot more fun than in real life. Since then nothing had happened.

This was all very interesting, thought Joli, and he was sure that it held a useful moral somewhere, but it didn't do much to help his more immediate food problem. He did, however, discover at the back of the library a cache of neobradz – a nonaddictive artificial derivative containing the active principle of the drug that had enslaved millions during the World's forgotten history – and through use of it was able to wing his way onwards to he knew not where, so long as it was somewhere with food and telecommunications.

Anya, arriving only a few tantalizing days later, roasted a fat pigeon over a blaze of public records she'd found left lying around in the library.

5

Right in the middle of the Great Eastern Continent, after a year-long trek on foot, Joli came to the city of Marg'-phelin, disputed capital of the disputed empire of Garaya, a place where for centuries competing warlords had battled for the wreckage of the imperial throne. Scarcely one stone now stood upon another within the city itself, but in the surrounding countryside life carried on very much as always, the minor lords having formed a union some centuries ago with the principal aim of having nothing to do with the wars among their betters. Here great fields basked beneath hot oriental sunshine. Well fed peasants harvested grain crops of every conceivable kind, including a form of maize that, on reaching full ripeness, attained mobility and thus could be sent to market in long caravans shepherded by only a few drovers mounted on alliberis. These latter were both beasts of burden and sources of a thin, vile-tasting but highly nutritious milk, the sole reason that they were tolerated, for their intelligence was sub-bovine, their temper unpredictable and vicious, and their mindless braying discordant and inestimably loud.

Joli found to everyone's surprise that he was distinctly simpatico with the alliberis, and so on arrival he was swiftly dragooned into becoming a herder of the creatures. He soon got into a routine of sleeping until mid-morning – alliberis shared his attitude towards dawn – then buckling on his all-over leather armour and heading out into the pastures, where he had little to do until dusk except stop his charges from killing each other and any fool who happened to pass nearby. For this he was well victualled, housed and wenched, the latter an especial incentive to remain there for the remainder of his years, as he had entered a sort of indian summer of the libido. However, news reached him that a Great Golden Priestess had raised an army in the west and was now leading a massacre-prone campaign directly towards Marg'phelin. *That's my girl*, he thought on hearing this, as he doffed his latest wench and his leather armour, in that order, for the last time.

As he was making his stealthy way out of the region of Marg'phelin he remembered that, yet again, he'd failed to find any means of communicating his location to Reen – assuming she still lived. He felt vaguely guilty about what he knew she would regard as his failure, but it had been a long time since he'd found himself anywhere near anywhere that could remotely have been described as a centre of civilization. He resolved to make his way yet further east, towards the coast, in the hope that the communities there might have escaped the societal regression that seemed to have afflicted so many of the cities of the continent's heartland.

The Great Golden Priestess missed him at Marg'phelin by well over a month, and had to content herself with bringing some measure of order to the region. Finally, accompanied only by a musical vampire bat to which she'd taken a fancy, she continued on her quest.

6

After leaving behind the cities of the Plain of Bears, Joli reached the coastal city of Jenny Hanniver, where at last he was able to send a message by holofax to Reen or, as he was gloomily beginning to assume, her successor. There was no reply.

The economy of Jenny Hanniver was based on its position beside a strait through which seventy per cent of the World's marine life had to pass during the annual migration. Fishing was such a central part of all life that the inhabitants, among whom the wearing of brightly coloured artificial gills was fashionable, had begun in many respects themselves to resemble the creatures upon whom they preyed. They had also entered into various forms of symbiotic relationship with one of the more intelligent marine species, a form of semi-sessile kelp, colonial aggregates of which functioned as solid construction materials in return for the nutrition they could derive from human bodily waste fluids, especially sweat and urine, which were rich in the ureic acid important to the kelps for the synthesis of long-chain polyproteins. Although it was stressed to Joli that it was indeed only his waste-products that the kelps desired, he nevertheless had to tank himself up on a hallucinogenic liquor distilled locally from crabmeat before he could find the courage to take ship aboard one of the Jenny Hanniverian kelpoid craft that carried passengers across the strait to the Anomalous Continent and, he hoped, a form of civilization that more closely accorded with that in which he had grown up.

The trouble was that he had by now become by no means certain that he would recognize his own civilization, or its like, should he ever come across it again. He was fairly sure that some of the things that he had seen and experienced since his flight, a decade and a half ago, from Whatever would have been impossible in the World as it had been then; the 'fairly' had to be stressed, because every time he now tried to remember anything his mind would offer him an array of alternative versions of his past life, all of which were equally implausible, and it was very hard to settle upon one of them in preference to its fellows. He had assumed, when first he'd noticed this phenomenon, that it was just another of the inevitable signs of his advancing years; but during a late-night drinking session with a semi-porpoidal philosopher who'd befriended him he'd discovered that, though there were still in existence history books that could be read conventionally, the vast majority were now written in the form of numbered paragraphs and came with a set of multifaceted dice and a selection of personal attributes for the reader to choose from.

Pondering this fact, which seemed to lessen in significance the more he became convinced that the bulkheads of the kelpoid ferry were *watching* him, he finished his first bottle of crabmeat liquor and cracked open the second.

Anya, watching the craft diminish to nothing more than a dot on the horizon, cursed creatively at the near miss and contented herself, during the days she had to wait before the ferry's next sailing, with attempting to foment a revolution.

7

The poets sang that Bantiarada was the ideal place in all the World to be in love, which was just as well, because City Ordinance #354, as amended before ratification, had made it a local bye-law that the state of being in love was compulsory among all the people of Bantiarada and its environs. Joli, on arrival, discovered to his vehement revulsion that there were no exemptions for visitors, no matter how short their intended stay. He had twenty-four hours to find a partner or it was the lynch-mob for him. Wondering if the simplest thing to do might not be to resume his journey at once, he'd made his way to the nearest fax shop only to discover that it was closed for the weekend. Duty vied with inclination for just as long as it took him to ascertain that the other person spitting and cursing on the shop's doorstep, a willowy young woman than whom he decided he'd met a lot worse, was a transient in the same predicament as himself. Finally they enacted a tearful departure, as prescribed in City Ordinance #477, before going on their separate ways.

Anya, more practical, simply placed a small ad in the *Bantiarada Daily Gazette*. A week or so later, on discovering that once again Joli had eluded her clutches, she listened patiently to her paramour's pleas that he would find it difficult to carry on living without her, and then took the obvious course of action.

Sometimes she missed the musical vampire bat that had served as her spiritual companion for so long, but on the ferry across from Jenny Hanniver it had got into conversation with a heavy-metal band that was looking for a bass player, and she hadn't had the heart to stand in the way of its career.

8

In the twin towns of Stereoville the distinction between animate and inanimate was blurred, a fact which did nothing to enhance Joli's increasing problems in coming to terms with his multifarious memory, which was now presenting to him such a broad array of alternatives each time he attempted to recall even what he had had for breakfast yesterday that selection from among them seemed to allow infinite possibilities. In terms of that particular category of data he wasn't too bothered: he was desperately short of money – had it not been for the fact that the jewel in his pocket featured as one of only three stable items in all the different scenarios of the past he might have been tempted to sell it – and so breakfasts generally consisted either of nothing or of something he didn't particularly want to be able to remember the next day. He was sure, however, that he must have undergone other, much more significant experiences that were now lost to him forever, and this he regretted deeply – even though he at the same time recognized that old pains, too, had vanished.

The second of the three permanent features of his past existence was the imperative to send details of his position in the World to Reen's holofax number as soon as he arrived somewhere new; and so, as soon as he'd established for himself a territory under one of Stereoville's expressway overpasses, he headed with some stolen trinkets for the nearest holofax shop. From there, after a short and inconclusive argument with the machine, he was able to send a message to Reen saying where he was and suggesting that she might see her way to MTing him some money. There was no reply, as there hadn't been for some years now. To make matters worse, on his return to his patch of hard-won territory he discovered that his position had been usurped by a solar-powered microwave oven and its gang of burly trashcans – street riffraff – and that he was de facto homeless.

It was then that his customary cheery pessimism collapsed into a nadir of despair, and he began seriously considering taking his own life, on the grounds that nobody else would want it. Except, he realized with a sudden rush of hope, the third shared feature of all his memory-strands: Anya. Accordingly he stayed for three months in Stereoville, living off the food he was able to pilfer from hypermarkets, learning to judge which cans would cooperate and which would shriek accusingly to the guards as he was trying to sneak them out past the tills. He could sense, however, that he wasn't really welcome in Stereoville – the way that the gutters kept trying to trip him up was pretty strong evidence. The trouble was that there was only one of him, which meant (obviously) that he could be in only one of the twin cities at any particular moment of time. Finally, with a heavy heart, he boarded one of the two hourly hoverbuses out of the place, not realizing that, had he endured the feelings of rejection for just a few hours longer, he would have had his heart's desire, for that was when Anya arrived, her bloodlust reaching impossible heights: she'd been hyping herself up to kill Joli for two decades now.

9

One day, after a long ocean crossing by whale, Joli found himself at the edge of an ethereal megalopolis that seemed to spread out over hundreds of square kilometres. The buildings were vast, their tops lost to sight among the clouds, and they were built of gauzy metals and blindingly white quasi-existent concrete-analogues: their windows had the transparency of thought. These architectural monstrosities looked as if they had no more substance than a feather, a hypothesis reinforced by the fact that they were sensitively balanced on bases that were vanishingly small – out of scientific curiosity Joli discovered that yes he could, indeed, put his arms right around one and still have several centimetres of embrace left over. The feeling of airiness was compounded by the fact that the dense, swiftly-moving traffic on the kilometre-wide thoroughfares was almost entirely silent, operating as it did on a principle of gravitic repulsion that worked only if the materials used were, like large parts of the architecture, merely quasi-existent.

Joli was not initially startled to discover that this megalopolis was called Ernestrad, because the fact that he'd ever been in a place called that before was lost among the myriad fibres of his memory. Nevertheless, as his first day in the city drew to its close he found that the name had a certain ring of familiarity to it, like that of a grandparent one has never known. After spending a night in Ernestrad – his body consigned to a left-luggage locker, his sleeping mind to a vacant niche in the city computer's databank – he became more and more convinced of the ancient travellers' adage that, no matter what point of departure you choose on the surface of the World, if you keep going long enough you will eventually arrive back home again, only to discover that home is a different place from the one you left.

This feeling strengthened all during his second day, especially since some of the street signs were now beginning to spark off that same sense of half-forgotten familiarity. That night, just before the kindly officials again separated his mind from his body, he discovered that the name of the country in which he'd arrived was Albion, and that clinched it.

On awakening the third day, he breakfasted well on a few whole-food tablets and set out into the streets with a new spring in his stride. A friendly robot directed him to Starveling Square (there being, according to the robot, no Starveling Street, Starveling Road or any other place under that name), and after a short journey by psychofacsimile translation Joli found himself looking up at the face of the sole edifice in the entire block, the mighty Syorco Building, whose scale dwarfed that of all the others around it and whose pinnacle Joli might have seen from tens of kilometres out in the ocean had it not been that he had come to Albion by such a cheap mode of transport.

Feeling numbed by the vastness of it all, Joli hitched a ride on a passing floater to the main entrance, where he let himself into a foyer the size of a cathedral and, having queued for half an hour for his turn with one of the fifty or more lobby receptionist terminals, typed into its grinning keyboard the message

JOLI'S HERE TO SEE REEN, PLEASE

At once all activity in the foyer ceased, the fifty or more receptionists simultaneously closing down as a result of a systems overload. All of the many humans in that vast echoing space – Joli was pretty certain he couldn't have counted up to a number that great – turned to look at him, some with blank resignation and others with blatant accusation that, through his actions, he had selfishly delayed their own transactions. Desperately trying to look as if he weren't embarrassedly waiting to see what would happen next, he embarrassedly waited to see what would happen next, which was that a waist-high blue holocyborg rabbit approached him, asked his name, requested that he follow, and led him to an internal psychofacsimile translation booth. Here the rabbit chanted a few numerals in its nasal voice, the lights dimmed, and

Chapter Six
MeN AT WORK OVeRHeAD

1

'Joli!' exclaimed Reen in a husk of a voice. 'We thought we'd maybe never see you again! Where in the World have you been all these weeks?'

The little man glared around him at the modest single-hectare office as the blue rabbit faded from beside him. He'd aged terribly in the months since Reen had last seen him: she wouldn't have recognized him had it not been that the look of bitter resentment on his face was exactly the same as always. The fact that his appearance had changed at all, let alone so drastically, concerned her, because Joli's face had always seemed quite ageless: even as a young child he must have looked old. Acting as the living bait in Reen's desperate fishing expedition must have been more arduous for him than she'd anticipated.

She glanced up at Barra 'ap Rteniadoli Me'gli'minter Rehan standing beside her, and saw similar concerns written on his face.

'Are you all right?' she said weakly to Joli.

'Yes,' he croaked, 'but no thanks to you, you old leather piss-bag.' He spat on the spotless carpet.

'Come over here and sit down,' said Rehan, gesturing at a chair. 'Do you want some coffee?'

'It's a long way to walk,' said Joli, truthfully, 'and what I want is a stiff drink.'

Reen smiled. 'I should think that can be organized,' she said, pressing a buzzer on her opal desk as Joli began his long trek.

The door behind her vaporized, and Kursten came into the office. She was dressed from head to foot in a modest pattern of fluctuating holographic tattoos. Joli's back straightened as soon as he caught sight of her, and a little of the old jauntiness returned to his gait. His preference not to notice Kursten was rather more blatant than a direct stare.

'Look, Kursten,' said Reen. 'Joli's returned to us.'

'Hi there, Joli.'

'Can you bring a bottle of the Glenlivet and some glasses? Cancel the rest of my appointments for the day.'

Joli sat down on a floating construction of black plastic and silvery synthetic metal that immediately altered its shape ergonomically to match his requirements; the result was excruciatingly uncomfortable. As the young woman retreated from the room he dragged his eyes away from her and stared at his old friends: Reen, still sitting behind the desk, half-leaning forwards across it towards him, her right hand holding some kind of wired stylus, looking crisp and clean in a navy blue dress with broad white lapels, her face hardly changed since last he'd seen it, the dark, dark eyes no older; Rehan, standing beside and slightly behind her, his dark suit making him seem even more slender than Joli remembered him, his arm across the back of her chair, his eyes seeming troubled above the over-large nose as he gazed back at Joli.

'I brought you a jewel,' said Joli weakly, digging into the pocket of his stained old coat. 'At first, when the pig brought it to me, I thought it was just a frippery bauble of some kind, but then, after I'd held on to it for long enough, I began to realize that it was more a matter of it holding on to me, and that you'd be wanting it.'

He tossed the gem onto the desk. It lay there, its pale grey and hazy blue now blended to render a soft, slightly sinister living misty hue, and all three of them just stared at it. 'Or maybe it was simply something extra added to the bait, to make it more appetizing to Anya?' he added.

'You . . . realized the truth of your rôle in this affair?' said Rehan hesitantly.

'Realized it?' Joli slapped his scrawny thigh and began to chuckle caustically. 'I knew what you two were up to as soon as I got Reen's telex, back in the hotel in Whatever. It was a bit bloody obvious, wasn't it? And even if I'd been too slow on the uptake to know what was going on then, I've had twenty-four years to think it over, haven't I?'

Reen exchanged a puzzled glance with Rehan. 'Uh, Joli,' she said carefully. 'You've only been travelling for a little over six months.'

He glared at her. 'Don't be preposterous,' he snarled. 'I spent five times as long as that in the Great Southern Continent alone. D'you think I'm crazy, or something?'

Reen put down her stylus and tented her fingers in front of her lips, breathing deeply in order to calm herself. That Joli might have lost track of time a bit in the confusion of his flight was plausible enough, but that he could have done so to such an extreme seemed impossible. Besides, there was the matter of how much he'd aged. Whatever the dangers and difficulties he'd faced, surely they couldn't have put all those extra lines in his face, whitened and thinned his hair – he was now almost completely bald – and crooked his back and shoulders so grievously. She threw a glance towards his hands, resting on his crossed knees, and saw the thinnings and liver spots of advanced years. Clearly, while she and Rehan had remained here at the Syorco offices, carrying on business as usual, the World had been playing yet another of its too-frequent temporal games, this time with Joli as its victim.

'No,' she said, 'I don't think you're crazy.'

Kursten reappeared at that moment, the drinks tray floating behind her, and so Reen was spared from having to make any further immediate comment. She gestured to the PA to summon a chair and join them. Once Kursten was settled and Joli was happily ogling her over the brim of his second glass, Reen began to speak again.

'I don't wish to carp,' she said, her gentle tone removing much of the sting from her words, 'especially since you are, as it were, the valorous hero returning, but why didn't you keep up your regular messages to us?'

'I tried, you bitch!' shouted Joli, his hand shaking with

fury as he refilled his glass. 'But half the time I didn't have any money, and the other half I still wouldn't have been able to contact you even if I'd been rolling. Let me tell you . . .' And he explained how in the Brooding Borough of Silence there had been nothing left functioning by way of communications equipment among the slumbering houses; and how in Marg'phelin, lost in the central wastes of the Great Eastern Continent, the same problem had applied, only significantly more so, as indeed it had done elsewhere. In Cvr'yotia, for example, the sole means of long-distance transmission known to the peacock-feathered citizens had been through differential plantings of the annual tulip crop; Joli had declined to wait there eight months for his message to be sent. 'And in other places I was more concerned about saving my own skin than about rattling off a postcard to you,' he growled a while later, 'and I'm not ashamed to admit it.'

'There aren't any places like that in the World,' muttered Reen to herself, 'and yet it's perfectly clear that Joli isn't merely raving.'

'I can't understand why you ran out of money,' said Kursten, who had been sitting calculating during most of his monologue. 'I established after you'd fled from Whatever that you had enough funds in traveller's cheques to last you for at least a year, assuming you didn't go too wild with your expenses. And, anyway, couldn't you have used your credit cards?'

Joli stared at her with the air of a person whose dearly beloved has just come out with a remark so intensely stupid that strangulation seems the only possible cure. 'I didn't *have* credit cards,' he snapped. 'You're talking about twenty-four years ago. That was around the time you look as though you were born, young filly. The height of technology was the telex: things have progressed very rapidly since then. Besides, you forget I was travelling all through the farthest-flung corners of the World: half the people I was mixing with weren't even people, and many of the rest of them didn't use anything that you would recognize as money. I wasn't equipped with breath-perfumes to exchange with the Aranassi, or the ability to dance myself to wealth among the people of the Filat Plains. Even if I'd had little bits of plastic, they wouldn't have done me much good, most of the time. And the funds I started out with at Whatever wouldn't have lasted me "at least a year" even if they'd been spendable, because they were locked up in the hotel manager's safe, like I'd been given strict instructions they should be. Does that answer your question?'

'What's this about twenty-four years?' said Kursten, looking at Reen for reassurance. 'You've only been . . .'

'There's a difference of opinion about that,' said Reen, getting to her feet, 'as I suspect there'll be a difference of opinion on quite a number of other things. Eh, Joli?'

She walked across to the wall, which was completely transparent, and, ignoring the fact that she seemed to be standing unprotected only a couple of centimetres above the edge of a vertiginous drop, looked out across Ernestrad. The air was clear, as always, but close to the horizon she could see what looked like a bank of cloud or fog. She frowned briefly, but then returned her attention to Joli.

'Can you remember much about what Ernestrad was like when you left it?' she said. 'Was it like . . . well, like it is today?' She turned to look at him and gestured towards the panorama behind her.

'I can remember a thousand different Ernestrads,' said Joli, irritated, 'but none of them like this. Come to that, I can remember a thousand different Reens as well, and Rehans, and, though all of them were certainly like the two of you, they weren't corporation executives dressed in smart suits or' – an appreciative sideways glance at Kursten – 'things.'

'I seem to remember . . . remembering like this,' breathed Kursten, her face working. 'I sort of recall that. Not properly.'

'I told you we might find something like this,' Rehan said to Reen. 'I said that if Joli were travelling he'd experience things differently from the way that we did, staying here. He's seen the evidence of so much change that it's told him about other changes. From the very diversity – the confusingness – of his experience he's been able to knit together a better picture of the truth than we could, staying in a single place, where nothing seemed ever to change.'

'And I only half-believed you,' she said. 'But at least it was half. Tell us something about our other selves, Joli.'

'Which of them? As I said, I can recall thousands of each of you.' Once more he topped up his glass, raising it in a silent toast to Kursten. 'I can even remember thousands of different versions of *me*.'

'Aren't some of your memories . . . stronger than others, Joli?' she insisted.

'It . . . it doesn't work that way,' he said, shaking his head annoyedly as if to clear it, 'but I know what you're trying to get at. The nearest thing I could say is that some of the Reens appear more or less the same in a lot of different memory-strands, whereas some of them are in only a few. Which is in various ways a pity.' He grinned suddenly, so that his face looked as if it were in danger of shattering. 'I don't suppose you recall a certain little tavern in Greenheart Lake Hamlet, and the way your eyes looked into mine in the candlelight as we dined on fresh-caught river trout, and then afterwards . . .'

'No,' she said bluntly, 'I don't.'

'Well, that's your hard luck,' he said. Then his smile faded. 'But you haven't been like that in most of my memories. None of you, nor Ernestrad either, have been much like the way I can see you today.'

'Tell us,' said Rehan quietly.

And so, criss-crossing his account with qualifications and amendments, acknowledging inconsistencies which couldn't be eliminated, Joli described to them a composite picture built up from many similar memory strands. He told Reen of how she'd been a brave warrior, temperamental yet stout-hearted, ruthless when she had to be yet astonishingly kind and gentle on other occasions, waspish with her tongue yet fiercely loyal to her friends. He described her love for Syor, and Syor herself, and how the two of them had raised Anya from infancy until Syor had taken her own life, and how Reen had then carried on bringing up the child on her own, and had served as her faithful lieutenant in the struggle to overthrow the Ellonia. Then he talked of how they had all been present at the time of the transmogrification of Syor and Nadar – here his words for a time sounded with greater certainty – and then he ran over the events that had taken place in the immediate aftermath. But all the time the qualifications: Reen had indeed been a warrior, but had she been fighting with swords and axes, or with stock-exchange manoeuvres, or was she instead an honest cop assisting in the expunging of the corrupt Mob led by her stepdaughter, or a circuit cowboy chasing Anya through cyberspace in the wake of the World's greatest computer scam, or . . . ?

All these differences, and yet the story told was essentially the same one: all the Reens essentially just the same Reen. It was as if she'd been an actress playing the same part in several productions of a play, each of the productions having the same script but different scenery. There was only the one story.

He patted Kursten affectionately on the knee, looking into her face. 'For what it's worth, poppet, although I never got to know you as well as I'd have liked to, you seem to be much the same in each of those memory-strands where I see you, although most times you've been . . . ah . . . unfortunately somewhat differently dressed.'

She forced a smile and shifted uncertainly in her seat.

'And you, Rehan,' Joli continued, switching his gaze, 'I can tell you the same as I told Reen.' Barra 'ap Rteniadoli Me'gli'minter Rehan, the singer whom Joli had in all of his memories initially regarded as something of an effete fop but to whom he'd slowly come to give as much of his grudging respect as Joli ever gave anyone. Sometimes he'd been a rock star, sometimes a street busker, sometimes a wanderer from village to village, bringing to the peasants through his music their history and their myth-making.

Yet he, too, had learnt to struggle for freedom and then been repelled by his own achievements on seeing them being turned to dust in Anya's hands, and had withdrawn from Albion to go out into the World. Again he'd been there when Syor had transfigured herself and her ancient enemy, but whether it was on a tabletop or an airstrip or somewhere else Joli couldn't say.

'I can still remember some of your ditties, though,' he remarked, easing back in his chair just long enough to fool it into adopting a new configuration before he jerked himself upright again. 'There was that bit of doggerel that ended up being on everybody's lips. Let me think now.' Moving into yet another position, to the chair's ill concealed fury, Joli used his thigh as a bodhran, beating it with the flat of his hand.

'*Seven women rode down through the town of Starveling that night*,' he sang:
'*Horses' hooves spitting galaxies in the pale moons' empty light.*
And their eyes sought out the corners where the shadows grew
As deep and as dark as wine . . .

Remember that one, eh, boy? Nobody ever knew what the fuck it was all about, of course, until Reen went and did her stuff – whatever her stuff was – but that didn't trouble the doxies much. All you had to do was sing a few verses of that, with your eyes looking all soulful, and they were in your bed more numerous than fleas. Begging your pardon,' he added abruptly, turning to Kursten and again patting her on the knee. 'The doxies bit is in only one of the memory-strands, and anyway I might have got it wrong.'

'The song seems familiar to me,' said Rehan stiffly, 'but I don't remember composing it and I don't remember singing it. In fact, I don't even remember being a musician, the way you said I was. All that I can find in my own mind is that I've served Syorco faithfully, as any vice-president should' – he nodded towards Reen – 'ever since the day of its founding. Before that I can recall' – another nod to Reen – 'liaisons, of course: who wouldn't? But never the sort of groupies you were talking about. No rock star me. No musician.' He looked down at his pale, immaculately manicured hands. 'No, certainly not a musician,' he said wistfully.

'But that is what you have been in almost all of my memories,' said Joli, looking baffled. 'Take away that and you're not really the same Rehan. Why, even Alyss thought you were a reasonably fair songster, and she's never been notably generous with her comp . . .'

He stopped, seeing Rehan's uncomprehending face. Reen and Kursten were looking equally blank.

'Don't you – any of you – even remember Alyss?' he said incredulously.

Rehan stared at his feet, Reen at the terminal implanted in her desk of opal, Kursten at her psychedelic fingernails.

'But Alyss is . . .' Joli began, then stopped. How to explain to people who'd never heard of her exactly who – or what – Alyss was? He gave up. 'You do remember Syor, don't you?' he tried instead.

'Of course,' said Reen, frowning. She waved a hand indolently, and behind her, at twice life-size, there appeared a full-colour psychopic of Syor, a pattern of electromagnetic fields that sparked the correct image in the minds of each of them. The eyes were a paler green than Joli had ever remembered, and surely Syor had never dressed in executive pseudo-tweeds. 'It would be almost heretical for any of us to forget our founder,' Reen said. 'Had it not been for her, this company could hardly have got off the ground, let alone have become what it is today, the largest corporation in all the World.' Her chest swelled with pride.

'Don't you recall her transfiguring herself as a god?' he said.

Reen smiled. 'I think you're becoming a little fanciful, my friend,' she said. 'I can remember her dying, yes. It's hard to forget tragedies like that. She was blown off the skyport on the roof when some clown of a hoverpilot screwed up his landing – her and some visiting executive from NADAR whose name I never did catch. It was the lead story in all the sensies for the best part of a week. As far as that goes, I can see the parallels with the various versions of her death that you've told us about. But as for her becoming a god . . . well, the dark days of superstition when gods could thrive are far behind us, Joli, and long may they remain so.'

'Or maybe Joli's right and we're wrong,' said Rehan quietly. 'Maybe I was a musician, once upon a time.' There was a tear in his eye as he gazed at his hands again; he made no effort to brush it away. 'If I can believe one, I can just as easily believe the other.'

'Why should we believe any of them?' said Kursten. 'How do we know that Joli hasn't simply been gallivanting around these past few months, having the time of his life on company expenses, rather than doing what he was supposed to be doing?'

'You'll become less sceptical . . . when you get a little older, lassie,' said Joli wearily. She twitched angrily, which delighted him. 'But for now, you cute little chickadee, you might take a few moments to explain to an old codger like me, old enough to be your grandfather, I'll bet you've been thinking, just exactly what it *was* that I was supposed to be doing. I've been running for twenty-four years, as far as I'm concerned, and all that time I've been assuming that I was acting as bait in order to lure a particularly vicious psychopath out into the open. All my other notions of my existence might keep changing, but that one stayed pretty bloody firmly implanted in the forefront of my mind – as you could imagine, if ever you'd been in the same situation yourself, which I hope you'll never be, because I'm a kindly old bozo, not a sharp-tongued little bitch. As it were.'

He smiled paternally at her, and again was rewarded by a flushed and furious glare.

'Yes, perhaps you could just outline,' he continued, 'the briefing that you're apparently so convinced I couldn't be bothered to fulfil.'

'Joli!' snapped Reen from the window. 'Leave the girl alone. Pick on someone your own size.'

'The old boot speaketh,' explained Joli lugubriously to Kursten, 'and I durst not do otherwise than she commands. All right,' he said, turning, bringing a whip into his voice, '*you* tell me.'

'According to the memories that we three share' – Reen looked quickly at the others for confirmation – 'Anya Ledbetter isn't just a sort of freebooting psychopath, the way you describe her, and, unless her people have discovered some way of jamming our intelligence devices that we don't know about, she hasn't left Ernestrad this past year or more except for properly accredited reasons connected with the functioning of this company. She's our Personnel Director.'

Joli stared at her, his mouth open, for once at a loss for words.

'You're kidding,' he breathed, finally.

'Not at all,' said Reen, shaking her head firmly and then turning to look out on Ernestrad again. The mist was coming closer, blowing in off the sea. 'Indeed, were it not for Rehan and his growing doubts about the . . . solidity of the reality that we're living in, I'd have fired you the moment you got back here with your wild tales, so that the corporation's health-insurance fund wouldn't have been faced with the bills of the white-coated gentlemen I'd immediately afterwards have summoned. The reasons for your dismissal would have been obvious, not that you'd have ever been able to challenge them: decamping with company funds and without permission, remaining out of contact despite strict instructions to report in regularly, spreading calumnies about a senior executive of the company – you name it. Half of them would have been lies, of course, because it was in accordance with my personal request that you went undercover, but it's a well known axiom that Syorco doesn't tell lies so no one would ever have queried the fiction.

'As it is' – she cleared her throat – 'as it is, there are too many crossovers between what you've been telling us and the version that we regard as fact for me to dismiss your descriptions of reality quite so readily. It was indeed because of my apprehension over the activities of Anya Ledbetter that I asked you to do as you . . . did. For some years now it's been a matter of concern to the board that she shows a little bit too much ambition, that her urge to reach the pinnacle has been rather too . . . naked, shall we say? Since the pinnacle of Syorco, that desk of mine in front of you, is one of the most powerful positions in the World, and since our founder must have had very good reasons for telling me not long before she died that Anya was not to be her heir in the corporation, my worries have been acute. Especially since, in her rise through the company ranks, there have been two or three rather convenient . . . accidents, at just the right time for her. Your colleague Ngur, for example, head of our Intherian franchizing agency: it was rather convenient for Anya that her ex died just at the moment when you might have wished to call on his help. If her mother's death was another 'accident', then it was horrendously ill gauged – far too soon for Anya's purposes – which is why I was so confident a little while ago in saying that it was, indeed, nothing more than a natural misfortune. But we can't be a hundred per cent certain of it, of course.'

'What you're saying,' grunted Joli, 'is that Anya may indeed be a killer, just like the Anya in all my memory-strands, but that if so she's been a lot more subtle about it.'

'Yes. And, remember, it's only a suspicion. A fairly strong suspicion, but a long way from anything proven.' Reen, still looking out of the window rather than at Joli, sighed. 'And the same could be said about her contacts with NADAR. For all we can be certain about, they may be totally above-board – nothing more than the natural diplomatic relations between senior executives of two large organizations whose rivalries are sometimes overridden by their common interests. But it could be that instead she's selling the ground out from under us. We just don't know.' She turned now to face him again and repeated: 'We – just – don't – know. Which is why we put you out on the run. To find out. To confirm the suspicion, or otherwise.'

'How?'

'By sending in imaginative confidential reports to me from all your randomly selected ports of call around the World, detailing any evidence you could find on the activities of our subsidiaries – manufactured evidence if you couldn't find anything real – that industrial-espionage cyber-cowboys sympathetic to NADAR had infiltrated our enterprise. Slowly your reports, which as I say were to be for my senses only, were to have built up a picture of exactly such infiltration, and at the highest possible levels within Syorco. About Personnel Director level, in fact.'

Joli grinned. 'You're an old bastard, you know that, Reen,' he said, 'to put the life of a bosom buddy in danger that way.' If Anya were betraying Syorco, she or her informants would certainly have found some way of hacking into Reen's personal databank – assuming they hadn't simply bribed some underling, like Kursten, perhaps, to pass them the information before it ever got that far. Joli's confidential reports would have been of particular interest whatever their content, since he was the executive who was supposed to have gone crazily AWOL – yet here he was maintaining contact with the boss. Then, when the nature of his covert mission had become clear, it would be natural enough that Anya would want a stop put to it. NADAR itself, assuming that she were indeed their highest-placed spy, would likewise wish to see him silenced – although quite the opposite would be true, of course, if she were innocent: then NADAR would have been content to sit back and watch Syorco destroying the career of one of its brightest luminaries. So all that Reen had to do was watch to see who if anyone started to move in on Joli. If they were NADAR operatives or associates, or if the NADAR cybernet was deployed to ensnare him . . .

Suddenly he was angry with Reen – with all of them. This wasn't so different from his own primary memory-strands, where he had been acting as bait for a psychopath to take. 'I could have been fucking killed!' he yelled.

'You volunteered for the job,' said Rehan mildly. 'I can remember it clearly. You put on a performance that would have doubled the ratings of any sensie soap opera – all courage and nobility – but you did volunteer.'

'What in hell can I have been thinking of?' said Joli, amazed.

Reen's eyes wandered briefly to Kursten's face. 'I don't know,' she said. 'I took it for granted at the time that it was company loyalty.' She coughed dryly. 'Besides, I may not have been entirely candid as to the true purpose of your mission. Whatever the truth of the matter . . .'

'There isn't any truth in the matter,' said Joli.

'Sorry?'

'There isn't any truth in the matter. All you have are your memories of what happened. But there isn't any Syorco, either: that's just another part of a single memory-strand.' He waved his hand at the vista beyond the window. 'That's just as unreal as any of the other possibilities. Syor wasn't merely the founder of a corporation who plummeted to her death as a result of an unfortunate hoverplane accident – she became a god, I tell you, a god. All of my own memory-strands are unanimous about that. Yours – yours must be an oddball, or an artifice, or some joke that the World's playing on you. I'd never have volunteered to risk my life for something as trivial as company loyalty – I'm not the type – or even to try to get into Kursten's pants, which is obviously what you think my motive might have been. I'm not the loyal sort . . . with some exceptions, corporations not being among them. If it had been a matter of *you* being at . . .'

He stopped suddenly, reddening.

Reen looked at him as if she'd never really seen him before.

'The results of the exercise,' said Rehan quickly, 'have unfortunately been equivocal, largely as a result of the fact that you were so rarely able to file your reports. I could show you some of those reports, if you like . . . no, it's hardly worth it – they're just what you'd expect them to be, although rather more cunningly concocted than we might have anticipated. You did a good job there, Joli. But we still don't know for sure . . .'

'Shut up, Rehan,' said Joli. 'I don't want to be a part of your fantasies any more.'

'They're not – oh,' said Rehan, subsiding into Reen's vacant chair, 'I see. From your point of view they are.'

'Soap-opera fantasies, like you were talking about,' said Joli. 'Spies and secret agents lurking in every corner. Hah!'

'I suppose so . . .' Rehan began.

'I want out,' Joli said. He took the jewel from where it still lay on the desk and returned it to his pocket. 'I want to get away from your slimy corporate politics and the people that it's turned you into. I want to go back into a World where you're a warrior, Reen, not a self-satisfied manipulator of power. A World where you're a musician, Rehan, not the office lickspittle. A World where I may be a selfish old bastard with vile habits and a lechery this failing body of mine is too feeble to cope with. A World that may have a million different faces to show me, so that I never know which of them is the real one, but at least a World that's honest.'

Reen shrugged. 'I'm not stopping you,' she said. 'Take the jewel – it's yours anyway. Kursten will give you a company credit card – it's yours to use as long as you want to. I wish I could come with you. But . . . well . . . responsibilities. You know.'

She shrugged, smiling sadly at him.

'Old boots are useful on rough roads,' he said.

'I'm sorry. I can't.'

She nodded at Kursten, who stood, holding out a hand for Joli.

'Maybe I'll see you again, then,' he said.

'You'll be welcome, any time.'

They shook hands, rather formally, knowing there

wouldn't be another time. Then Joli, pausing only to grab the half-empty bottle, obediently followed Kursten's swirling colours towards the door at the rear of the office, which vaporized for just long enough to allow them through.

'A World where you're a brave warrior queen,' said Rehan after a while, attempting a smile. 'It's a pleasant enough dream, I suppose.' He looked up at Reen, who had returned to staring out of the window. He was glad he couldn't see her face. 'A World in which Syor has become the God of Good – and some obscure minion of NADAR her counterbalancing principle of Evil, I guess. It can't make any sense, of course. If she'd become a god, rather than merely dead, we'd have seen some signs of change in the World these past few months – wars stopping, maybe . . .'

His voice drifted off.

'Gods have never made much difference to the way that we behave,' said Reen dully. Fog was blotting out more of Ernestrad's towers now. 'Only the arguments about them.'

She sighed. 'Good and Evil,' she said. 'We know what Good is. Good is what is good for Syorco's profits. And Evil is what will harm the company in the marketplace.'

Rehan didn't hear her. He was looking at his hands again.

'A World in which I'm a musician,' he said.

2

Kursten fixed him up with a credit card, implanting a digital analysis of his right retinal pattern in a thin magnetic strip around the edge of the rectangle and a psychopic of his face into its centre. Removing his hands from where they were straying, she chucked the now-empty Glenlivet bottle into a recike chute and opened the hospitality cupboard. That had been the last of the whisky, but there was an unopened litre of gin, so she put it in a polibag along with some boxes of smokesticks and gave them to him. Then she threw her arms around him, hugged him tightly, and covered his face and lips with polychromatic kisses, and he noticed that for some reason the stupid bloody tartlet was crying. She was still crying, a few seconds later, when she delivered him into the custody of the blue bunny.

The building's lobby was still quite crowded, and Joli let the po-faced throng have the benefit of one of his more spectacular sneers. He fished into his polibag and got out the bottle of gin, opened it, and took a healthy glug.

'Piss on the lot of you!' he bellowed as he screwed the cap back on.

He dodged the advancing grim-visaged rabbits adroitly and made an erratic beeline for the great plexiglass doors.

Outside, the World waited for him.

3

'The Personnel Director wishes to see you,' said the polycom on Reen's desk.

'In person?' she responded, surprised. Syorco executives rarely bothered going to each other's offices, even for meetings, since holo link-ups through the net were much easier. Rehan was different, of course: her office was more or less his as well.

'In person,' the machine confirmed.

Reen's eyes narrowed.

'Then I suppose you'd better confirm to her that I'll see her,' she said. 'When does she want to come?'

'Right now, if that is possible.'

'Right now it is, then.'

The words had hardly left her lips when there was a glow from the psychofacsimile translation booth at the far end of the room. Anya appeared there, smiling ingratiatingly, posing herself theatrically beside the rapidly disintegrating holographic image of a throttled blue bunny.

'Greetings, Anya,' said Reen cautiously, wishing she knew where Rehan had gone.

'Greetings, *dear* Reen.' Anya patted her bright blue

neowool dress as if to make sure it was still there, then smiled again. 'We might as well stop pretending, mightn't we?' she continued brightly. She brought her fist crashing down on the booth's control switch, smashing it. 'That's the last of the entrances – and exits – closed. Kursten and Rehan are trying their damnedest to get the other doors to function, but some curious electronic malfunction has put everything around here haywire, as it happens. Isn't that a pity, Reen? That means there's just the two of us in here to keep each other company. Can you think of any parlour games that we could play, just in case we run out of conversation?'

'What do you want, Anya?'

Anya walked lazily towards the desk. As always, she seemed to be able to move her body with much less than the required expenditure of muscular energy.

'I think it's about time we had a talk,' she said, settling uninvited on the floating chair in front of the desk.

'What about?'

'What you were discussing earlier today with Rehan and his floozy, not to mention our publicly discredited executive, rot him.'

'How did you . . . ?' Reen started. She glanced at the bug tell-tale on her desk console, but it was unlit, as was its back-up in the arm of her chair.

'Aw, come off it, Reen. Don't be so naïve. A great big picture window like that?' She pointed. 'Don't you think I have lasers trained on it from outside? You can actually *see* the NADAR building from here, so finding a suitably private location for the equipment wasn't exactly difficult.'

'I had the window tested for total molecular stability only a week ago.'

'A week is a long time in corporate politics,' Anya drawled. 'It only takes a few seconds to destabilize a molecular window again, you know.'

'So you know my suspicions about you,' said Reen heavily.

'And I know that they've been amply confirmed by the

510

few reports that Joli managed to send in to you,' said Anya, complacent hands in her lap, 'which is something that not even Rehan knows. Yet.'

'I still wasn't a hundred per cent certain,' said Reen, 'but I suppose I am, now. I still can't quite believe it, though. That you should betray all the aspirations of your mother . . .'

'Syor? Shit, but I hate having that name shoved at me the whole time. She was a neurotic mess, as you well know. If it hadn't been for you and that drooling toady of yours propping her up the whole time, she'd have been nothing. She almost killed herself when I was a child, you know, or have you conveniently chosen to forget all about that? She was a fruitcake, a psychiatrist's field-day.'

'Would you talk about her like that if she'd been a cripple?' Reen said. 'If she'd been born without arms or legs? Sure, she was a manic depressive – that was obvious enough to anyone who knew her. But that doesn't mean she wasn't worth a dozen of you . . .'

'Aw, uddy-duddy-wuddy,' said Anya, fingering her lower lip. 'I keep forgetting that you lurved her, don't I? How tacty-wactless of me.'

'There was a time when we both "lurved" you.'

'A stupid mistake. Besides, she betrayed me. She pretended to be something that she wasn't, and she was too much of a wimp even to keep up a good pretence of it. I was always much stronger than she was. The two of you were fools to "lurve" me.'

'I'm beginning to think so, Anya. After all this time, I'm beginning to think so.'

'Anyway, you'll understand that it would be impossible for both of us to carry on in our current positions,' remarked Anya, her face, which for a while had lapsed into a spoilt-child pout, now shining again. 'The *status quo ante* simply wouldn't be tenable, would it?'

'What do you suggest?' said Reen, putting her hands – her old, old hands – on the desk in front of her and pushing herself to her feet. Without waiting for an answer, she strolled over yet again towards the window, to her favourite vantage point, where she could see the megalopolis of Ernestrad seemingly thrumming with tireless industry. Except that now she couldn't see even as far as the slab on the far side of the street: the fog was thick enough that the two of them seemed to be sealed inside a cocoon of grey cotton wool. 'That I resign, and hand over the reins of the corporation to you? It wouldn't be that easy, you know.'

She positioned herself carefully, the toe of her left shoe just a centimetre away from the button under the carpet.

'No,' said Anya. 'Look at me, Reen.'

'Because you can't bring yourself to shoot me in the back? Come, come, Anya, you're softening a bit in your old age, aren't you?'

'I haven't got a needler or a laser, Reen.'

Reen turned her head.

Anya was holding a primitive dagger. Primitive, but the shine of its blade told Reen that it was razor-keen. There was a tight smile on Anya's lips, and her eyes were alight.

'Sometimes I used to dream about a time when things were settled differently, Reen,' she said. 'They were dreams which seemed almost as concrete as real memories.'

Reen stared fascinated at the blade.

'They weren't dreams, Anya,' she said as a flood of confusing images – colours, sounds, smells, tastes, movements – came into her. 'They genuinely *were* memories. There's only ever the one story, you see, however much the details might differ.'

She pressed the button with her toe and the window behind her vaporized, so that the fog came creeping in. She edged to one side, her hands automatically checking the hilt of her sword in its scabbard at her left side and the dirk at her belt.

She moved across the short turf of Starveling-stage, her eyes never leaving Anya's green-clad figure, only peripherally aware of the cairn to her left and the curlew perched atop it, watching both of them. There was blood covering

Anya's hands and clothing, even a smudge of it on the tip of her nose, like some bizarre attempt at cosmetics. All around the mountain the fog rolled, so that the two of them could have been the only people left in the World.

No.

Not just the two of them.

Reen knew that Syor was with her, as the god of the World, and that Nadar was with Anya, as its principle of Evil, and that somewhere Alyss would be observing them.

'You stupid old turd!' Anya hissed. 'I can kill you as easily here in the World as anywhere else!'

What was Anya meaning by 'anywhere else'? Where else was there but the World?

'You've killed far too many people in your life,' said Reen, using the words to cover the fact that she was ever sidling towards Anya. She wished that her body felt twenty years younger. 'It's time, now, for it to stop.'

Anya would probably go for the throw first. That's what Reen herself would likely have done, and Anya had learnt the arts of combat from Reen – but she'd never learnt sufficient subtlety in their use to realize that this very fact was like an extra weapon at Reen's belt.

'Who do you think could stop me?' Anya snarled. She waved with her dagger-hand towards the opaque barrier of mist. 'Those are *my* people out there. They worship *me*. I can feel the strength of all of them in my body, willing you to die, old witch. You haven't the spring left in your antique muscles to thwart me any longer. Tough carrion for the crows, you'll make.'

Anya, too, was circling. Reen reminded herself that her own underestimation of Anya's abilities might more than counteract her additional insight, if she weren't watchful.

'Too tough,' she said. 'So I'll spare the crows their indigestion.'

With a complicated double-movement of her wrist, Anya threw the dagger with blinding speed directly towards Reen's chest. Reen was able to duck sideways and down only at the last possible moment, the blade of the weapon spitting her through the flesh of her upper arm. She controlled the pain with an effort, shaking the heavy-hilted dagger free. *I taught you well*, she thought, despite herself. *I thought you might have been in enough of a frenzy to go for either the face or throat, but you had enough sense left to choose the bigger target.*

'First blood, Anya,' she gasped, righting herself. 'But now you're a weapon down.'

'I could kill you with my bare hands.' Anya made a fist. 'Shall I try, or shall I be merciful and take you out with my sword?'

Reen took a couple of scampering, dancing paces forward and swung her sword around in a whooping arc. Just in time Anya saw the blow coming and was able to swivel her body away from the hips, bringing her own weapon up to guard herself. Steel clashed on steel. The shock jarred up Reen's arm, but she didn't have the time to pay it any attention because already Anya was feinting away from her, grabbing up some sheep-droppings and flipping them up towards her face as a distraction. Reen refused to be distracted, allowing the pellets to ricochet harmlessly off her forehead and cheeks. She took another step forwards and Anya retreated.

'I'm not quite the fossil you thought, eh, Anya?' she said, the words irrelevant, the diversion everything. Sure enough, Anya's eyes wandered slightly as she thought of some suitable abuse to hurl back at her. Reen took the moment to flick her sword in a viper-swift downwards dart, its tip catching Anya on the unguarded inside of her wrist, so that the redness leapt onto the grass.

Anya made no sound, but her face contorted from the pain. 'A cheap trick,' she grunted.

'Not so cheap,' said Reen. 'Been a long time since someone pinked you, hmmm, Anya? But then you've always taken care, these past years, to pick on people who can't fight back, haven't you? Now you've screwed up in your selection of easy targets, haven't you? And you're just beginning to realize it, aren't you?'

Reen's goading was rewarded by a look of uncertainty that momentarily clouded Anya's eyes. *That's right*, Reen thought. *She's younger than you and she's fitter than you, so you're going to have to use weapons she doesn't have. Misgivings, for example.*

Anya abruptly half-crouched, whipping her sword around in an attempt to slash Reen's ankles. Nimbly Reen jumped back, twisting her own blade in the air for a blow at Anya's head, but already Anya was back upright and was parrying with ease, so that the two shafts of the weapons slid up together until their guards locked, the edge of Anya's blade neatly trimming off Reen's earlobe as she pulled her head away a fraction of a second too late. Then Reen was shoving with all her strength against the bond and bringing her knee up towards Anya's crotch, feeling it impact with satisfying force. A man would have been demolished; as it was, Anya staggered away from her, her face pale, her mouth moving in silent imprecations.

'Out of practice, Anya? You never used to be so coy about how you fought.'

'Fuck off, you old buzzard!'

Another futile fusillade of sheep-droppings in her face. Another scamper towards Anya, who was moving much less fluidly now. Clearly the blow to the groin had debilitated her more than Reen could have hoped, and the flow of blood from her wrist was continuing unabated.

Reen relaxed slightly, an oversight that almost lost her her life. Anya spotted the momentary loss of concentration and plunged forward, sword outstretched ahead of her, shrilling at the top of her voice, watching her old mentor moving slowly, too slowly, to one side to evade the blow. But Reen had managed to raise her sword, just – it was all in the wrong grip but it was raised – and it was sufficient to deflect Anya's lunge although the blade got caught in the hand-guard of Reen's sword, which maybe would be as much as was needed because the momentum of the thrust was tearing the hilt of Reen's sword out of her grip so that Anya could flip it all the way to the other side of the tabletop where it tumbled a couple of times before lying still.

But Reen had anticipated being disarmed and was swinging round with her dagger towards Anya's side and Anya was 'way off-balance in the follow-through and there was nothing she could do except twist her body so that she fell over, but at least it was away from Reen. Keep rolling a couple of times. Confuse Reen – remember she's only got a dagger now so if she wants to kill you she'll have to get right down here on the ground beside you and . . .

Anya looked up, slightly dizzy, and saw to her horror that, reckless now of her own life, Reen had sprung through the air and was flying towards her, lips peeling back, the knife like a great fang out ahead of her. Anya tried desperately to roll just a little further, but her sword had somehow jammed itself underneath her so that she couldn't get out of the way quickly enough and Reen was on her and *oh the pain the pain oh Nadar the pain of it please help me Nadar I never knew there was this much pain in all the World* . . .

It was some minutes before Reen could prise her body away from Anya's and haul herself to her feet. She looked down at the shambles.

Her first blow – the fatal blow – had taken Anya in the lower abdomen and ripped upwards, cutting her flesh apart until the blade was stopped by the base of the ribcage. But then – and here Reen's memory of events was covered in a red haze – she had wanted to make sure that not just the woman was dead but also the long-ago child Anya whom she'd loved, whom she'd learnt how to make smile, and the Anya whom she'd instructed in sword-play and wrestling and archery, and then the older Anya who'd led the peasant troops against the Ellonia and so opened up Albion to the World, and then the ruthless tyrant that Anya had become, and then . . .

Her knife had risen and fallen many times, doing brutal work.

Under the stony eye of the curlew, Reen staggered away a few paces and threw up.

She was right: you really are getting too old for this sort of thing, she thought as the red colours in her eyes dimmed. *Treat it like just another slightly unofficial execution – a job that had to be done – and you'll be all right, old girl. You'll be all right. And in the holy name of Syor by fuck my arm and head hurt!*

She looked back on the wrecked body.

No, there was more to be done. One last rite. Then she'd be finished.

She limped across the stained turf and, straining the sinews of her back until she thought they must surely crack, she lugged Anya's body up in front of her, cradling it like a baby. She began to weep, but she forced her legs to take her, one step at a time, to the edge of the plateau, to the lip where the sharp drop began almost as cleanly as if Syor in her wisdom had carved it with a spatula.

'Anya,' she said through the tears. 'Anya, I'm sorry.'

Mustering the last dregs of her strength, she hurled Anya's corpse out into the engulfing mist, so that it was lost forever.

4

'Reen! Reen!'

She heard someone shouting her name.

Rubbing the blood-soaked sleeve of her jacket across her eyes in a poor attempt to clear them, she turned and saw Rehan running across Starveling-stage towards her, Kursten a few paces behind him.

5

'Reen! Reen!' Rehan shouted, running across the great office floor towards her, Kursten just behind him.

Reen was standing right on the precipice where the window would normally have been. She was half-lost to his view in the grip of the fog.

'Reen! Get back from there!'

It had taken them the best part of half an hour to trace the malfunction – or sabotage, as it had proved to be –

517

and make the necessary repairs so that they could get into Reen's office. Even through the soundproofing they'd heard the screaming and the heavy sounds.

'She's gone,' said Reen stupidly, swaying.

She looked a mess. There was blood all over her blue dress with the white lapels. More of it was slowly pulsing from a place just below her shoulder and – yuk! – there was part of her left ear missing.

'Reen, come away from there.'

'She's gone,' Reen repeated, staring out into the fog. 'She's lost in the mist of unrealized possibilities. The mist of the wishes of the gods. It's very much the same thing.'

'Get back from there!' he yelled.

Kursten, quicker-thinking, dived for the correct part of the carpet and thumped her hand down several times until she located the button. With the slightest of hisses the window rematerialized.

Reen lethargically punched the edge of one fist against the monomolecular glass. The other was clutching a dripping stylus.

'She's gone,' she kept mumbling. 'I should have gone with her.'

Rehan took her in his arms, and she turned in towards him and began to weep on his shoulder.

Kursten, getting up onto her knees, began fully to appreciate for the first time quite the devastation to which the office had been subjected. Large areas of the carpet were stained, and there were red wipe-marks on the walls. Most of the equipment had been torn out of its recesses on Reen's opal desk, so that loose wires trailed in crazed directions. One of the seats was floating at a drunken angle, performing a slow uncertain circle, its semi-intelligent plastiform upholstery shredded.

And then, as she turned her gaze back to the fog fumbling at the window, all of this seemed completely unimportant.

'The World,' Reen was saying, her shoulders now better under control, 'the World we belong to is dying, Rehan.'

'I've got to get a physiodroid here,' he said.

'Not worth it, oldest friend. Neither you nor I have very much longer left for this existence. Why bother patching up this deteriorating old bag of bones for just an hour or two?'

'Nonsense, you've got . . .'

'No, Rehan.' She put up a bloodstained finger to seal his lips. 'No. I haven't got years of life ahead of me still. And neither have you. As you'd know, if you would stop to think about it.'

'I don't know what you're . . .'

'Hush, Rehan, hush. Lian's long dead. Marja's long dead. The Despot's dead. Syor's in her heaven and Nadar's in his hell. Ngur's dead. And now Syor's final wish has been fulfilled: Anya's dead. Every tile of the mosaic is at last in its correct position. And that's an end of the story, except for you and me. The World that gave us all birth is dying, too: it's been dying since the moment that Syor began her act of creation. The World was some of the clay that she took with her to her potter's-wheel to cast a pot with. It'll be reborn, of course, but not as the World . . . maybe as something much finer, much more complete . . .'

'Kursten's not dead. She's . . .'

He broke off. Kneeling, Kursten was quite motionless, seemingly transfixed by what she saw at the window.

'Leave Kursten,' said Reen. 'She was born from the Mistdom, from Syor, not from the World. She's not of the same kind as you and I, my friend: she's of the kind that'll live in the world that the Mistdom will start to create, now that our World has so nearly run its course.'

'She . . .'

'Don't argue, Rehan. I haven't got the energy left to persuade you. If you don't want to believe what I'm saying, then just shut up about it – all right?'

She smiled at him, and kissed him on the lips. He kissed her back, feeling the surge of memories of the times – long ago – when the two of them had been comfortable lovers, loving not passionately, not unwisely, but well enough for their love to have lasted them the rest of their lives.

'Do an old woman a favour, Rehan,' she said at last, 'and take me down to the river.'

6

And so they either went through the vaporizing door into Kursten's office and down via the psychofacsimile translation booth to the foyer, or they climbed down the steep, fog-enshrouded side of the plateau, and it took them either the smallest fraction of a nanosecond or hours of hard labour. Either way, they then seemed to walk for a long time through the muffling fog or the Mistdom, she leaning into the warmth and protection of his arm for support, until finally they were down by the side of the river, far from the nearest houses, squelching along in the mud.

They saw no one except a crazed old man swilling from a bottle and yelling a stream of incomprehensible syllables towards the sky. Rehan paused for a moment, muttering that by some magical coincidence it might be Joli. But it wasn't, of course, and so they carried on their way.

'Joli's not dead,' said Rehan after a while. The lights of the buildings on the far side of the river glowed spectrally through the mist at them. It was hard to imagine that those lights could belong to anything moored to the ground: they seemed to be independent, free-floating. 'Not that we know of, anyway. Isn't he a piece of the final mosaic?'

'Syor wasn't perfect in life,' said Reen, hugging herself and then him to keep the cold off them. 'You can't expect her suddenly to discover perfection in all things just because she's a god now, can you?'

He laughed.

Reen smiled. No, that wasn't the truth of it that she'd just told him. She'd known Syor well, much better than anyone else ever had, and she appreciated the way that Syor's mind worked. Whatever the new universe that

Syor was building would be like, Reen knew what one of its fundamental characteristics would be: into everything, no matter how great or small, there would be built some imperfection, for Syor had the wisdom to know that it is the imperfections in things that give them their beauty. She would leave the mosaic trivially incomplete – or, at least, the version of it that was reproduced in mortal minds. The god had taken Joli partly to herself, made him partly, like Kursten entirely, her own.

'We're almost there now,' Reen said.

'Almost where?'

She shrugged. 'Almost at the place the World ends,' she said lightly. Her wounds had stopped hurting her a while ago. 'Come on down to the water's edge with me.'

Still not fully understanding, he followed her squashy footsteps down through the mud until they were kneeling beside the slow-moving, oily water. The mist was thick and affectionate all around them. Now there were no lights bright enough to shine to them all the way from across the river.

'Look,' said Reen, crouching down even lower and pointing along the water in the direction of the flow. 'Can you see, along there?'

Far in the distance, framed by arms of fog, Rehan could see what looked like a field of stars.

'That's the new universe,' she whispered in his ear. 'That's why the World is dying, so that the new universe can be born. Let your soul gaze on it through the windows of your self.'

Rehan looked, sensing his soul staring directly at the stars, which tickled his eyes. He felt his body becoming less substantial, as if it were no longer knitted together by bonds of flesh and sinew.

'Give me your eyes,' whispered Reen.

He reached up and took the eyes from his fading face. 'I love you,' he said through lips that were mere shapes in the mist.

'And I love you,' she said. 'Always have. Silly of me, really.'

She took their eyes – her own and his – and, just as her hand was disappearing, cast them out onto the water, where they bobbed once or twice before beginning to float gently with the current down towards the field of stars.

Chapter Seven
eMPIRe

1

Alyss sits in a place that is not a sun-mottled glade on a shallow hillside, where birds do not sing and insects do not flutter or hum about their inscrutable errands, where the sound of a distant stream does not mingle with the prying of the wind through the leaves and branches of the lazing trees, where there is no tang of resin in the nonexistent air, where the sky does not arch overhead in a glowing opaque blue, where the flowers do not cluster together to form blotches of argumentative colour, where the heather does not bristle clannishly and the bracken does not breathe (although the hillside of the whole might seem to, as if it were the flank of a basking creature) – and yet where all of these things are nevertheless the case, because she has decreed that it shall be so.

She frowns, and nervous broods of white and yellow daisies spring into existence across the coarse, spiky grass. She waves a painterly hand, and a backdrop forms of distance-empurpled hills; she puffs a breath to shroud their peaks in mist.

For a few moments she's quite still, knees up in front of her, her elbows making points as she leans on her forearms. She looks out over the landscape that she's conjured into existence, appreciating the distance that she's created. She winks a couple of clouds into the sky: extra, seemingly casual embellishments to make the whole perfect.

No.

Not quite perfect.

She frowns, puzzled for a moment. She's not

accustomed to this strange experience, forgetfulness, and it both fascinates her and irritates her, so that she finds she's doing three things at once: trying to remember whatever it is that she should have remembered; poking around inquisitively among her own mental patterns to watch the way that her absentmindedness functions; and chafing annoyedly at herself for allowing herself to have fallen into the trap of forgetting. Exasperated, she finally tweaks a few details of recent reality so that the forgetting never happened in the first place.

Now there's a brown, clayey road – there always has been – leading down towards the velvet valley beneath her. Trudging up through the dust towards her is a mousy-haired woman of indeterminate age, dressed in coarsely spun browns and greens; on her feet are crumpled, soft leather boots. The woman clearly senses that Alyss is watching her, for she stops walking and stands for a few seconds with her hands on her hips, gazing uphill frankly, expressing a mixture of petulance and defiance. Then, shoulders down, she resumes her climb.

Alyss turns to watch a small cloud spiralling towards the sun. When at last she turns her attention back again, Syor is sitting beside her, brushing the dust from the creases of her dress. There is dust in the creases of her face, too, but that she leaves alone.

'You summoned me,' she says. Her annoyance would be less obvious were it not so impeccably disguised. She carries on sweeping at the rough cloth.

'I suggested that we meet.' Alyss corrects her very precisely, the fingers of her own small hands moving as if in resonance with Syor's. 'I don't think that I *could* summon you, now, even if I were as discourteous as that. I may make requests of you: I cannot command you.'

'Hmmm,' says Syor absently. 'You have a way of making your requests more difficult to refuse than your orders. Besides, you never asked my permission to use a part of me to create . . . this.' She gestures at the landscape around her.

'Nor Nadar's,' Alyss agrees. 'You and he will have to get used to people not wanting to worry you about petty matters.'

Syor smiles, but the smile rapidly fades. 'The thing I'll have to get accustomed to,' she mutters suddenly, addressing one of her knees, 'is the fact that I'm responsible for Nadar's presence here.'

'You never had any choice,' says Alyss with a laugh. 'If it hadn't been Nadar it would have been someone else, or perhaps you would just have had to endure the other aspect of your*self*. Whatever the wishes of creators, it always ends up like this – that there's some kind of principle of Evil to counterbalance the principle of Good. It's not something that gods can escape from, because Good and Evil aren't qualities that gods are really capable of having, or even understanding. They're *mortals*' qualities, and it's mortals that bring the universes into existence just as much as the creators do.'

Syor says nothing for a little. Her eyes roam the mountainsides.

'If you'd told me, back when I was just another peasant child growing up in Albion, that one day I'd be responsible for creating a new universe,' she murmurs at last, 'I'd probably have believed you, but any time after that in my mortal life I'd just have laughed, thought you were crazed. But the child-me would have taken the notion seriously. She'd have sworn solemnly to make the very best universe as ever she could, and then to reign as a loving god, so that all the little mortals would live lives of unremitting happiness. That much of the child still survives in me, you know: I still *want* to be a benevolent god.'

'There's no such thing as a benevolent god.' Alyss speaks impatiently. 'No benevolent god would allow religion to thrive, yet they all need to be worshipped: mortals require it of them.'

'Do they? Do they have to in *my* universe?' Syor's haughty glance matches ill with her peasant dress. 'I don't *wish* to be worshipped. I've always believed that the desire to be worshipped belongs only to children, the insane and the stupid.'

'Mortals create gods in their own image,' says Alyss quietly. She plucks a dandelion clock from the stubbly grass and, between words, puffs idly at the spores, watching them as they flutter away on newly sprouted green wings. 'You mustn't forget it – that they create you every bit as much as you have created them. That's a matter of plain fact. Their perceptions mould the universe in which they dwell, and, as the gods are so intricately entwined into the fabric of the universe, they're indistinguishable from it: therefore they're moulded by mortals' perceptions, too. That's why you have to have another aspect, something like a Nadar, to share the godhead with you, to be the joint ruler of your empire.'

'I have no wish to rule any empire.'

'You – have – no – *choice*.'

Another long silence from Syor; then: 'And you? Where do *you* fit into the scheme of things?'

Alyss grins and puts her head on one side; there's a self-deprecatory gleam in her eyes.

'Me?' she says. 'Oh, if you two are the monarchs, then I suppose I'm the jester who fools around with an inflated bladder at the foot of your throne. I'm the one who can say things to you that nobody else would be allowed to. Maybe, every now and then, you listen to what I'm saying, and that changes your minds about something you were planning to do. Perhaps once every millennium or so you allow me to reign for a day in your stead, so that you two can spend a day as my jesters. Who knows?'

'I want you to be more than just my clown,' says Syor earnestly, putting her hand on Alyss's thin shoulder, staring intently into that small mobile face. 'Guide me, Alyss. I ask you to guide me in my empire. I *command* you.'

'You may not do so,' Alyss responds, once again speaking very precisely. She shakes off Syor's hand. 'I am not yours to command, because I am not altogether a part of your empire. No universe can logically be complete – complete and discrete – without some element within it that comes from outside it. Here, in your creation, I'm that element – or, for all I know, just one of many. I'm a product of the polycosmos, not of any one of its universes in particular. I am not, and of necessity cannot be, bound by the laws that govern the individual universes in which I manifest myself: I can act according to the rules of whichever universe I happen to be visiting, but even if I wished to I couldn't conform to them in their entirety. I'm surprised' – she grins again – 'that you haven't, um, noticed this.'

Syor shares the smile, but sadly. 'You're a very versatile jester,' she says.

'Let us hope that you'll prove to be an even more versatile god,' Alyss retorts. Now it is her turn to reach out, to touch. 'I'll be here in your universe often,' she adds. 'Indeed, I'll never really be not-here. I'd like to say that you'll always be able to rely on me, that you can trust me as a steadfast friend who'll ever be at your side when you need me; but I'd be lying if I did, making a promise I couldn't keep. It's your inescapable responsibility to make the laws that govern this universe of yours: whether you like it or not, your motives, conscious or unconscious, will be built integrally into its structure. Already your ethics – yours and Nadar's – have been appropriated to serve as its foundation stones. Busy little masons are already buzzing around, snatching from you a wisp of a thought here and an unnoticed emotion there, and using whatever bits they can of the two of you as bricks to raise the universe. I can be here to assist you only insofar as there's an overlap between your motives and mine; that overlap is indescribably tinier than you'll ever be able to realize. Just because I choose to don forms that mortals can recognize doesn't mean that that's what I really look like, or what I really am. Oh' – an angry little shake of the head, stirring her short hair briefly – 'I'm not talking about outward appearances: they're irrelevant. What I'm getting at is the bit that you see when you look at *me*, not at the body I've chosen to reify. Even then, the "me" you see is just a tiny part of me, the intersection between my true, whole self and the universe I happen to be in – like a thin slice taken through an infinitely complex shape. You're seeing the flat surface of the slice; it is quite literally impossible for you, constrained within the bounds of a single universe, to comprehend the remainder of my true form: there is no possibility, limited as you are by the substrate laws of your own universe, that you can predict my next action. But the rest of me does exist, it is still *there*, and it controls what this slice of me can do. When the things that I do seem to you to be nothing more than capricious, that's just because you're unable – will forever be unable – to see anything more of me than this little part. The little part that coincides with a segment of your universe. The little part that's speaking to you now.'

'What if I don't want to make any limiting rules like that?'

'I told you. You've no choice.'

'But what, then, if I create rules that accord with the ones *you* conform to?'

'That's impossible.'

'Why?'

'Because it's a contradiction in terms. The polycosmos as a whole doesn't have anything that you'd recognize as rules – not in a single universe, you couldn't. All that holds sway in the polycosmos is randomness. At the most fundamental level of all things, that's all you can find: complete arbitrariness. Things like rules and motives and realities – and mortals, and gods like you yourself – are only transient, wraith-thin structures built upon that. The only soul that the polycosmos has has been grafted onto it by beings like the creators; the only souls the universes have are those that mortals have foisted onto them. Mortals like to believe that their universes have the potential to be benign, that somehow there's a guiding principle inbuilt into the universe that will ensure that somehow, always, even when the circumstances are at their grimmest, the outcome will be some form of overall improvement. But that's not the case. The arbitrariness has no motives: it is neither clement nor inclement: not Good, not Evil. And, when mortals mould it partially, to create their creators just as their creators have created them, they adjust the arbitrariness towards their own image: which is not benign.'

'You don't actually *like* mortals very much, do you?' says Syor, after a long time.

'That's a curious question,' says Alyss after a few moments' thought. 'As you'll discover for yourself, gods neither like nor dislike the . . . the fungal growths that occupy their domains. In any case, on their own terms they're not exactly very likable, are they? Look at them. They're driven almost entirely by the need to satisfy various transitory greeds. They delight in inflicting infantile cruelties upon individuals among themselves; they describe as triumphs their contributions towards perpetuating the misery of the mortal state as a whole. You said that only the stupid and the immature and the insane would find gratification in being worshipped: how, then, can you describe the mortals who want to *worship* these crazies? Fools? Defectives? Misguided children? They seek gods to justify themselves; and, if they can't find gods, they select from among themselves what they call "strong leaders" – the school bullies.'

Alyss shakes her head wearily. 'There was a moment, you know, when I glimpsed the first ReLM that you'd so carefully constructed for me, that I wanted to blame the creators for all this . . . mess, but that was unjust of me. It's mortals who create their own hells, then bring those hells into reality, and then finally ensure that the hells will endure for eternity. And you ask me if I like mortals.'

'I ask you again,' says Syor, very softly.

Alyss looks at her intently, seeming to peer right inside her. 'You're more perceptive than I thought,' she says slowly. 'Perhaps you'll make a better god than the mortals who will live in this universe have any right to expect. Yes, to use words loosely, there's a bit of my aspect here that experiences some analogue of love for some of them. I "loved" you when you were a mortal; and I "love" Reen – yes, and Rehan and Ngur and Joli, and even Anya and

Nadar and your first creation, Kursten. I even sprinkled some of the part of me called "love" on them – on you – and was prepared to overlook your astonishingly boorish discourtesy when you didn't even notice the gift I was giving you. Illogical of me, I know, but then' – a sudden switch back to the puckish Alyss to whom Syor was accustomed – 'illogicality has always been a part of my charm, don't you think?'

Syor says nothing; just turns her gaze away.

Much later, after Alyss has thoughtfully lowered the sun in the sky, reddening the ambient light tastefully, she speaks to Syor again.

'You've trapped your mortals in here, you know,' she says.

'Don't blame me. How was I to know any better? You might have . . .'

'Don't immediately leap to the defensive: that's a mortal habit. I wasn't trying to blame anybody or anything: blaming's another mortal habit. I was just telling you something; I'm being the messenger, not the news itself. The news is that the mortals in this universe are trapped here, thanks to the fact that you've created this universe the way you have. You're trapped here, too. Elsewhere in the polycosmos, mortals can travel from one of the reified universes into the others, through their visions or through "dying". But not from this one. You've made sure there aren't any gates through its seamless shell. When mortals die in this universe, they'll die; there'll be no escape for their spirits into the next reality. The seven ReLMS will be all there is – all seven of them, mixed into the one. That'll be all there is. No next existence for "your" mortals.'

'Then, at least in one respect,' says Syor wistfully, 'you've been wrong in what you've been saying. At least in a small way, I'm a benevolent god.'

She hauls herself to her feet, her eternally young legs seeming age-stiff. She smiles wanly down on Alyss, who is still sitting with her arms wrapped around her bony, childlike knees. Alyss glowers back up at her; the scowl inadequately disguises something like the mortal sensation of pain, but infinite and eternity-long.

Not knowing quite why she's doing so, Syor stoops down impulsively, cradles Alyss's face in her rough peasant hands, and kisses her on the forehead, as one might bid a child goodnight.

'I'll be seeing you,' she says, straightening up again.

'I'll be around,' mutters Alyss tersely.

Syor shrugs, then turns and begins the long trek back down the dusty road-that-isn't-a-road, descending from the nonexistent hillside towards the vacuum of a valley.

Alyss watches her go.

Finally she mimics Syor's shrug, then stretches her body in various ways until she has become a curlew. For a few moments longer she struts among the grass (which now seems more like thick, coarse hair) and the bright flowers (which could easily be mistaken for beads of perspiration). She turns a shining, blinkless little eye to drink in the sight of branches waving where there is no breeze.

Then, with a couple of paces, she launches herself into the air and tucks her yellow feet up beneath her. She extends her wings and, with a few powerfully controlled beats, drifts away in lazy arcs towards the radiant, limitless, tireless airs of the polycosmos.

2

And, of course, once she has gone the hillside wakes and stirs. It gathers itself up until it is standing on its four thick legs, then shakes its head and shoulders a few convulsive times to rid itself of sleep. It snuffles once or twice, appreciating its final solitude.

At last the pig turns its inquisitive snout to the fresh-smelling emptiness.

Elsewhere & Elsewhen

four

Here is the final experiment you can perform in this first session with the equipment you have constructed. The demonstration is an intriguing one, so you may wish to try it at other times.

Very carefully, keeping your hand as steady as possible, spin the pyramid as rapidly as you can on its pivot.

There.

What do you see as you watch the blurring succession of paper surfaces passing before your eyes?

That's right.

You can see all of the World at once.

Bibliography

Readers interested in following up some of the ideas and images that form the subtexts of this book might enjoy these:

Barrow, John D.: *Theories of Everything: The Quest for Ultimate Explanation*, London and Oxford, OUP, 1991

Bohm, David: *Wholeness and the Implicate Order*, London, RKP, 1980

Davies, Paul: *God and the New Physics*, London, Dent, 1983

Davies, Paul: *Other Worlds*, London, Dent, 1980

Davies, Paul: *Superforce: The Search for a Grand Unified Theory of Nature*, London, Heinemann, 1984

Gleick, James: *Chaos: Making a New Science*, London, Heinemann, 1988

Gribbin, John: *In Search of Schrödinger's Cat*, London, Wildwood House, 1984

Herbert, Nick: *Quantum Reality: Beyond the New Physics*, New York, Anchor/Doubleday, 1985

Jones, Roger: *Physics as Metaphor*, London, Wildwood House, 1983

Schrödinger, Erwin: *My View of the World*, Cambridge, CUP, trans, 1964

Then again, in an equally valid reality, they might not.

A selection of bestsellers from Headline

BURYING THE SHADOW	Storm Constantine	£4.99 ☐
SCHEHERAZADE'S NIGHT OUT	Craig Shaw Gardner	£4.99 ☐
WULF	Steve Harris	£4.99 ☐
EDGE OF VENGEANCE	Jenny Jones	£5.99 ☐
THE BAD PLACE	Dean Koontz	£5.99 ☐
HIDEAWAY	Dean Koontz	£5.99 ☐
BLOOD GAMES	Richard Laymon	£4.99 ☐
DARK MOUNTAIN	Richard Laymon	£4.99 ☐
SUMMER OF NIGHT	Dan Simmons	£4.99 ☐
FALL OF HYPERION	Dan Simmons	£5.99 ☐
DREAM FINDER	Roger Taylor	£5.99 ☐
WOLFKING	Bridget Wood	£4.99 ☐

All Headline books are available at your local bookshop or newsagent, or can be ordered direct from the publisher. Just tick the titles you want and fill in the form below. Prices and availability subject to change without notice.

Headline Book Publishing PLC, Cash Sales Department, Bookpoint, 39 Milton Park, Abingdon, OXON, OX14 4TD, UK. If you have a credit card you may order by telephone — 0235 831700.

Please enclose a cheque or postal order made payable to Bookpoint Ltd to the value of the cover price and allow the following for postage and packing:
UK & BFPO: £1.00 for the first book, 50p for the second book and 30p for each additional book ordered up to a maximum charge of £3.00.
OVERSEAS & EIRE: £2.00 for the first book, £1.00 for the second book and 50p for each additional book.

Name ....

Address ....

....

....

If you would prefer to pay by credit card, please complete:
Please debit my Visa/Access/Diner's Card/American Express (delete as applicable) card no:

Signature ....Expiry Date ....